MEDIUM ÆVUM MONOGRAPHS
NEW SERIES

I0649385

SERIES EDITORS
A. J. LAPPIN, N. F. PALMER,
C. SAUNDERS, J. H. M. TAYLOR

MEDIUM ÆVUM MONOGRAPHS
NEW SERIES XXIV

ESTORIA DELOS GODOS

Critical edition and introduction

by
AENGUS WARD

The Society for the Study of
Medieval Languages and Literature
Oxford
2006

THE SOCIETY FOR THE STUDY OF
MEDIEVAL LANGUAGES AND LITERATURE
http://mediumaevum.modhist.ox.ac.uk

ISBN-13: 978-0-907570-17-2 (pb)

ISBN-13: 978-0-907570-53-0 (pdf e-bk)

British Library Cataloguing in Publication Data

A catalogue record for this book
is available from the British Library

CONTENTS

ACKNOWLEDGEMENTS

I have had the good fortune to benefit from the help of a large number of friends and colleagues. I would like to record my particular thanks to Enrique Jerez Cabrero for drawing my attention to the previously unknown manuscript BNM Res/278, and also for his many helpful comments on the translations of the *Historia Gothica*, not all of which I agree with, but all of which were offered with an admirable sense of the importance of academic and intellectual exchange. I would also like to thank Julián Martín Abad, Joe Snow and John O'Neill for their help in accessing the manuscripts of the *Estoria*; and Fernando Gómez Redondo, Inés Fernández-Ordóñez and Leonardo Funes for their knowledge and wisdom. Particular thanks must go to Anthony Lappin, who read repeated drafts with remarkable good humour; Jane Taylor and Simon Barton for their thoughtful insights. I would also like to recognize the help offered in various ways by Georges Martin, Juan Carlos Conde López, Trevor Dadson, Manolo Hijano Villegas and CarolAnn van der Walt.

My thoughts on the *Estoria* have evolved enormously in the last few years, principally as a result of comments offered by those present at the Medievalia conference at the Universidad Nacional Autónoma de México, the Medieval Chronicle conference at Utrecht, the Colloquium on Rodrigo Ximénez de Rada at the Ecole Normale Supérieure, Lyon, and at seminar papers at the University of Reading and Queen Mary, London. My thanks to all, and particularly to Alan Deyermond and Barry Taylor for their insights on the subject of textual editing.

I would also like to record my gratitude to my colleagues in the Department of Hispanic Studies at the University of Birmingham. While the production of this edition has not been swift, it would have been rather slower without the help of my colleagues and also a period of study leave granted to me in the second half of 2003.

And last, but certainly not least, to Solange, Lois and Sé.

INTRODUCTION

The recent proliferation of works dealing with the flowering of vernacular historiography in the Peninsula has concentrated almost exclusively on the Alfonsine chronicles and their direct successors, for perfectly sound academic reasons.[1]

It is generally recognised that the vernacular chronicles owed a large debt in terms of concept of history, and also in terms of questions of source material, to a number of Latin chronicles, amongst which Rodrigo Ximénez de Rada's *De rebus Hispanie* is perhaps the shining example.[2] In addition to providing the Alfonsine teams with both inspiration and raw material, *De rebus* also was to spawn a separate tradition of Iberian historiography in the form of translations into romance.

[1] Amongst the most notable works in this respect are the following: Diego Catalán, *La 'Estoria de España' de Alfonso X: creación y evolución*, Fuentes Cronísticas de la Historia de España, 5 (Madrid: Seminario Menéndez Pidal, Fundación Menéndez Pidal & Universidad Autónoma de Madrid, 1992); Diego Catalán, *De la silva textual al taller historiográfico alfonsí: códices, crónicas, versiones y cuadernos de trabajo*, Fuentes Cronísticas de la Historia de España, 9 (Madrid: Seminario Menéndez Pidal, Fundación Menéndez Pidal & Universidad Autónoma de Madrid, 1997); Inés Fernández-Ordóñez ed., *Alfonso el Sabio y las crónicas de España* (Valladolid: Centro para el Estudio de los Clásicos Españoles & Fundación Santander Central Hispano, 2000); Leonardo Funes, 'Las variaciones del relato histórico en la Castilla del siglo XIV: el período post-alfonsí', in *Estudios sobre la variación textual: prosa castellana de los siglos XIII a XVI* (Buenos Aires: SECRIT, 2001), pp. 111–34; Fernando Gómez Redondo, *Historia de la prosa medieval castellana, I: La creación del discurso prosístico; el entramado cortesano* (Madrid: Cátedra, 1998); Georges Martin, *Les Juges de Castille: mentalités et discours historique dans l'Espagne médiévale*, Annexes des Cahiers de linguistique hispanique médiévale, 6 (Paris: Séminaire d'études médiévales hispaniques de l'Université de Paris-XIII, 1992); Georges Martin ed., *La historia alfonsí: el modelo y sus destinos (siglos XIII-XV): Seminario organizado por la Casa de Velázquez (30 de enero de 1995)*, Colección de la Casa de Velázquez, 68 (Madrid: Casa de Velázquez, 2000); Aengus Ward ed., *Teoría y práctica de la historiografía hispánica medieval*, (Birmingham: University of Birmingham Press, 2000).

[2] *Historia de rebus Hispanie* is the title given to the collection of Ximénez de Rada's historical works, the *Historia Romanorum, Historia Ostrogothorum, Historia Hugnorum, Vandalorum, Sueuorum, Alananorum et Silingorum, Historia Araborum, Historia gothica*). In addition it is often used as shorthand for the part of his works more correctly known as *Historia gothica*, the direct source for the *Estoria delos godos*. For the purposes of this edition, and to facilitate reference to the 1987 edition, the title *De rebus Hispanie (DRH)* will be used to refer to the *Historia gothica*.

One such translation is that known as the *Estoria delos godos*. Of all the
medieval translations of *De rebus*, it is the one that has been best served and
most widely known, and it has been available to scholars in two separate
editions since the end of the nineteenth century. However, there are a
number of reasons why a full critical edition and detailed study have become
necessary. First, the text has never been studied in any great detail and its
importance as a key piece in medieval Iberian historiography never truly
established. Second, the previous editions have provided what is effectively
no more than a transcription of the principal manuscript and the current
edition benefits from the accumulated scholarship of the the last century or
so, a time in which our knowledge of the dynamics of Iberian historiography
expanded enormously.

It is widely accepted that the *Estoria delos godos* is a vernacular translation of
Ximénez de Rada's *magnum opus*. Beyond this simple, and ultimately
deceptive, datum, there is little accord among those who have sought to
examine it.[3] To begin with, the nature of the text as translation is
problematic, as it can scarcely be described as an accurate rendering in one
language of a text originally composed in another, even if we were to assume
that such be an appropriate definition of the nature of translation. However,
the greatest source of academic disagreement lies in the content and
significance of the *Estoria* itself, as manifested in a number of key areas.

To date, the most acute method of analysis of medieval chronicles in
Castilian is that provided by Leonardo Funes. This involves an examination
of the inter-relationship between three key elements, defined by Funes as '(i)
[el] lugar de enunciación cronística, (ii) [el] sistema de modelos cronísticos y
(iii) [los] modos concretos de configuración narrativa del hecho histórico'.[4]
What we are therefore concerned with is the complex relationships between

---

[3] There have been few studies of the medieval translations of Rodrigo's work. See for
example Benito Sánchez Alonso, 'Las versiones en romance de las crónicas del
Toledano', in *Homenaje ofrecido a Menéndez Pidal. Miscelánea de estudios lingüísticos, literarios e
históricos*, 3 vols. (Madrid: Hernando, 1925), I, 341–354; Diego Catalán, 'El Toledano
romanzado y las estorias del fecho delos godos', in *Estudios dedicados a James Homer Herriott*
(Madison: HSMS, 1966), 9–102; and the now very dated José Amador delos Ríos, *Historia
crítica de la literatura española*, Gredos reprint (Madrid: Gredos, 1969). Linda Elizabeth
Lassiter's *An Etymological Vocabulary and Study of La Estoria de los Godos, 1243*, Spanish
Studies 25 (Lewiston, Queenston, Lampeter: The Edwin Mellen Press, 2004) adds almost
nothing to our knowledge of the chronicle, as the author relies principally on Amador
delos Ríos for her information about the *Estoria*.
[4] Funes, 'Las variaciones', p. 117.

the internal and external contexts of composition of the chronicle, where the former is understood as the specifically textual dynamics of composition and the latter the historical background at the time of its composition. The manner of analysis, then, involves the careful collation of data, both internal and external, provided by the chronicle itself with what is known of the social and political conditions which gave rise to it.[5] This necessarily gives rise to a series of hypotheses which fall broadly into Funes's categories. The primary area of interest with respect to the *Estoria* derives from its relationship to the source text, with reference both to questions of form and content (e.g. version of the Latin text employed, analysis of what is included, omitted and added etc.) from which it is possible to arrive at some tentative conclusions about the nature of the text.[6] First, however, it is necessary to situate the *Estoria* in its most immediate contexts: those of the surviving manuscripts and the date of its composition.

The Manuscripts

There are four surviving manuscripts of the *Estoria*.

Madrid, Biblioteca Nacional ms. 302 (*Olim*. Toledo, Archivo de la Catedral ms. F196, 26–23.)

BN 302 is the sole complete medieval codex of the *Estoria*, and until the recent appearance of BN Res/278 (see below), the principal source of information on the text. The physical characteristics of the text, as described by Faulhaber, Simón Díaz and the catalogue of the Biblioteca Nacional are as follows: 75 folios of vellum, with two paper guard sheets at the beginning and one at the end. Folio size 225mm × 140mm, text box 162mm × 109mm. 28 lines per folio. There are 9 octavo cuadernos and one cuarto at the end. A nineteenth-century binding has been added (for full detail see Faulhaber).[7]

---

[5] While one must always bear in mind Diego Catalán's comments on the priority of textual criticism, and the dangers associated with prioritising the 'ideological' elements in the construction of any text, it is still possible to reach tentative conclusions. Diego Catalán, 'Monarquía aristocrática y manipulación de las fuentes: Rodrigo en la *Crónica de Castilla*. El fin de modelo historiográfico alfonsí', in Martin ed., *La historia*, pp. 75–94, esp. pp. 75–6 and p. 94.

[6] It is not my intention to comment on the linguistic nature of the translation, although this is not an indication of the lack of value of such an exercise.

[7] http://sunsite.berkeley.edu/Philobiblon/BETA/1390.html

The hand is a Gothic miniscule, and rubrics are picked out in red ink. A later hand has added chapter numbers and foliation.[8] The same hand has also made some corrections and marginal additions, principally concerning the numbering of the councils of Toledo. These alterations must be from the eighteenth century, or prior to it, as they have been incorporated into the text of Madrid, Biblioteca Nacional ms. 12.990, which dates from that century. The codex also contains some comments from the pen of Amador delos Ríos on the nature of the text. One minor oddity of the text is the presence of paragraph marks, usually to mark sense divisions. These disappear abruptly at folio 23v in the chapter entitled, 'Delos bienes de España'. Initial capitals are picked out in red and blue ink, the two colours generally alternating in successive chapters. Initials are generally two lines high, although letters with significant descenders appear adorned in the margin. The later hand has also numbered the chapters and provided foliation.

BN 302 resided for some considerable time in the library of the Cathedral of Toledo, and may indeed have been copied there, although there is no evidence beyond the circumstantial to confirm this. BN 302 was probably one of the two hundred manuscripts moved to the Biblioteca Nacional from the Cathedral of Toledo in 1869.[9] Although it is the earliest of the manuscripts of the known codices of the *Estoria*, it is not an original copy. On the contrary, comparison with BN Res/278 shows that BN 302 suffers from a significant number of defective readings. However, it has been chosen as the base text for the current edition, as it does contain the complete text of the *Estoria*. It also served as the base text for the Lidfors edition and the Paz y Melia transcription which is based upon it.[10]

Madrid, Biblioteca Nacional ms. Res/278

In 2001 the Biblioteca Nacional acquired a further version of the *Estoria delos godos* from Subastas Velázquez, with an ex-libris of José Menéndez Pidal y Álvarez. The codex consists of 105 folios of paper, 262mm × 172mm, the text box is 27 lines per folio, 220 × 140 mm, in what is thought to be a fifteenth-century hand. Rubrics are picked out in red ink, and initials in what is now a faded lilac. The section beginning 'Que peccados…' sees the use of

---

[8] The later hand which numbers the chapters in BN 302 omits a number of them and, in error, leaps directly from 79 to 90.
[9] For a history of the manuscript collections of the BN see http://www.bne.es/esp/comanuscritos.htm
[10] See p. 47 below.

paragraph marks picked out in red. Foliation is provided in both Arabic and Roman numerals. The opening folio is badly damaged as are the final folios, and folios 18, 19, 21, 39, 40, 42, 59 and 90 are missing. The text of the *Estoria* runs from folio 2r to 100r, and the remaining folios are occupied by the beginning of a further chronicle which starts; 'Esta es la generacion delos Reyes τ delos primeros padres como uino de padres en fijos...' and ends '...moujera por don Lacmedon que los tanmal recibio τ mandol...', of which more below. The manuscript is of particular interest as it contains the text of the *Estoria* supplemented by additional sections translated directly from *De rebus* and which the copyist presumably felt were rather badly served by the text of the original *Estoria*.[11] The points at which BN Res/278 employs its own translation are marked in the footnotes of the present edition. In general, however, it can be said that the newly translated section covers the history of the Goths; it is employed directly from the beginning of BN Res/278 until the text corresponding to folio 12v of BN 302, from which point the new translation is intertwined with the *Estoria* text. It is particularly noticeable that the copyist of BN Res/278 accepted the *Estoria* text for the early years of Bamba's reign. From folio 24r of the BN 302 text ('Que peccados fizieron los reyes godos') onwards the two codices are all but identical, with the exception of minor errors of readings. BN Res/278 is therefore much more of a history of the Goths than is the *Estoria*. However, given that the copyist of BN Res/278 must have had the *Estoria* text to hand, and that the BN 302 text is more consistent in its editorial policy, it is the BN 302 text that has been followed for this edition. The additional translations, which are far more faithful to the *De rebus* than is the BN 302 text and which maintain the chapter structure of the Latin,[12] are worthy of further examination, but this falls outside the scope of the present study.

Where the manuscript follows its own translation of *De rebus* it mirrors the Latin chapter structure. Subsequently, the rubrics are similar to those of BN 302. The rubricator has made an attempt to imitate the Gothic script of the source text for some of the rubrics deriving from the 'original' *Estoria delos godos*. The folio beginning 'Que peccados...' (fol.43) is the first in a new gathering, and as the previous folio is missing it is impossible to say where the definitive move away from the 'new' BN Res/278 translation of *De rebus* occurs. Curiously, the use of paragraph marks in BN Res/278 from this

[11] Enrique Jerez Cabrero, 'La Historia gothica del Toledano y la historiografía romance', *Cahiers de linguistique et de civilisation hispaniques médiévales*, 26 (2003), 223–40 (pp. 230–33).
[12] For the chapter structure of *De rebus* see Inés Fernández-Ordóñez, 'La técnica historiográfica del Toledano. Procedimientos de organización del relato', *Cahiers de linguistique et de civilisation hispaniques médiévales*, 26 (2003), 187–222.

point corresponds almost exactly to their disappearance from BN 302. However, the possibility of a textual boundary at this point in a putative common source is somewhat unlikely as BN Res/278 obviously had access to the 'original' *Estoria* text in previous sections. It seems most likely then, that both BN Res/278 and BN 302 derive from a common, now lost, archtype. This impression is added to by the presence at the beginning of BN Res/278 of a title page in which Rodrigo is described as 'Confirmador delas Españas'. This is drawn from the opening lines of the 'original' *Estoria* text, and the equivalent passage does not appear in BN Res/278.

The remaining text at the end of the codex also merits comment. Brief inspection of the five folios in question reveal a significant similarity with the *Liber Regum*/*Livro das Linhagens*/*Libro de las Generaciones* group of texts. Similarity, but not identity, for the BN Res/278 text shares features with each of these texts in different proportions. The fact that the text is compiled in Castilian has implications not only for the whole of BN Res/278, but also for the textual relationships of the *Liber Regum* tradition. It is most likely that the fragmentary text here is the beginning of the so-called LR$_2$, that is, the Castilian version of the *Liber Regum* probably composed in Toledo in the 1220s. If this is the case, the presence of details shared with the *Libro de las Generaciones* and the *Livro das Linhagens*, but not with the *Liber Regum*, suggests that there must have been a Navarrese LR$_2$ which served as archtype for all of them. Once more, the question falls outside the current study, but again merits further consideration. However, the presence of another 'Toledan' chronicle in the same codex emphasises the origins of the *Estoria* in the see of Toledo.

Madrid, Biblioteca Nacional ms. 12.990 (N)

This manuscript, 195 folios of paper, appears to be a copy of BN 302, as it states on the title page 'Historia de España Escrita en Latin por Rodrigo Ximenez, Arzobispo de Toledo Y traducida en castellano antiguo por un Anonymo Sacada de un Ms antiguo en pergamino en forma de 4o que se guarda en la libreria de la Santa Iglesia primada de Toledo Caj 21 num 15 Año de M.DCC.LII'. CarolAnn van der Walt says of this that '[t]he codex reference given here does not equate to any known reference for BN 302. However, as Sánchez Alonso notes, 'no es de extrañar que en aquella librería se multiplicasen las copias de obras de un prelado tan esclarecido'.[13]

---

[13] Sánchez Alonso, 'Las versiones', p. 342. This section was completed thanks to the generous help of Carol Ann van der Walt. See Carol Ann van der Walt, 'A critical edition of the Toledano Romanzado', Unpublished PhD. thesis (University of Birmingham, 1999).

Nonetheless, the similarities between BN 302 and BN 12.990 are such as to render unnecessary the positing of another codex in the Toledo library. Furthermore, as van der Walt points out, a later note at the end of BN 12.990 seems to suggest that BN 302 was indeed the source for the later text. The readings supplied by BN 12.990 generally follow those of BN 302, though on occasion they are rather clearer. As such, BN 12.990 has occasionally been employed in the edition to clarify defective readings in BN 302.

Hispanic Society of America HC 385/274

This manuscript is described by Faulhaber in *Medieval Manuscripts in the Library of the Hispanic Society of America. Religious, Legal, Scientific, Historical, and Literary Manuscripts*, I, pp. 484–86, item 485; it is dated 1752 and states it was copied in Toledo by Francisco Javier de Santiago y Palomares. It consists of 140 folios on paper, 304mm x 201 mm, text size 235mm x 140 mm, with a guard sheet at the beginning and end. From my examination of the text, it can be identified as a copy of BN 302. As a codex descriptus it was not employed in the current study.

It is possible that both BN 302 and BN Res/278 are drawn from a common archetype, the latter supplemented by its own translation and the former, in places, poorly copied. However, in the absence of a wider textual tradition it is not thought appropriate to provide either a more categorical statement of the relationship between the extant manuscripts and putative missing manuscripts, nor a rather bare stemma codicum.

Previous editions:

There are two previous editions, both of which appear to confine themselves to transcription: E. Lidfors, *Acta Universitatis Lundunensis*, 7 (1871) and 8 (1872); A. Paz y Melia, *Colección de documentos inéditos para la historia de España*, LXXXVIII (Madrid: 1887).

Date of composition

The *Estoria delos godos* appears to be a product of the thirteenth century, as the earliest manuscript can be plausibly dated to this period. The first significant attempt to posit a date of composition for the *Estoria* is that of Amador delos Ríos, who suggested that the translator was none other than Rodrigo Ximénez de Rada himself, as no-one else would have had the authority to alter the Archbishop's words so radically. This view, rejected in turn by Paz y Melia and Sánchez Alonso, would place the translation some time in the mid- to late- 1240s. Enrique Jerez Cabrero has demonstrated quite convincingly that the source text for the translation was one of the manuscripts of the *primera redacción* of *De rebus*, that version of the chronicle completed in 1243, and not the *segunda redacción* which was completed in 1246/7.[14] This leaves a potentially suitable period of four years between the completion of the first version and Rodrigo's death in the waters of the Rhône on 10 June 1247 within which the Archbishop could conceivably have composed the translation. Could have, but did not. For the translation refers specifically to Alfonso X as the king of Castile, ('do*n* Alfonso rey de Castiella, fijo del rey do*n* Fernando' p. 134)[15] in which case the *terminus a quo* for the scribe putting quill to parchment must be 30 May 1252, the date that Alfonso acceded to the throne. Enrique Jerez has suggested that the *terminus ad quem* must be 8 July 1253, the date of the death of Teobaldo I of Navarra. The rationale for this is quite straightforward: while dealing with the genealogy of the kings of Navarra, the translator refers to near contemporary events in the following way:

> La te*r*cera fija, doña Bla*n*ca, caso co*n* Tibaldo, co*n*de de Cha*m*paña, τ
> ouo en ella a do*n* Tibaldo. Este Tibaldo caso co*n* fija del co*n*de delas
> Marchas τ despues partiero*n* se por ygle*s*ia a gra*n*d pesar della; pues
> este do*n* Tibaldo caso co*n* fija de do*n* Guisart de Belioc τ de doña
> Sebilia, fija de Felip, co*n*de de Fra*n*dria; τ desta muge*r* ouo una fija
> doña Bla*n*ca, q*ue* despues caso co*n* do*n* Iuha*n*, duc de Bretaña. Pues
> este Thobaldo caso otra uez co*n* doña Margarita, fija de un noble
> p*r*incep Arche*n*bad, e ouo en esta dos fijos, do*n* Thobaldo τ do*n*
> Ped*r*o τ ot*r*os. Este do*n* Tibaldo, por faze*r* se*r*uit*i*o a Dios, pasose a
> ultra mar et en aiuda de la t*i*e*r*ra sa*n*ta, τ gano ala uillas τ castiellos q*ue*
> dio a c*hr*ist*i*anos, fizo mucho bie*n* a cauale*r*os me*n*guados, τ pues torno
> asu t*i*e*r*ra. Este heredo Nauarra. (p. 128)

---

[14] Jerez Cabrero, 'La Historia', p. 223.
[15] All references to the text of the *Estoria* are to page numbers in the current edition.

There are two objections to this. Although it is clear in the Latin text that the last line refers to Teobaldo I, it is not so clear in the translation. Indeed, a subsequent historian of the kingdom, basing himself on this passage of the *Estoria*, came to the conclusion that it is Teobaldo II (1253–1274) who is being referred to here.[16] Furthermore, the logic of Jerez's argument is that had the text dated from after 1253, the translator would have included mention of Teobaldo's death, and, presumably other events which he knew to have taken place outside the framework of *De rebus*. However, the translation ends at precisely the same point as the Latin, and in almost identical fashion, even to the point of including Ximénez de Rada's explicit. It therefore appears to have no pretensions to be anything other than a version of Ximénez de Rada's words, and it in no sense brings the narrative up to the present of the translator. The absence of any reference to the death of Teobaldo therefore tells us nothing more than the fact that the translator did not include it, but we cannot be sure *why* he did not do so. This absence, in itself, is not proof of anything. The sole datum we are left with is therefore the present tense reference to Alfonso X as king. But this, of course, would permit a date of composition as late as 1284.

There are a number of reasons for positing a date of composition in the last 12 years of Alfonso's reign. First of all, if we are to read as significant possible references to contemporary events, then we must take *all* such references as significant. One such reference is that to the infanta Aldonza, daughter of Alfonso IX, who is described as one of the offspring of the king, all of whom die 'sin fijos' (p. 155). Aldonza died in 1267. Another such reference is to Alfonso X's sister Berenguela (1235–79), for whom the present tense of the Latin has become a past tense in the translation (p. 180). A nun in Las Huelgas, she was buried there in 1279. A third reference of this type is the removal of the phrase 'hodie principatur' (p. 181) in reference to Muhammad I, the first Nasrid king of Granada, who died in 1273. Taken on their own, of course, such data are no more conclusive than the absence of reference to the death of Teobaldo.[17] However, there are other, internal, factors which suggest a late date of composition, certainly one following the Conjuración de Lerma and the nobles' revolt against Alfonso, and perhaps even so late as to come within the bounds of the 'corte molinista' described

[16] See García de Eugui, *Crónica d'Espayña de García de Eugui*, ed. Aengus Ward (Pamplona: Institución Príncipe de Viana, 1999), p. 391.
[17] Diego Catalán comments on the hazards of using the last attested date as a reliable method of dating chronicles in his *La Estoria*, p. 72. Most such judgements rely on circumstantial evidence, the importance of which lies in the identification of trends.

by Fernando Gómez Redondo, and broadly associated with the figure of the Archbishop of Toledo, Gonzalo García Gudiel.[18]

The *Estoria delos godos*, *De rebus Hispanie* and the history of Iberia

Although it is ostensibly a version in Iberian romance of *De rebus Hispanie*, the *Estoria delos godos* is, in many ways, a radically different chronicle. For the purposes of the following discussion the *Estoria* has been compared and contrasted with its source under a number of significant headings, some suggested by the content of the text itself, and others of a more general nature. These, in the main, represent major differences between the two, and cover the following areas: abbreviation of the Latin text; textual organization of the translation; and additions and modifications to the Latin text. These last, in turn, are grouped under the following sub-headings: heightened interest in religious matters, and particularly in the see of Toledo; a distinct perspective on material deriving from legendary or epic sources; an altered rhetorical style, with particular emphasis on direct speech; a raising of the profile of Alfonso VII; a modified view of the relationship between king and nobility; and a notable interest in the non-Castilian kingdoms of Iberia, with particular reference to Aragon and the lordship of Albarracín.

Abbreviation of the source text

There can, of course, be no doubt that the *Estoria* represents a significantly abbreviated version of *De rebus*, as the disparity in length between the two amply attests. However, it is entirely reasonable to suggest that the nature of such abbreviation is of itself worthy of comment, as it must be assumed that in reducing the scope of his text, the translator would either remove significant detail or provide a summary of Rodrigo's eloquent words. In fact, as might be expected, he did both, but an examination of the former may help to suggest a motive for the very compilation of the translation in the first instance.

Before dealing in depth with such examples it is worth examining the former phenomenon, that is, the replacement of lengthy passages of Latin

---

[18] See below p. 45.

by rather more laconic romance, without losing a great deal of primary information. This method of translation accounts for a sizeable proportion of the difference in scale between source and translation. The following passage serves as a useful example:

Pues passo por Cartagena τ prisola τ destruyola. E don Chaco moraua estonçe en Celciberia o Carpecia, este fue dicho fijo de Ulean τ moraua en Moncayo, e por esso le diçien hoy assi en latin Monscatus, el Mont de Caco τ era muy rico de ganados; a este uençio don Hercules. Despues Cacus fuxo en Lauinia en un mont quel dizien agora Auentino, τ metiosse en una cueua mucho estrecha τ cercola con cadenas. (p. 56)

Procedensque per Cartaginensem prouinciam occupans deuastauit et Cacum, qui en Carpentania et Celtiberia morabatur, bello contritum in fugam coegit. Hic digitur Vulcani filius, cuius habitatio principalis in monte Carpentanie, qui adhuc hodie mons Caci dicitur, celebris habebatur, cui armentorum et gregum et uenationum copia famulatur et in Sirrio iugo sublimior inuenitur, cuius principium prope Lermam Tirreno prope Socorbicam terminatur. Cacus autme bello inferior, fuge prodigus, Lauiniam peciit et inmonte qui nunc Auentinus dicitur, in spelunca saxea, profundissima, tenebrosa metu Hercules se recipit, cuius aditum garuis moles cathenis appensa ferreis protegebat, quam ipse paterno artificio fabricarat. (I.v.15–27).

The technique employed here is scarcely that of word-for-word translation. The translator is interested in toponyms and personal names, and the set of relations between them but little else. Indeed, he goes on to excise Rodrigo's gloss on the legendary description of Cacus altogether, along with mention of its source (Lucan) to deal instead with the next in the series of events forming part of the narrative chain. Although the translator has attempted to retain as many significant details as possible, it is noticeable that this effort comes at the cost of a high degree of polysyndeton. This stylistic phenomenon, scarcely unknown in thirteenth-century Castilian chronicles, nonetheless contrasts strongly with the stylistic fluency of Ximénez de Rada's text. The translation therefore represents an attempt to retain the principal factual information of the source in an embryonic written language which is still searching for a style to match that of Latin prose. Similar examples can be seen all through the text. A fine example of typical abbreviation by the translator comes in his account of the doings of Count Sancho of Castile:

Muerto el co*n*de do*n* Ferrand, **finco** co*n*dado a su fijo do*n* Sa*n*cho, τ salio muy bueno τ dio muy buenos fueros τ tolio los malos q*ue* falo; τ firmo su amor co*n* el rey de Leon τ co*n* el de Nauarra como fiziera su padre, τ co*n* ayuda delos mouio sus huestes τ paso por Toledo, q*ue*ma*n*do τ destruyendo, τ por Cordoua otrosi. Pues diero*n* le gra*n*d auer, τ fincaro*n* q*ue*bra*n*tados, τ asi ue*n*go asu padre. (p. 124)

Hic succesit in comitatu Sancius filius eius, uir prudens, iustus, liberalis, strenuus et benignus, qui nobiles nobilitate pociore donauit et inminoribus seruitutis duriciam temperauit. His patris iniuriam impaciens sustinere, iuxta fedus cum patre initium Nauarrorum et Legionensum exercitus conuocauit, et ingressus cum eis ad partes Toleti cede et clade cuncta uastauit, et predis abductis, que remanserant flama consumpsit. Nec ab hiis stragibus fuit regnum Cordube alienum; set utroque regno uastatione consumpto et munera optulerunt et indignationis faciem donariorum copia placauerunt; et sic patris iniuria uindicata gloriosus et inclitus remeauit. (V.xviiii–12)

Once more the concerns of the translator are plain. The major narrative elements are preserved in all their brevity and the flowing, elegant prose of the Latin converted into a series of consecutive data. The comparative concision of the *Estoria* is due, in no small measure, to this key principle of the translator: retain as much of the factual detail as possible and make no attempt to reproduce the style of the source.[19]

Although the manner of translation described above accounts for a large part of the abbreviation characteristic of the *Estoria*, more significant qualitatively, if not quantitively, are those sections of the Latin which fail to appear under any guise in the *Estoria*. That the translator engaged in such editing is apparent from the very beginning; that it is accomplished systematically becomes clear from a detailed overview. The first major excision of *De rebus* material from the *Estoria* comes right at the outset. Following Rodrigo's address to Fernando III, copied in Latin in the *Estoria*, the translator removes almost all of Rodrigo's prologue. What remains of the archbishop's account appears in the form of a truncated statement of why Rodrigo was writing, accompanied by mention of his principal sources. In consequence, all of the archbishop's commentary on the nature of history, and the nature of its writing, is removed. So when the translator has Rodrigo explain that his aim is 'componer mi libro delos fechos de España', there is little doubt that it is precisely this that the translator has in mind for his own work. As we have seen, the translation's concern is the recounting

[19] Of course, this may be due to the non-existence of such stylish prose in the vernacular, but in the end it makes little difference.

of factual information, and Rodrigo's occasional philosophising, as in the case of the prologue, will be left to one side. Of course, the reader without access to the Latin would never know the difference, and would, presumably, take the *Estoria* as a faithful rendering of Rodrigo's words. For the fortunate well-informed few, however, the differences are revealing.

There are a number of specific thematic strands of *De rebus* which led the translator to wield his editorial pen in systematic fashion. The first of these is particularly interesting as it led to a major difference between the two earliest surviving codices of the *Estoria*. The most cursory examination of the earliest of these manuscripts, Madrid, Biblioteca Nacional MS. 302, reveals that the most widespread abbreviation and excision of source material takes place in the first half of the chronicle, in the text covering the beginning of the chronicle up to the account of the Visigothic kings of the Peninsula. For example, when dealing with the sons of Noah (p. 53), the translator has retained most of the toponyms, but cuts the *De rebus* material dealing with the actions of Tubal outside the Peninsula. Similarly, the extra-Peninsular doings of Hercules (p. 55); Ximénez de Rada's commentary on the origins of the Goths and his sources (pp. 58–9); his detailed account of various of their battles (e.g. pp. 60, 62); his interest in Alaric (p. 62 ff) and his commentary on Theudis, to mention just some, all but disappear in the *Estoria*. It is in precisely these sections that the other major medieval manuscript, Biblioteca Nacional Res/278, differs substantially to BN 302. This latter codex replaces most of the early sections of the *Estoria* with a translation of *De rebus* which is, in the main, an accurate rendering in Castilian of the Latin. The difference between the two is clear: despite the title accorded to it, the version of the *Estoria* preserved for us in BN 302 is less of a history of the Goths than, as the codex itself points out, an account of the 'fechos de España'. By contrast, whoever was responsible for BN Res/278 must have decided that a full account of the Goths was necessary, and so provided one to replace the original, much abbreviated translation.[20] Nonetheless, the version of the text of most widespread diffusion, that of BN 302, retained the title *Estoria delos godos*, and despite the significant

---

[20] It could perhaps be suggested that although Res/278 is a later manuscript it could represent an earlier stage of composition. However, the sections unique to Res/278 are the only sections in either manuscript which are so closely translated, and they do not therefore fit quite so well with the editorial policy of the whole as do their BN 302 equivalents. From this, it seems logical to deduce that they are additions to the BN 302 text on the part of someone who regarded the BN 302 history of the Goths to be insufficient.

disjunction between title and content, it seems reasonable to maintain the title by which it has always been known. The original intent, it seems, was to provide a history of Spain, translated from Ximénez de Rada's Latin chronicle, and not a history of the Goths.

Although it can seemingly be demonstrated that the translator's view required a chronicle of Spain in which, implicitly at least, *neogoticismo* is reduced in importance by comparison with *De rebus*, the excision of lengthy extra-Peninsular Gothic detail is not the sole systematic editorial act in the *Estoria*.[21] For there are other parallel indications to be found elsewhere in the translator's trimming of his source material. His interest in Roman affairs (already dealt with in cursory fashion by Rodrigo) is all but nonexistent (p. 62). In addition, he fails to replicate Rodrigo's interest in Islamic matters, methodically removing all of the archbishop's accounts of, for example, the origins of the Almohads (p. 157) and the actions of Almanzor (p. 121). However, his eagerness to remove characters from the lens of history is not confined to non-Christians. The non-Spanish troops who (briefly, at any rate) turned up for Las Navas de Tolosa come in for similar treatment as that accorded to Almanzor (pp. 167–8); and, perhaps not surprisingly, Rodrigo's words on the subject of Arianism are also consigned to the historiographical dustbin (p. 64). There are two other major suppressions worthy of comment. The first concerns the aforementioned tendency of the translator to remove those passages in which Rodrigo breaks the narrative flow to engage in religious or philosophical discussion, one such example being Ximénez de Rada's commentary on the nature of faith (p. 160). Such concern to maintain the narrative thread is accompanied by a regular removal of the Biblical quotations of which Rodrigo was so fond. The second notable suppression occurs in the later stages of the *Estoria* when Ximénez de Rada's paeans of praise for two different Castilian kings, Alfonso VI (p. 145) and Alfonso VIII (p. 168) respectively, are entirely removed, as is a similar passage in praise of Fernando III's mother Berenguela (p. 182). As will be seen below, the attitude to Alfonso VIII is very different in the translation, but the removal of more than one such commentary is scarcely an accident.

In this light, we might be justified in suggesting that not only was the translator's expected audience interested solely in the chain of events of a specifically Spanish history in which the role of monarchs is not overplayed,

---

[21] *Neogoticismo* is understood as that trend in political and historical discourse which saw the medieval monarchs of Iberia, and in particular those of Castile, as the inheritors of the kingdom of the Visigoths. See for example José Antonio Maravall, *El concepto de España en la Edad Media* (Madrid: Instituto de Estudios Políticos, 1954).

but also that the same audience was not expected to recognise Biblical quotations in Latin. Of course, this might seem to exclude the possibility of an ecclesiastical readership, but then, they might have been expected to have access to Rodrigo's Latin chronicle in the first place.[22]

Textual organization of the *Estoria delos godos*

There is some disagreement over the extent to which it can be said that *De rebus Hispanie* was compiled in the formal manner with which we are today familiar, that is, in a series of well-defined books and chapters. Nonetheless, there is little doubt that the textual organization of Rodrigo's work fulfilled Vincent de Beauvais' dictum that capitulation should be made so that 'operis partes singule lectori facilius eluscenant'.[23] Inés Fernández-Ordóñez has demonstrated the organizational principles of the Latin text in such a way as to confirm the rigorous nature of its structure. On the face of it, however, the *Estoria delos godos* could not be more different. In the place of the 219 chapters divided into nine books provided by *De rebus*, the *Estoria* presents us with 105 chapters, or perhaps 'rubrics' would be a better term, with no higher divisions into books or sections. Furthermore, unlike their equivalents in the source text, the chapters of the *Estoria* rarely correspond to the lives of significant figures, nor are topical elements dealt with in the same manner as is frequently the case in *De rebus*.

The correlation, or lack of it, between the formal structure of the two texts is revealing. On many occasions the *Estoria*'s rubrics correspond to formal breaks in *De rebus*, although the rubrics bear little resemblance to their Latin equivalents. Indeed, from the chapter entitled 'De la muerte del conde don Iulian' onwards, almost all the chapter breaks in the *Estoria* occur at similar chapter breaks in *De rebus*, although the converse is obviously not the case.[24] Previous to this point however, there is very little correspondence.

The choice of divisions on the part of the translator reveals not a little about his priorities. Of the new chapter breaks provided by the *Estoria*, no less than eighteen are, in one way or another, related to various councils of Toledo; two others deal with archbishops of Toledo; and three more are related to the preservation of the holy relics, their transfer from the city and

---

[23] Quoted in Fernández-Ordóñez, 'La técnica' p. 205.
[24] Part of the reason for this is, of course, that the *Estoria* does not follow *DRH* particularly closely for its history of the Goths.

an explanation of why Toledo is the primatial see, taking the argument to those who suggest that Seville might have a better case. In the entire narration of the history of Iberia up to 711 only two named kings have a chapter/rubric to themselves. However, in one of these cases, that of Chindaswinth, the content of the chapter is concerned almost exclusively with the question of the primacy of Toledo. The second, that of Bamba, is in majuscules; this section will be dealt with in detail below. After the Muslim conquest, the rubrics tend to follow a more traditional pattern of mentioning individual monarchs by name, although this is by no means always so.[25]

The divisions may, on the surface, appear somewhat idiosyncratic. There are many cases of lengthy chapters in the *Estoria* which cover material drawn from large numbers of *De rebus* sections. For example, 'De la batalla de Roncasvalles' [sic] takes material from eight chapters of *De rebus*, 'De las batallas de Almonzorre' from six and 'Delos reyes de Asturias' from ten. What is more puzzling are the rubrics themselves. The aforementioned chapter on the battles of Almanzor sees the death of the great Muslim warlord after about half of its length, and that ostensibly dealing with the death of Julian eventually comes to a halt with the accession of Alfonso el Casto. It is true that certain sections appear to possess a rather higher degree of textual unity. For example, the kings of Navarra, Aragon and Portugal are given their own sections, although the reader might struggle to ascertain the rationale behind the division of the text in this manner.[26] In certain circumstances, it seems, the translator has made an effort to highlight particular historical phenomena, as in the case of the Councils of Toledo, which are therefore marked out as of particular importance. The same might also be said of the divisions given to the *Estoria*'s account of the battle of Las Navas, or indeed the sections dealing with the non-Castilian/Leonese kingdoms. Elsewhere it is hard to imagine the rationale for such textual organization. It may, in fact, be the case that the author or copyist had no greater motive for the rubrics than that of aide-mémoire or brief indication of what is shortly to come.[27] The presence of the rubrics themselves, in

---

[25] A full list of the rubrics can be found in Appendix 1.

[26] I discuss this point further in my 'La *Estoria delos godos*: ¿la primera crónica castellana?', *Revista de poética medieval*, 8 (2002), 181–98.

[27] This is a point made by Keith Busby in repsect of *Perceval* manuscripts: "That rubrics, like miniatures and other markers functioned as bookmarks and helped the reader or performer orientate his or herself is perfectly plausible". Keith Busby, *Codex and Context. Reading Old French Verse Narrative in Manuscript*, 2 vols. (Amsterdam, New York: Rodopi, 2002), vol I, p.347. Busby is here following Manfred Gunther Scholz's notion that rubrics

many cases, reflect the chapters of *De rebus*, so we must assume that where the translator has chosen to divide the text in an alternative manner, that this must have some significance. The wording of the rubrics themselves may be of rather less consequence.

One final element of organization of discourse merits attention: the presence within the text of the translator himself. In fact, the translator has not only gone to great lengths to remove himself from the narration, but many of the first person asides of Ximénez de Rada are also elided. Such personal comments as there are generally take the form 'direuos', 'esta es la uerdad', or the plaintive 'qui mas sabe, diga' at the end of a commentary on the resting places of a number of saints. There is also one specifically actualising comment: 'et el dio et establesçio que Santiague ouiese una caualleria en sus caualgadas que fue por costumbre, τ asi es oy en dia en algunas fronteras' (p. 107). However, it is not clear which 'fronteras' in particular the translator had in mind, nor, obviously, why he might have been familiar with them. Perhaps the only remotely extended intervention by the translator in the course of the narrative comes in the section dealing with the death of Hercules.

> En la fin don Hercules fue coytado por amor de su muger, que non pudo yr tan ayna aella como querie, ca de dolor τ de grand amor fizo fazer muy grand fuego τ echose alli τ assi mato asi mismo el que mato a muchos otros. Esta fue la uerdad maguer la faba dize que Dexanara por conseio de un encantador fiziera una camisa enuenada τ que la enuiara por quel fizieran entender que amaua otra muger. τ dizien que luego que la uistio començo de arder. Otros dizen quela camisa era estrecha τ al uestir que le afogo τ asi mismo yo digo que la camisa fue la dueña τ la estrechura fue la firmedumbre τ el atreuimiento de la bien querencia τ el ueneno fue el fuego dela grand amor, τ asi murio. (p. 56–7)

In this case, the first person voice is not that of Ximénez de Rada. Beyond indicating a certain talent for literary analysis and an eye for the allegorical solution, the presence of the 'yo' figure in this case tells us precious little about the translator and his motives for writing. In truth, such motives can only be deduced from the content of the chronicle, as the material concerning the translator himself is pretty thin stuff.

---

can serve as guides to silent readers, performance readers or even serve as indicators to illustrators. As the *Estoria* codices are all unadorned (perhaps they aim, in Busby's words, for the "weightiness and seriousness approaching that of the chronicle" which he sees in the unbroken text of certain *Renart* manuscripts, *Codex*, p.259), it may be that they were intended to be functional rather than decorative. The nature of the 'guide' offered to readers of the *Estoria* remains somewhat enigmatic.

Additions to, and modifications of, the source text

The *Estoria* has been written off in the past as a poor relation of *De rebus*, principally on the grounds that, unlike the *Toledano romanzado* for example, it is not an accurate rendition of the source text. The abbreviated nature of the translation has led to a, perhaps understandable, reluctance to treat the *Estoria* as a significant piece in the historiographical puzzle. There are many reasons why such an attitude could be challenged, one of which is that this is to miss the subtle shifts and changes of ideological outlook contained within it. Some of these have been dealt with above, but amongst the most important are those which are represented by the additions to the Latin text. Equally important an indication of authorial world view is that provided by those sections which the translator chose not to abbreviate or cut, but rather translate in full. Many of these are, on the face of it, minor, but taken together they suggest a radically altered viewpoint from that offered by *De rebus*, or indeed by other late thirteenth-century historical writings.

The Estoria, matters ecclesiastical and the Archdiocese of Toledo

Peter Linehan, writing of the version of the *Estoria de Espanna* completed in 1289 under the auspices of Sancho IV, commented that it was written 'in the service of a view of history which was neither "coherently monarchical" nor "aristocratic" but ecclesiastical' and goes on to point out that, in fact, its 'ecclesiasticization' of the historical record actually implied its 'Toledanization'.[28] A text such as *De rebus*, imbued to its very core with Rodrigo's advocacy for his archdiocese might well be considered to fall into the same bracket. For this reason, the presence in the *Estoria* of material similarly advocating the importance of Toledo might not be considered to be so strong an indication of Toledan sympathies, as their absence would be viewed as advocacy of the contrary position. Nonetheless, the question of 'ecclesiasticization' and 'Toledanization' merits examination.

As mentioned above, the translator seems to have a particular interest in highlighting the Councils of Toledo which took place in the Visigothic period. Indeed, with the exception of detailed consideration of the early career of Bamba, there is little in the *Estoria*'s account of this period which is not explicitly related to matters ecclesiastical in one way or another. Thus, for example, while not adding major sections to Rodrigo's narrative, the

---

[28] Peter Linehan, *History and the Historians of Medieval Spain* (Oxford: Clarendon Press, 1993), p. 471.

translator chooses to retain in great detail the victory over Arianism (p. 64); papal letters confirming the metropolitan status of Oviedo and the establishment of Santiago and a lengthy list of bishops which follows them (p. 110 ff.); as well as the aforementioned debate over the primacy, resolved in Toledo's favour (pp. 72, 98, 144). In a work in which abbreviation of source material is the order of the day, retention of large-scale passages cannot but be significant. Here it is clear that the translator is not interested in the niceties of ecclesiastical argument, but is determined to include in his account of the Peninsula any material relating to the strategic position of the Church, and also the relative importance of its (arch)dioceses. It is true that in one of the cited examples, that of Oviedo, the inclusion of detailed information is not to the advantage of Toledo. However, in almost all the other cases, the explicit retention of ecclesiastical detail raises the profile of the primatial see and sets it above all others.

Such interest in the fate of Toledo is not confined to its relationship with other bishoprics. On a series of occasions the *Estoria* moves away from the forms of abbreviation outlined above and translates the words of Ximénez de Rada with what might seem surprising attention. Examples of this are to be found in the reign of Alfonso VI (pp. 144–47) when the fate of Toledo is described in full detail; in the *Estoria*'s account of the doings of Archbishop Bernard (p. 146) and also in the reign of Bamba, a king destined to be associated with Toledo, and whose regulations governing the see are reproduced (pp. 78–84), albeit not to the extent of copying the *Cum longe lateque* canon which is faithfully translated in BN Res/278. What is more, towards the end of the chronicle, the policy of abbreviation of the source text appears not to apply to those sections dealing with Toledo. Whereas in other sections the translator showed no particular interest in the minutiae of historical detail, where privileges accorded to the see of Toledo are concerned the manner of translation changes. This can be seen in the post-conquest account of the donations to Toledo by Alfonso VI (p. 144); again in the very final lines when the siege and capture of Lucena and Quesada are passed over in cursory fashion but their consequences, principally to the benefit of Toledo, are carefully preserved. There may even be a hint of personal familiarity with the archdiocese on the part of the translator as he translates 'uille ecclesie Toletane que Sanctus Torquatus dicitur' as 'Santo Torcat, cabo Alcala τ Guadalfaiara' (p. 174), although of course it is ill-advised to exaggerate the importance of such small details.

Although the specific arguments outlined by Peter Linehan in favour of a 'Toledanization' of the *Estoria de Espanna* are not directly applicable to the

Estoria delos godos,[29] nonetheless, the weight of textual evidence provided by the latter is such that it is reasonable to posit the existence of a translator who, at the very least, had an interest in highlighting the importance of the primatial see, and for whom 'ecclesiasticization' and 'Toledanization' were almost certainly synonymous.

Legend and epic in the Estoria

The question of the presence of legendary and epic material in the *Estoria* has been dealt with recently by Fernando Gómez Redondo. In an acutely observed article, he makes a series of general points on the implications for the chronicle of the inclusion of such material, and constructs a closely argued analysis of one legend in particular: the division of the kingdoms of Sancho el Mayor, following the calumny of his wife on the part of his sons.[30]

The text of the translation contains all the basic elements outlined in *De rebus*, and it therefore conveys the fundamental message of Rodrigo's version, which is an explanation of how Fernando I came to inherit Castile ahead of his first-born brother García, who, in the words of the *Estoria* 'lo deuie todo heredar como fijo mayor' (p. 129).[31] The detail, however, reveals significant additions in the *Estoria*. The key figures in the *Estoria*'s version are the Castilian knight who advises the queen, and the queen herself. It is she, rather than Sancho, who devises the succession of the kingdoms, and Fernando is seen as less blameworthy than in the Latin version. The conclusions Gómez Redondo draws from this concern the implications of the *Estoria*'s version for our understanding of the epic, and also for the understanding of the context of writing of the *Estoria*. First, and in line with the *Estoria*'s account of the subsequent death of García in the fratricidal wars, the *Estoria* highlights the evils of 'soberbia'. In the case of García, he will subsequently die at the hands of those of his knights who went into

---

[29] The coronations (or not) of Alfonso VII, Enrique I and Fernando III, and the presence of clergy (or not) at said events, do not figure so prominently in the *Estoria*, although in the case of Fernando III it is clear that his accession takes place in Toledo in the presence of the clergy. See also Aengus Ward, 'Rodrigo Ximénez de Rada: auteur et acteur à Castile du fin du treizième siècle', *Cahiers de linguistique et de civilisation hispaniques médiévales*, 26 (2003), pp. 283–94 (p.290).

[30] Fernando Gómez Redondo, 'La materia', 273–76. See also David Pattison, 'The legend of the sons of Sancho el Mayor', *Medium Aevum*, 51 (1982), 35–52.

[31] Fernando, the second born, inherited Castile in the traditional fashion, i.e. by division of his father's realms in which the firstborn received the father's own inheritance. This seems not to have been accepted by a host of chroniclers, hence the 'reina calumniada' story. This detail does not appear in *De rebus*.

voluntary exile in the face of the king's disdain for them. The message here with regard to the relationship between monarch and nobility is clear. A parallel conclusion concerns the *Estoria*'s concern for the necessity to, in Gómez Redondo's words, 'castigar el conducto de los primogénitos', a concern which will be brought into sharp focus in the *Estoria*'s account of Fernando's own children, and which could not be more relevant to the political context of the last quarter of the thirteenth century in Castile. Given that the 'reina calumniada' can be summed up as an indication of the weakness of royal power, the necessity of noble support for effective royal governance and, by extension, the importance and vitality of 'second' lines, its appropriateness to the burgeoning 'corte molinista' of which Gómez Redondo has written so eloquently, can hardly be overstated.

As Gómez Redondo also notes, there are many other occasions on which epic material appears to be present in the *Estoria*. Thus the *Estoria* contains due reference to Rodrigo and the loss of Spain; Bernardo el Carpio; Carlos Mainete; Fernán González; el Infante García; the Judges of Castile and the Cerco de Zamora. Not all of these are dealt with differently by the *Estoria*. The tale of Carlos Mainete, for example, follows the Latin text quite closely, as does that of the Infant García (within the confines of the *Estoria*'s standard manner of abbreviation). However, it is possible to suggest that where such changes do appear, they are far from being random. The first such case surrounds the opening by Rodrigo of the famous palace of Toledo. The brief *De rebus* account is factual: 'palacium a multorum regum temporibus semper clausum et seris pluribus obseratum' (III.xviii.11), which appears in the *Estoria* as 'un palacio q*ue* un rey fiziera ete*n*der, τ puso y un cañado τ puso por fuero τ por ley que nu*n*qua abriessen aq*ue*l palacio τ cada rey q*ue* uiniese q*ue* pusiese y su cagnado' (p. 87). King Rodrigo's curiosity here becomes the breach of 'fuero' and 'ley', with a rather obvious moral for what happens to an ill-advised king who should risk such proud behaviour. Not that the King Rodrigo of the *Estoria* has anyone to blame but himself, as the *De rebus* comment that his decision was taken 'contra uoluntatem omnium', becomes the rather more specific 'no*n* q*ui*so escuchar por co*n*seio delos suyos'. The *Estoria* by comparison with its source places a heavier premium on wise conduct of the monarch generally, where wise conduct is understood to involve assuring the place of the nobility in the smooth running of the kingdom.

The legend of the Judges of Castile has, of course, been dealt with in exhaustive fashion by Georges Martin.[32] In tracing the trajectory of the Judges in Peninsular historiography Martin was able to advance some hypotheses about the nature of the ideological projects the legend was destined to serve. On the basis of the Judges sections in the *Estoria* he states of the *Estoria* that 'ce n'est plus [...] l'aristocratie identifiée sous le rapport de son état naturel qui est portée au devant de la scène, mais la noblesse en tant qu'état hiérarchique', and goes on to say of the 'rôle spécifique que jouait la noblesse dans *De rebus Hispanie*' that the *Estoria* 'exalte ce rôle jusqu'à réserver à l'état nobiliaire toute la scène de l'histoire'.[33] The text of the Judges legend in the *Estoria* follows that of *De rebus* quite closely. However, Martin's conclusions, which are in line with much of the other textual evidence outlined above and below, demonstrates the extent to which what are ostensibly the same texts can vary significantly in meaning by virtue of the language employed.

To complete the overview of epic material, it is worth mentioning that both in the case of Bernardo el Carpio and in the case of the siege of Zamora, the translator displays a notable sympathy for those who suffer at the hands of, if not tyrannical, then certainly unjust, monarchs. In the case of the Zamora references, it should also be mentioned that this is perfectly in line with Gómez Redondo's comments on the subject of bastard or second-born sons. And, finally, mention should also be made of Rodrigo Díaz de Vivar. The Cid appears little in the source text. Although to nothing like the same extent as in the *Estoria de Espanna*, for example, the Campeador does make something of a comeback in the *Estoria delos godos*. It may be the case that the additional detail provided derives from epic sources, in particular the mention of his conquests and victories across the Peninsula. Although the Cid could fall into the category of 'knight harshly treated by unjust king', the translator appears rather more ambivalent about the Cid's rectitude. For although the sections of *De rebus* dealing with him are gathered together to provide a more coherent biographical sketch, the image given is not entirely positive. A possible reason for this is given at the outset of the first chapter dealing with him:

---

[32] See Martin, *Les juges* and 'Paraphrase (transcription/traduction; approche lexico-sémantique)', in his *Histoires*, pp. 69–105.
[33] Martin, 'Paraphrase', pp. 87 and 103.

Esto*n*z Ruy Dias era mal q*uí*sto del rey do*n* Alfonso, τ echolo de ti*er*ra, lo uno por su co*n*seio se guiaua el rey do*n* Sanc*h*o co*n*tra dese*re*dar sus he*r*manos τ por q*ue*l agutio ta*n*to la iura. (p. 147)

The translator appears to be unwilling to forgive Rodrigo's association with Sancho, and Alfonso's ire is explained as being caused not by the scene of Santa Gadea, but because he stepped forward to enforce the oath 'auiendo y meiores que el'. The sympathies of the *Estoria* in this period lie with Alfonso VI alone, and the *Estoria* surpasses the extent of the *Poema de Mio Çid* by pointing out that Valencia fell once more to the Moors, after the death of Rodrigo.

Direct speech and immediacy of narration

A further characteristic alteration of the text of *De rebus* by the translator of the *Estoria* is one which, as in the case of the legend of the Judges, involves little or no adaptation of the basic narrative elements of what is recounted but rather significant presentational and rhetorical difference. Frequently, the translator places in the mouths of the *dramatis personae* words which appear in the Latin in reported speech. The following, drawn from one of the first true set-piece moments in the chronicle, the confrontation between Bamba and the defeated Paul, is a fine example of the phenomenon:

A terçer dia aduxiero*n* a Paulo co*n* sus ueladores ante B*a*nba, las manos legados, τ dixol Banba: 'Co*n*uiertete, t*ra*ydor, por Dios q*ue* te fizo, q*ue* digas la uerdad: ¿q*ue* te fiz por q*ue* te me alcases co*n* la ti*er*ra τ co*n*tra mi?'. Dixo Paulo: 'Señor, c*ri*este me τ feziste me onbre, el diablo melo co*n*seio τ falsos amigos, muert*e* meresquo τ mas si seer pudiere; faz de mi lo q*ue* tu q*ui*sieres, nu*n*qua ta*n*to faras q*ue* mas no*n* meresca, τ nu*n*qua de mi auras ue*n*ga*n*ça qual deues τ yo meresco'. (p. 82)

Tercia feria post uictoriam Paulus cum aliis qui erant custodie deputati ligatus principi exhibetur. Cumque uinculatus cum suis tribunali assisteret: 'Adiuro te perfide', inquit princeps, 'ut si te lesi in aliquo aut tibi malum occasione malicie procuraui, hic edissere coram cunctis, ut contra me tantum fascinus cogitares et regni etiam apicem atemptares'. Mox Paulus coram omnibus protestatur se a principe nunquam lesum nec in aliquo molestatum, set suis beneficiis plus merito exaltatum, et quod fecerat instinctu diaboli se fecisse. (III.viiii.14–22)

The effect in the *Estoria* is two-fold: the extent of Paul's perfidy and the depth of his abjection are emphasised by their description in his own words; and the scene presented to the audience becomes all the more immediate in consequence. The translator is extrapolating meaning from Rodrigo's terse sentence and creating a heightened sense of dramatic tension as a result. The modern reader may, while praising a skill of a specifically literary order, object to the breach of the rules of historiography. However, the boundaries between such categories were presumably rather more fluid, if they existed at all, in the minds of thirteenth-century writer and audience alike.

There are many such examples of the creation of an effect of immediacy in the *Estoria*, the following being an indication that not all of them occur in the course of key episodes in the chronicle:

Un dia, mirando el rey la obra dela yglesia, penso de fazer una cruz rica τ estraña τ preçiada; τ fizo demandar buenos maestros, τ aparescieron le dos angeles en semblante de omnes τ maestros. Dixieron: 'Rey nos te faremos obra qual tu demandas, τ meior τ mas rica τ ayna'. Dioles el rey oro τ plata τ piedras preciosas quantas demandaron, τ dioles una casa apartada que les non enbargase ninguno. (pp. 101–2)

Ad hec cum rex preciosos lapides coram aspiceret, cogitauit crucem de auro et eisdem lapidibus fabricare, ipisque ab ecclesia ad palacium uenienti occurrerunt duo angeli in effigie peregrina se esse aurifices asserentes. Rex autem datis auro et lapidibus etiam dedit domum in qua secrecius operari. (IIII.viiii.1–6)

Here again, the introduction of direct speech does not alter the chain of narrative events, but rather alters our perspective of them. Further examination of the moments in which the translator permits the creation of such immediacy may, however, shed some light on the motivating force behind the chronicle as a whole. In addition to the abovementioned, these are:

the address of the barons of Spain to Alfonso el Casto (791–842), threatening him with a variety of ills as a result of his promising the kingdom to Charlemagne, as a result of which he sees the error of his ways (p. 103);

the address of Santiago to Ramiro I (82–850) before the battle of Clavijo (844), when he appears to the king in a dream (p. 107);

the rationale by which Íñigo Arista (c.810–851) comes to be chosen king of Navarre (he is seen as the most war-like among the Navarrese elite, and therefore most appropriate as a leader) (p. 125);

the reasoning behind the decision not to take Pedro Atares as king of Navarre (1134), as a result of which Navarre returns to its autochthonous monarchy (p. 126);

the approach of the Muslim Toledans to Alfonso VI, lamenting the loss of their mosque following the reconquest of the city in 1085 (p. 145);

the encounter between Alfonso VI and his barons following the death of Alfonso's heir Sancho at the battle of Uclés (1108), in which the counts state that they put the future of the kingdom before their own lives (p. 150);

the assurance given to García Garcés de Asca that the Lara clan will secure his interests in the minority of Alfonso VIII (1158–1166, p. 159);

the defiant response of Manrique Pérez de Lara to Fernando II of León when the former removed the infant Alfonso VIII from harm (p. 160);

the advice of the barons of Castile to Alfonso VIII following the disastrous defeat at Alarcos (1195), assuring the downcast king that he will have revenge (p. 164); and,

the battle crises at Las Navas de Tolosa (1212, pp. 171–2), which are analysed more fully in the section below.

In addition to these moments of drama, there are also occasions on which the *Estoria*'s text, while not re-creating scenes in direct speech, do appear to be rather more vivid and immediate than their equivalents in *De rebus*. One such example of this can be seen in the advice of some monks to Vermudo II (984–999), suggesting that he release the wrongfully-imprisoned bishop Gudesteno of Oviedo. He fails to heed their advice, and the catalogue of misfortune which succeeds includes his own death (p. 123).

What these examples generally share is an emphasis upon the wisdom of the upper nobility. In most of these cases their interest is in securing the future of their kingdoms, and they fulfil their role of providing good counsel for frequently wavering monarchs. Generally then, it can be said that the *Estoria* creates a heightened interest in those set-piece occasions in which the importance of a dynamic and wise nobility for the good governance of the kingdom is made apparent, frequently to the detriment of the image of the king. The future of the kingdom is seen to depend on the inter-relationship of monarch and nobility, and the translator presents to the audience in vivid tones those occasions which are the most patent demonstrations of the necessity of such a symbiotic relationship.

The king, the archbishop and the nobility

In the light of the above comments, it is instructive to examine the treatment accorded the figure of the king in the *Estoria*. The most prominent of monarchs are Alfonso VI, Alfonso VII and Alfonso VIII. Alfonso VI appears to be something of a model for the translator. As indicated, the *Estoria* comes down firmly on the side of the second-born in his battle with his elder brother, Sancho. Nonetheless, the removal of Ximénez de Rada's extended praise of the king, and the emphasis on the role of the nobility at the end of his reign might lead us into thinking that the translator's approval of the monarch is rather more wary than effusive. While it is true that the *Estoria* takes the opportunity to mention the name (and indeed title) of

Alfonso VII 'el Emperador' at the first chance, the figure of the king himself is rather less prominent than in *De rebus* and the emphasis on the emperor is explicable in the dynastic terms outlined for other texts by Georges Martin.[34] Perhaps the sole additional detail we are provided with concerns the role of the emperor in the upbringing of Urraca/Petronela, the future queen of a united Aragon and Barcelona, significant in its indication of Castilian superiority over Aragon perhaps, but scarcely a major re-writing of the Castilian past (p. 131). Where there is significant addition to the Latin text in the reign of the emperor, it concerns not the king himself, but his knights. The brief note of praise for Spain's 'cauallería' by the king of France in *De rebus* is extended in scope in the *Estoria* (p. 157).

One of the principal indications of difference of outlook between the translation and *De rebus* appears in the treatment accorded to the figures of Alfonso VIII and Rodrigo Ximénez de Rada himself. As mentioned above, there are occasions on which the image of the king is diminished, only to be saved by the wisdom of his nobles. The most remarkable example of this occurs in a section of the chronicle which deals with the various crises of the battle of Las Navas de Tolosa, in effect, the high-point of the chronicle as a whole. The key passage appears in *De rebus Hispanie* VIII.10, 'De victoria christianorum et strage sarracenorum', the chapter dealing with the battle crisis and ultimate victory of the Christian armies at Las Navas de Tolosa. In Rodrigo's account, the initial repulse of the Christian assault, and the attempt to flee on the part of some of the Christians, 'non tamen de magnis', of course, gives rise to a reaction on the part of the king: 'Archiepiscope ego et uos hic moriamur'. Re-assured by the archbishop, the king 'inuictis animo' has to be restrained by Fernando García from entering the fray himself. Although he again weakens momentarily, it is with the comment that such a death would at least be a noble one. Once more reassured by the archbishop, the king, described by Rodrigo as 'inmo uiriliter et constanter, ut leo imperterritus, aut mori aut uincere firmus erat', goes on to win the day, in a battle which is seen as the key moment in the recovery of the Peninsula. One might ask if Rodrigo's comment at this point is in response to the suggestion that Alfonso's comportment was other than lion-like, but this is enter into the realms of speculation. The view that we are given is that of a king in charge of a mighty enterprise occasionally re-assured that all is well.

By contrast the narration of the same scene in the *Estoria delos godos* is considerably different. This time the king bemoans his fate no less than three times, and in considerably different manner. The phlegmatic Alfonso

---

[34] Martin, *Les juges*, pp. 186–90.

consoling himself with the prospect of an honourable death is replaced by a tearful king for whom Spain is on the verge of being lost. Here Rodrigo provides rather more reassurance to the king than in his own Latin text, standing out from the crowd of weeping bishops and reminding Alfonso of his place in history. The narration continues with a reminder of Alarcos, Alfonso's greatest defeat, a reminder nowhere to be seen in the equivalent passage in *De rebus Hispanie*, and the *Estoria* also refers to the important role played by Aragonese and Navarrese forces in the battle. Alfonso's second crisis is a plea to God, a plea for help for Christianity; and in the face of his third crisis, it is again the clergy who are seen to put steel in the back of the wavering king. One final point: there is no mention of Alfonso's qualities, for it is the bishops, and principally the archbishop of Toledo, who save the day. And crucially, the scene with Fernando García is reversed: it is not he who restrains the king from wielding his sword, but the other way around. A very different vision of the key moment of Reconquest and one in which the figure of Rodrigo himself is key, in a way which his own words do not suggest.[35]

There are a number of conclusions to be drawn from this section. First, the prominence given to Rodrigo is far greater than that which the archbishop was willing to give himself (Peter Linehan has questioned the extent to which Rodrigo's own description of his role can be considered in any way reliable);[36] it is the figure of the king which is diminished by comparison. Second, and in consequence, the relative importance given to the clergy and the *militia Dei* in the successful outcome of the battle is therefore extended far beyond Rodrigo's own perspective. It is Alfonso who is seen as restraining the bellicose urges of the nobility, rather than the reverse. In short, we have presented to us a dramatically altered outlook on the balance of power in Castile. The king, we are led to believe, and Spain itself, are lost without the moral backbone provided by the episcopate and the bravery of the nobility. It can be no coincidence that the source of the victory hails from the see of Toledo.

Equally, the view the *Estoria* gives us of the aristocratic defenders of Zamora in the face of Sancho's siege, or that of the role of Count Pedro in the minority of Alfonso VII, suggests a rather more positive view of the nature and role of the nobility in the history of the Peninsula than that

---

[35] These points are also made in Ward, 'Rodrigo', pp. 287–88; my translation.
[36] Peter Linehan, 'D. Rodrigo and the Government of the Kingdom', *Cahiers de linguistique et de civilisation hispaniques médiévales*, 26 (2003), 87–99 (p. 99).

suggested by other historiographical texts. This is a view which is
emphasised in the figures of those warrior kings who attain, and retain,
power through their military prowess and dependence on their nobility.
Íñigo Arista springs to mind as one such case, but perhaps the most
significant of all is that of Bamba. Of all the Visigothic kings, Bamba is the
one given most attention by the *Estoria*, and whose reign is most adapted by
the translator for his own ends. At the outset we are told of Bamba:

> Este fue muy noble, τ de buen seso, τ de buenas maneras, τ de linage de los
> godos, τ ya ante auie fecho munchos buenos fechos en batallas; τ non como
> algunos que dizen que fue de uill natura, ante fue muy noble. (p. 78)

That is, he was chosen as king for his characteristics as a noble; and
unlike the readers of *De rebus* we are left in no doubt that his lineage was
appropriately aristocratic. But perhaps the most significant information
provided in Bamba's reign comes in the king's own voice, in his address to
his army in the face of Paul's rebellion:

> 'Uarones, uos sodes godos, uos τ uuestra natura siempre fustes leales τ buenos,
> τ siempre uençistes. Yo uno solo non ualo mas que otro omne, el mi mal τ el mi
> daño τ mi honta uuestro es, τ lo uuestro mio. Pese uos de lo que faze Paulo,
> griego de mala natura, que siempre fueron tales, ya se me [a] alçado con la tierra
> en onta delos godos, delos muertos τ de los biuos que oy son τ que an de
> nasçer, esforçad τ prended coraçon como sienpre fezistes. Uayamos cobrar lo
> nuestro τ uengar esta honta, aiudar nos a Dios con la uerdad que tenemos τ
> cofonda a ellos con su mentira. Pero si lo fazen con ayuda delos franceses, que
> alas cuytas siempre demandaron aiuda de los godos, non lo se, mas
> comencemos lo con Dios τ uençremos'. (p. 79)

The equivalent of this passage in *De rebus* emphasises the glorious history
of the Goths and the perfidy of the French, but nowhere is there an
indication of the role of king as *primus inter pares*. 'Yo uno solo no ualo mas
que otro omne' from the mouth of one of the most successful of Peninsular
kings can be seen as a possible rebuke to overweening monarchical power in
the context of the vernacular chronicle's composition, all the more so in the
light of the other examples of a suitably co-operative and mutually beneficial
relationship between monarch and nobility that the *Estoria* provides.[37]

---

[37] Peter Linehan comments on the importance of Bamba in the 1270s, *History and the
Historians*, pp. 455–462. Were the *Estoria* to have been compiled in the 1250s it would
have been ahead of the Bamba game by some distance. The figure of Wamba would
become particularly important for Alfonso X in the 1270s, to the extent that the driving
force behind the *Estoria de Espanna* had his predecessor re-interred. No doubt Alfonso
was not alone in realising the value of Wamba in the construction of historical argument.

Albarracín, Aragón, Portugal and Navarra

Amongst the more striking additions to the text of *De rebus* by the translator are a number of references to Albarracín. This small territory managed to attain and protect an independent status in the twelfth and thirteenth centuries, thanks in great part to the talents of the various members of the Navarrese Azagra family who succeeded in taking advantage of its strategic position between Castile and Aragón. Enrique Jerez Cabrero has contended that the interest in Albarracín is a function of the translator's focus on the east of the Peninsula, and in particular, on the kingdom of Aragon (for which see below). The lords of Albarracín, it is true, were frequently engaged in dealings with their occidental neighbour, and indeed one of the relevant additions to the Latin text concerns the role of the bishop and lord of Albarracín in the early reign of Jaume I of Aragon (1213–1276) (p. 133). The other additional references are: (i) an account of the aid offered by Fernando Ruíz de Azagra, (lord of Albarracín 1186–1196), to Alfonso VIII after the battle of Alarcos at the prompting of his Castilian wife Teresa (p. 164); and (ii) the despatch to Morocco of Ximen Gómez de Azagra (p. 165). The history of the lordship of Albarracín is, however, not so straightforward as to suggest that whoever was responsible for these additions must perforce have been of Aragonese origin. At the outset, and until the end of the twelfth century, it was in fact the king of Castile who exercised the greatest influence over the territory. Pedro Fernández de Azagra, son of the abovementioned Fernando Ruíz and lord of Albarracín from 1196 to 1246, was placed in the care of the Order of Santiago as a child. Even more crucially, the Archbishopric of Toledo had a major interest in the founding of the diocese (described by Almagro Basch as the 'creación del metropolitano de Toledo'),[38] and Archbishop Martin is described as possessing a document from the bishop of Albarracín confirming that this was the case. This interest would remain all through the thirteenth century, to the point that Sancho, the (ironically Aragonese) archbishop of Toledo, would, with the help of a Papal Bull, confirm Toledo's interest in Albarracín in 1258, and through it, implicitly, in its dependent churches in Segorbe and Valencia, no doubt much to the ire of those who propounded the claims of the see of Cartagena in this regard.[39] Albarracín, then, was important to the

[38] Martin Almagro Basch, *Historia de Albarracín y su sierra*. III: *El señorío soberano de Albarracín bajo los Azagra* (Teruel: Instituto de Estudios Turolenses, 1959), p. 223. Toledo's interest in Albarracín is also commented upon by Julio González González who notes the importance of the 'hitación de Bamba' in the matter: Julio González González, *El reino de Castilla en la época de Alfonso* VIII, 3 vols (Madrid: CSIC, 1960), pp. 401–2.
[39] Almagro Basch, *Historia*, p. 278.

see of Toledo. There are two other indications of Castilian interest in Albarracín. One concerns the references themselves. When the translator comments approvingly on the actions of 'do*n* España, obispo de S*an*ta M*ari*a de Albarraçi*n*', whose actions frustrate the scheming of Simon de Montfort and lead to the return of Jaume to his vassals, he is commenting on none other than Raimundo Hispano, former Dean of the Chapter of Toledo, who would subsequently strengthen both the bishopric of Albarracín and its ties to the Archdiocese of Toledo.[40] The second reference is again related to Castile. When Fernando Ruíz, husband of Teresa Ibáñez and uncle by marriage of Diego López de Haro, comes to the aid of the king of Castile, it is at the prompting of his wife, the daughter of Juan Vélez, herself Castilian.[41] Shortly afterwards we are told that another member of the Azagra clan, Ximen Gómez, son of Gonzalo Ruíz de Azagra, is sent as a hostage to the Moors, never to return. This case is particularly revealing. Gonzalo Ruíz de Azagra, according to Almagro Basch the son of Rodrigo Pérez de Azagra, had been standard-bearer to Sancho VI of Navarra. His subsequent career would see him serve the kingdoms of León and, crucially, Castile. His service to Alfonso VIII would make him highly thought of in the latter kingdom.[42] In other words, the references to Albarracín all concern, in one way or another, relations with Castile, and frequently Toledo. A further reason for suggesting that the references to Albarracín may not have been due to any particular interest in Aragon lies in the subsequent history of the lordship. Upon the death of Álvaro Pérez de Azagra the lordship fell to his daughter Teresa. Teresa Álvarez de Azagra

[40] These ties would remain important. As Peter Linehan and Francisco Hernández note, Albarracín and Segorbe would still exercise the mind of the Archbishop of Toledo, in this case Gonzalo Pérez Gudiel, in the 1280s: Francisco J. Hernández and Peter Linehan, *The Mozarabic Cardinal: The Life and Times of Gonzalo Pérez Gudiel* (Firenze: Sismel, Edizioni del Galluzzo), pp. 226–29.

[41] The sieges in question took place in 1197, according to Almagro Basch a year *after* Fernando Ruíz died. The wording of the *Estoria* (minus the reference to Fernando Pérez) account mirrors that of the *Anales Toledanos Terceros*, quoted in Gonzalo Martínez Díez, *Alfonso VIII, Rey de Castilla y Toledo*, Colección Corona de España, Serie Reyes de Castilla y León, 21 (Burgos: La Olmeda, 1995), p. 160. Martínez Díez also notes the presence of Fernando Ruíz in the Castilian army which resisted the advance of Alfonso XI in the Tierra de Campos the previous year.

[42] Almagro Basch, *Historia*. The agreement of Ágreda (1186) between Castile and Aragón specifically mentions him as exempt from the ban on receiving members of the Azagra clan in the two kingdoms. See González González, *El reino*, I, p. 823 and Martínez Díez, *Alfonso VIII*, p. 229. His son is not mentioned by either as being an element in the truce of 1197 between Castile and the Almohads. González González describes Gonzalo as 'más afincado en Castilla que su hermano Pedro' (p. 792).

was to marry none other than Nuño González de Lara in 1260.[43] Given my contention above that the interest of the translation lay in asserting the rights of the nobility rather than those of the crown, and also that the translation is a product of the last third of the thirteenth century, then it is far more likely that the references to Albarracín indicate an interest in the politics of Castile rather than those of Aragon.[44]

Mention of the kingdom of Aragon cannot, however, be confined to the references to Albarracín. As has been pointed out by previous scholars, the kingdom of Aragon features rather prominently in the *Estoria*. In particular the *Estoria*'s narration of thirteenth century Peninsular history seems to have a disproportionate interest in Aragon. It has even been suggested that the language of the chronicle indicates that the translation is of Aragonese origin. Of especial interest in this regard are the genealogies of Navarra, Aragon and Portugal. As in the source text, these are dealt with in their entirety as an interlude in the narration of Peninsular history generally. However, the latter two of these have significant additions, which are worthy of more detailed examination.

The first of these, the genealogy of the kings of Aragon (p. 130 ff.) begins as a faithful version of Rodrigo's words on the subject but subsequently veers off in various directions unknown to the archbishop. The section dealing with the proposed elevation of Pedro Atares is removed by the translator from its position in the Aragonese section of *De rebus* and replaced in the genealogy of the kings of Navarra. It might be suggested that the addition of certain details could be indicative of local knowledge on the part of the translator. For example, the death of Pere I of Aragon at the siege of Huesca is given in more vivid detail, reference is made to the death of Alfonso I at Fraga, and a nickname for Ramón Berenguer (Cap d'Estopa, on account of his hair colour) is alluded to. Of these, however, only the last is truly original, as the death of Pere bears more than a passing resemblance to that of Alfonso V at Coimbra (in addition to which, the translator frequently demonstrates a capacity for vivid description not drawn from *De rebus*); and the link between Alfonso and Fraga is mentioned elsewhere. It is true that the genealogy that follows demonstrates a wider frame of reference

---

[43] For a history of the Lara family, see Simon Doubleday, *The Lara Family: Crown and Nobility in Medieval Spain* (Harvard: University Press, 2001); for the marriage reference see p. 76.

[44] The lord of Albarracín naturally features in the *Llibre dels Feyts* although in a somewhat different light as the emphasis here is on the links between Albarracín, Navarra and Aragón. See for example *Llibre dels feyts* §1–16, 20–22, 131–133, 136–137.

than that of *De rebus*. Individual cases do not necessarily suggest an Aragonese bias, however. The first of these cases is the comment that Urraca, daughter of Ramiro el Monje, was brought up by Alfonso VII, which is yet another allusion to the importance of this *Castilian* king. The additional characters mentioned by the *Estoria* are: (i) the wife of Nuño Sánchez, nephew of Alfonso II of Aragon, and grandson of Count Nuño de Lara. She was none other than the daughter of Lope Díaz de Haro. Regarding this couple, the *Estoria* merely says that their marriage was dissolved. (ii) The full antecedents of the wife of Alfonso VII, doña Rica, are given ('la enperadriz doña Rica, q*ue* fue fija del duc de Polloño τ h*er*mana del enp*er*ador de Co*n*sta*n*tinopla'); this last does not appear in *De rebus*. (iii) The marriages of the four daughters of Alphonse of Provence are given in full; only two are mentioned in *De rebus*. Although the translator omits Raymond's tenure of the County of Provence, the mention of Beatrice brings the chronicle up to 1245, at least, when she acceded to the County of Provence. (iv) The marriage of the youngest daughter of Alfonso II, described variously as Juana and Sancha (see p. 132 for the confusion caused as a result). The reason for her inclusion appears to be to explain quite why the County of Toulouse comes to fall into the hands of Alphonse, brother of the king of France. This occurs on the death of Raymond VII of Toulouse in 1249. (v) The previously mentioned description of the involvement of the bishop and lord of Albarracín in the early years of Jaume may be considered an indication of Aragonese bias in the composition of the chronicle. However, as already outlined, the expansion of the role of the bishop alluded to by Rodrigo as 'Hispano Secobricensi' is readily explicable as a function of the translator's interest in Albarracín. As Rodrigo himself notes, this chain of events would subsequently permit first the marriage of Jaume to Leonor of Castile, and then his second marriage, to Violante de Hungría (1208–1251), mother of Alfonso X's wife Violante de Aragón.

The following description of the early years of Jaume's reign, the brief rebellion, appointment and later rejection of three governors, is, however, a significant addition to the text of *De rebus*. The additional text reads as follows:

τ pus entro por la ti*er*ra como lo yuan iura*n*do sus uillas yua el entra*n*do fasta andido todo el regno, τ los q*ue* se q*u*isiero*n* alçar no*n* ouiero*n* o yr pues fuero*n* **en Terue**l; el rey yua p*ar*a ala, saliero*n* ende τ delos fuero*n* a Uale*n*çia, q*ue* era de moros, τ delos a Castiella. Pues p*er*donolos el rey, τ tornaro*n* ala ti*er*ra. El Rey estonz, por conseio de sus vasallos que era niño para gobernar la tierra, p*ar*tiola fasta fuese de edat τ fizo tres goue*r*nadores: el uno de Catalueña τ el otro de Ebro aqua, el te*r*cero de

Ebro alla; estos fuero*n* los q*ue* touiero*n* sie*m*pre co*n* el a tie*m*po por *con*seio
τ por ruego destos p*er*dono alos echados del regno τ qu*an*do fuero*n* y
fuero*n* bie*n* uenidos, τ los goue*r*nadores fuero*n* mezclados τ fueles muy
mal gradescido, como q*ui*en sirue a niño q*ue* no*n* a edade. (p. 133)

The question of the three governors is one which has a lengthy history in
works dealing with the kingdom of Aragon. It is a question which has been
dealt with most effectively in Ferran Soldevila's account of the early years of
Jaume.[45] Soldevila says of the councillors that recognition of their existence
goes back to the papal bull of 23 January 1216, 'la qual devia haver deixat
flotant en la tradició la idea d'uns quants personatges que havien intervingut
en el govern dels regnes, al costat del comte Sanç'.[46] Subsquently, he goes
on:

> Es més que probable que aquesta nominació de consellers per a
> Catalunya i Aragó donés origen a una versió singular, recollida per le
> Crònica de Sant Joan de la Penya i després, extreta d'ella, per nombrosos
> historiadors de tots el temps.[47]

An examination of the text of the *Crónica de San Juan de la Peña*, reveals
that the Aragonese section, supposedly drawn from *De rebus*, says the
following:

> El sennor d'Albarrazin clamado don Pedro Ferrandez de Çagra et los
> poblos del regno contradeianlo, guardando dreyto de naturaleza por el
> infant don Jayme que devia ser rey. [...] Et quando el dito infant fue en
> edat que pudo regir por sí mismo su tierra, feyta solepnidat fiesta et
> honor por la su nobleza cavallería, la qual recibió en Taraçona, se levantó
> rey et sennyor de la tierra et los que eran seydos contrarios al alçar
> fueronse a Teruel et el rey que hira por allá, fueron algunos pora Valencia
> quer era de moros, otros pora Castiella. Después a tiempo perdonoles el
> rey et tornoron a la tierra del rey.

> En aquella ora, por consello de algunos, los governadores fueron
> mesclados et mesturados con el rey don fue muerto don Pero Ahones et
> los otros malgrazido et por esto dizen: 'qui a ninno sierve, pierde su
> tiempo'.[48]

[45] Ferran Soldevila, *Els primers temps de Jaume I* (Barcelona: Institut d'estudis catalans, 1968), pp. 15–137.
[46] Soldevila, *Els primers temps*, p. 99.
[47] Soldevila, *Els primers temps*, p. 98.
[48] Carmen Orcastegui Gros, ed. *Crónica de San Juan de la Peña: versión aragonesa* (Zaragoza: Institución Fernando el Católico, 1986). The references are from Chapter 35, lines 15–16 and 42–52, p. 87. The editor comments (p. 5) that the chronicle was probably originally

A comparison with the equivalent text in the *Estoria* leaves no room for doubt. The Aragonese text is borrowing from the *Estoria* at this point and not from *De rebus*, as the Latin text does not contain these details. But who, one might ask, are these councillors, and why do they appear here? Soledevila gives us a hint:

> Un dels noms, el de Pere Ahonès, s'havia conservat; però un altre, el de Pere Ferrández d'Azagra, s'havia infiltrat subreptíciament, a causa de la gran importància del personatge i de la seva real intervenció en els afers dels regnes durant aquest període turbulent.[49]

The missing councillor is therefore none other than the lord of Albarracín. Once more then we are presented with an addition to the text of *De rebus* which foregrounds the role of the lords of Albarracín, this time Pedro Fernández de Azagra, son of the Fernando Ruíz de Azagra mentioned above. It is reasonable to suggest, then, that the compilers of the *Estoria* must, at the very least, have had some knowledge of Albarracín and some interest in emphasising its importance. Some tentative conclusions in this regard are outlined below. It is worth mentioning, however, that the picture with which we are presented is that of wise councillors who calm the social tensions between king and nobility and who are unjustly treated by a capricious monarch as soon as he has attained the reins of power. This is, of course, an outlook which fits in well with the editorial policy revealed by close reading of the remainder of the chronicle and might suggest that the Albarracín additions are integral to the translation and not a later attempt at supplementing it.

It might be suggested that the presence of a copy of the *Estoria* at San Juan de la Peña suggests an Aragonese translator. There are a number of reasons for suggesting this is not the case. First, there is no suggestion that the *Estoria* was translated solely for the purposes of serving as a source for the *Crónica de San Juan de la Peña*. Second, there is no widespread indication of Aragonese elements in the language of the *Estoria*. A comparison with the text of the *Crónica d'Espayña de Garcia de Eugui* shows that the undoubtedly Navarrese copyist of Eugui's chronicle left a light, but perceptible, linguistic imprint on the language he was copying.[50] However, the text of the *Estoria*,

---

compiled in Latin and subsequently translated into romance. This would account for any siginifcant differences in language between text and source. Unlike the *Estoria*, the *CSJP* displays significant evidence of Aragonese origin in the language used...
[49] Soldevila, *Els primers*, p. 99.
[50] Eugui, who employed the *Estoria* as a source, may well have come across it at San Juan de la Peña.

as we currently know it, bears no such imprint, and it seems rather more probable that the translation was originally made in Castile, if not in Toledo itself.[51]

The provision by the *Estoria* of additional details does not appear to stop at those related to Aragon, however. It is equally noticeable that the translator adds to Ximénez de Rada's account of the genealogy of the monarchs of another Peninsular kingdom: that of Portugal. In this case there are two significant additions. The first is awareness of Sancho II's deposition and his replacement by his brother Afonso III. This occurred in 1248, and was therefore beyond the temporal scope of *De rebus*. It is not necessary to propose a Portuguese source for this information as it would have been widely known in the Peninsula at the time. The translator does not mention the end of Afonso's reign in 1279, and the translator's assurance that an account of the replacement of one brother by another will be provided is never fulfilled (p. 155). The second major addition to the text of *De rebus* is an extended reference to Pedro, younger brother of Afonso II:

> El yfañt do*n* Pedro, q*ue* dixiemos, q*ue* caso *con* fija del *con*de d[e] Urgel, no*n* ouo fijos; la mug*er* ouo de morir τ delexo el *con*dado a do*n* Pedro en q*ue* uisq*u*iese, depues q*ue* tornase as*us* he*r*ederos; el rey do*n* Iayme de Aragon, muerta la *con*desa, por q*ue* ael p*er*tenesçie el *con*dado, temie*n*do q*ue* sele malmet*er*ie, fizo co*m*pusiçio*n* co*n* el yfañt do*n* Pedro q*ue*l diese el regno de Mayorga *con* su *con*q*u*ista por s*us* dias, τ q*ue*l dex*a*se Urgel, τ asi fue. Des pues el yfañt enoiose de mar pasar a tie*m*po τ fizo co*m*posiçio*n* q*ue*l diese Muruiedro τ Sogorue τ Moriella τ ot*r*os logares por s*us* dias, τ q*ue* delex*a*se Mayorga, τ asi fue. Pues los dio al yfañt do*n* Alfonso, fijo del rey de Aragon, q*ue* las touiese por el. Otrosi digamos como p*er*dio el regno el rey do*n* San*ch*o, τ como lo ouo su he*r*mano el *con*de de Boloña. (pp. 155–6)

As it transpires, the prince in question was frequently involved in affairs in the East of the Peninsula, although not always to the satisfaction of

---

[51] The *Estoria* is described by Diego Catalán in *El español. Orígenes de su diversidad* (Madrid: Seminario Menéndez Pidal, 2002), as a 'versión aragonesa' (p. 40, n.35) and the work of 'un aragonés al servicio de don Pero Ruíz de Azagra' (p. 25, n.20), a view which will be eluciadated further in a promised forthcoming monograph. In another work, *El Çid en la historia y sus inventores* (Madrid, Fundación Menéndez Pidal, 2002), p. 120, n.133, the same author alludes to a 'romanzador aragonés que en 1252/3 tradujo la *Estoria delos godos*'. As mentioned above, Pedro Ruíz de Azagra died in 1196, a year before the date given for his defence of the Castilian frontier after Alarcos, and considerably in advance of the composition of the *Estoria*.

Jaume. As the *Llibre dels feyts* tells us, Pedro was indeed involved in the capture of Majorca, however, his value to Jaume appears to have been greater than merely that of military force.[52] For Pedro, himself related to Jaume, had been married to Aurembiaix, heiress to the County of Urgell, and one-time possessor of a concubinage agreement with Jaume. On her death in 1231 Jaume seized upon the opportunity to incorporate Urgell into his kingdoms by exchange: in return for Urgell he enfoeffed Majorca and Minorca to Pedro. In 1244, Pedro left his kingdoms for various towns and castles in Valencia, which he was to hold for a further 10 years. It may be that the reference to these events does indicate a particular interest in, and knowledge of, Aragon on the part of the translator. It might reasonably be asked why, in this case, the translator chooses to recount the doings of a Portuguese warlord rather than those of one of the most significant players on the Iberian stage, Jaume. The evidence provided by the *Estoria* is not clear. Two items of circumstantial evidence may point away from Aragón, however. The first is that amongst the towns in Valencia to which Pedro was now entitled was Segorbe. As Almagro Basch points out, this is one of the areas which was confirmed by papal bull as falling into the jurisdiction of the see of Toledo, precisely because it was subordinate to the bishopric of Albarracín.[53] And the archbishop of Toledo who confirmed this in 1258 was the aforementioned Sancho (archbishop from 1256–75) who, as an Aragonese prince, might be expected to know about the matters referred to. The other piece of evidence concerns the infante Alfonso, son of Jaume I and Leonor of Castile, and mentioned by the *Estoria* as holding the Valencian towns for Pedro. Alfonso's rights to the crown of Aragon were confirmed in 1231, as outlined by Jaume himself in the *Llibre dels Feyts*. However, as Almagro Basch points out, Alfonso was to be less than enamoured of the division of Jaume's kingdoms, and his struggle to overturn Jaume's decision on the matter was supported by various parties, amongst whom the lord of Albarracín, the infante Pedro of Portugal and the king of Castile stand out. In other words, the only events provided as evidence for Aragonese interest in the *Estoria* can equally be shown to be linked with Albarracín, and by extension, with Castile.

Indeed, if the structure of the translation is taken into account, then the kingdom of Navarre is just as important as Aragon and Portugal. It is true that there are precious few additional details beyond what is recounted by Ximénez de Rada, the description of Sancho el Fuerte's raid as far as Burgos

---

[52] See *Llibre dels Feyts*, §109–110.
[53] Almagro Basch, *Historia*, p. 275.

which also appears in later versions of the same events being one such. Nonetheless, in structural terms within the chronicle, each of the kingdoms is given its own self-contained chapter, perhaps as a way of highlighting the equality of Peninsular kingdoms. Whether or not this is the case, the thematic unity of the sections dealing with Navarre mark them off from the narrative flow of the remainder of the text, not least because the translator engages in some neat textual editing to bring together elements dispersed through the pages of *De rebus*, as is the case of the reference to the erstwhile king of Navarra, Pedro Atares (p. 126). These chapters, at least, must have been written explicitly in such a manner. If the focus of the translator lies between Toledo and Albarracín, it is worth remembering the influence of the Pyrenean kingdom in that part of the Peninsula in the late twelfth- and early thirteenth century. The *Estoria delos godos* is more of a history of Spain than is *De rebus*, and not solely because it systematically edits out extra-Peninsular references, but also because of the structural significance it accords to all of the Peninsular kingdoms.

Conclusion

In a preliminary study of the *Estoria delos godos*, I advanced a series of tentative conclusions which coalesced around a number of general headings.[54] While some of the details of the earlier examination of the text can be discarded, the general organizational bulwarks underlying the analysis remain the same. These are: a study of the nature of the past created by the *Estoria* by comparison with that of the source text; an examination of the *Estoria* as a discrete element in the canon of medieval Iberian historiography; an analysis of the present served by such a past and, in consequence, an attempt to propose an underlying ideology in the writing of the chronicle.

The nature of the past created by the *Estoria* is, despite its categorization as a translation of *De rebus Hispanie*, significantly different to that of its source. As outlined above, the abbreviations, additions and deletions undertaken by the translator can be seen to have been achieved in a systematic manner, and in such a way as to suggest that the writer of the *Estoria* was quite well aware of the effect that such changes would have on the past of the Peninsula presented to the reader. In the first instance, the *Estoria* is a history of the Goths in name only, as the extensive narrative of the origins of the Goths

---

[54] Aengus Ward, 'La *Estoria delos godos*'.

provided by Ximénez de Rada is, in large measure, reduced to almost nothing. The compiler of BN Res/278 obviously felt the need to restore the early sections, by means of a bespoke translation of the archbishop's words. But in doing this he created a different text, in which the focus of the translation shifts back to the Goths. In truth, the two manuscripts offer very different visions of Peninsular history, and serve as yet another reminder why Bernard Guenée so eloquently suggested prioritising the study of codices, rather than 'oeuvres', for despite their similarities, the two are radically different.

There are a number of implications which flow from this. Despite the title by which it is known, the translation does not truly share the *neo-goticismo* of *De rebus*. The 'original' *Estoria delos godos*, that represented by BN 302 and its descendants, is a history of Iberia, understood not so much as the preservation of the same line of royal descent, but rather as a collective enterprise on the part of its Christian inhabitants. In consequence, the only truly relevant information is that which concerns the internal affairs of the Peninsula and the emphasis placed on the Goths concerns not their relevance to the existence of an unbroken royal bloodline, but rather their example as good, or indeed poor, governors of a realm in which the city and cathedral of Toledo play a steadfast, and starring role.

A more self-consciously 'Iberian' chronicle (the term is the most appropriate given the *Estoria*'s interest in all of the Christian kingdoms of the Peninsula) than its illustrious predecessor, the *Estoria* is not merely a pale imitation of it. Although it is not a history in the modern sense of the word, and its author is not the critical historian that Ximénez de Rada was, nonetheless the manner of compilation of the *Estoria* suggests a particular view of the preservation of the past. There seems to have been a quite conscious effort on the part of the translator to erase any of the philosophical and indeed historiographical musings of which the archbishop was so fond. The *Estoria*, rather, is characterised by the preservation of the narrative chain. History for the writer of the *Estoria* is a series of individual events to all of which must be accorded their due chronological place. On occasion, and following the example of the source, parenthetical sections appear, most notably in the case of the genealogies of the kings of Navarra, Aragon and Portugal. These, being 'mini-histories' in their own right, are accorded their own sections (significantly, the textual unity of the chapters in question is remarkable by comparison with its absence in other chapters), but even here, as in the case of the erstwhile king of Navarre Pedro Tares, the translator performs some minor surgery to the text of *De rebus* in order to put a more logical, and chronological, order on the elements recounted.

The past recounted by the *Estoria* is also one which must have been both more familiar to the average medieval reader (if it is possible to speak of such a category...) and more vivid in its portrayal than that of *De rebus*. One possible reason for this lies in necessity for each history to include, in the words of Leonardo Funes's felicitous phrase, 'el grado cero de la historia', understood as all that which is commonly believed to be true of the past, and the absence of which would impact on the verisimilitude of the chronicle.[55] In the case of the *Estoria* the allusions to legendary matters can be explained in this way: they must be included or the story will not be believed. Of course, in consequence these legendary elements attain their own hallowed status in ironically circular fashion: they are included because they are believed to be true, but, it is also the case that they are believed to be true precisely because they are included in histories.[56]

As has been pointed out above, however, the *Estoria* is not limited to a filleted version of narrative events drawn from *De rebus*. On the contrary, by means of an examination of its construction of the past, and also the additions made to the thread provided by Ximénez de Rada, it is possible to show that the world view advocated by the *Estoria* is significantly different to that of the Latin text. In particular, the interest in Albarracín and Toledo, and its suggestion of a relationship between crown and nobility rather different to that posited by other, better known, thirteenth-century Castilian chronicles, point towards the creation of an historical focus almost unique in thirteenth-century narrative history in the Peninsula. The *Estoria* is therefore a narrative of particular story elements combined in ways that hint at the underlying ideology it serves. Much the same could be said for any chronicle, but what is unique about the *Estoria* (or any other chronicle) is the interrelationship between its production and the context that gave rise to it.

Possible solutions to this question (the 'why?' of the *Estoria*) will be dealt with below. First, however, the second of the promised analytical conclusions, the historiographical context (the 'why in this way?'), must be dealt with.

---

[55] Funes, 'Variaciones', p. 131.
[56] This point is dealt with by Peter Ainsworth in his synthesis of previous works on the subject, see *Jean Froissart and the Fabric of History: Truth, Myth and Fiction in the 'Chroniques'* (Oxford: Clarendon Press, 1990). The nature of medieval histories has been particularly well studied with respect to French chronicles. See, in particular, Bernard Guenée, 'Y a-t-il une historiographie médiévale?', *Révue historique*, 258 (1977), 261–75; Bernard Guenée, ed., *Le métier d'historien au moyen age: études sur l'historiographie médiévale* (Paris: Publications de la Sorbonne, 1977) and Benoît Lacroix, *L'historien au Moyen Age* (Paris, Montreal: Institut d'études médiévales, 1971).

Examination of the form of the *Estoria* must address the question of why translate in the first instance, rather than compose a vernacular history which does not pretend to owe so great a debt to a source text.[57] There are a number of possible answers to this question. First, and most obviously, the Latin of *De rebus* may not have been accessible to a significant proportion of those it might have affected. The provision of the text in Castilian may have been conceived as a manner of fulfilling the most basic requirement of propaganda: that it be understood by those it is designed to affect.[58] Second, and perhaps more importantly, although the *Estoria* presents itself as such, it is not truly a translation of *De rebus Hispanie* in the admittedly simplistic sense outlined in the beginning of this introduction. For although it claims to be Rodrigo's chronicle, even to the extent of translating, in part, the archbishop's address to his patron and his explicit, as we have seen, it is far from representing an accurate version in Castilian of Ximénez de Rada's words, and still less the ideology that underlay Rodrigo's chronicle. For this reason, the *Estoria* can claim for itself all the authority of Rodrigo, even then, one suspects, a very weighty authority indeed, without being encumbered by the necessity to reflect faithfully Rodrigo's sentiments. It therefore gains all the advantages of association with the canonical historian of medieval Spain, and creates a significantly altered world view in his name. A better demonstration of translation as a creative process of unlimited possibility it would be harder to find.

Allusion to the *Estoria de Espanna* above is a reminder of the greatest of all medieval Iberian chronicles, and the one which inevitably influences any view of other such chronicles. The weight of tradition and the volume of study dealing with the Alfonsine chronicle may lead us into imagining that matters were always thus, and that all medieval Iberian chronicles must perforce owe some sort of debt to it. However, the *Estoria delos godos* appears, on the face of it, to belong to an entirely different tradition, a tradition which therefore deserves due recognition in the canon of Iberian historiography.[59] Recent studies have expanded our understanding of the range of works included in that canon, as well as the conceptual framework that

---

[57] This question is also addressed in part in the aforementioned article. Ward, 'Rodrigo'.

[58] Similar points are made by Gabrielle Spiegel, *Romancing the Past* (Berkeley: University of California Press, 1993), Funes 'Las variaciones' and Martin, *Les juges*.

[59] This point is developed further in Aengus Ward, 'Iberian Historiography and the Alfonsine Legacy', *Hispanic Research Journal*, 4 (2003), 195–205.

underpinned each one of them.[60] Although the best known of these have concentrated almost exclusively on the *Estoria de Espanna* and its descendants, at least two, those of Vones and Funes, have sought to explain the development of romance historiography in its historical context as an evolutionary process covering a variety of genres.

In his classification of the historiography of the period, Funes follows the monumental studies of Diego Catalan and Inés Fernández-Ordóñez for the Alfonsine period, and characterises the immediate post-Alfonsine period as a stage of diversification of forms (such as the *crónica castellana, historia nobiliaria, crónica particular*, etc.). In part this derives from the time of the Conjuración de Lerma and what he describes as the existence of a cultural 'foco ajeno a la corte'. Based around oral testimonies encoded frequently in *fueros*, such aristocratic history refers back principally to the 'Edad heróica' of the nobility, principally during the reign of Fernando III in which Reconquest is the lauding of a *militia Dei,* and serves as a counterpoint to the Alfonsine histories and their particular view of social organization. In his comments on this phenomenon, Funes notes a move away from the Alfonsine 'exemplum' to the use of the 'fazanna, leyenda y anécdota', the 'puntos de encuentro de lo histórico y lo jurídico'. These acute observations of the early post-Alfonsine period might also be usefully employed in the study of the translations of *De rebus Hispanie*.[61]

That there was a flowering of historical writing from the late thirteenth century onwards is not in doubt. Funes's study throws further light on the motivations for it. Rather than seeing all chronicles, and indeed legal texts, as necessarily poor imitations of an Alfonsine exemplar, Funes sees in the vast panoply of prose vernacular histories an attempt to seize control of the present by dominating the past on the part of political forces external to, and at times antagonistic to, the Crown. Alongside this, Martin's characterisation of *De rebus* (or at least its Judges of Castile section) as an effort to 'sauver l'image de la noblesse', cannot but be seen as significant.[62] I will return

---

[60] See for example Catalán, *La 'Estoria', De la silva*; Fernández-Ordóñez, *Alfonso X*; Gómez Redondo, *Historia*; Funes, 'Las variaciones', and also Ludwig Vones, 'Historiographie et politique: l'historiographie castillane aux abords du XIVᵉ sicle', in *L'Historiographie médiévale en Europe* edited by Jean-Philippe Genet (Paris: CNRS, 1989), 177–188.

[61] These points are also made in Ward, 'Rodrigo', pp. 285–86.

[62] Martin, 'Paraphrase', p. 87. Spiegel, *Romancing*, makes a similar case for a defeated French nobility.

below to the question of a specifically 'noble' history; however, the point made (that the diversification of forms of historical writing is redolent of more than merely superficial difference) is an important one, for each text treated on its merits can reveal surprising differences in ideological outlook. With this in mind, the existence of an early translation of the words of Ximénez de Rada takes on an even greater significance. Of course, given that it has proven impossible to provide a definitive date of composition, it is equally impossible to situate the *Estoria* in the Iberian historiographical tradition. Nonetheless, the contention of the current study is that the *Estoria* is likely to have been composed sometime after 1272, in which case it would reasonably be seen as a part of the flowering of vernacular prose histories rather than preceding it.

Furthermore, as Georges Martin points out,[63] in addition to the linguistic difference between the two, there is a significant conceptual difference between the forms of historical writing represented by *De rebus Hispanie* and the *Estoria de Espanna*. In the case of the former, a named individual historian provides a named monarch and patron with an account of the past of the Peninsula. In the latter, the agency of the writer is dissolved into the anonymity of a team of researchers and compilers writing, nominally, in the name of the king and at the service of a wider socio-political project. In this particular context, the *Estoria delos godos* does not fit either of the paradigms on offer. Although the translation has a named author, it is markedly different to the text of which it is a nominally a translation. On the other hand, it shares with the *Estoria de Espanna* only the language in which it is expressed and the most general of subject matter. In consequence, the *Estoria delos godos*, if written after 1270, would represent a double rejection of the mode of history represented by the Alfonsine histories, that is, a rejection both of the all-encompassing form of the *Estoria de Espanna*, and its encyclopaedic content. [64] In this light, the *Estoria delos godos* can be seen as an implicit rejection of the Alfonsine political project itself.[65]

---

[63] Martin, 'Le pouvoir historiographique (l'historien, le roi, le royaume. Le tournant alphonsin)', in *Histoires*, pp. 123–136.

[64] See Georges Martin, 'El modelo historiográfico alfonsí y sus antecedentes', in his *La historia alfonsí*, pp. 9–40.

[65] The nature of Alfonso X's political project and efforts to encode it in historical writings of the period is most clearly outlined in Georges Martin (ed.), *La historia alfonsí*, in particular in the article by the editor: 'El modelo historiográfico alfonsí y sus antecedentes', pp. 9–40. The key elements of Alfonso's project were the centralisation of power in the figure of the monarch and his parallel attempt to accede to the title of Roman Emperor. Both would end in failure; nonetheless the extensive cultural project,

The particular ideological project served by the *Estoria delos godos* provides the final conclusion for this study. The weight of evidence outlined above points in two principal directions. The changes made to the base offered by *De rebus* suggest that the translator had an interest in promoting the Archdiocese of Toledo (and the city generally) as well as advocating a form of political organization in which the role of the nobility in the effective and corporate governance of the kingdom is emphasised.

The first of these may come as no surprise. One of the principal aims of Rodrigo's own chronicle was precisely that of underpinning the importance of his own archdiocese, at a time in which its role as primatial see was to be questioned as never before. Although Ximénez de Rada himself died before the capture of Seville by Fernando III (1248), he was more than aware of the impact that this would have on the position of Toledo. That some of his carefully constructed case in favour of Toledo came across into the translation is to be expected. However, a detailed look at the *Estoria* reveals that whoever was responsible for writing it was particularly concerned to preserve any advantageous references to Toledo. Although Rodrigo himself died long before the writing of the *Estoria* and cannot therefore have had any part in the translation it does not seem unreasonable in the light of the above evidence to suggest that the translator also was in some way associated with the cathedral of Toledo. And indeed, given Georges Martin's characterisation of Rodrigo himself as a 'grand seigneur', it is equally reasonable to suggest that the interests of the cathedral of Toledo and those of the nobility were not incompatible, at least towards the end of the thirteenth century.

It is notoriously difficult to identify political projects associated with the upper nobility. As Julio Escalona Monge points out in respect of the *Crónica de Alfonso X*, it is usually the case that the views of the nobility have to be assumed from their negative characterisation in royal chronicles.[66] And even where this is possible, as Simon Doubleday succinctly observes, historians who have a modern view of the state are reluctant to see in the exercise of noble power anything other than self-interest and greed at the expense of sound government.[67]

---

encompassing history, science and the law among others, stand as eloquent testimony to the scale of the political project they supported.

[66] Julio Escalona Monge, 'Los nobles contra su rey. Argumentos y motivaciones de la insubordinación nobiliaria de 1272–1273', *Cahiers de linguistique et de civilisation hispaniques médiévales*, 25 (2002), 131–162.

[67] Doubleday, *The Lara Family*, p. 61. Doubleday quotes Otto Bruner's work on medieval Germany in this regard.

Any survey of the nobility in the thirteenth century inevitably comes across a recurring problem for the class described by Ignacio Álvarez Borge as the 'clase dominante extractadora', that of economic crisis.[68] That prices had been rising for some time to the detriment of the nobility is undeniable. That the squeeze on noble incomes could give rise to grievances with the crown is equally plausible. If the necessity to defend the position of the nobility in the form of control of the past was a response to economic difficulty then, of course, the *Estoria* could be a product of any historical moment after 1252. However, it is more likely that a specific moment of crisis, on the face of it political, but also with economic inspiration, provided the background to the writing of *this* history.

The period of Alonso X's reign which follows 1270 is marked by a number of important events, all of them inter-linked. The first is the *fecho del imperio*, Alfonso's attempt to gain for himself the imperial throne, and which after great expense was abandoned in 1274. The second was the 'Conjuración de Lerma', the noble revolt of 1272, occasioned in part by the additional economic hardship brought about by the *fecho del imperio*, but also by the perceived threat to the rights and privileges of the nobility. The third was the death of Alfonso's first-born son, Fernando de la Cerda, in 1275, and the succession crisis that would ensue. The mid-1270s then provide us with a series of moments in which the way in which the kingdom was to be governed, and the relationship between crown and nobility suddenly come into sharp focus. When placed alongside the, admittedly limited, internal evidence for a late date of composition, and the fact that this is precisely the moment in which large-scale royal histories at the service of a unabashedly monarchical world view appear on the scene, the historical context of the late 1270s appears far more likely as a background to the composition of the *Estoria*.

That there were attempts to counter royal propaganda in this period is confirmed by Leonardo Funes's study of what he terms a 'foco ajeno a la corte, ...[una] aristocracia rebelde [que] impulsó la redacción y la fijación por escrito de su propia versión de la historia'.[69] The *Estoria delos godos* would fit comfortably into such a pattern of reclaiming of the legal and historical record.

What then of the details of the chronicle itself? The vision of the relationship between Crown and nobility which we are given in *De rebus* is, as

---

[68] Ignacio Álvarez Borge, *La plena edad media: siglos XII-XIII* (Madrid: Editorial Síntesis, 2003), p. 144.
[69] Funes, 'Variaciones', p. 119.

Martin and Funes both point out, significantly different from that which would appear in the Alfonsine chronicles. There can be seen in the words of Ximénez de Rada a more harmonious relationship between the two, at a time when the *militia Dei* of the nobility felt itself to be valued. In Martin's study of the *Estoria* the relationship between crown and nobility emerges as a co-operative one, a state of affairs borne out by Gómez Redondo's characterisation of the reign of Sancho IV as 'monarquía nobiliaria'. The aspiration to such a state of affairs is clear in the *Estoria*, to the point that the Bamba it presents its readers with could see himself as only being the equal of his barons. If we examine in detail other such hints provided to us by the translation we are left with an number of key indications of its underlying ethos. In addition to the aforementioned interest in the lordship of Albarracín, the most significant may be those arising from Gómez Redondo's comments on the importance of second-born sons.

The latter of these, of course, has a particular resonance in 1270s Castile. If we are to see the *Estoria* as supporting the extensive group of rebels which coalesced around the figure of the future Sancho IV, then its composition must have taken place between 1275 and 1284. Gómez Redondo has argued eloquently for the existence of a 'corte molinista' responsible for the production of a series of works supporting the position of Alfonso's second-born son. The *Estoria* could quite plausibly have been the product of the early stages of such a cultural imperative. Indeed, given the importance to the 'corte molinista' of the erudite figure of Gonzalo Pérez Gudiel, we would not have to look far for a link to the cathedral of Toledo either.[70] Gonzalo Pérez was the archbishop of Toledo in the 1280s and 1290s, ably supported during his absences in Rome by his nephews, one of whom would succeed him as archbishop. As Linehan also points out, up until the beginning of his sojourn abroad from 1279 to 1284 (an absence which ensured he would not have to make awkward choices between father and son in the latter years of Alfonso's reign), he was also heavily involved in a variety of intellectual projects associated with Alfonso's court. He had also been a dean and archdeacon of Toledo. As such, he would have had access

[70] For the importance of cathedral of Toledo and the 'corte molinista', see Fernando Gómez Redondo, *Historia de la Prosa*, Chapter V, 'La corte de Sancho IV (1284–1295)'; Germán Orduna, 'La élite intelectual de la escuela catedralicia de Toledo y la literatura en época de Sancho IV', in *La literatura en la época de Sancho IV*, edited by Carlos Alvar and José Manuel Lucía Megías (Alcalá: Servicio de Publicaciones, Universidad de Alcalá,1996), 53–62; Peter Linehan, *History and the Historians*, Chapter 13.

to all the appropriate people and documentation.[71] Of course, he was not the only agent of Toledo at work in the latter thirteenth century. Jofré de Loaysa, archdeacon of Toledo, was to write, in Castilian, a continuation of Rodrigo's chronicle.[72] Although the original romance version is lost, we can be sure that Jofré's continuation is not based wholly on the *Estoria delos godos*, as the chapter numbering in Jofré's text mirrors that of the Latin, and not that of the *Estoria*. Nonetheless, the existence of this text indicates the awareness in Toledo of the importance of control of the past through the medium of the vernacular, especially when the author to be translated is Rodrigo Ximénez de Rada. Jofré's Aragonese antecedents, though almost certainly not the motivation behind the appearance of Albarracín in the *Estoria*, nonetheless indicate that knowledge of the east of the Peninsula was scarcely lacking in Toledo.

It is therefore quite reasonable to suggest that the late 1270s could have thrown up circumstances in which the interests of Toledo and those of the nobility could have come together.

However, the question of the prominence of Albarracín cannot be ignored. Once more, the date of the chronicle is key. For the lordship of Albarracín became far more relevant to the kingdom of Castile after 1260 when the heiress to the lordship married Nuño González de Lara. The following thirty years would see a lengthy struggle for control of Albarracín, in the course of which the Lara claim would wax and wane considerably. And, of course, Nuño González himself was one of the prime movers in the Conjuración de Lerma and the ongoing noble revolt. Furthermore, the links between Albarracín and Toledo were already such as to present no barrier to the possibility of a joint enterprise in the writing of history. Against this suggestion of a Lara link to the *Estoria delos godos* could be laid the evidence of considerable hostility to the Lara family on the part of Ximénez de Rada, only partially mitigated in the *Estoria*. Furthermore, as Jofré de Loaysa points out, principally in chapters 19, 20 and 21, the Laras were alone in supporting

---

[71] Gudiel, described in Hernández and Linehan's monumental biography of the Archbishop as the spiritual heir of Ximénez de Rada, was certainly behind the Toledanization of the *Estoria de Espanna*. Hernández and Linehan, *The Mozarabic Cardinal*, pp. 267–277. Clerics at Toledo had cast their lot in with Sancho at an early stage, while Gudiel, in exile, tried to maintain a balancing act between the king and his rebellious son. Although the interests of Toledo and Sancho coincided, they were not synonymous. There is no direct suggestion that Gudiel had any part in the *Estoria*, rather the circumstances of the time, in which he played a part, and the internal evidence of the translation, lend themselves to the tentative conclusion of a link between the *Estoria* and those in the 1270s and 80s with the interests of the Cathedral at heart.

[72] For Jofré's chronicle, see Hernández and Linehan, *The Mozarabic Cardinal*, pp. 327–331.

the Infantes de la Cerda immediately following the death of Alfonso's heir Fernando, and the Lara family could hardly have been over-enamoured at Sancho's altering of his father's agreement with the king of Aragon over Albarracín at Ágreda in 1281. All of which indicates that the interest in Albarracín on the part of the *Estoria* is unlikely to have derived from a connection with the Lara family. Nonetheless, there is no shortage of links between Albarracín and Castile, and particularly Toledo.

None of the foregoing is confirmation of the involvement of any of the named historical figures in the composition of the *Estoria*. However, the fact that the *Estoria* is a history specifically of Spain; that it advocates a more equal relationship between nobility and crown; that it foregrounds the place of Toledo, and that of Albarracín; that it is written in Castilian while claiming the authority of Ximénez de Rada; all point towards a time when such matters were of pressing importance.

The writing of history is not a neutral business. Elsewhere I have described the *Estoria*, and another early translation of *De rebus* (that known as the *Versión leonesa*, or more correctly the *Sumario analístico de la Historia gothica*), as an attempt to take on Alfonsine history in its own territory.[73] Perhaps it was an effort destined to be swamped by the attention accorded the Alfonsine texts, although it undoubtedly had something of an influence on subsequent histories. But, at the very least, close reading of the *Estoria* provides us with an indication of the importance of control of the past for the struggles of the present.

Norms of this edition:

The aim of the current edition is that of providing a readable text of the *Estoria delos godos* while respecting scholarly convention and permitting the reader to see where emendations have been made. To this end, the base text for the edition is that of BN 302, as this represents the translation as originally conceived before the addition of the supplementary translations which appear in BN Res/278. It is also the earliest of the extant manuscripts, although it is not a translator's autograph as comparison with BN Res/278 reveals that many readings of BN 302 are defective. Emendations have been made as follows: where the readings provided by BN 302 are considered defective, this judgement being made principally by comparsion with the text of *De rebus Hispanie*, better readings have been obtained from BN Res/278. These appear in the edition in bold print and in

---

[73] Ward, 'Rodrigo'.

the cases where the manuscript permits, the defective reading appears in the endnotes. When emendation from BN Res/278 is not possible, better readings are provided from BN 12.990 (in italics and underlined) or by editorial addition after comparison with *De rebus Hispanie* and the previous editions (additions in braces and emendations in italics). Where there is no endnote to indicate the defective reading the text in question is either missing in BN 302 or illegible. Line divisions in BN 302 are marked by a subscript vertical line, and folio divisions are also indicated in subscript. Footnote references contain indications of source material and additional information necessary for the understanding of the chronicle, but in the main editorial matter is confined to the endnotes.

I have aimed, where possible, to retain the original orthography of the manuscript. The tironian sign is represented by τ, and the graphs c, ç, i, j, u and v have been retained according to scribal practice. Although this will present the reader with occasional difficulty, it was felt better to remain as close to medieval practice as possible and to avoid excessive emendation. For this reason, I have not attempted to employ accents following modern practice. In a similar spirit of keeping editorial intervention to a minimum, punctuation and capitalization are used as sparingly as possible. The truly Bédieriste edition would, of course, preserve original punctuation; however, since modern readers are less likely to train themselves to follow medieval norms of punctuation (or their absence) than is the case for orthography, I have not maintained the punctuation of the manuscripts, with the sole exception of the *calderones*, represented here by the character ¶.

From the foregoing, it might be concluded that the present edition aims to cover a variety of uses. In the light of the ongoing debate over editorial practice, and indeed the value of editions in the first instance, it might have been considered appropriate to take either a fully paleographical approach or a fully Lachmannian one. I have chosen neither. In part this responds to the growing dissatisfaction with the nature of critical editions which do not take account of the materiality of manuscripts.[74] While attempting to remedy this perceived flaw in editions, I have also aimed to acknowledge the benefits accorded by the tools of philology. In the first instance then I have tried to indicate the form and content of the base manuscript. However, I have also attempted to indicate better readings where there is suitable, medieval

---

[74] This dissatisfaction is most eloquently expressed by Keith Busby's injunction to medievalists to employ manuscripts rather than editions in their study of medieval texts. It should be noted however, that this does not render the critical edition obsolete, on the contrary, Busby calls for a renewal of the "great editorial enterprise" in a manner which foregrounds the codicological dimension of medieval texts. Busby, *Codex*, Introduction.

authority for this, usually by comparison with the Latin text.[75] In all cases, I have made editorial practice as transparent as possible, so that the edition can plausibly be employed for a variety of scholarly functions. In consequence, it may reasonably be pointed out that the readability of the resulting edition suffers somewhat. This is an inevitable consequence of the approach taken and it is one that I have chosen to accept since (i) the edition is intended for scholars who should be able to arrive at satisfactory understanding with a minimum of effort, and (ii) it permits me to take account of some of the material dimensions of the manuscripts concerned.

Editors, like scribes, are human, and the act of editing necessarily implies alteration and/or error. The authority for this I have borrowed from medieval sources, without their permission: such is the nature of scholarship. The responsibility is, of course, mine.

---

[75] It might be pointed out that the resulting text looks remarkably like an archetype, however, the edition does not claim this as an aim.

ESTORIA
DELOS
GODOS

[fol.1r] | Aqui enpiesça¹ la estoria delos godos τ conpusola don Rodrigo ar-
|çobispo de Toledo et confirmador delas Espannas.

| Serenissimoⁱ et inuicto semper augusto domino suo Ffernando, Dei gratia
Re-|gi Castelle et Toleti, Legione, Galleçie τ Cordube atque Murcieⁱⁱ | et
Giennij Roderico indignus cathedre Toletone sacerdos hoc opusculum | regi
regum perpetua adherere.

| Sennor,ⁱⁱⁱ pues ala uuestra real magestad plogo enuiarme preguntar | si sabia
algunas cosas delos fechos que acaesçieran en España,ⁱᵛ | tan bien delos
presentes como delos pasados, que me trauiasse² de uos | fazer bien çierto o
por libros o por oydas o por mj mismo; yo non fuy osado | de uos non
responder maguer bien se que ensaye de responder a grand cosa, | como omne
non abastado de seso nin de rraçon.ᵛ

|Pero asi es, trauaie³ de componer mi libro delos fechos de Espa-| ña del
tiempo de Iahet, fijo de Noe, fasta el nuestro tiempo segund yo | pud saber por
los libros de Sant Ysidoro τ de Sant Yldefonso τ de Ysi-|doro el menor τ de
Ydicio, obispo de Galliçia τ de Selpicio⁴ | τ delos conçilios toledanos τ de
Iordan que fue chanceler de la corte ma-|yor τ de Claudio Tolomeo que escriuio
el mundo τ sus fechos τ Otonᵛⁱ | que escriuio la estoria gotica τ Porpeyo Trogi⁵
que escriuio las estorias de | orient τ de muchos epitafios.

Del diluuio de Noe

| Asi como la escriptura dize τ afirma el Genesi, nuestro señor for-|mo el
ome asu semeianta τ pora su seruiçio de limo dela tierra. Et co-|mo dado de
uil materia τ corrompible, ouo de se corromper τ ouo de pecar | τ de
perseuerar en mal. Et nuestro senor que crio çielo et tierra non lo quiso sofrir,
| τ por derecha uengança τ por dar enxienplo alos que auian de uenir quiso |

ⁱ The dedication mirrors those of the majority of the Latin manuscripts.
ⁱⁱ No mention is made of Sevilla here. The addition of Jaén follows certain of the DRH manuscripts.
See Fernández Valverde's edition, p. 3 and Jerez Cabrero, 'La Historia'.
ⁱⁱⁱ Most of the DRH prologue has been excised, including the extensive passage of comment on the
nature of history. What remains therefore is mention of sources and Jiménez de Rada's first-person
address to the king. See above p. 10.
ⁱᵛ This is a loose translation of DRH prologue 153. ff. 'Quia igitur…' although the translator has
altered the order of the elements mentioned.
ᵛ DRH: Prologue. Once more the translator has greatly reduced in length the sentiments of Ximénez
de Rada.
ᵛⁱ DRH: 'Dionis', the marginal commentator of N has 'dion' although this may of course have been
by comparison with a manuscript of the Latin text. Amador delos Ríos's mention of 'Astacio' here
and suggestion of a different source for the Estoria delos Godos can probably be discounted.

destruyr por agua τ enuio el diluuio sobre la *tierra*. τ no*n* rremanescio |
ho*m*bre biuo si no*n* fue Noe co*n* sus fijos, Sem, Cam e Iaphet, q*ue* esca-
|paro*n* enel arca ellos co*n* sus mugeres.

De fijos de Noe

[fol.1v] | El*i* diluuio pasado, ffinco la gene*ra*tion de Noe por habitar[6] en Cal-|dea
τ en Damasco τ Siria τ en Armenia la mayor τ en Siria, q*ue* | es agora dicha
Ninjue. Las otras *tie*rras, como es Asia τ Affrica e Eu-|ropa, eran yermas
fasta q*ue* por su peccado la gene*ra*tion de Noe por cuydar | se enparar si ot*ra*
uez acaeçiesse el diluuio, comença*ro*n de faz*er* una tor- | re. τ peso a N*ues*t*r*o
Señor τ departio y los lenguaies q*ue* se no*n* entendie*n* unos | a otros. Entonz
se departiero*n* por la *tie*rra ¶ los fijos de Sem he*re*dero*n* Asia, | mas no*n* toda;
los fijos de Cam a Affrica; los fijos de Iaphet,[7] de Ama*n* τ de | Tauro los
mo*n*tes de Celiçia τ de Siria, q*ue* son en Asia τ toda Europa | fata los moiones
de He*r*cules,*ii* q*ue* son en España. ¶ Maguer que assi | partiero*n* la *tie*rra,
semeio q*ue* los no*n* abastaua τ comença*ro*n se de guerre-|ar τ de matar. En las
*tie*rras q*ue* poblaua*n* τ q*ue* ganaua*n* metie*n* les sus | no*n*bres, de todos diremos
τ mas de Iaphet, pe*ro* si fijos de Cam ouiero*n* | algo en España creo q*ue* lo
ouiero*n* por batalla. ¶ Europa*iii* comiença | del rio de Canay,[8] dela una part el
mar Terreno, dela otra el mar | Septe*n*t*ri*onal, dela ot*ra* el mar Gaditaneo.
Este te*r*mino de Asia τ de Eu-|ropa es muy famoso, mar Gaditaneo es dicho
delos godos, tanto di-|ze como delos moiones de He*r*cules q*ue* es enlas
entradas de Ga-|liçia. ¶ El mar *septentrional*[9] ha muchas islas: Scançia, Frisia, |
Socia, Anglia, Tu*n*ra*n*,[10] Albetaia τ otras menores. ¶ Aque*n*t el mar | Terreno
son Maiorica, Minorca, Euica, Frumentaria, Corsica, Sar-|deña, Sicilia,
Mutilena, Venescia e otras menores. Costantino-|pla es en Europa. Todos
estos te*r*minos son fasta Gadita*n* e que | encierra de Cappalin.

Los fijos de Noe que generation ouieron

|Los*iv* fijos de Iaphet: Gomer τ Magos τ Maday τ Iaua*n* τ Tu-|bal[11] τ Mosac τ
Tiras, cada uno ouo su *tie*rra ensu le*n*guaie. | De fijos de Gomer, Asanet;
deste uiniero*n* satmatos q*ue* son di-|chos g*ri*ego reginos, destos uiniero*n*

---

i *DRH*: I.i.19. The translator maintains only the basic details of narrative, removing the opening
section of condemnation.
ii *DRH*: 'Gades Herculis'
iii *DRH* I.ii, the details of the extra-peninsular doings of Hercules are cut.
iv There is no equivalent chapter break in *DRH* here, although the narrative details are the same.

ficlos[12] τ apulos τ satinus, q*ue* habi- [fol.2r] | taro*n* en Lascia. ¶ De Iaphat[i] uiniero*n* plafagones, on*de* es dicha | Phafigonia[13] q*ue* se tiene*n* en Galliçia. Dize[14] Cornelio Nepos q*ue* los plago-|nos uiniero*n* en Lonbardia τ fuero*n* dichos pues uenetos τ los | lengures τ los emilios. ¶ De Togorma uiniero*n* frigios, ende | es dicha Frigia. ¶ De Yua*n* *ui*no[15] Yelisa, deste son dichos griegos | eolides, deste uiniero*n* cilicos, estos habitaro*n* en Silicia. Aqui es | Trasso, çiudad metropolitana q*ue* es arçobispadgo. Deste uino Cetim on-|de son dichos cichios, e segu*n*d estos Ciprus de fijas de Iauhet ui-|no, no*n* de Sem, ende es dicha Cicio una cibdad. Ende son dichos ro-|dos de los quales es dicha toda una çibdat. ¶ De Gomer uino | Galante, q*ue* en lati*n* es dicho de Gala, estos galos conq*ue*riero*n* una par-|tida de Gr*e*cia, por ende ouo de amas no*n*bre de galos τ de Gr*e*cia ouo | no*n*bre Galliçia. ¶ De Magog uiniero*n* los scithos, ende son dichos | masegotos τ godos uandalos τ sueuos, alanos τ hirignos.[16] De | Maday uiniero*n* los medros, ende es dicha Media. ¶ De Yua*n*[17] es | dicho Yanes, ende es dicho marganeo τ son dichos yanes gr*ie*gos. | Destos gr*ie*gos q*ue* habitaro*n* en Troya pues q*ue* Troya fue destroyda | saliero*n* ende dos h*er*manos: Pr*i*amos τ Ant*e*nor. τ con so nauio[18] ribaro*n* | en Uenescia. Pues murio Ant*e*nor τ fue enterrado en Padua. Pue*s* | Pr*i*amo priso Germania τ fue dicha G*er*mania en lati*n* por el τ por | su h*er*mano τ agora es dicha Teutonia por do*n* M*er*curio, q*ue* es dicho | en lati*n* Teutos τ los latinos dizie*n*le Alimania por un rio q*ue* a | no*n*bre Lemano en lati*n*. ¶ Este rio co*n*tiene estos t*ie*rras: Lothorin-|gia o Braba*n*çia τ Uestefalia τ Frisia τ Turi*n*gia τ Saxonia τ Sueuia | τ Bauaria τ Franchonia τ Cori*n*tia τ Austia τ Galias. Esta Galias | por q*ue* fue partida a dos h*er*manos es dicha Fra*n*cia *a fractione*[ii] en la-|tin. Otrossi Bruto ueno de Troya en Anglia, e pusol no*n*bre Breta- | nera q*ue* fue ante dicha Siluaria, aq*ue*nte el mar es dicha B*re*taña | [fol.2v] | la Menor. ¶ De Mosach, fijo de Iaph*e*t, uiniero*n* los capadoçes. Deste | Mosac es dicha una çibdat arçobispal Mozacha, pues Tib*er*us Çesar le | puso no*n*bre Cesa*r*ea. ¶ De Tiras son dichos *Tracie*[19] ende es dicha Fa-|zie. Todo esto auemos dicho delos q*ue* abita*n* en Europa por co*n*tinuar la | estoria.[iii]

---

[i] The toponyms and personal names given are frequently corrupted (comp. *DRH*: I.ii.18 ff.) although the details are generally unchanged.
[ii] The Latin term is maintained by the translator along with the close attention to geographical detail.
[iii] Translation of *DRH*: 'Hec ideo dixi quia cogit hystoria quam assumpsi de incolis Europe aliqua declarare', although the statement is also correct for the *EG* also.

De Espan e los que uinieron a Tubal[i]

ǀ De Tubal, fijo de Iahuet, uinieron los españoles, fijos de Tubal. Ui-ǀnieron en occident en España[ii] τ creçio ende grand gent τ lamaronse ǀ celtiberes. ¶ Et por que catauan su hora en un estrela espero que se pone ǀ con el sol, pusieron nonbre a España Espera. Europa ouo nonbre dela ǀ fija de Antenor, la que canbio[20] don Iupiter. ¶ Delos fijos de Iaphet que ǀ fincaron en Europa τ aca cada unos uinieron sus lenguiaes: fijos de ǀ Tubal ouieron latino, griegos otro lenguange, blancos τ bulcos otro, go-ǀmanos scilanos[21] otro, boemios otro, polonios otro, ungaros otro, Iber-ǀnia otro, Socia otro, Teutonia τ Uerodacia τ Nouergia τ Suescia τ Frandia ǀ τ Anglia otro. Scancia τ las otras yslas de septentrion que son en Europa ǀ han los lenguaies, Nalia, Anglia τ Bretaña la menor τ Bascoles[22] ǀ τ Nauarros han otros lenguaies. ¶ Estos fijos de Tubal aribaron ǀ cerça un rio que es dicho Yberus, que es Ebro τ por esto es dicha essa tierra ǀ Celtiberia. E ali en Carpentania ha quatro castiellos:[iii] Auca, Calaforta, ǀ Taraçona, Auripa, ¶ ala cual Çesaragustus, por excellenia delas ǀ cuydales de España, pusol nonbre τ dixol Caragoça, en latin Çesara-ǀgusta. Esta, como dize Plinio, perteneçie la prouinçia de Cartagena, ǀ desent se partieron por la tierra τ poblaron τ pusieron sus nonbres a sus ǀ poblationos. ¶ De Phalec Fato[23] y Jedeon, so qui nascie Hercules, fueron ǀ m.cc.lxiiij. años; de la muert de Hercules fasta la prision de Tro-ǀya fueron xiij años; dela prision de Troya fata Romulo, el qual a- ǀ poblo Roma, ouo ccc.xlij[iv] años; de Romulo fasta los con-ǀsules ouo cc.xli. De Tarquinio soberuio rey postrimero gouer- [fol.3r.] ǀ naron los consules cccclxiij años; pues regno Gayo Iulio Cesar iiij° ǀ años τ vj meses. ¶ En tienpo delos consules Affrica τ España fueron des-ǀtruydas de Scipion; Telamon τ Bruto fizieron Toledo en çient τ viij años ǀ ant que Iulio Çesar regnase en tienpo de Tolomeo, fijo de Uergetis del ǀ rey de Egipto.

De Hercules τ delos griegos[v]

ǀ Pues que Hercules ouo conquistado fasta toda Asia auie[24] consigo un es-ǀtrologiano muy sabio que dezien Achias, sobrino del gran Alanth ǀ de qui conta el Ouidio que fizo omes de lodo. Otrossi era un mont que era dicho ǀ

---

[i] *DRH* I.iii Lidfors emends this to "De espan[o]les que uinieron a Tubal".
[ii] The translator cuts the Latin references to the wanderings of Tubal and to the Pyrenees, retaining in preference a rather closer narrative of Spain.
[iii] *DRH*: 'oppida'. Although some details have been removed here, *EG* follows the text of *DRH* closely in the list of toponyms and genealogical detail.
[iv] *DRH*: 'ccccxlii', the other dates in this passage are transmitted correctly.
[v] *DRH* I.iv, the details of the extra-peninsular doings of Hercules are cut.

Athas. Hercules auie un estrument^i q*ue* era bueno co*n*tra el ca*n*to delas ₁ serenas τ maguer q*ue* ouo muchos periglos en la mar aribo τ uino ₁ en España Esp*er*ia τ ffizo y torres por meter sus naues. Aq*ue*l logar ₁ dizie*n* los Gades alos moiones de He*r*cules. ¶ Era ento*n*çe un om*n*e ₁ en Esp*er*ia²⁵ q*ue* dizie*n* Gerio*n*, rico om*n*e de ganados τ señor de tres reg-₁nos de Gallizia τ de Lusitania τ de Betica. Este por q*ue* era gra*n*d τ fie-₁ro τ señor de tres regnos dizie*n* q*ue* auie dos cabecas por los tres ₁ regnos so un cuerpo q*ue* era*n* so un señorio.^{ii} Aeste gentio ue*n*çio He*r*cules ₁ τ matolo τ p*r*iso esos .iij. regnos τ diolos a poblar alos q*ue* uiniero*n* ₁ co*n*el. ¶ Los gallates poblaro*n* Galliçia τ dende ouo no*n*bre esta ₁ Gallizia q*ue* es la v.ª p*r*ouincia de Espa*n*a. ¶ Pues^{iii} He*r*cules fue en Lu-₁sitania q*ue* es çerca de un rio q*ue* dize*n* Aña τ por q*ue* ue*n*çio cerca ₁ ese rio, ma*n*do fazer y iuegos en reme*n*brança de Oli*m*piades, la qual ₁ so rio Pellapio establecio en Olimpo en aq*ue*l mo*n*t. E pues ouo no*n*-₁bre aq*ue*l lugar Lusitania a lusu en lati*n* τ Aña aq*ue*l rio, porq*ue* fizieron ₁ iuegos cerca aq*ue*l rio. ¶ Pues He*r*cules fue a Bethica τ en la plana ₁ q*ue* es regada de u*n* rio q*ue* dizie*n* Bechi alli poblo Seuilla, q*ue* es en latin ₁ Yspalis, por q*ue* al comienço del poblar fazie*n* chozas de palos e si no*n* ₁ q*ue* es meior por q*ue* la poblaro*n* los palos q*ue* uiniero*n* de çerca Stichia, ₁ por esto ouo no*n*bre Ispalis. Pues passo por Cartagena τ prisola [fol.3v] ₁ τ destruyola. ¶ Don Chaco moraua estonçe en Celcibe*r*ia o Carpe-₁cia, este fue dicho fijo de Ulea*n*²⁶ τ moraua en Mo*n*cayo, e por esso le ₁ diçie*n* hoy assi en lati*n* Monscatus, el Mo*n*t de Caco τ era muy ₁ rico de ganados; a este ue*n*çio don He*r*cules. Despues Cacus fuxo ₁ en Lauinia en un mo*n*t q*ue*l dizie*n* agora Aue*n*tino τ metiosse en ₁ una cueua mucho estrecha τ cer*g*ola²⁷ co*n* cadenas.^{iv} ¶ Pues Her-₁cules ala rayz desse Mont Acayo poblo una çibdad delos o*m*es ₁ q*ue* uiniero*n* co*n* el de Tiro τ de Ausonia τ puso ala ciudad el ₁ no*n*bre dellos: Tirasona. τ poblada delos de Tiro τ de Ausona ₁ esta dize*n* oy Taraçona. ¶ Pues fue gana*n*do las fortalezas de ₁ Celtibe*r*ia τ por q*ue* co*n*strinie las t*ie*rras τ los o*m*es por batalas τ ₁ por fuerça de urgeo, q*ue* es en lati*n* por constrenir, poblo entonz ₁ una uilla τ pusol no*n*bre Urgel. ¶ Pues p*r*iso gra*n*d t*ie*rra τ dio ₁ la a poblar alos ausones q*ue* uinie*n* co*n* el, por esso ouo no*n*bre ₁ essa t*ie*rra Ausonia τ su cibdad ha no*n*bre hoy Uic.^{v} ¶ Despues ₁ do*n* Hercules enuiaua ix barcas por mar a Grecia τ ouiero*n* de ₁ periglar asi q*ue* se partiero*n* e las .viij. barcas ribaro*n* a Gallizia τ ₁ la nouena al puerto de Celtibe*r*ia τ ali poblo

---

^{i} Translation error, *DRH*: 'Habebat etiam secum Traxillinum...'.
^{ii} The translator removes *DRH* references to sources 'De quo Ouidius...in libro Heroydum...in VII Eneydos'.
^{iii} *DRH* I.v
^{iv} The translator adopts a policy of retaining basic detail while reducing background detail. Compare *DRH* I.v.15 ff.
^{v} *DRH*: 'cuius ciuitas Vicus hodie nuncupatur'.

una uilla τ pu-₁sol no*n*bre en lati*n* Barchinona, por q*ue* ali ribo la barca
nouena ₁ τ dize*n*le Barcilona. ¶ Ahe q*ue* do*n* Hercules co*n* los griegos asi ga-
₁no España τ poblaro*n* la ellos τ echaro*n* ende alos cetubeles ₁ Q*ue* era*n* de
natura de Tubal, q*ue* como no*n* era*n* osados de batalar ₁ ni nu*n*qua ouiero*n*
cuydado de auer armas τ fuero*n* uençidos. ₁ ¶ Pues do*n* Hercules entro en el
mar de Bretaña τ delexo por ₁ cabdielo ensu lugar a Sp*er*ia τ a Celu*n*bia, un su
c*r*iado τ su uasa-₁lo q*ue*l dizie*n* Yspanus.²⁸ Este Yspano salio muy bueno τ
por su ₁ no*n*bre τ por sus buenos fechos mudaro*n* ala t*ie*rra su no*n*bre τ ₁
dixiero*n* le Espanna.

De fechos de Hercules[i]

[fol.4r] ₁ Pues *don*²⁹ Hercules uino en Lonbardia τ do*n* Ticius,[ii] un su ome, ₁
curiaua el ganado enel mo*n*te τ q*ue* do*n* Hercules toliera a Gerion³⁰ ₁ en
Celetabia enla ribe*r*a de Ebro. τ el andando por el mont, do*n* ₁ Cacus, q*ue*
fuxiera de Mo*n*t Cayo por miedo de Hercules q*ue* se uiniera ₁ esconder alas
cueuas de Aue*n*tino, falo este ganado de do*n* Her-₁cules τ furto ende q*ua*tro
uacas τ q*ua*tro toros τ por amatar rast*r*o ₁ pusolas en su cueua por la cola.
Pues andando el ganado por el ₁ mo*n*t mudiendo τ echa*n*do bozes al alua del
dia, una uaca e-₁cho un bramido delas dela cueua τ fizo gra*n*d sonido la
cueua ₁ τ el mo*n*t. τ uiniero*n* τ asmaro*n* τ dixiero*n* a do*n* Hercules q*ue* ali
tenie*n* ₁ sus uacas. Pues ente*n*dio q*ue* ali era el furto, paro³¹ ala τ p*r*iso ₁ una
maça τ q*ue*bra*n*to las cadenas τ las ligaduras dela cueua ₁ τ entro ala τ co*n*peço
de lidiar co*n* Cacus a piedras τ co*n* dardos.[iii] Pues ₁ lo no*n* podia sofrir do*n*
Cacus, come*n*ço de fazer fuego τ fumo. Don Her-₁cules no*n* dio por ello
nada, passo por el fuego τ esta*n*colo τ assi ₁ lo mato a don Cacus. Ahe toda la
t*ie*rra de Lonbardia destruyda ₁ τ los o*m*es subiugadas asu s*er*uiçio, do*n*
Hercules uino en Grecia τ ₁ despues Troya. ¶ Ali fallo do*n* Antenor³² τ lidio
conel τ q*ua*ndo lo ₁ tenie por matar cobraua Antenor su fuerça τ su uida, q*ue*
atal ₁ era su fado[iv] solame*n*te q*ue* co*n* el alma alca*n*çasse a t*ie*rra de no mo-₁rir;
estonz do*n* Hercules alçolo ensus braços de t*ie*rra τ touolo tanto ₁ ap*re*tado
fasta q*ue*lo mato τ assi murio Antenor. ¶ Pues restauro ₁ los juegos de
olimpuedes en reme*n*brança de do*n* Pelayco*n*. En ₁ la fin do*n* Hercules fue
coytado por amor de su mug*er*, q*ue* no*n* pudo ₁ yr ta*n* ayna aella como

---

ⁱ *DRH*: I.vi
ⁱⁱ Translator's error: *DRH*: 'Cumque ad loca ubi nunc Rome gloria principatur Hercules peruenisset
et heros Tyrincios, unus ex magnibus heroybus...'.
ⁱⁱⁱ This is a summary of *DRH* I.vi.20 ff, and in consequence the translation loses most of the drama
of the source passage.
ⁱᵛ *DRH*: 'et uastatis partibus Italie et subiectis in Greciam transfretauit et resumpto exercitu uastauit
Ylium et Antheum palestre inuentorem, cum non posset interra, eleuatum in ere interfecit'. The
additional details appear to be drawn from the imagination of the translator.

querie³³, ca de dolor τ de gra*n*d amor fizo | faz*er* muy gra*n*d fuego τ echose alli
τ assi mato asi mismo el | q*ue* mato a muchos ot*r*os. Esta fue la u*er*dad
maguer la fabla diz*e* | q*ue* Dexanara, por co*n*seio de un enca*n*tador, fiziera una
camisa [fol.4v] | enuenada³⁴ τ q*ue* la enuiara por q*ue*l fiziera*n* ente*n*der q*ue* amaua
ot*r*a muger. | τ dizie*n* q*ue* luego q*ue* la uistio come*n*ço de arder. Otros dize*n*
q*ue*la camisa era | estrecha τ al uestir q*ue* le afogo τ asi mismo yo digoⁱ q*ue* la
camisa fue la | dueña τ la estrechura fue la firmedu*n*bre τ el atreuimiento de la
bie*n* | qu*e*rencia τ el ueneno fue el fuego dela gra*n*d amor τ asi murio. Visco |
do*n* Hercules lij años τ asi fino el ensu fecho. ¶ A esse tie*n*po inbio³⁵ A-
|lixa*n*de, fijo de P*r*iamo, a Helena τ come*n*ço la guerra de Troya, por q*ue* des-
|pues fue destruyda por traycion τ por fuego, como dize do*n* Dareo.ⁱⁱ | Don
Españos,ⁱⁱⁱ q*ue* fizo por señor en España, fue co*n*plido de todas | buenas
costu*n*bres τ fue de buen seso τ restauro toda la t*ie*rra q*ue* era | pe*r*dida τ fizo
mucha buena obra asi como paresce oy en torres de | Galliçia τ enlos
moiones q*ue* dize*n* de Hercules; ala fizo una çibdad | en unas altas sierras por
q*ue* pasaua al pie un rio q*ue* dizie*n* Cabia, | pusol no*n*bre en lati*n* Scobia como
q*ue* es cerca de Cobia. Esta es oy Se-|gouia τ por alli por las sierras fizo uenir
el agua ala çibdad por | arcos τ por canal, fizo su obra como oy paresce τ
otras muchas | q*ue* bie*n* paresce de antigo τ q*ua*les era*n* los o*m*s estonz atales
paresce*n* | hoy sus obras cont*r*a las de agora. ¶ Asi fico España en poder de |
g*r*iegos, ca echaro*n* ende a fijos de Tubal τ de Iaphet q*ue* era*n* dichos | en lati*n*
cetubeles, co*n*pañeros de Tubal, o celtib*er*es, co*n*pañias de çer-|ca Ebro τ fue
España en poder de g*r*iegos fata los tie*n*pos delos | romanos por me*d*io
tie*n*po el regno partido.

Dicho como fijos | de Dabal poblaron España pues como los echaron ende los grie- gos, agora delos godosⁱᵛ

| Pues auemos dicho delos g*r*iegos como | toliero*n* el regno alos Tucebeles τ
fincaro*n* en España al rue-|go delos señores, dire algo delos godos onde
uiniero*n* τ como e-|charo*n* alos g*r*iegos d'España. Mag*ue*r muchas opiniones
diga*n* los o*m*es | delos godos, esto es la uerdad:ᵛ dize Tolomeo, q*ue* esc*r*iuio el
mu*n*do [fol.5r] | τ sus fechos, q*ue* cont*r*a Septe*n*trion ha una ysla q*ue* dize*n*

ⁱ Editorial comment on the part of the translator who finds a metaphorical message in Hercules'
fate. This is one of the few first person comments by the writer of the *EG*. See above p. 17.
ⁱⁱ The marginal corrector of N has 'Dares Phrigio', although no such authority appears in *DRH*.
ⁱⁱⁱ *DRH*: I.vii
ⁱᵛ *DRH*: I.viii, the first person narrative reflects that of *DRH*. The same basic details are recounted
by the *EG*, albeit with a considerable reduction in rhetorical flourishes and an altered introduction.
ᵛ The authorial voice here is that of the translator, not Ximénez de Rada.

Sta*n*cia³⁶ τ de ali sal-|le*n* muchas ge*n*tes e de alli saliero*n* los godos,ⁱ ellos uesegodos, ellos³⁷ | ostragodos, e los daños, e los archos, e los chamios. | ¶ Destos fue el p*r*imer rey aso salida Rodulpus. Este oyo el poder de | Theudorico τ diose a cauall*er*ia por la famadia q*ue* oyo de aq*ue*l. Esta Scan-|çia es muy fria ti*er*ra: alli enel tie*n*po del estiuo .xl. dias τ .xl. noches | es escuro a man*er*a³⁸ de noche. ¶ Desta misma ti*er*ra se leua*n*taro*n* los | ostragodos q*ue* losⁱⁱ echaro*n* de ti*er*ra. ¶ Pues desse mismo lugar dize*n* | q*ue* se leuantaro*n* los godos co*n* su rey q*ue* ouo no*n*bre Ueric, e pues | q*ue* ribaro*n* ad aq*ue*l logar pusiero*n* le su no*n*bre τ dize*n* le oy dia Goris Scan-|çia. Pues ue*n*çiero*n* alos ulmerogos τ ot*r*osi alos uandalos sus uezi-|nos τ fiziero*n* mu*n*chos reyes de su natura. ¶ Murioⁱⁱⁱ Ueric τ | regno Guadariç, este co*n*qui*r*io muchas fortallezas en Daçia. ¶ Mu- | rio Guadaric τ regno so fijo Philimer τ maguer los godos mucho gana-|se*n* los gou*er*nadores τ su señorio mayor en Scicia lo dexaro*n*.ⁱᵛ ¶ Dize Y-|sidie q*ue* godo ta*n*to q*u*iere dezir como fortaleza, otrosi los godos ouiero*n* | no*n*bre getas τ citas, no*n* de natura mas de sus moradas. Ellos | ganaro*n* Sacia τ pusiero*n* le no*n*bre Gothia. ¶ Nunq*ua* fuero*n* o*m*es q*ue* asi lidiase*n* | como q*ue* ala p*r*imera salida ganaro*n* Sca*n*cia, upmetaigas τ delos ue*n*dalos | τ ue*n*çiero*n* los τ desterraro*n* por batalla al rey Uesase de Egipto τ | ganaro*n* Asya la mayor partida, ca mucho y finco ¶ onde dize q*ue* sal-|liero*n* los porcheos. Estos delexaro*n* sus mug*er*es τ ellos començaro*n* | de lidiar τ ganaro*n*³⁹ gra*n* p*a*rtida de Asia. τ subiugaro*n* Armenia, | τ Siria τ Salicia,⁴⁰ τ Gallizia τ Pisidia τ Y*n*conia. τ *despues*⁴¹ Chele-|phus, rey delos godos, ue*n*çio alos g*r*iegos τ alos danos τ mato a The-|sandre, enpues el murio Dorio Y*n*daspis τ su fijo Xersos, e fuero*n* | fallados enla batalla de Ançito, rey delos godos. Estos mando [fol.5v] | Alixa*n*dre esq*u*iuar de su co*n*paña, [Piru]s⁴² ouo pauor τ Cesar. Ento*n*z P-|onpeyo mouio guerra cont*r*a Iullio Cesar por ganar el p*r*incipado de | Roma, mas lidiaro*n* meior. Creba*n*taro*n* Tracia⁴³ τ desgastaro*n* Lonbardia | e p*r*isiero*n* Roma τ fiziero*n* Uerona q*ue* dize*n* en lati*n* Uay Roma, en on-|ta delos romanos. ¶ Pues entraro*n* por Fra*n*çia τ [con]q*u*isiero*n*,⁴⁴ uiniero*n* ot*r*o-|si en España τ ganaro*n* la τ fiziero*n* su siet τ cabesca de su regno en | Toledo. ¶ Pues q*ue*l lexaro*n* Sicicia no*n* ouiero*n*

ⁱ Most geographical detail here is excised, including mention of the River Vistula ('Instulam fluuium').

ⁱⁱ The referent of 'los' is unclear in the *EG* text, as the mention of the 'Herulos', described by Fernández Valverde (*Historia*, p. 74) as a people of Jutland and the south coast of the Baltic is not maintained. *DRH*: 'Ostrogothe autem et Dani ex ipsorum stirpe progressi Herulos propriis sedibus expulerunt'. The following passages are greatly reduced in rhetorical flourishes by comparison with the Latin text.

ⁱⁱⁱ *DRH*: I.viiii

ⁱᵛ Ximénez de Rada's comments on his sources are omitted, as are lengthy comments on the Goths; the translation then resumes at the reference to Isidore, although what follows is greatly summarised from *DRH*: I.viiii.41 ff.

cuydado de retener vil-|las ni*n* castiellos ni*n* lo q*ue* ganaua*n*, mas pero uinie*n* matua*n* τ destru-|yen τ q*uan*do fazie*n* su morada choças en q*ue* habitaua*n* τ no*n* hauie*n* cuy-|dado de auer sino*n* semnar τ coier τ yr adela*n*t, p*re*nder τ matar τ des-|truyr. Pues q*ue* conosciero*n* los om*ne*s fuero*n*se cabdila*n*do τ mesura*n*-|do τ fiziero*n* su rey τ fiziero*n* maestros dela ley por q*ue* se guyasen. | Pues[i] ya q*ue* Europa los ouo miedo los sueuios p*re*ndiero*n* lo q*ue* auie*n* | en España en tie*n*po de Hercules, asi fue q*ue* lo todo ganaro*n* por mar | τ por ti*e*rra e ffuero*n* muy temidos fata q*ue* uino el rey Sisebuto q*ue* | lo touo todo en buena paz. Estos fuero*n* fuertes τ poderosos τ | muy sabios. Dest*ru*yda Grecia τ Macedonia τ Po*n*to τ Asia τ Illirico | touiero*n* τ Macedonia bie*n* .xv. años τ descendiero*n* de los Alpes on | q*ue* moraua*n* enla p*ri*mera siet. Ouiero*n* rey a Fephilimit en la scul*er*a[45] | en Tacia ouiero*n* Hactut enel philosopho, pues a do*n* Diceneo, pues | a do*n* Zalmoxe*n* q*ue* fue muy sabio, on segu*n*d dize*n* los esc*ri*ptos por | barbaros seer no*n* ouo en mu*n*do ta*n* sabios omes como godos co-|mo q*ue* por si fiziero*n* maestros τ señores de ley por q*ue* se guyasen.[ii]

Delos fechos delas almazonas[iii]

| Dicho delos godos, | direuos delos almoçonas[46] sus mug*er*es. Uesa su rey de Egip-|to come*n*ço guerra τ m*a*taro*n*[47] le los godos. Auie*n* estonz a do*n* Canatisus, | este gano fascas toda Asia τ deuino su uasalo do*n* Formi, rey | de Media. ¶ Pues se q*u*itaro*n* mu*n*chos delos godos por morar [fol.6r] | en Asia τ son dichos oy porq*ue* se partiero*n* delos sos. Muerto[iv] Ca-|canusso fue[ron]se[48] ala otra gent τ lexaro*n* y las mug*er*es. | ¶ Fincaro*n* en Sicia dos ninnos muy poderosos de liñage de Plinio τ | de Scolapio q*ue* fuero*n* reyes. Estos, q*uan*do uiero*n* q*ue* los uaro*n*es era*n* | ydos, come*n*çaro*n* de matar los q*ue* falaua*n* delos godos τ come*n*caro*n* | a pasar alas mug*er*es delas por fuerça τ delos por grado, e las | ouiero*n* de consentir. τ qu*an*do paria*n* fijo mataua*n*lo τ qu*an*do fija | c*ri*auala τ taijaua*n* le la teta siniestra por meior leuar escudo τ | por ue*n*gar su despecho τ su onta. E pues q*ue* oyero*n* dezir delas al-|maçonas fuero*n* para ellas τ fiziero*n* dos cabdiellos a doña Lla*n*-|pete τ a doña Marp*er*sia, estas ganaro*n* Asana, dela por fuerça | τ dela por grado. τ despues ganaro*n* Armenia τ Siria τ Silicia τ | Galliçia τ Pissidia τ Asia;[v] τ uillas τ

---

[i] Having followed *DRH* closely, the translation returns to to summarise Ximénez de Rada's comments on Europe and the Sueves.

[ii] As previously, mention of Classical authors is removed.

[iii] *DRH*: I.xi, the extensive explanation of the background of the Amazons is greatly reduced. In 302, this rubric is embedded in the end of the previous line.

[iv] *DRH*: I.xii

[v] In an indication of the priorities of the translator, all significant details of these conquests, with the exception of toponyms, have been removed.

castiellos τ asi touieron Asia ǀ bien por .c. años. E pues uieron que mucho menguaua τ corrieron ǀ se a Caucesso τ rogaron asus vezinos que casassen con ellas τ lexa-ǀsen el lidiar τ al cabo de año que tornase por sus fijos τ asi lo fi-ǀzieron. ¶ Mientreⁱ ellas conquerien Asia τ la destruyen uino una ǀ hueste de Persia e lidio con las almazonas τ murieron delas ǀ bien xl. mil τ murio con ellas doña Marpessia e pues ella ǀ regno su fija Sipnac. ¶ Fino Sipnac τ regno doña Ortidia que ǀ començo guerra contra Hercules Meneldo τ fue uençida mas por ǀ engaño que por fuerça . τ fue presa Occidia con bien .c. mill al-ǀmas que murieron con Hercules. Enuio a doña Occidia asu hermana ǀ Anpabi que regnaua con ella, ¶ Arpedo regnaua en Sicia τ Ortri-ǀolia enuiol demandar ayuda por lidiar con Hercules. Otra uez Ar-ǀpedo ouo dolor delas almaçonas que eran dela natura delos ǀ godos enuioles su fija con ayuda τ don Hercules, si ouo miedo o ǀ uerguença non uino ala batalla mas tornose a Graçia τ mu-[fol.6v] ǀ rio Occidia τ regno Pentisselea. Esta uino en ayuda delos de Troya con ǀ lxx. mill. armados τ lidio muy bien τ matola Piro, fijo de Achilles; τ murio Pen-ǀtiselia τ regno depues Talisar τ destas fueron siempre fermosos τ ba-ǀtallerosas τ touieron el regno fasta agora enla tierra que dizen Femi-ǀnia. Estos son de la noble natura delos godos

Delos reyes go- ǀ dos de Chepreⁱⁱ

Ya es dicho delas almazonas, mugeres ǀ delos godos, agora dire delos reyes que ouieron ante Telepho:ⁱⁱⁱ ǀ Uederic τ pues Gadario τ pues Filime τ pues Zalomoxen τ pues ǀ Tanauso τ pues longo tiempo Athepho, fijo de Hercules. ¶ Don Her-ǀcules fue en tiempo de Gedeon que gouerno el pueblo de Israel .c τ .lxxx. ǀ τ .v. años τ por este conto paresce τ es uerdat que grand tiempo ante que ǀ Gedeon sallieron los godos de Scithia. ¶ Thelepho, fijo de Hercules, que ǀ casso con la hermana de Priamo τ murio quando uinie en ayuda de ǀ Troya; e pues su fijo Eufilus regno en Messeia, que es dicha una parti-ǀda de Femina. ¶ Puesⁱᵛ Darius, fijo Ydaspus,⁴⁹ rey de Persia, rogando τ ǀ menazando, demando por su muger la fija del rey Antiro delos godos, ǀ τ non gela quisieron dar τ començo el la guerra τ passo con sus naues ǀ τ lidio con los godos τ de doze mill armados que leuo perdio los ǀ ocho mil τ fuyo en Troya τ murio τ su fijo don Xermes quisolo ven-ǀgar τ ouo delos suyos dos mil

---

ⁱ Summary of DRH: I.xii. The translator's interest in, and accurate reproduction of, numerical data is maintained.

ⁱⁱ DRH: I.xiii, the rubric in 302 appears at the ends of two consecutive lines.

ⁱⁱⁱ References to, and quotations from, Orosio and Juvenal are not translated, although the subsequent lists follow DRH accurately.

ⁱᵛ DRH: I.xiiii

armados τ de ayuda .ccc. mill.[i] | τ passo mar τ no*n* oso co*n* ellos lidiar τ asi se
ouo de tornar. | ¶ Philpo, padre de Alixa*n*dre, fizo paz co*n* los godos τ p*r*iso
por mug*er* | a doña Madupa, fija del rey Gudiella, por q*ue* se afirmase bie*n* en
| el regno de Maçedonia. τ pues q*ue* Filipo fue en Maçedonia τ | la q*u*iso
co*n*bater, los godos q*ue* era*n* y abriero*n* le las puertas con | gra*n* gozo τ
reçibiero*n* le por señor porq*ue* se era mas de la t*ie*rra | mas natural. ¶ Qua*n*do
lo sopo Sithacus, el cabdiello delos godos, | pesol deste engaño τ troxo bie*n*
.c. mill armados.[ii] Entonze reg-|[fol.7r] | naua en Athenas Perdica, Q*ue* era dado
por señor por mano de Alixa*n*dre. | Este Sicaus[50] co*n*batio Athenas τ deuasto
Maçedonia τ asi sie*n*pre uencie-|ro*n* los godos. ¶ Desende[iii] regno delos
godos do*n* Buruista[51] τ uino a el | Deçeneus al tie*n*po q*ue* do*n* Sitilla[52] tenie el
senorio delos romanos de | Diçenea,[iv] diol el regno de Germania, q*ue* agora
es dicho Fra*n*cia. Mag*uer* | q*ue* Cesar fue señor fascas de todo el mu*n*do τ
Gayo Tib*er*erio otro si, no*n* pudi-|ero*n* ganar el regno delos godos. Los
godos p*r*isiero*n* por co*n*seiero τ | por no*n* salir de ma*n*dimie*n*to de do*n*
Diçeneus; este era maest*r*o en philo-|sofia, en fisica, en teoria, en p*r*atica, en
logica, en astrolaguia τ del | cosso[53] del sol τ dela luna τ delas estrellas τ por
su seso era*n* obede-|çidos de gra*n*des τ de chicos. Este establecio maestros
de ley en the-|ologia. ¶ Muerto Diceneo contaro*n* por rey τ por obispo a do*n*
Errano-|sicus, pues a tie*n*po regno do*n* Dorpa*n*cus. ¶ Delos[v] xiij años ante
de | la era fasta la era de çient .xxv. en q*ue* regnaua Domiçiano, q*ue* son |
cxxxvij, no*n* falo esc*r*ipto delos fechos delos godos τ por tanto lo | delexe.
Era cxxv, q*ue* regnaua Domiciano, los godos no*n* q*u*isiero*n* | seer enel pleyto
q*ue* pusiero*n* co*n* los ot*r*os p*r*incipes τ uiniero*n* con | su poder τ destruyero*n* la
rib*er*a del Danubio q*ue* era*n* en possesio*n* delos | romanos τ uiniero*n* en Opio
de Sabina τ destruyero*n* uillas τ cas-|tiellos, pues uio Q*ue* asi p*er*die lo suyo,[vi]
mouyo su poder | don[54] Fusco, prelado de Roma τ p*a*so el Danubio τ ouo
su fazie*n*-|da co*n* los godos τ murio Fusco τ fue ue*n*çido Domiçiano. Ma-
|guer todos auie*n* no*n*bre godos, los q*ue* moraua*n* en Sicia era*n* dichos |
godos, los de orie*n*t ostrogodos, los de occide*n*t uesegodos. Los q*ue* |
moraua*n* en Scicia semp*r*e *man*touiero*n*[55] bie*n* lo suyo τ obedeçiero*n* | los
ua*n*dalos τ Margomanus, p*r*incipe delos esquadros. Fastidia, | rey de
Geppida, enuiol dezir a ostragodo Q*u*el delexase la t*ie*rra | si no*n* q*ue* yria

---

[i] The translator's previous interest in numerical detail is maintained here while other background information is removed.
[ii] A *DRH* paragraph I.xiii.23 ff. detailing the deception involved is cut.
[iii] *DRH*: I.xv
[iv] The emphasis in the translation remains on the Goths to the almost total exclusion of the Romans.
[v] *DRH*: I.xvi, the translation maintains the first person narrative of Ximénez de Rada.
[vi] *DRH*: 'respublica', details of the battle narrative are greatly reduced.

sobrel, paro[56] su dia[i] τ fue uençido Fastida τ fincaro*n* [fol.7v] ǀ los godos e[n]lo suyo. ¶ Murio Ostrogote τ regno su fijo Gina. Este ǀ fizo dos huestes: la una enuio a Messia deuastar, co*n* ella fue ala ǀ Philipolin τ prisola τ deueno su uasallo Prisscus q*ue* era prjncep dende. ǀ Pues lidio co*n* Decius q*ue* començo regnar era mill τ ccLxxvij τ fue ǀ luego ferido do*n* Illico, fijo de Decio τ el padre q*ue*riendo se ue*n*gar el fi-ǀjo murio y. Muerto[ii] Decio τ su fijo Uolu*n*siano, ouiero*n* los godos ǀ el regno delos ruanos por dos años enla era de clxx, pues ǀ Gallieno por si priso el prjncipado enla era .cclxxij,[iii] τ passo e*n* ǀ Assia τ destruyo muchas uillas τ el te*n*plo de doña Diana q*ue* fizie-ǀro*n* las almaçonas τ destruyo Calcedonia, pues trepalo Cornelius; ǀ τ fue p*ar*a Troya τ lo q*ue* rec[onstruyeron] dela destruycio*n* de Agameno ǀ todo lo q*ue* destruyo; τ moraro*n* [en] Antenas, una çibdad q*ue* poblo ǀ Sardana Paulus, rey delos asyrios τ pues torno ensu t*ier*ra.[iv] ¶ De ǀ mei*n*tre ellos desgastaua*n* el jmperio de Roma, Claudius, q*ue* començo ǀ regnar enla era de clxxxvj,[v] lidio co*n* el τ fiçolo tornar a Sicia ǀ onde saliera*n*. τ los romanos a onor de Cladio, *ficiero*n[57] una estatua τ un ǀ escudo de oro τ pusiero*n* lo enel capitolio por q*ue* uençio los godos. ǀ ¶ Costa*n*ti[no][vi] Cesar [regno] era cccxxvij τ uiniero*n* contra el los godos τ ǀ ue*n*çiolos τ fizo los pasar el Danubio onde fue muy loado. Otra ǀ uez a tie*n*po tornaro*n* los godos co*n* dos sus cabdielos, Ariacho τ ǀ Autico τ degastar Ytallia τ Panonia τ alli fiziero*n* Uetona, otros ǀ dize*n* q*ue* fue Sica*n*bria τ moraro*n* y much*os*. E apus[58] Ariaco τ Aurico reg-ǀno Gabe*n*t enel .xxvij. años de Co*n̄stantin*, enla era de cccliij. Pues ǀ Yemar τ los uandalos fuero*n* echados de su lugar τ uiniero*n* en ǀ Panonia; τ moraro*n* y bie*n* lx años τ como desterrados auie*n* de ǀ obedeçer alos enperadores. ¶ Pues Yemar τ los ua*n*dalos ouiero*n* ǀ de pre*n*der Gallias τ qua*n*do q*u*isiero*n* no*n* pudiero*n* tornar en Panonia, ca ǀ murio Goberido[59] τ regno Hermonarico enlos godos, el ij° año de ǀ [fol.8r] ǀ Costa*n*cio, era ccclvij. Este fizo mucha bueña fazie*n*da τ co*n*q*u*irio los ǀ esclauos τ los ue*n*cianos. Este H*er*manarius, rey delos godos, fue ǀ *muy* batalareso, fue una uez plagado y desto fue sie*n*pre tolido.[vii] ǀ¶

---

[i] Once more the lack of interest of the translator with respect to close detail of the Goths is clearly shown. Compare *DRH*: I.xvi.26 ff.

[ii] *DRH*: I.xvii. 'Defuncto autem Decio Gallus et Volusianus filius eius regnum adepti sunt Romanorum et regnauerunt annis duobus era CCLXX'. The translator fails to follow the logic of the Latin text.

[iii] *DRH*: 'cclxxi'.

[iv] These two words are unclear in 302, and the copyist of N has also left question marks at these points, suggesting that N is a copy of 302. The text of BN Res/278 is following its own translation at this point.

[v] *DRH*: 'cclxxxvi'

[vi] *DRH*: I.xviii

[vii] A significant comparsion with Alexander the Great is removed, along with the end of the chapter.

En^i ta*n*to Hala*n*ber, rey delos unguones, fue destruyr los ost*ro*-｜godos τ los uesegodos q*ue* se era*n* p*ar*tidos delos godos τ qu*an*do lo ｜ oyo He*r*manaricus, ouo peoria de su plaga co*n* el pesar q*ue* ouo τ co*n* el ｜ dolor ouo de morir τ uisco .cx. años τ por esta muert puiaro*n* ｜ et ualiero*n* los ugnones. Los godos q*ue* fincaro*n* sin cabdiello τ ｜ los ostrogodos q*ue* escaparo*n* enuiaro*n* dezir a do*n* Uale*n*s, el enpe*r*ador, ｜ q*ue* los diesse Tracia τ Nicessio, el otorgo*lo* τ passaro*n* el Danubio ｜ τ alli fincaro*n* τ fiziero*n* y su m*orad*a. Era^ii ccclxxij come*n*ço de ｜ regnar Atanarico sobre los godos τ regno xiij años. Este qua*n*-｜tos chris*t*ianos fallaua, los q*ue* no*n* q*ue*rie*n* adorar ydolos, luego los ma-｜taua, pues q*ue* se enoio de matar ma*n*do los passar enla p*ro*ue*n*çia ｜ de Roma, era cccLxxxvijj.^iii Pues acuscio bandos entre lo go-｜dos τ los unos obedesciero*n* Atanarico τ los ot*ro*s Stredigno τ ｜ matosse entresi, pe[ro] Atanarico ue*n*çio a Fredetigno, q*ue* Uale*n*s qu*e*l ｜ dio ayuda, pe*ro* Fredierigno por rey andaua. Pues q*ue* se no*n* p*er*dies-｜se el regno τ la glo*r*ia delos godos, acordaro*n* se Fridegno co*n* los ｜ ostrogodos τ Atanarico co*n* los uexegodos τ fiziero*n* un obispo ｜ qu*e*l dizie*n* do*n* Gudilla q*ue* les amostro la fe ch*r*istiana. ^iv Este traslado ｜ los euangelios τ la ley τ el nueuo testame*n*to τ el uieio enla ｜ letra toledana τ en esta les amostro la ley τ delexaro*n* los ydo-｜los^60, los qu*al*es usaua*n*. ¶ Elos cuydaro*n* q*ue* Uale*n*s era bie*n* ca*tho*lico, ｜ τ enuiaro*n* le rogar q*ue* les enuiase maest*ro*s q*ue* les demostrase*n* ｜ la fe catolica. Et el enuiol cle*r*igos arrianistas por co*n*fonder ｜ la fe catolica encubierto, q*ue* tenie*n* los godos, ｜ ellos,^61 como era*n* nueuos en la fe no*n* ente*n*diero*n* como les amos-｜[fol.8v] ｜ traua*n* la sec*t*a de Arriano τ firmaro*n* y su fe τ fiziero*n* sus ygl*es*ias. ^v ｜ Esta fe ma*n*touiero*n* fasta el te*r*cio co*n*cilio de Toledo, q*ue* fue celebrado so ｜ Recaredo, p*r*incep τ pues coñosçiero*n* su error, tornaro*n* ala fe catolica era ｜ ccclxxx. ¶ Los^vi godos q*ue* echaro*n* de ti*er*ra alos ch*r*istianos, pues Atan-｜arico τ Frede*re*gño, sus reyes, co*n* ellos fuero*n* echados alie*n*de el Danu-｜bio, pues co*n* coyta ouiero*n* se de tornar uasallos de Uale*n*s el enpe*r*a-｜dor. A tie*n*po delos romanos sacaua*n* los de fuero, ento*n*z cayo fa*n*bre ｜ enla ti*er*ra asi q*ue* el om*n*e se ue*n*die por un pa*n* τ sus fijos ue*n*die*n*, q*ue* mas ｜ q*ue*rien ue*n*der sus fijos q*ue* morir de fambre. Ento*n*z Dictator, q*ue* era de ｜ los romanos, enuido a yantar a Friderigno, rey delos godos, por ｜ engeñio: qua*n*do fuero*n* en casa aparto dellos τ come*n*ço de matar delos ｜ godos. Ente*n*diolo Friderigno τ ouo miedo de si, fuxo co*n*

---

^i *DRH*: I.xviiii
^ii *DRH*: II.i. 'ccclxxi', the passage between two books of the source text goes unmarked in the translation.
^iii *DRH*: 'ccclxxxviiii'.
^iv The translation follows *DRH* closely here thereby revealing something of an interest in religious matters.
^v A passage dealing with Arianism has been removed, *DRH*: II.i.35 ff.
^vi *DRH*: II.ii this is something of a summary of the Latin equivalent.

los q*ue* pudo ┊ ende τ com*en*ço de guerrear co*n* los romanos por estas dos razones ┊ τ mato a Lapiscino τ a Maximo, duq*ue*s de Roma. Ento*nz* co*n*braro*n* otr*a* ┊ uez los godos τ ma*n*dauan como señores q*ue* ante era*n* sieruos τ ga-┊naro*n* todo lo de septe*n*trio*n* fata el Danubio. ¶ Vale*ns*, qua*n*do lo oyo, mo-┊uio hueste τ fue co*n*tra ellos en Tr*a*cia τ ue*n*çiero*n* lo los godos τ fue ┊ ferido τ fuyendo τ esco*n*diosse en una casiella, los godos en alca*n*ço ┊ daua*n* fuego a qu*an*to falaua*n* τ no*n* cuyudaro*n* q*ue* alli serie τ diero*n* le fue-┊go τ alli murio co*n* los otr*o*s q*ue* era*n* y. Pues los godos fallaro*n* los *chri*st*ia*-┊nos q*ue* echaro*n* de si τ recibiero*n* los por h*er*manos como de p*ri*mero, ┊ τ partiero*n* la gana*n*çia τ ganaro*n* gr*an*des t*ie*rras τ ouiero*n* co*n*cordia entr*e*si ┊ τ fincaro*n* ala fe catolica.[i] ¶ Muerto[ii] Uales com*en*ço de regnar su ┊ sob*ri*no Tr*a*çiano,[62] era de cccLxxxxj τ regno vj. años. Este T*ro*çianus al ┊ vº año q*ue* com*en*ço de regnar fico a Teodosio, q*ue* fue español ¶ et ┊ fijo de Theodosio, el conde enp*er*ador de orie*n*t τ fizo a Ualer*i*ano, su ┊ h*er*mano el menor, enp*er*ador de Roma. Este Uale*n*tiniano regno ┊ viij. años co*n* Theodosio τ salio de bue*n* seso τ co*n*q*u*írio mas[63] por ┊ [fol.9r] ┊ bue*n* sentido q*ue* por armas τ por seso. Deste cobraro*n*[64] los romanos τ e-┊charo*n* alos godos de Traçia. ¶ Pues *que* Teodosio enfermo a muert τ Fre-┊derigno p*ar*tio su hueste τ robo toda Thesalia τ Acaye τ alos theos; τ ┊ co*n* su gana*n*çia uino a Panonia. τ Tracianus el enp*er*ador, q*ue* era ido a ┊ Gallias, oyolo τ torno τ lidio co*n* ellos, mato a Frederigno, los su-┊yos fuero*n* a Tanarico. Traçiano fue p*ar*a el τ fizo paz co*n* el τ ouiero*n* ┊ entre si co*n*cordia. Pues guareçio do*n* Theodosio desta paz τ fir-┊mola τ fue muy amigo de Atanarico τ rogol q*ue* uiniese co*n* el a Cos-┊ta*n*tinopla. τ qu*an*do uio tamaña riq*ue*za de omes τ de auer τ cibdad tan ┊ bie*n* puesta, dixo q*ue* nu*n*qua lo creyera ni*n* uiera ta*n* famosa riq*ue*za. Es-┊tonz enfermo Atanarico τ murio τ fizol mayor hondra Th*e*odosio ┊ en muert q*ue* en uida τ asu enterramie*n*to, calo enterro muy on-┊dradame*n*t. ¶ Murio[iii] Atanarico era ccclxxxxiiij, pues los godos ┊ diero*n* se al imperio de Roma por la bondad de Theodosio τ fuero*n* ┊ sin rey xxviij años. Pues Thedosio p*ri*so bie*n* xx. mill armados[iv] ┊ τ fue contr*a* Eugenio, q*ue* matara a G*ra*çiano τ subjugara Gallias τ ┊ lidio co*n*el τ matolo. En tie*m*po de Todosio entraro*n* en España los a-┊lanos τ los ua*n*dalos τ los sueuios.[65] τ los alanos entraro*n* Carta-┊ageña τ Lusitania, una p*ar*t delos ua*n*dalos τ delos filignos[66] fin-┊caro*n* en B*e*tica. ¶ Pues q*ue* *Theodosio*[67] co*n*peço regnar co*n* Graçiano, era ┊ ccclxxxxij τ regno co*n* el .v. años τ Ualentiniano regno en Ro-┊ma .vij. años; τ Theodosio,

---

[i] *DRH*: II.ii.34 ff. *EG* attributes to the Goths an attitude to the Christians which is diametrically opposed to that indicated by *DRH*. This is almost certainly due to a failure to comprehend the Latin.
[ii] *DRH*: II.iii
[iii] *DRH*: II.iiii
[iv] *DRH*: 'federati'.

pus la muert de Uale*n*tiano el me-|nor, regno el solo por si x años τ fue co*n* todo xxiij. años. Este | fizo paz τ bie*n* delos godos τ murio era ccccxiij. ¶ Regna-|ro*n* pues el Archadio τ Honorio, sus fijos, xxv. años τ come*n*ça-|ro*n* de beuir suziame*n*t τ de menos p*re*çiarlo los godos,[i] elos | no*n* lo pudiero*n* sofrir. ¶ Querie*n*do esleer rey el xj. años de | Archadio τ de Honorio, enla era de ccccxiij, partiero*n* se, los [fol.9v] | co*n*uie*n*to co*n* Radagayso los co*n* Alarico τ ouiero*n* entressi guerra τ muri-|ero*n* y muchos. Pues acordaro*n* se como regnasen amos τ p*a*rtie-|ro*n*se, Alaricus por yr a Ytalia p*re*nder.[68] ¶ Radagayso, q*ue* era nath*u*ral | de Scicia, salio crudel τ ydolat*ri*a τ co*n* cc. mill armados fue a Y-|tallia cont*ra* los *chris*tianos. Pues Stiloco*n*, duc de Roma, ouolo | de çercar τ p*re*nder por fambre τ ouolo de matar. ¶ Alatius,[69] *chris*tia-|no de no*n*bre h*er*ege de uelu*n*tad, pues q*ue* murio Tadayguso[70] co*n*peço | de regnar τ ouo miedo delos romanos τ enuio al enp*e*-|rador de Roma do*n* Honorio q*ue* si morarie*n* los godos en Lonbar-|dia[ii] si el q*u*isiese en paz, si no*n* q*ue* lo aurie*n* por armas. El enp*er*a-|dor ouo su acuerdo co*n* el senado τ ma*n*do alos godos q*ue* sali-|esen de Lonbardia, q*ue* no*n* q*ue*rie q*ue* y morasen τ q*ue* se fuesen a Gal-|lia o a España. Plogo alos godos τ ellos uiniero*n*. Scilico*n*,[71] sue-|g*ro* de Honorio q*ue* mato a Tadagayso, dioles salto enlas Al-|pes τ lidio co*n*los godos. Ue*n*çiero*n* lo τ diero*n* tornada τ robaro*n* | a Lio*ri*a[72] τ Milia τ Cuscia o ante no*n* auie*n* fecho mal, q*ue* se yua*n* en | paz. ¶ Creçio[iii] co*n* ta*n*to Alarico por ue*n*gar la muert de Tadagayso, | come*n*ço guerra co*n* los romanos cerca Soa*n*,[73] τ p*ri*sola τ destruyo | la cibdad q*ue* solie los otros destruyr, p*er*o Alarico τ los godos asi | fuero*n* mesurados, q*ue* no*n* q*u*isiero*n* meter mano esqua*n*tra la ygl*es*ia·| ni*n* faz*er* mal a qua*n*tos y fallaro*n* de*n*tro ni*n* fuera qua*n*tos se lama-|ro*n* por *chris*tianos. Un om*n*e muy poderoso delos godos anda-|ua por la cibdad τ fallo una u*ir*gen τ dema*n*dol si sabie*n* algunos | tesoros,[iv] ella amostrol los uasos de Sant Pedro q*ue* iazie*n* esco*n*-|didos τ dixo ella: "Estos son dela ygl*es*ia, yo no*n* telas dare, p*re*nd*e*lo | tu si tu osas". Fue este τ dixolo Alarico, el enuio por los uasos τ | por la u*ir*gine*n* τ dixo el rey: "Yo co*n*los romanos lidio, no*n* co*n*la | [fol.10r] | ygl*es*ia no*n* co*n* Dios ni*n* co*n* sus s*an*c*t*os". Co*n* gra*n*d gozo tornaro*n* los uasos | ala ygl*es*ia τ la u*ir*ge*n* otrosi. Alas uozes saliero*n* muchos *chris*tianos q*ue* | estaua*n* escondidos τ muchos moros τ ge*n*tiles[v] τ h*er*eges escaparo*n* | de muert por no*n*bre de *chris*tianos.

---

[i] The lengthy rhetoric of *DRH* is greatly reduced, and *EG* removes *DRH* implicit indication of the superiority of Goths over Romans.

[ii] *DRH*: 'ytalia'

[iii] *DRH*: II.v

[iv] The editorial policy of the translation reveals an interest in basic details, and little else. In this case the terror of the ambassador is entirely removed, and the passage as a whole is significantly abbreviated.

[v] *DRH*: 'etiam τ pagani'

Fue p*re*sa Roma de Alarico[74] | clxxxxij. años q*ue* fue fecha Innoce*n*cius papa el p*ri*mo. Por no*n* uer es-|ta destruycio*n* de Roma, q*ue* fue mas por ue*n*dicta de Dios q*ue* por ar-|mas, uino se .i. p*ar*a Taue*r*na. ¶ La uilla p*re*sa τ destruyda, los go-|dos p*ri*siero*n* a doña Plaçida, fija del emp*er*ador Teodosio τ h*er*mana de | Archadio τ de Onorio τ co*n* gra*n*d aue*r* uiniero*n* se p*ar*a Ca*m*paña[75] τ B*ri*çia | τ Luchania τ q*ui*siero*n* entrar en mar por yr a Cecilia τ perdiero*n* mu*n*-|chos om*n*es, p*er*o ta*n* gra*n* era el gozo delo de Roma q*ue* por la p*er*dida | no*n* diero*n* un dine*r*o. ¶ Viniero*n* a Gusançia q*ue* ellos destruyera*n* τ a-|li fino Alarico, era ccccxxvij τ regno xiiij. años. τ fiziero*n* le | fuesa en medio de un rio q*ue* es dicho Barsentho τ ali lo enter-|raro*n* co*n* muchas ioyas τ tornaro*n* el agua sobrel por q*ue* mas nu*n*- | qua lo fallasen τ mataro*n* los catiuos q*ue* fiziero*n* la fuesa. ¶ En-|terraro*n*[i] Alarico, alçaro*n* rey asu sobrino[ii] Ataulfus τ salio | muy graçioso τ torno a Roma τ destruyo qua*n*to y fallo τ destruyo | a Lo*n*bardia.[iii] Honorio nol podie controlar en nada, pues Ataulfus | caso con Plaçida, fija de Th[eod]osio, h*er*mana de Archadio τ de Onorio, lo | uno por su fermosura lo ot*r*o por su linaie. τ lexo Lonbardia ha Ho-|norio como por co*n*dado τ el fue a Gallias. Los ot*r*os τ los borgu*n*do*n*es[76] | q*ue* ante *costra*naua*n*,[77] ouiero*n* miedo τ obedeçiero*n* le τ co*n*firmaro*n* el | regno delos godos. ¶ Et oyo dezir dela maláda*n*çia delos de Es-|paña τ uino p*ar*a acorer en Barçilona τ degollaro*n* le los suyos | mismos, era ccccLv, regno xxxij años. τ no*n* dexo fijos, en ta*n*-|to Saliçio, el co*n* q*ue* dixiemos,[iv] q*ui*so echar del imperio a Honorio | [fol.10v] | por faz*er* enp*er*ador asu fijo, ouiero*n* fazie*n*da [e murieron el y] Beuterio. ¶ Murio[v] Ataul-|fo sin fijos fiziero*n* los godos rey a Sige*ri*cho, era ccccLv τ regno un | año τ fue bueno τ sabio τ piadoso,[vi] τ ouo v fijos: Gise*ri*co τ Onorico | τ Cu*n*thema*n*do[78] τ Trasamu*n*do τ Histe*ri*co τ por q*ue* el regno fincase asus | fijos en paz, auino con[79] los godos. E*n*qua*n*to esto ente*n*diero*n*, los godos ma-|taro*n* lo en fabla, era ccccLvj. Murio Siguerico, fiziero*n* los godos | rey a Ualia. Este regno iij años τ ouo co*n*cordia co*n* Onorio el enp*er*-|ador τ re*n*diel co*n* gra*n* aue*r* asu h*er*mana Plaçiçida, la q*ue* tenie cati-|ua. Pues Uallia uino en España τ q*ue*branto los ua*n*dalos[vii] τ los ala-

[i] *DRH*: II.vi
[ii] *DRH*: 'consanguineum eius', *EG* omits the physical description of 'Ataulfus'.
[iii] *DRH*: 'ytaliam'.
[iv] *DRH*: II.vi.27 The Biblical reference to the Book of Daniel on which Ximénez de Rada casts doubt is excised entirely here. The translation therefore appears more economical and less prone to editorial comment than the Latin.
[v] *DRH*: II.vii
[vi] This is the direct opposite of Sigericus's characteristics as recounted by *DRH*. It is also noticable that the narrative is reduced again here, to the point that the sole details fully preserved are those of the names of the protagonists.
[vii] The *EG*s narrative is reduced to almost annal proportions by comparison with the analysis of the *DRH*.

¡nos τ los sueuos; τ torno con uictoria en Tolosa τ ali fino asu tienpo ¡ por si. Murio[i] Ualia τ regno Theudedos en era CcccLviiij τ reg-¡no xxx. años.[ii] τ començo guerra con los romanos, pues çerco ¡ Narbona τ pusolo en grand fanbre, pues leuantolo ende Latorius, prin-¡çeb de la tierra de Roma, pues Lathorius enganando por dichos delos ¡ ydolos[80] τ lidio conlos godos τ mataronlo. ¶ Murio Liturio τ Theudo-¡do fizo paz con los romanos τ lidio con Catilla,[81] rey delos ugnones, ¡ e[n] los Canpos Catalonicos τ ayudauan a don Achila los francos τ los ¡ burgundiones τ los sayones[82] τ briones, que fueron dela caualeria de ¡ Roma. Sangibanos, rey delos alanos, prometio ayuda [a] Achila τ ¡ Theuderdus τ Chirus, que lo sopieron, mandaron bien curiar las puertas que ¡ non passase Sanguibanos. Don Achila, rey delos ugnones, demando ¡ asus ydolos[83] τ asus adeuinos de conseio: "que matarie aun prin-¡çep dela otra parte τ que uencrie". El dia uino τ fizieron sus hazes, San-¡guibano uino en ayuda de Achila, dela otra part Turisebundus, ¡ fijo de Theudero; τ Elius, duc delos romanos; τ Orderico,[84] rey de ¡ los ostrogodos. τ fue con grand batalla que el rio yua cubierto de ¡ sangre o Theudedeus fue ferido de un dardo[iii] τ cayo del caualo τ asi ¡ murio entre pies; τ murio y Laudarico, cuñado de Achila. Partieron ¡ [fol.11r] ¡ se los godos τ los alanos τ lidiaron muy fuert, don Achila a pocos mu-¡riera τ si non que fuxo τ puso se enlos caros que trosxiera; Tarisbundius,[85] ¡ fijo de Teudereto, cuydaua tornar seguro asu alungada τ firiolo un ¡ cauallero enla cabeça τ pero escaparon lo los suyos que non murio luego ¡ y. Pues que uino la noche los godos demandaron su rey τ fallaron muer-¡to entre otros muchos τ Turismundus su fijo, con conseio de Echeus, quiso ¡ yr uengar muert de su padre. Echicius conseiol que fuese a reçebir ante ¡ el regno τ ordeno lo de su padre. ¶ Murio Theudero, alçaron rey asu ¡ fijo Turismundus enlos Canpos Catolonius.[86] Uençio la batalla era cccc ¡ Lxxxxij. τ regno un año τ con su padre dos. Este conbro bien su tierra ¡ pero murieron en esta batalla bien .ccc. mill omes,[87] menos de bien xv ¡ mill entre frances τ cepidos[88] que murieron ante la batalla.[iv] Pues con ¡ Atila estoruose un tienpo de guerra. E pues començo Thurismundus ¡ τ uino a Tolosa, don Efamus que era obispo enterro muchos delos. Pues ¡ Achilla paso el Danubio guerrear con los alanos τ uençio Turis-¡mundus. Tornose para Tollosa τ fizo paz conlos suyos enel ij° año que ¡ regnaua; el, que se sangraua del braço por conseio delos suyos fue ferido ¡ de muert, el entendio que era de muert con curauet[89] que traye mato algu-¡nos desus

---

[i] DRH: II.viii
[ii] DRH: 'annis xxxiii'.
[iii] This passage provides another fine example of the reduced rhetorical style of the translation, which nonetheless manages to retain the principal details.
[iv] The significance of the battle is diminished by EG and its lengthy aftermath is greatly reduced.

traydores q*ue* esta esta[uan] y. Uincio Turismu*n*dus τⁱ fiziero*n* rey asu her-
｜mano do*n* Theudorico enla era .cccclxxxxiij τ regno iiijⁱⁱ años τ co-｜me*n*ço
guerra de Rechiario. Pues q*ue* Rechiario caso co*n* fija de Teude-｜ro, he*r*mana
de Theuderico, asmo q*ue* España suya deuie ser por dere-｜cho, el auia
Gallezia τ Lusitania τ come*n*ço de correr a España. Teudo-｜rico enuiol rogar
mu*n*chas uezes q*ue* lo no*n* fiziese, q*ue* el uernie a Tho-｜losa τ uerie q*ue* era.
Ouiero*n* de au*er* fazie*n*nda entre Astorga τ Leon τ fue ｜ ue*n*çido Rechiario.
Fuxo por mar τ aribo en Portogal τ fue y p*re*so ｜ τ aduxo a Teudorico τ por
esto p*er*dio el cuerpo τ al regno. Pues Thu-｜dorico d[i]o el Regno asu c*r*iado
Alu*n*phus, este era de Alumna τ no*n* era ｜ [fol.11v] ｜ bie*n* godo τ por co*n*seio
delos sueuius leua*n*tose co*n*tra Eudorico. Teudorico ｜ uino sobrel, ue*n*çiolo,
p*r*isolo τ matolo. ¶ Ento*n*z los p*re*lados uiniero*n* a ｜ el τ recibiolos muy bie*n* τ
otorgoles q*ue* esleyesen rey desu natu*r*a. ｜ ¶ Pues Teudorico q*u*iso rapar⁹⁰ la
çibdad de Emeriça τ ouo miedo ｜ de Sant Ollala τ delos martires q*ue* son y τ
no*n* oso. τ fizo tres p*ar*tes ｜ de su hueste: la una lexo τ por retener lo q*ue*
ganara en España; co*n* ｜ la ot*ra* uino ala Uethica; τ la ot*ra* enbio a Gallizia τ
dioles por cab-｜dielos a Sime*r*ico τ a Nepoçiano. Estos destruyero*n* los
sueuios fata ｜ Lugo, de ento*n*ze aca fuero*n* los duques delos godos en
España. ｜ Qua*n*do ouo co*n*q*u*isto los sueuios uino Teudorico en Gallia
Gothica. ｜ ¶ Egipnus, por au*er* ayuda delos godos, dio Narbona a
Theodorico. ｜ ¶ Pues desa muert partiero*n*se los sueuios, los unos co*n*
Muyde-｜ta, fijo de Masilla, este regno .ij. años; τ los ot*ro*s co*n* Frata*n*. Murio ｜
Ma*n*stra τ regno su fija Remismu*n*dus τ este co*n*cordo co*n* Fianta*n*⁹¹ τ ga-
｜naro*n* amos Lusitania. ¶ A dos años passados murio Frata*n* τ ｜ los suyos
fiziero*n* rey a Frunario, este gaño Flauia por guerra. ｜ Remismu*n*dus robaua
mu*n*cho τ Auria. ¶ Depues ij años Remis-｜mu*n*dus acordo co*n* los galleçios τ
ouo el regno τ fiziero*n* lo rey los ｜ suyos. Paso Lusitania τ gaño Coynbria τ
destruyola τ gano Ulix-｜bona, ca gela dio un cibdadano Lucidio Q*ue* la tenie.
¶ Pues Remis-｜mu*n*do firmo su paz co*n* Ce*n*durico τ el enuio mug*er* co*n*
Salario, ｜ un su c*r*iado. Pues torno Solano τ falo muerto a Thurdoricco, q*ue* lo
ma-｜to su he*r*mano mismo Elerico. ¶ Murioⁱⁱⁱ Thudorico τ regno su her-
｜mano q*ue* lo mato, era de vi τ regno xvij. años. τ destruyo ｜ mu*n*cho de
Lusitania τ gano Pa*n*plona τ Caragoça τ Tirgana τ ｜ su p*ro*ue*n*çia τ España la
de suso. ¶ Pues oyo dexir q*ue* finara Ua-｜le*n*tiniano, ca lo matara un su
p*r*ínçep τ uio el romano impe-｜rio co*n*coruado, come*n*ço guerra, gaño a
Arlech τ Masil τ ue*n*çio a Rio-｜[fol.12r] ｜ timej, rey delos bretones, q*ue* uino en
ayuda delos romanos. ¶ Seye*n*-｜do en Atelalaro⁹² uio las armas delos godos

---

ⁱ *DRH*: II.viiii
ⁱⁱ *DRH*: 'xiij'.
ⁱⁱⁱ *DRH*: II.x. As is frequently the case, *EG* fails to include 'd' in the subsequent date.

camiar colores.[i] So este rey ǀ delos godos τ despues se escriuieron los estatutos que ante por costumbre ǀ iudgauan. Don Heurico murio en Arelato. ¶ Murio[ii] Heurico τ regno su fi-ǀio Alarico en Tolosa, era de [d].xxiij. Este lidio con Flugdigino, princep delos ǀ frânçes τ matolo[93] τ peyelo. ¶ Murio Alarico τ regno en Narbona .iiij. ǀ años Gaufalxus, era de [d]xlvj. Este Eusaleyto fue njeto de Alarico, ǀ fijo de Amalarico, fijo de Alarico, el que ouo en Amalasuente,[94] fijo de ǀ Theuderico rey delos otrogodos. τ fue fijo sempre malapreso τ perdio ǀ el regno τ la cabeça. τ murio Alarico τ su madre auie un fijo cicho[95] ǀ τ menospreçiaua ael τ aella τ[iii] ella dio elogar de rey a sobrino Thudo, ǀ era de lxx τ regno xvij. años. Este dio liçençia que alegasen los obispos ǀ τ que se acordasen asu ley τ asus conçilios. Este echo los francos que ǀ auien Destrian Tharugona. ¶ A tiempo este Thudis fizo afogar enel ǀ baño Alamalasuncris[96] que fizo regnar. Oyo esta aleuosia Iustino, que te-ǀnia su fija della en comienda que deuie regnar τ el enuiola morar ǀ con Belesario. Quando el plogo mataron la los romanos Theudo.[iv] τ regno ǀ Teudisco, era de [d]xxvij τ regno un año τ vj. meses. Esse salio malo ǀ τ facie asus uasallos cornudos τ iuntaron se contra el τ uinieron todos ǀ τ afogaron lo como a señor desleal τ malo contra sus uasallos.[v] ǀ ¶ Murio[vi] Thudisco τ regno Aguilla, era de .lxxxviij τ regno .v. años. ǀ Este uio gerra contra Cordoba τ en esta delos christianos fizo echar ǀ los fuesos de Sant Acisolo el martir por los muradales; e pues ǀ cofondiol Dios[vii] que partie[97] el fijo τ quanto traye τ fuxo a Merita τ toliel ǀ el regno Achindagildus. Los de Merida uieron que les podrie uenir mal ǀ por ello τ mataron lo τ[viii] dieron la uilla a Thagisilo; ya ante muchas ǀ uezes le quisieran toler el regno con ayuda de Iustiniano τ non pu-ǀdo fasta que los suyos le tolieron el regno τ lo mataron. ¶ Murio ǀ [fol.12v] ǀ Agilla τ[ix] alçaron rey a Thigildo, era de lxxxxiij τ regno xiiij. años. ǀ Fino Athagildo en Toledo, uaco el regno .v. meses. ¶ Pues dias de Acha-ǀgildo regno Luyba en Narbona, era de vij τ regno tres años. Al [segundo][98] ǀ año fizo elongar de fijo de su hermano Leouigildo τ partio con el la tierra τ ǀ diol España τ retouo la Gallia. Leuodegildo casara con Thodosia, ǀ fija del duc de Cartagena, que fue fijo de Theodicco. Fino[99] Luyba τ su ǀ hermano

---

[i] The narrative of military campaigns is drastically foreshortened, however Ximénez de Rada's references to legal matters survives in translation.
[ii] DRH: II.xi
[iii] DRH: II.xii, the details removed from what follows gives the EG an annalistic feel.
[iv] A lengthy anecdote concerning the doing of Theudis fails to appear at this point.
[v] Mention of Seville in DRH is silenced in EG.
[vi] DRH: II.xiii.
[vii] DRH: II.xiii.6: 'sanctis inferentibus'.
[viii] DRH: II.xiiii, though recounted in a slightly different order, the details are the same.
[ix] DRH: II.xiiii. Again, basic detail is maintained and DRH authorial comment cut.

Leouegildo heredo Gallia τ España, que ante [a]uie era de x. τ re-|gno .xviij. años. Este quiso guerrear τ ganar tierras τ priso Caura-|bina τ Arigna τ conbro muncho delo quel tolieran. ¶ Este salio arriano, | masco τ segudo τ destoro los christianos.[i] Este echo de tierra a Leandro, ar-|cobispo de Yspalis τ de Seuilla; τ a don Mesana, arçobispo de Ora | τ otros muchos; τ tolie alas yglesias sus posesiones τ los pri-|uilegios τ los tesoros; τ fazie[ii] rebatizar alos catolicos τ fizo | a fuerça apostatar a **Vicencio**,[100] obispo de Cartageña τ de Caragoça τ | echar de tierra τ matar los principes que eran catholicos. ¶ Este fue el | primer rey que uistio paños realles τ comio solo asu mesa, lo que | ante non fazien que asis comie con[101] otros τ non fazie meiorie de paños | de otros. Este poblo una uilla en Celtiberia τ pusol nonbre desu fijo | Rebcapolim. Este emendo los istatutos de Eurico lo mal fecho τ lo | soberano. Pues uino a muerte τ repintiose τ mando asu fijo Rega-|redo que tornase los **xpristianos** desterados τ a Leandro asu hermano Fulge-|nuo, obispo Astigitano; τ que los **ouiese**[102] como padres τ señores; | τ fino en Toledo. Murio[iii] Leouegildo, fizieron rey asu fijo Reca-|redo, era de [d]xxviij τ regno xv años. Este fue muy catholico | τ muy bueno, enuio por Leandro τ por Fulgencio τ tornolos **en sus estados**[103] | τ fizoles seer en paz.

El primer concilio de Toledo[iv]

| Este[104] Recardo fizo fazer concilio de clerigos τ de legos τ de sus | principes τ fueron y lxij. obispos a estempnar la openion τ la | fe[105] de Arriano τ crouo la catholica τ firmola el τ sus uarones | [fol.13r] | τ mandola predicar. Pues uençio alos uascones τ alos nauarros τ a | los francez[106] que uinieron contra el. **Esti** dio mucho a pobres τ fizo por Dios τ | murio en Toledo muy bien confessado.

Que concilio fizo Recaredo

|Enel iiijº año que regno este _glorioso_[107] don Regardo, idus de mayo, fue | fecho otro[108] concillo en Toledo. τ ouo entrel ijº cocilio τ este[109] tercero Lxij. años contados.[110] |

---

[i] A lengthy paragraph on the subject of Hermenegild has been excised by the translator, thereby indicating his interest in a continuous narrative without religious comment.
[ii] The text of BN Res/278 (fol. 27r, line 8) seamlessly corresponds to that of 302 from this point onwards. See above pp. 4-5.
[iii] _DRH_: II.xv, there is a chapter division in BN Res/278, with the corresponding _DRH_ rubric translated. See above pp. 4-5 and 13-15.
[iv] This rubric does not correspond to a _DRH_ chapter. See p. 15 above.

Enel ij° concilio de Toledo[111]

Este co*n*cilio fue fecho | en tie*m*po de Helladio τ fuero*n* y estos arçobispos: τ *de Merida*[112] Ma-|usona, de Taragona do*n* Eufemio, de Seuilla do*n* Leandre, de Narbona do*n* | U*n*ge*n*çio, de Braguena do*n* Pardardus τ de sus sufraga*n*eos mu*n*chos. En este | co*n*cilio fue co*n*de*m*pnada τ amortiguada[113] en España la fe τ la opinio*n* | de Arriano, q*ue* auie aturado en España del tie*m*po de la era de ccclxxx | viij°,[i] en q*ue* regnaua Atanarico τ Uale*n*s el enp*er*ador, fasta este co*n*cilio | q*ue* nu*n*qua fue ende salida, pues aca fuero*n* bie*n* catholicos. Esto*n*z fizo | Leandro una omilia a loor dela co*n*uersio*n* delos godos q*ue* tornaro*n* ala fe | catholica. En este co*n*cilio ouo Lxij. obispos menos de uicarios τ | de esçusados.

De fechos delos reyes[ii]

| Murio Recaredo τ regno su fijo Li*m*bre, era de [dc]Lxiij τ regno dos años. | No*n* fue noble[114] de madre pues Uectius matolo en edad de xvj. | años. Fino Luyba, era de [dc]Lxv τ regno Uiterico, el Q*ue* lo mato. Este reg-|no vij. años τ fue sie*m*pre ue*n*çido τ mal ap*re*so τ por derechos[115] q*ue* | mato asu señor[iii] seyendo me*n*ino. En cabo el mur[i]o de gladio τ fue | uil miente enterado, era de **dclxxiiij**.[116] Pues este regno Ga*n*demato[117] | ij años τ deuasto los uascones τ fino en Toledo. ¶ Pues[iv] de | Ga*n*demato regno Sisebuto, era de [dc]Liiij τ regno viij. años τ | vi meses. Este fizo batear los iudios delos por fuerca delos | por grado τ por razo*n*,[v] ca era y letrado; τ gano uillas τ castiellos | q*ue* los romanos tenie*n* en España τ dema*n*do τ ensayo los obispos | si era*n* bie*n* catholicos. Esto*n*z era arçobispo en Toledo do*n* Heladio | τ en Yspanis[118] Ysidoro. Este rey co*n*uertio a Sire,[vi] q*ue* era obispo de | [fol.13v] | los arianos τ subiugo asi los ro*n*caleses τ fizo las ygl*es*ias de Santa Leo-|cadia. ¶ Murio Sisebuto, unos dize*n* q*ue* de pozones ot*r*os q*ue* por si τ de-|lexo un fijo chico de un año τ vij. meses τ fino luego pues su | padre. ¶ A este tie*m*po de Sisebuto p*re*dicaua Mahomat so su seta τ so | ley de nueuo. ¶ Pues[vii] Sisebuto diero*n* el regno a Suintilla q*ue* fue fijo | del rey Rechadeo, era de [dc]lxxxiij τ regno x años. Este gano las ciu-|dades q*ue* los romanos[119] tenie*n* en España τ

---

[i] The translator's close attention to detail here, particularly significant in the light of surrounding passages, indicates heightened interest in the city of Toledo and its synods.

[ii] *DRH*: II.xvi, a return to the doings of monarchs sees a parallel return to the *EG*'s characteristic brevity of expression and paucity of detail.

[iii] *DRH*: 'in morte autem gladio periit quia gladio fuerat operatus', *EG* omits the moral dimension of Luyba's life and death.

[iv] *DRH*: II.xvii

[v] *DRH* quote from St. Paul removed. *EG* takes a less exemplary view of the past.

[vi] *DRH*: 'atque per ueridica doctorum testimonia Syrum...'.

[vii] *DRH*: II.xviii, 'Suyntila...suscepit diuina gracia regni sceptra...'.

fue bie*n* señor d'España ǀ del mar ocorano aqua τ subiugo[120] los uascoles q*ue* guerreaua*n* τ cos-ǀtriñien a Taragona, fata q*ue* uiniero*n* asu me*r*çed. Ellos[121] iuraro*n* **obedie*n*cia**[122]ǀ τ fieldad τ en voz de paz poblaro*n* asus misiones τ asu costa ǀ Olit, pe*r*o ot*r*os dize*n* q*ue* Oloro*n*. En uida deste rey regno bien paz[123] τ co*n*cordia ǀ enla t*i*e*r*ra τ fino en Toledo, era de [dc]Lxxxxiij τ regno so su fijo Rechi-ǀtapar[124] τ salio en sembla*n* τ en meñas[125] al padre τ murio a pocos dias, ǀ pero delexo dos fijos:[i] Siseñadus τ Ci*n*dasuynudus. De pues Suyntila τ su ǀ fijo Rechiniro, regno[ii] su he*r*mano Siseñandus, era de [dc].Lxxiij,. τ regno .v. ǀ años τ xj. meses τ fue bue*n* rey.

El tercero concilio de Toledo

ǀ El[iii] te*r*cero año q*ue* regno Sise*n*adus fizo faz*er* co*n*cilio en Toledo en Sa*n*ta ǀ Locadia τ sobre los artic*u*los dela fe τ ot*r*as muchas cosas τ ǀ fuero*n* y todos los p*r*incipes de Gallia τ de España. Era ento*n*z Ysido-ǀro, q*ue* fizo mu*n*cho bue*n* libro; era arçobispo en Toledo do*n* Iuste τ Y-ǀsidoro de Seuilla τ **Cilia** de Narbona τ do*n* Iulio de Barguena τ do*n* Au-ǀdix[126] de Cartageña τ do*n* Imirus, uicario de Emerita τ sus sufraga*n*eos. ǀ τ fuero*n* y Lxviij. obispos q*ue* se sosc*r*iuiero*n* τ pusiero*n* los no*n*bres, menos ǀ delos uicarios τ delos escusados.

El quarto concilio de Toledo[iv]

ǀ El q*u*arto co*n*cilio fue en Toledo en dias de Eugenio, arçobispo ǀ τ p*r*imado. τ fuero*n* y xxiiij obispos τ el arçobispo de Car-ǀtageña τ estos sosc*r*iuiero*n*, menos delos uicarios τ delos escusa-ǀdos. τ[v] maguer pocos qua*n*to de bie*n* fue y falado ta*n* bie*n* delo tinre-ǀnal[127] como delo espitital, no*n* lo podrie o*m*ne sofrir dezir, como es ǀ [fol.14r] ǀ esc*r*ipto enlos cañones, ent*r*e los q*u*ales Braulo, obispo de Çaragoça, ǀ τ dixo ta*n*to q*ue* fue marauilla por q*ue* la ygle*s*ia fue τ es muy hondra-ǀda, ta*n* bie*n* en Roma como en España.

---

[i] BN Res/278 adds text translated directly from *DRH* to the previously existing translation and then resumes the narration in the style of 302 albeit with the continued addition of translated *DRH* rubrics.

[ii] *DRH*: II.xviiii. Once more the *EG* rubric indicates a different order of priorities to that of the source.

[iii] Once again, BN Res/278 adds text directly translated from *DRH* to the 302 narrative. The text concerns the accession of Suynthila. For the implications of this and the translation of rubrics, see above pp. 4–5 and 15.

[iv] *DRH* has no chapter division at this point. *EG* again divides its narrative according to its own criteria.

[v] *EG* provides a resumé of the *DRH* narrative.

El quinto concilio de Toledo[i]

| El[ii] v⁰ concilio de Toledo fue fecho en tiempo de Cuntila,[128] que era princep, | τ su Eugenio, eso mismo primado, sobre la disciplina τ sobre | la fe catholica. Escriuieron τ pusieron nonbres Scula, arçobispo de Nar-|bona τ Iuliano τ Braguena τ Honorato de Yspalis, o de Seuilla τ | Protasio de Taragona τ sus sufraganeos τ sus uicarios, los que pu-|dieron y uenir.

Delos reyes godos[iii]

| Murio Cintilla τ regno su fijo .i. Tulgans, rayz delos godos, | era de [dc]Lxxxiij τ regno ij. dos años τ murio sin fijos. | Dolieron so los godos mucho desu muert, que tenie la tierra en bien | τ en paz, por que murio tan niño que non lexo fijo que heredasse el regno. Pues[iv] Tulgas regno Cindaespandus, et envadio et destruyo el regno | delos godos, era de [dc]Lxxxv τ regno x años τ fue rey bueno | τ piadoso.

El sesto[129] concilio de Toledo[v]

| El[vi] quinto año que regno, fizo fazer concilio .xv. kalendas de nouien-|bre en Toledo sobre los _herejes_ τ los iudios τ los falsos | christianos τ fueron y los principes τ los uarones de España τ Eu-|genio, ese mismo primado de Toledo; τ Tantio, arçobispo de Emerita; τ | Antonius de Yspalis, τ Protasio de Cartageña; τ con sus sufraganeos fueron | xxx obispos τ x uicarios, menos delos escusados. τ todos estos | sobscriuieron en este conciilio τ el rey mando catar τ requerir todos los | libros delos sanctos padres.

De Taio, obispo de Cartageña[vii]

| Estonz falaron menos en España un libro Moralia de Gregorio, que fizo a | ruego τ a peticion de Leandro τ ouieron su acuerdo τ enuiaron los | prelados de España a don Taio, obispo de Caragoça, que fuese a Roma de-|mandar este libro al papa, que lo non auien en España. τ fue τ demandol | que con otras cosas que auie de ueer la cort que lo non falauan entre otros mu-|[fol.14v] | chos. Moraron y gran tiempo seyendo y muy enoiado, fue una noche uelar | ala yglesia de Sant Pedro **τ rogo a los sacristanes que lo lexassen hy velar**

---

[i] _EG_ chapter structure again follows its own imperatives, as there is no _DRH_ division at this point.
[ii] BN Res/278 returns to its own, more comprehensive translation at this point.
[iii] No _DRH_ division at this point
[iv] _DRH_: II.xx
[v] No _DRH_ division at this point.
[vi] BN Res/278 resumes the 302-style narration.
[vii] No _DRH_ division at this point.

τ aparesciol una uision como en sueños, pero ui-|eron lo los que guardauan el
tesoro. Leuantose una grand claridad en la | yglesia τⁱ entraron dos, mano a
mano, cantando τ luego otros dos con ellos |τ el uno uieio τ caño. Este uiño
a¹³⁰ Taio τ dixo: "¿como andas aqui?". | Respuso Taio: "¿quien eres que lo
preguntas?" τ dixo: "Yo soy Gregorio cuyos libros | tu demandas τ por tu qui
lazras,¹³¹ τ nuestro señor enbiome que telo mostra-|se, sepas que este libro
fallaras enel penultimo armario delos libros | ala parte diestra solos otros
libros." Dixo Taio: "¿que quien eran aquellos dos que yuan | delant τ los que
uienen¹³² despues?". Respuso [que]¹³³ el uno era Sant | Pedro¹³⁴ τ el otro
Sant Paulo, "los otros son compañas que quearienⁱⁱ aqui enla cib-|dad". τⁱⁱⁱ
pregunto Taio si andaua y Agustin τ dixo que non que mas alto estaua | que
ellos, que mas alto fablara. Taio echo sele¹³⁵ alos pies por lo adorar, |τ non uio
nada dela uision. Los sacristanos ouieron pauor dela claridat |τ dela uision τ
fizieron roydo que lo sopo el papa τ enuio por Taio τ mandol | dezie esta
uision en uirtud de obediencia. τ contola τ falaron el libro asi como | el dixo τ
en ese lugar τ enuiaron lo con su libro a España.

Del rey Cidasyundoⁱᵛ

| Enᵛ tiempo deste rey Cindasyndus non fue fallado herege nin mal | christiano
en España. Este fizo demandar los libros delos sanctos padres |τ confirmo
los de Ysidoro. ¶ Este gano priuilegio del papa que ouieron en | España la
primacia o ante solien, o si querien en Toledo. ¶ Este por la senten-|çia del
conçilio general desterro a Teodistino, arçobispo de Yspalien τ pri-|uolo dela
primacia que fue antiga τ tornola en Toledo τ confirmola, y con pri-|uilleios τ
otorgamiento del papa, maguer ante auien fechos concilios | que iazie mas en
comedianedo. Este mantouo la tierra en bien τ en paz. | Este alço asu fijo
Rensesuyndo rey delos godos. El regno por si vj. | años . τ x. meses τ conel
fijo iiij. años τ xv dias. Esteᵛⁱ murio | τ fue enterrado en Toledo. ¶ Puesᵛⁱⁱ
Cidasmundo [regno Retensuydo],¹³⁶ era de [dc]Lxxxxv τ | [fol.15r] regno este
xviij. años τ xj. meses por si τ con el padre v, fizieron | xxiij. τ onze meses τ
fue muy bien rey.

ⁱ BN Res/278 returns to its own, more comprehensive translation of *DRH*.
ⁱⁱ *DRH*: "qui in ista basilica requiescunt"
ⁱⁱⁱ BN Res/278 translation again returns to the 302 text.
ⁱᵛ *DRH*: II.xxi, *EG* shows similar Toledan interest in the question of the primacy to that of the source.
ᵛ BN Res/278 returns to its own, closer, translation of *DRH*.
ᵛⁱ BN Res/278 translation again resumes the 302 text.
ᵛⁱⁱ *DRH*: II.xxii

El septimo concilio de Toledo[i]

| Este Rete*n*suydo en sus dias fizo faz*er* iij. co*n*cilios en Toledo. En el p*ri*-|mero[137] todos sus p*ri*ncipes τ sus uarones τ ouo y xlvj. obispos, | menos de ot*ro*s cle*ri*gos τ delos abbades τ de ot*ro*s me*n*sageros τ delos ui-|carios τ delos escusados τ soscr*i*uiero*n* τ pusiero*n* sus no*n*bres. Este co*n*ci-|lio fue co*n*tra los ereges τ los malos xp*ri*st*i*anos τ sobre la fe dela t*ri*nidad τ fue el vij° co*n*cilio q*ue* fue en Toledo so[138] | Eugenio τ el rey Recusoyndo.

El viij. concilio de Toledo

| So esse mismo rey τ Eugenio fue el viij. co*n*cilio en Toledo τ fuero*n* | y arçobispos Ore*n*çio de Eme*ri*ta; Antonio de Yspalis; P*ro*chanio de | Braguena τ sus sufraneos τ **fueron hy arçobispos** τ fuero*n* y Lij. obispos τ x. uicarios τ | mu*n*chos abbades τ mu*n*chos p*ri*ncipes de España. Estos soscr*i*uiero*n* | τ pusiero*n* sus no*n*bres τ ta*n* bie*n* obispos como los p*ri*ncipes.

El ix° concilio de Toledo[ii]

| So ese mismo rey, al vj. año q*ue* regno ese mismo tropo-|litano Eugenio, fue el ix co*n*cilio en Toledo τ soscr*i*uiero*n* y los p*ri*nci-|pes de España τ xvj. obispos, menos delos uicarios τ delos abse-|tens τ delos escusados.

El x. concilio de Toledo

| So ese mismo rey τ ese mismo p*ri*mado, al[139] viij. año q*ue* come*n*ço | de regnar, fue el x co*n*cilio en Toledo. En este soscr*i*uiero*n* los arço-|bispos Fugitiuo de Yspalis; τ Fructuoso de Bragena τ ent*re* sus sufra-|neos τ uicarios de ot*ro*s obispos fuero*n* y xxv.

Del bien de Reçesuydo

| Este[iii] rey fue cathelico τ amo fe τ ley τ delectauase fablar en | ela τ oyrla departir. τ el mismo pues dema*n*daua alos niños | τ alos legos la fe τ el q*ue* no*n* la ente*n*die bie*n* el le amost*ra*ua. ¶ En su | tie*n*po ouo el sol eclipsi q*ue* a m[e]d[i]o[140] dia parescie*n* las estrellas. Este | echo alos uascones de España τ fue muy bie*n* rey mucho amado | τ temido. ¶ Este rey fino en Banba q*ue* solie*n* auer no*n*bre esto*n*z Gerçigas, | en te*n*mino de Pale*n*çia, **murio kale*n*das de setie*n*bre τ fue ally soterrado en** era de [dccxx] xiij.

---

[i] Although the *EG* follows the *DRH* text closely, the revised set of editorial priorities leads to very short sections. See above pp. 15–17.
[ii] 302 rubric is split across line ends.
[iii] This detail of religious import is preserved from source.

De la uida de Sant Illefonso[i]

| [fol.15v] | El ix año q*ue* regno fue arçobispo de Toledo Ildefon*so* τ fue de bue*n* | linage τ descipulo de Sant Ysid*g*ro. Este come*n*ço en niñeza τ sie*m*pre | p*er*seuero τ delecto en officio de San*t*a M*ar*ia. A tie*m*po uiniero*n* de Gallias He-|luidius τ Pelagio en España, por denostar la ui*r*ginidad de Santa Maria. | τ uiniero*n* ante Illefon*so* τ a razo*n* τ a prueua τ ue*n*çioles τ cofondio | los co*n* muchos esc*ri*ptos, p*r*oua*n*do su ui*r*ginidad τ seer leal[141] τ u*er*dad*er*a | τ li*m*pia **por derecho τ por la escriptura.** ¶ Pues ala fiesta de Santa M*ar*ia q*ue* el establecio, xvº.[ii] ianua-|rij, enel mes de nouie*m*bre,[142] Illefonso q*ue* ca*n*taua la misa, a uista de | todo el pueblo q*ue* era en la ygle*s*ia aparesçio uesible mie*n*tre Santa M*ar*ia | a Ellefonso τ co*n* ella co*m*pañas de angeles τ de apostoles τ marti-|res τ co*n*fessores τ ui*r*gines τ dixol esta razo*n*: "Por q*ue* co*n* p*ur*a ui*r*gi-|nidad τ co*n* linpia co*n*cie*n*cia ceñiste tus renes de ligamie*n*to de uir-|ginidad τ castidad τ te lecteste en mio oficio, p*r*ende esta uesti-|me*n*ta del trasoro de mio fijo q*ue* la uistas las fiestas de mio fijo | τ mias".[143] Esto dixo τ tornose al çielo asu fijo. Esto uiero*n* τ oyero*n* to-|do el pueblo, de*n*t recibie este dono Ildefon*so* τ uistiolla τ ca*n*to co*n* | ella. Despues el nu*n*qua la uistio ni*n* ne*n*guno si no*n* fue Sisebe-|rto, q*ue* por su culpa **fue** exulado τ echado de t*ie*rra. ¶ Visco Illefon*so* ix | años τ dos meses en su cathedra arçobispal τ fino xº k*a*l*en*das fe-|broarij, el xvij. año q*ue* Reseuydo regnara sin su padre τ fue | enterrado en Santa Leocadia, a pies de Sant Eugenio su antecesor; τ fizo | muchos libros τ algunos delexo por acabar, por esto fue dicho o | autor[144] como q*ue* ouo boca dorada. ¶ Ysidoro esc*ri*pso el nascimie*n*to delos | godos fasta el q*uí*nto año ¶ del rey Suintilla. Yllefon*so* sc*ri*pso los tie*n*-|pos[145] delos godos τ delos alanos τ delos ua*n*dalos τ delos sueuios | del v año. de Suintilla, o lo delexo Ysidoro, fata xviij. años de Rece-|seydo. Ysidoro el menor sc*ri*uio q*ue* come*n*ço la cronica del comie*n*ço del mu*n*-|do fata el xviij. años de Recesuydo τ fata la destruçio*n* d'España | [fol.16r] |q*ue* fiziero*n* los arabes.[146]

---

[i] This does not correspond to a *DRH* chapter. Unlike the source the *EG* does not equate chapters with the reigns of individual monarchs.See above p. 15 ff.
[ii] 'in festo gloriose Virginis, quod in Hispaniis XV kalendas Ianuarii celebratur', Ildefonso's part in the celebration of this feast is the initiative of the translator.

DEL REY BAMBA[i]

₁ Fino[ii] Roscesido τ fizieron rey por election a Banba. Este fue muy no-₁ble τ de buen seso τ de buenas maneras,[147] τ de linage los godos τ ya ₁ ante auie fecho munchos buenos fechos en batallas; τ non como algu-₁nos que dizen que fue de uill natura, ante fue muy noble. Uerdad es que fue rey ₁ mas por fuerça que por grado, que sera bueño omne τ temie su alma τ non a-₁uie cuydado de regnar nin de mandar tierra. τ maguer que con todo esso, non quiso ₁ que lo clamasen rey fata que uino en Toledo τ fue y alçado rey y confirmado ₁ τ iurado. τ el iuro τ dio bueños fueros τ camiar los malos. τ otrosi iu-₁raron le[148] τ fizieron le omenaie quel obedeçiesen τ quel fuesen[149] fieles, entrelos ₁ quales uino don Paulo, que depues fue su traydor. Uino Bamba en Toledo τ ₁ iuraron lo τ el fizo dar buenos fueros τ tener la fe catholica; alcaron lo ₁ rey τ pusieron lo cerca el altar de Santa Maria, ali seyendo a uista de todo el ₁ pueblo uieron quel salie dela cabeça baho como fumo τ salie ende una ₁ abeia τ bolaua contra el çielo τ semeio que ala suuio τ uieron las gentes ₁ que serie rey dulz τ bueno τ pisadoso τ Dios que serie conel τ que porel se al-₁carie el regno la yglesia τ la fama delos godos. Esto fue era de .xiiij.[iii] ₁ τ regno nueue años τ un mes. ¶ Luego[iv] al primero año que regno, ouo ₁ discordia ensu regno: el dicho conde de Euinas, con ayuda de don Gil, obis-₁po de Magalona τ del abad don Ramiro, alçose con la tierra τ fizo tornar ₁ alos godos alos iudios, que eran exulados por derecho delos godos τ ₁ comenco de guerrear alos que esperauan por rey a Banba. τ por que Origio,[150] obis-₁po de Nuemas, non lo quiso consentir, echolo dela tierra τ toliol el obispadgo ₁ τ fizo obispo al abad don Remiro que tenie con el τ consagraronlo otros ₁ dos obispos que eran de su parte. Quando lo oyo **Banba**, lego sus huestes τ enuio ₁ los sobrel τ enuio por cabdiello a don Paulo, que era de natura delos ₁ godos τ fue entrado enla tierra por nonbre de Banba por sus cartas ₁ τ con su hueste. Pues que fue apoderado enla tierra que a fuerça que a grado ₁ [fol.16v] ₁ con ruegos τ con menazas τ con dos torno la tierra asi, que dixieron que non querien otro rey ₁ si non a Paullo, que non auien nada con Bamba. Eso mismo otorgo don Tanosindo que era de ₁ su conseio. Don Argebalo, obispo de Narbona, uido esta traycion τ non lo quiso con-

---

[i] Unique rubric in capitals, mirrored by N. This corresponds to a new book in *DRH* III.i. For the rubrics in *DRH* see Inés Fernández Ordóñez, 'La técnica'. The attributes of Bamba here are slightly different, and the translator is both aware of comments over Bamba's alleged 'uil linage' and keen to deny them. See above p. 28.
[ii] BN Res/278 returns to its own translation of *DRH* at this point.
[iii] In contrast to previous practice *EG* retains most of *DRH* detail, albeit in slightly different configuration.
[iv] *DRH*: III.ii, BN Res/278 resumes its account of the 302 text.

|sentir¹⁵¹ a don Paulo τⁱ començol de mouer guerra. Los otros obedescieron a
Paulo τ | juraron lo como fizieron en Toledo a Bamba τ el fizo dar buenos
fueros τ que nunqua | obedescrie a Banba τ los otros otrosi. Pues que a fuerça
τ que a grado gano en su a-|yuda alos francos τ alos uascones τ los pireneos
del Puerto de Aspa, | τ fizo otrosi su conuiniencia¹⁵² con los otros traydores,
con el conde Hysindico τ con don | Guillen, obispo de Magalona τ con don
Ramiro, obispo de Nuemas, que fue abad, | que fuesen todos en uno. τ
destruyo Gallia Gotiga τ una partida de Celtiberia, | τ los uascones τ los
pirencos destruyeron mucho en Cantabira, maguer | a tiempo *Bamba* los echo
dende. Haheuos con toda essa conpana, don Paulo con su ban-|do cuydo
uenir bien seguro en España contra el rey Banba. ¶ Banbaⁱⁱ era | estonz en
Cantabria τ sus partidas de Gallia τ oyo la traycion de Paulo τ | partio sus
gentes, los unos que se uinieron adobar la tierra τ los otros que fuesen | luego
conel. τ dixoles: "Uarones, uos sodes godos, uos τ uuestra natura siempre |
fustes leales τ buenos τ siempre uençistes. Yo uno solo non ualo mas que |
otro omne, el mi mal τ el mi daño τ mi honta uuestro es τ lo uuestro mio. Pe-
|se uos de lo que faze Paulo, griego de mala natura,ⁱⁱⁱ que siempre fueron tales, |
ya se me [a] alçado con la tierra en onta delos godos, delos muertos τ de | los
biuos que oy son τ que an de nasçer, esforçad τ prended coraçon como si-
|enpre fezistes. Uayamos cobrar lo nuestro τ uengar esta honta, aiudar nos | a
Dios con la uerdad que tenemos τ cofonda a ellos con su mentira. Pero si lo
fa-|zen con ayuda delos franceses, que alas cuytas siempre demandaron aiuda |
de los godos, non lo se, mas comencemos lo con Dios τ uençremos". Plogo |
atodos; mouieron se, pasaron por Calaforra τ por Huesca τ por el Ual | de
Aspa, quemaron τ destruyeron la Guascueña τ sus fortalezas, que | siempre las
fizieron de madera τ **priso**¹⁵³ por fuego los que obedeçien a Pa-|[fol.17r] | ulo τ
fizieron le omenage; τ dieron le estages los fijos τ fueron con el. Paso **a
Gallias** | τ fizo tres huestes: la una contra Turheno τ Alba dela çibdad de
Esqu ita-|nia, ala qual dieran por **caudiello**¹⁵⁴ un so sobrino **Disiderio** que
estonz era enla prouen-|çia de Narbona; la otra hueste contra Ausoniaⁱᵛ a los
que tenien con Pau-|lo; la otra por el plano de Tolosa contra Narbona τ a
Bitrin τ Agatha; Banba con la mayor conpaña yua enpos los que yuan ad
Ausonia. Començaron los | de Bamba forçar los mugeres τ dixo les alos suyos:
"Uarones, siempre | los godos fueron τ sodes buenos τ leales, tened uos con

ⁱ *DRH*: III.iii. Similar details are recounted albeit at significantly reduced length.
ⁱⁱ *DRH*: III.iiii
ⁱⁱⁱ The lengthy harangue by Wamba is different to that of *DRH*, Wamba's words in *EG* emphasise
the equality of the Goths, king and counts, and the divine right associated with his side. See above p.
28.
ⁱᵛ *DRH*: 'Ausoniam'

Dios τ no*n* ₁ lo fagamos yrado, no*n* forq*ue*des mugeres. U*er*dad tenemos, Dios nos ai-₁udara co*n* armas τ co*n* lealtad, no*n* co*n* mal". P*r*ísiero*n* su co*n*seio τ no*n* p*r*ísi-₁ero*n* mal desen*d*. Luego p*r*ísiero*n* Barçilona, q*ue* se alçara τ p*r*iso q*ua*tro aleuo-₁sos:[155] Euradi*n*o τ Pande*r*io τ Gu*n*tiferedo τ Ulfo diache*r*o τ Manfredo; τ **esso mismo** ₁p*r*ísiero*n* **Girona** τ **alli le presentaron** unas letras[156] que Paulo enuia-₁ra a do*n* Amador, obispo de Giro*n*da, q*ue* era de su p*a*rte τ dizie*n* asi: ¶ "Oy ₁ dezir q*ue* el rey Banba q*ue*rie uenir sobre nos τ no*n* lo creo τ no*n* temas, ₁ τ dote por señal q*ue* es u*er*dad; el p*r*íme*r*o q*ue* tu uieres uenir co*n* hueste ₁ aqu*el* es el señor τ aqu*el* deue seer rey τ daquel deues obedesçer". Leyo ₁ Banba las letras τ dixo: "Mesq*uí*no do*n* Paulo, no*n* cuydando τ p*r*ofetizo ₁ τ^i adeuino de su mal τ dixo u*er*dad q*ue* yo deuo seer rey por q*ue* yo ₁ ui*n* p*r*íme*r*o co*n* hueste". Pues el enuio las letras τ ouiero*n* gra*n*d sa-₁bor. Salio^ii Banba de Giro*n*da τ p*r*íso una bastida enel Puerto de Aspa q*ue* ₁ dizie*n* **Collibre**,[157] τ p*r*íso Xultuaria τ subiugo a Silibia; el q*ue* uinie auer ₁ castiello, q*ue* es cabesca **Cardaña**,[158] fallo y a do*n* Ia*n*çinto de Hielenesie*n*, ₁ a do*n* Arçisdo*n* q*ue* se y[ba]n por p*r*ender aq*u*est castiello. Dela ot*r*a p*a*rte los de Ba*n*-₁ba p*r*ísiero*n* a Ranosindo, Hiltegiso τ ot*r*os malos q*ue* uiniero*n* y por p*r*en-₁der este castiello de p*a*rte de Paulo τ los manos atadas diero*n* ₁ los a Banba. Uicamuro,[159] el rey traydor, q*ue* tenie Sardenia[160] τ lexo la ₁ uilla τ uiño se a do*n* Paulo a Narbona τ dixol nueuas de Banba, ₁ [fol.17v] ₁ q*ue* de amos ouiero*n* miedo de su uenida. Esto*n*z come*n*do Narbona a ₁ Uictimiro τ lexo co*n* el do*n* Remi*r*o, el falso obispo τ do*n* Argemu*n*do τ do*n* ₁ Cult*r*ion P*r*ímoçerio. Este obispo do*n* Remi*r*o qu*a*ndo uido la hueste de Banba no*n* ₁ oso fincar τ fuxo dela uilla τ pe*r*o fue preso fuyendo τ aduxo al rey Banba. ₁ Las ot*r*as huestes p*r*ísiero*n* muchas fortalezas, pues uiniero*n* se p*a*ra Banba, ₁ τ folgo dos dias, q*ue* era*n* todos ca*n*sados. Pues enuio una hueste q*ue* guer-₁reasen Narbona por mar τ qu*el* uedasen la entrada τ co*n*dicho; enuio otra ₁ hueste co*n* qu*a*tro p*r*íncipes q*ue* **lidiasen**[161] por tie*r*ra. Qua*n*do llegaro*n* al muro los de ₁ la uilla q*ue*rie*n*se re*n*der a me*r*çed del rey Banba, mas no*n* q*uí*so Uictomiro q*ue* a-₁yudaua a Paulo, ante come*n*ço de denostar a Banba τ los godos. Esto^iii peso ₁ alos godos τ fuero*n* co*n*bater Narbona a manos τ a piedras τ **con sayetas** τ co*n* fondas ·₁ τ diero*n* fuego alas puertas dela uilla τ asi entraro*n* por fuerça. τ Uic-₁timiro pusose enla ygle*s*ia de Sa*n*ta Ma*r*ia τ come*n*ço de defenderse por armas ₁ no*n* por ruego; τ fue y preso el co*n* sus aiudadores τ los manos atados ₁ fuero*n* aduchos antel rey Banba. P*r*ísiero*n* Magalona τ Bitans,[162] q*ue* era*n* cib-₁dades τ fuero*n* contra Magalona; do*n* Gil, el falso obispo, fuxo ende, ui-₁nose p*a*ra Paulo a

---

^i The direct speech is again significantly different from that of the source. See above pp. 23–25.
^ii *DRH*: III.v
^iii *DRH*: 'Quod Gothorum animositas impaciens tolerare...'.

Ueninaso;[163] el rey Banba cerco Magalona τ prisola por ｜ fuerça. Pues[i] Banba
enuio su hueste con quatro principes τ que auie bien ｜ xxx mill armados τ
fueron adelant de guissa que suso al alua fueron enlas ｜ puertas de Neunoso.
Era y Paulo con poder grand de francos, quel uinieron ｜ aiudar τ otros muchos
aleuosos quel ayudauan: el obispo don Guillen τ ｜ Frusco τ Flodeorio τ
Uictimiro τ Rauerinrudo τ Adosindo τ Adulfo ｜ τ Maximo τ Gothila; empero
uieron que eran pocos non osaron salir al canpo, te-｜miendo otra sobreuienta τ
posose uno al muro en uoz de conseiero τ ｜ dixo alos godos de fuera:
"Uarones,[ii] uos sodes pocos nos muchos｜ τ demas esperamos gran aiuda oy o
cras, andad uos en paz a uuestra tierra ｜ τ non uos querades perder, que si non
uos ualdredes a Banba nin Banba a uos". ｜ Por esto creçio coraçon alos
godos, pero non por los dela uilla, mas por ｜ [fol.18r] ｜ otros si uiniesen; enuiaron
demandar ayuda a Banba τ el enuioles, a-｜si que otro dia al alua amanescio y
el duc Uandemiro con x mill arma-｜dos. Paulo suvio en una torre por ueer la
hueste τ dixo alos su-｜yos: "Non temades, que yo ueo ali Banba τ es poca
conpana τ en de mas ｜ ya fue tienpo que lidiaron los godos, mas agora non son
nada, salgamos ｜ aellos que uençidos son". τ dizen los otros: "Ued como uino
Banba sin ｜ seña, por dar a entender que ayuda espera, uayamos para ellos que
uençidos ｜ son". Entanto[iii] los godos comencaron lidiar τ **combater** la uilla a
manos τ a piedras ｜ τ a dardos τ **sayetas** τ con fondas τ fueron maltrechos **los
de Paulo τ comencaron de desconortar τ Paulo ouo miedo entre si.**
Los de Banba non quisieron ｜ tardar la batalla otro dia τ lidiaron la uilla fasta
nona τ legaron al ｜ muro τ dieron fuego alas puertas τ entraron la uilla por
fuerca. τ ｜ Paulo con los suyos alçose en una fortaleza de Areñas que los
godos ｜ fizieran contra los romanos τ los cales todos yazien leñas de ｜
muertos. En tal dia a cabo de un año como Banba fue rey alcado ｜ en Toledo
kalendas setenbris fue preso Neuinaso. Aheuos[iv] don Paulo en ｜ cuyta en quela
su fortaleza de Arenas τ cayo entre elos descordia, ｜ los unos dizien que por
derecho les contescie que fizieran traycion asu se-｜ñor τ que los cofondie
Dios. Dixolo a Paulo un su criado: "Señor, bien se ｜ que moro mas, ¿on son
tus consegeros τ tus ueledores que te conseiaron ｜ alçarte con la tierra?, non
son aqui mas los que y son nin ellos ternan para ti ｜ nin tu aellos". Paulo
despuso la corona τ el señorio τ demando conse-｜lo que que farie. τ[v] non
pudieron[164] fallar **conseio** lo meior que enuiasen ｜ a don Argebaldo, obispo

---

[i] DRH: III.vi, the translation policy returns to that of recounting basic detail and little else.
[ii] The direct speech is again more immediate in EG, although the content is broadly similar.
[iii] DRH: III.vii
[iv] The address to readers is that of the translator.
[v] DRH: III.viii. The bishop's supplication, and its plea for the mercy of God, is more vivid in EG.
Compare III.viii.12 ff.

de Narbona q*ue* fuese pedir me*r*çed a Banba | por el. El obispo ca*n*to misa τ
asi uestido salio ala carera al rey Banba, | τ echosele alos pies τ dixo: "Señor,
tus traydores somos, en tu | me*r*çed somos, p*re*ndate de nos piedad por aq*ue*l
señor Ihe*s*u Xp*ris*t*o q*ue* | p*ri*so muerto por ti τ por nos τ pe*r*dona alos q*ue* tu
q*ui*sieres τ aue do-|lor de la t*ie*rra τ no*n* los astragues q*ue* finq*ua* la t*ie*rra
yerma". Banba ouo dolor | [fol.18v] | τ piedad τ pe*r*dono al obispo τ al pueblo
menudo dela uilla, mas no*n* a | Paulo ni*n* asus ualedores ot*r*osi. Acorero*n* se¹⁶⁵
las huestes q*ue* enuiara Ban-|ba, todos co*n* el τ fuero*n* los lidiar de muert. τ
fue p*ri*so Paulo co*n* sus p*ri*nci-|pes q*ue* y era*n* τ ma*n*do recabdar bie*n* a do*n*
Paulo fata te*r*çer dia, q*ue* fuese iud-|gado por corte. Los fra*n*cos τ los suiuos
q*ue* fuero*n* y presosⁱ redimiero*n* | se luego, q*ue* no*n* era*n* basallos de Banba
mas era*n* soldados de Paulo τ a-|yudaua*n* lo. Pues Banba ouo dolor dela
çibdad τ fizo faze*r* los muros | τ renouar las puertas τ soterrar los muertos τ
sanar los lagados | τ dema*n*dar los tesoros τ los q*ue* Paulo τ los otros prisiera*n*
alas y-|gle*s*ias, fizo los y tornar; ot*r*oⁱⁱ si una corona q*ue* Recuredo, p*ri*nceb de
Giro*n*-|da, ofreçiera al altar de Sant Felizes τ p*ri*siera la P*au*lo τ q*ue* la pusiera |
ensu cabeça, fizo la dema*n*dar τ tornar ala ygle*s*ia. ¶ A te*r*çer dia a-|duxiero*n* a
Paulo co*n* sus ueladores ante B*am*ba, las manos legados τ | dixol Banba:ⁱⁱⁱ
"Co*n*uiertete, t*r*aydor, por Dios q*ue* te fizo, q*ue* digas la ue*r*dad: | ¿q*ue* te fiz por
q*ue* te me alcases co*n* la t*ie*rra τ co*n*tra mi?". Dixo Paulo: "Señor, | c*ri*este me τ
feziste me onbre, el diablo melo co*n*seio τ falsos a-|migos, muert*e* meresquo
τ mas si seer pudiere; faz de mi lo q*ue* | tu q*ui*sieres, nu*n*qua ta*n*to faras q*ue*
mas no*n* meresca τ nu*n*qua de mi | auras ue*n*gança qual deues τ yo meresco".
Ot*r*osi la cort τ el pueblo | τ los p*ri*ncipes, por la ue*r*dad τ por su iudiçio
mismo, iudgaro*n* τ otorgaro*n* | q*ue* merescie muert el co*n*los suyos; τ pues q*ue*
Banba p*r*ometiera al o-|bispo τ los seguraua de muert, ma*n*dol sacar los oios
τ ten[er]los en | p*ri*sion. Pues*ⁱᵛ* dixiero*n* a Banba q*ue* los fra*n*cos τ los
theotenicos ui-|nie*n* co*n*tra el τ no*n* fue nada q*ue* ploguiera al rey Banba, pues
q*ue* | Banba ouo desterrado la uilla de Neninaso de muros τ de torres, | τ de
puertas; dixiero*n* q*ue* do*n* Lobo, un om*n*e noble, degastaua el ter-|mino de
Bite*r*eno τᵛ fue Banba cont*r*a el. El ot*r*o, enq*ue* lo oyo, desma*n*pa-|ro los
suyos τ fuyo, asi q*ue* muchos fuero*n* y p*re*sos τ muertos τ | [fol.19r] | pe*r*didos,
q*ue* se esco*n*die*n* por las cueuas τ nu*n*qua mas paresciero*n*. ¶ Esto*ⁿ*ⁱ fe-|cho,

---

ⁱ A lengthy passage of *DRH* material is omitted.
ⁱⁱ BN Res/278 returns to its own translation of *DRH*.
ⁱⁱⁱ *DRH* extensive narration is omitted. *EG* presents a more dramatic face-to-face scene in direct
speech. See above pp. 23–25.
ⁱᵛ *DRH*: III.x. The *DRH* passage on peace with the 'francos' has been removed and others greatly
reduced in extension.
ᵛ All details of Lupo's rebellion removed.
ᵛⁱ *DRH*: III.xi, extensive *DRH* passages are reduced to their main narrative events.

uino a Narbona τ ordeno la çibdad τ la prouincia Tureno τ Alba, que estonz |
a ella pertenesçie τ restauro los muros τ fizo uenir los que fuxieron de miedo, |
τ meioro los fueros, mando tener bien la ley τ mando salir de la tierra alos |
iudios τ los hereges τ los malos christianos τ dio al pueblo buenos cab-|diellos
τ piadosos τ batalerosos. ¶ Pues desto quiso uenir a España, | τ quando fue
en un lugar que dizen Canabath, lego su poder τ sus caualleros ·| τ
grandescioles mucho los quel auien fecho seruicio τ leoles como fueran |
buenos τ dioles licençia que tornasen asus casas τ dioles sus ioyas τ sus |
mercedes.¹⁶⁶ Bien acabo de vj. meses que salio d'España torno con uictoria τ
con | grand fama. Pues aduxieron a Toledo a Paulo τ sus compañeros,
esquilados | barbas τ cabescas, çiegos, desnudos τ descalcos τ Paulo otrosi
mas con | corona de pez en su cabeça τ asi entraron por la corte. ¶ Pues[i] que
Ban-|ba torno a Toledo con grand preçio que uençio los enemigos τ cobro su
tierra, fi-|zo refazer los muros dela uilla τ fizo fazer epitafios en las pu-|esta a
honor de Dios τ dela fe catholica τ delos santos, que y eran | presentes.[ii]

El xj. concilio de Toledo

| Enel iiij. año que regno Banba fizo fazer concilio en Santa Maria de Tole-|do
τ este fue el xj°. Estonz era [Quirico] primado en Toledo, que ouo xxvj. |
obispos que soscriuieron τ muchos uicarios delos otros obispos τ a-|li
repitieron los dichos τ los fechos delos otros concilios que fueran ante | fechos
τ alli establecio Banba que todos los obispos touiesen obde-|mada en Santa
Maria de Toledo τ que non cantase y ninguno enel altar | mayor si non el
obispo τ, si non a cueyta, un abad por uicario.[iii] Estonz | ribaron a España
Lxx. naues de arabes τ enuio ala Banba su | poder τ uençieron τ mataron τ
prisieron dellos τ quemaron las na-|ues τ tornaron se al rey con grand gozo que
uençieran. ¶ En tiempo del | rey Sidasuyndo uino de Greçia don Atdauasto
ayrado en su enpera-|[fol.19v] | dor τ arribo en España τ recibiolo bien
Çindasuyndo τ diol su sobrina por | muger τ ouo en ella un fijo Eutigio; este
fue criado entonz τ fizieron lo | conde. Pues este dio y[er]bas¹⁶⁷ al rey Banba
que perdiese el seso τ asi fue. | Quinto, que era arçobispo τ primado de
Toledo,[iv] τ todos sus uasallos uieron | que el rey perdie el seso, puñaron en
encobrirlo τ fizieron lo confesar co-|mo meior pudieron τ fizieron le su
unçion τ murio τ fue enterrado en | Pampliega. Uisco Banba enel regno .ix.

---

[i] *DRH*: III.xii
[ii] The full text of these is quoted in *DRH*, III.xii.7 ff.
[iii] *DRH* mentions the *Cum longe lateque* canon, although its implications are not fully explained. *EG* chooses a rather more obvious demonstration of the importance of Toledo.
[iv] *EG* follows *DRH* account of Wamba's death very closely, although this differs from the version provided by BN Res/278.

años τ uisco enel monesterio ₁ vij. años, asi fino. ¶ Murio[i] Banba e regno Eutigio, por q*ue* era sob*ri*no de ₁ Çindasuydo, p*er*o mas lo recibiero*n* a fuerça que a grado, q*ue* Resesuyndo lexa-₁ra un fijo chico por no*n*bre Chufredo q*ue* deuie regnar por derecho. P*er*o co*m*pe-₁co Eurigio de regnar, era de [d]ccxxxiij τ regno .vij. años. Pues ouo ₁ miedo Q*ue* Chufredo dema*n*darie a tie*m*po el regno τ caso su fija Cisilona ₁ co*n* Eriga, p*ri*ncep sob*ri*no del rey Banba. Ensu tie*m*po ouo gra*n*d fam[bre][168] en ₁ España

El xij. concilio de Toledo[ii]

Enel ij° año q*ue* regno Eurigio fi-₁zo faz*er* co*n*cilio en Toledo; este fue el xij° τ fue v°. idus de mayo τ ouo ₁ τ xxx obispos, menos delos uicarios q*ue* fuero*n* x. τ los escuderos τ ₁ todos los p*ri*ncipes del regno. Era estonz arçobispo τ p*ri*mado en Tole-₁do Iuliano,[iii] τ estos sosc*ri*uiero*n*: Iuliano Yspalis, Luyba Brachare*n*se τ Este-₁fano τ Eme*ri*ten τ sos sufraneos τ sus uicarios q*ue* fuero*n* y en este co*n*ci-₁lio de Toledo.

El xiij. concilio de Toledo[iv]

₁ Enel iiij. año Q*ue* regno Eurigo, Flauio p*ri*ncep, fizo faz*er* el xiij° co*n*-₁cilio en Toledo, [bajo][169] Iuliano p*ri*mado τ ouo y xLviij. obispos τ ₁ sosc*ri*uiero*n* y Liuba de Braguena, Steua*n* de Eme*ri*ta τ Sp*er*ando abbad, p*ro*cura-₁dor de do*n* Sunifredo de Narbona τ ot*r*os obispos d'España τ de Gallia co*n* ₁ los uicarios delos absentes.

El xiiij.[170] concilio de Toledo[v]

₁ El v° año Q*ue* regno Eurigio, fizo faz*er* el xiiij°. co*n*cilio en Toledo so esse ₁ mismo p*ri*mado do*n* Iulia*n*; τ sosc*ri*uiero*n* y do*n* Uitaliano, p*ro*curador de ₁ Sunifredo de Narbona τ do*n* Maximo, p*ro*curador de Steua*n* de Me*ri*ta τ do*n* ₁ [fol.20r] ₁ Recesindo, uicario de Li*u*ba de Braguena τ do*n* Gaude*n*cio, uicario del ₁ de Yspalis τ ot*r*os xvj. obispos τ los uicarios delos ot*r*os. Esto fue en dia ₁ deca.[171] .xij. ka*lendas* dece*n*bris.

---

[i] *DRH*: III.xiii
[ii] This is not a *DRH* division, see above p. 15ff.
[iii] *DRH* 'Iuliano urbis regie primate'.
[iv] See p. 16. above.
[v] See p. 16 above.

En este concilio escusaron al de Narbona[i]

Egica, yerno de Euregio, recibio el regno era de xxx. τ regno x. | años. τ pues
que regno lexo la fija de Eurigio por la muert de Ban-|ba τ este quiso siempre
mal alos godos. En tiempo deste cayo el mal delos | ignes enla prouincia de
Narbona τ por esto fueron escusados los obis-|pos dela Prouincia de pus aca,
que non auiniesen a conçilio para que recibiesen | los estatutos τ que fuesen
toda uia obedientes al primado de Toledo.

El [xv] concilio de Toledo[ii]

| El iº. año que regno Egica, fizo fazer el xvº. concilio en To-|ledo, vº. idus de
mayo τ fueron y todos los principes del regno. Era en-|tonz primado en
Toledo ese mismo Iulian τ ouo y Lxx. obispos τ soscri-|uieron y arçobispos
Simefredo de Narbona, Floresindo de Yspalis, Faus-|tino de Braguena,
Maximo de Emerita, Sisullo, uicario de Taragona, que | era estonz arçobispo
don Ciprian, con sus sufraganeos τ ouo y uicarios | delos escusados Lxj. Alli
demando Egica licencia alos prelados que soltas-|sen el omenaie de su muger
y fue luego y soltado.[172]

El xvjº. concilio de Tole- do[iii]

| El vjº año que regno Egica Flauio, fizo fazer el xvj. concilio de Tole-|do,
nonas de mayo, so Felix, primado de Toledo; τ soscriuieron y ar-|cobispos
Faustino de Yspalis, Maximo de Emerita, Uera de Tarrago-|na, Felix de
Braguena τ sus sufraneos τ sus uicarios.

El xvij conci- lio de Toledo[iv]

| El[v] vijº año que regno Egica, fizo fazer el xvijº concilio en | Toledo en Santa
Leocadia, o iazie su cuerpo τ fue so Felix primado, | que fue buen omne τ
santo τ sauio τ soscriuieron y Faustino de Yspalis | τ Maximo de Emerita τ
Uera de Taragona τ Felix de Braguena τ[vi] sus | sufraneos τ los uicarios delos
que non pudieron uenir.

---

i DRH: III.xiiii, the council referred to is dealt with in the following chapter.
ii See p. 16 above. The rubric in 302 appears across the end of two lines. The translator edits out the
contents of the papal letter described in DRH.
iii See p. 16 above.
iv See p. 16 above.
v BN Res/278 returns to the use of the 302 text as far as '...ordenamiento del regno'.
vi DRH details of the Council are omitted, although the names of those present are retained.

Delos reyes godos Egica[i]

| Pues[173] Flauio Egica, iij. años ant*e* q*ue* muriese, pu-|so asu fijo Uatiza, el q*ue* ouo en Çisilona, enel regno _de_ Gallazia τ | [fol.20v] | ma*n*dol q*ue* morase en Tuda, la mas uiciosa ciudad de Gallia. Ali **auia esterrado**[174] a do*n* Fafila, | padre de _P_ellagio. ¶ Pues Egica, por razo*n* de su mug*er*, ouo de ferir co*n* un pa-|lo en la cabeça τ a Fafilla τ desso murio τ fue enterrado en xij. **manos**[175] Q*ue* es | agora dicho Pa*n*pliga. ¶ Murio do*n* Egica en Toledo de su muert*e* τ regno Uati-|za, era de [d]cc τ xL. τ regno ix años. Este come*n*ço bie*n* τ torno los exulados | Que[176] Aqu*el* rey echara de ti*er*ra τ p*er*dono alos Q*ue* el padre q*ue*rie mal τ fizo co*n*cilio | sobre ordenamie*n*to del regno, maguer no*n* es esc*r*ipto. ¶ Pues q*ue* come*n*ço | en todo mal, echo de ti*er*ra a Pelayo, fijo de Fafilla, q*ue* pues lidio bie*n* co*n* mo-|ros, este fizo por saña q*ue* ouo co*n* su padre Fafilla. Come*n*ço Uatiza de seer | luxurioso, p*re*nder se las mug*er*es de sus uasallos τ delos otros por fuer-|ça. Era[ii] esto*n*z p*r*imado en Toledo Gu*n*derico, bueno τ sabio τ fue pus el Sin-|dendo,[177] bueno τ sabio, este duro fasta el tie*n*po del rey R*o*d*r*igo, q*ue* se p*er*dio la | ti*er*ra. Uatiza[iii] q*ue* crescio en todo mal τ uio qu*el* contr*a*llaua qu*el* paraua rebel do*n* | Sidendo, el p*r*imado de Toledo τ por los males Q*ue* fazia aporfazaua τ q*ue* se | enuiaua q*ue*rellar τ apellar ala cort del p*a*pa, ouo miedo qu*el* podrie uenir | daño de Roma, fizo su cort τ ma*n*do alos cl*er*igos Q*ue* casassen τ tomasen | qua*n*tas mug*er*es q*ui*siesen por seer bie*n* co*n* ellos τ ma*n*do q*ue* no*n* obedesciesen | a Roma. ¶ Haeuos el regno delos godos, Q*ue* era alto τ pod*er*oso, Q*ue* tenie de | mar a mar de **Tanger**,[178] cibdad de Africa, fasta el Ruedano, regno noble de | buenos p*r*incipes τ de catholicos p*r*elados τ de buenos dichos, asi como de | Leandro τ Ysidoro τ de _C_ladio, de Eugenio τ de Illefon*so* τ de Iuliano | τ de Fulge*n*cio τ de Martino Dumie*n* τ de Ydalio de Barcilona τ de Taio | τ de Caragoça τ[iv] delos sabios de Cordoua,[v] tornado a mal τ apoco seso | τ a sobeiania τ a discordia τ a luxuria, ta*n* bie*n* los cl*er*igos como los le-|gos, los gra*n*des τ los chicos, los buenos τ los malos. Pus Eutiza,[179] | por si no*n* teme del regno Q*ue* se leua*n*ta su guerra co*n*tra el, fizo derribar | los muros delas uillas τ tornar les armas en reias τ en lego-|nes τ en lauores, q*ue* no*n* se temiesen de usar su peccado τ su mal. | [fol.21r] | ¶ Dios[vi] ouo dolor del regno delos godos τ ouo de crescer Thufredo, fijo | de Recesuy*n*do, q*ue* deue por derecho h*er*edar τ era bue*n* niño

---

[i] _DRH_: III.xv
[ii] BN Res/278 returns to the 302 text.
[iii] _DRH_: III.xvi
[iv] _DRH_ detailed commentary and editorial comment excised, though, as always, the narrative thread is retained.
[v] At this point BN Res/278 resumes its own translation of _DRH_.
[vi] _DRH_: III.xvii

τ de bueña uentura ╷ τ amado de todos. A tienpo, por que quiso regnar,
echolo de tierra don[de] naçiera τ uino ╷ se Thufredo a Cordoua τ alli seyendo
caso con Tacisilana que era noble τ de ╷ grand liñage τ ouo en aquela muger a
Rodrigo. Regno Uatiza pues su padre ╷ Egica τ segudo de mas a Thufredo τ
prisolo τ sacol los oios. Otrosi quiso ╷ fazer a don Pelayo, fijo de Fafilla a
quien el ouo ferido de un fuste por que mu-╷rio τ non lo pudo prender, que
Dios non quiso; τ fuyose en Cantabria τ ala esca-╷po τ retouo los Dios asu
seruicio. ¶ Estonz Uatiza toliol el arçobis-╷padgo de Toledo a don Sidendo
en su uida τ diolo asu hermano que don ╷ Oppa, arçobispo de Yspalis, ca era
su hermano τ factor en todo mal τ ╷ en toda luxuria; τ reuoco los iudios τ
tolio τ quebranto los priuileios alas ╷ yglesias del regno. Dios, que se nunqua
pago del mal fizo y uieredicta, crescio ╷ Rodrigo τ por amor del padre era muy
amado delos romanos τ dieron ╷ les ayuda τ leuantose contra Eutiza. Lidio
con el τ prisolo τ cegolo τ asi ╷ como ael fizo al su padre Thufredo τ exulolo a
Cordoua τ toliol[180] el re-╷gno τ asi murio, era de ccLj. τ maguer dos fijos,
Sisberto τ Eban, non reg-╷naron, que los non quiso el pueblo por el padre que
les fue malo τ cruo. ¶ Con ╷ ayuda delos romanos, uiuiento Eutiza, regno
Rodrigo el vijº. año del reg-╷no de Eutiza, enla era de ccxL.ix., enel iiijº año que
regnaua Ulith, en ╷ la era delos arabes Lxxxxjº; regno Rodrigo .iij. años .i. por
iij. uiuiendo ╷ Uatiza. Rodrigo[181] echol de tierra τ a Siseberto τ a Enba, fijos de
don Uatiza, ╷ τ reçibiolos don Reçilla, cuende de Tingitania, por amor que ouo
con ╷ su padre don Uatiza. ¶ Auie estonz en Toledo un palacio que un rey ╷
fiziera etender,[182] τ puso y un cañado τ puso por fuero τ por ley que ╷ nunqua
abriessen aquel palacio τ cada rey que uiniese que pusiese y ╷ su cagnado;[ii] τ asi
fasta el tienpo del rey Rodrigo. Pues el non auiendo gue-╷rra nin coyta nin
mengua, creciol coraçon por saber si auie tesoro en aquel ╷ [fol.21v] ╷ palacio τ
non quiso escuchar por conseio delos suyos τ fizo abrir el pa-╷lacio. τ non
falaron y mas de una arca τ ya alli no pudo ser grand te-╷soro como el cuydo
τ abrieron el arca τ fallaron y un paño de seda pre-╷çiado, a formas de omnes
τ escripto aderedor las formas delos omnes ╷ que eran con barbas luengas τ
tocas enlas cabeças τ uestidos anchos ╷ como almexias; las letras eran griegas,
abraecas τ latinas τ araui-╷gas τ todas dizen[183] esta razon: "el tienpo que este
palacio sera abierto τ esta ╷ arca catada τ este paño sacado, se perdera España
τ perderan los godos ╷ su regno τ ganaran ientes desta façion que son aqui". El
rey Rodrigo, en que ╷ uido esto, non fallo tesoro como el cuydaua, de mas

<hr>

[i] DRH: III.xviii
[ii] This detail, along with various other which follow, is not drawn from DRH. The legend
surrounding Rodrigo is recounted at greater length in the translation than in the source. This is the
first indication of interest in legendary matters in the EG. See above pp. 20–23 and Gómez
Redondo, 'La materia'.

oyo ta*n* mal man-|dado, ouo miedo τ pesol; fizo el paño tornar asu arca τ cerraro*n* el | palatio como ant*e* era. ¶ Estonz[i] era cosu*n*bre *Que* los altos omes enuia-|ua*n* sus fijos a cr*i*ar a casa del rey, por cr*i*arse de meiores man*er*as. | Otrosi enuio una su fija el co*n*de do*n* Iulia*n*, a tie*n*po esposola co*n* el rey | R*o*drigo. ¶ Pues[ii] el rey ouo su co*n*seio sobre la demostra*n*ça *Que* falaro*n* enel | paño, dema*n*do *que* om*n*es era*n* τ falaro*n* asi leua*n*to en Arabia moros *que* | creyan[184] la pr*e*dicato*n* de Mahomad τ maguer poco tie*n*po auie *que* se | leua*n*taro*n*, *que* uençiero*n* muchas fazie*n*das. Sobre esto enuio al co*n*de do*n* | Iulia*n*, *que* era bue*n* cauall*er*o τ mu*n*cho ardit τ lidiador, *Que* fue pon*er* paz | τ co*n*cordia τ amiztad co*n* los moros de Arabia τ ala tornada *que* casa-|rie co*n* su fija. El co*n*de pasaua la mar por recabar fazie*n*da de su señor | o por muerte o por uida *Que* acaesçiese, come*n*do su fija τ la mug*er* τ qua*n*to | auie. Enta*n*to paso la mar τ uidose co*n* los arabes τ puso su amiz-|tad buena τ firme co*n* ellos τ qua*n*do torno fallo su mug*er* q*ue*relosa | del rey: unos[185] dezie*n* *que* se yogo el rey co*n* la co*n*desa,[iii] los otr*o*s *que* co*n* la fi-|ia, otr*o*s *que* co*n* amos, p*er*o qu*a*lq*u*ier *que* fuese todo era mal. Oyolo el co*n*de | τ pesol de coraço*n* *que*, anda*n*do en su s*er*uicio, ta*n* mal gualardo*n*; p*er*o en-|cubriose como *que* lo no*n* sabie τ uino al rey τ co*n*tolo como recap-|[fol.22r] dara su me*n*saie τ el gradeciolo qua*n*to y fiziera. ¶ Ala yeu*e*mada dema*n*-|do su fija al rey R*o*drigo, *que* leuase asu madre *que* enfermara co*n* deseo della, | pr*i*sola co*n* su mug*er* τ co*n* su co*n*paña paso la mar τ pusolas en Cepta. | Esto*n*z tenie Iulia*n* Algeçira Tafrada τ dende fazie much*o* mal alos | moros τ[186] alos de Africa. Esto*n*z Muca Auenocair, un pr*i*ncep en Africa, | τ Uelit era Amitamo*n* τ Iulia*n* dixoles la ho*n*ta qu*e*l auie fecho el rey | R*o*drigo, anda*n*do en su s*er*uicio τ a pr*o* dela *ch*r*i*sti*a*ndad; τ pesoles por el desguisa-|do del rey R*o*drigo τ plogoles por la discordia delos *ch*r*i*sti*a*nos τ pr*o*me-|tiero*n* le ayuda por se ue*n*gar τ puso pleyto co*n* ellos *que* les darie Espa-|ña si ellos q*u*isiesen τ plogoles de coraço*n* *que* conosçiesen *que* Iulia*n* era | bue*n* cauall*er*o τ muy poderoso. τ maguer co*n* todo eso dubdaua*n* en | Julia[n] τ ouiero*n* su acuerdo *que* enuiasen co*n* el algunas co*n*pañas apr*e*n-|der le*n*gua τ uerie*n* como falarie*n* la t*i*er*r*a τ ali uerie*n* si dezie u*er*dad Iulia*n*. | Asi lo fiziero*n*: do*n* Muca, *que* era pr*i*nceb de Africa τ enuio au*n* moro Ra-|fet Auencara co*n* Iulia*n*, *que* uiniese a España τ g*u*isaro*n* y .ij. naues τ | enuio co*n*ellos .c. cauall*er*os τ cccc peones de Africa. Esto fue en | el Lxxxxj°. año delos arabes, en la era de c.L., enel mes *que* es di-|cho Ramada. Esta fue la pr*i*mera entrada *que* moros ouiero*n* en España, | aribaro*n* en Algezira Rafef τ ali moraro*n* fasta *Que* se ajuntaro*n* los pa-|r*i*e*n*tes de Iulia*n* τ sus amigos τ sus ueladores τ aqu*e*llos *Que* pesaua | el su

---

[i] *DRH*: III.xviiii
[ii] The link between the two events is given more overtly here and more Arabic detail provided.
[iii] Again, more extensive detail given here by comparison with *DRH*.

q*ue*bra*n*to. ¶ La p*ri*me*ra* corrida fue ad Gezira Tafrida τ ganaro*n* y mu-|cho τ
qua*n*do q*ui*siero*n* τ no*n* ouiero*n* co*n*struto ni*n* p*er*diero*n* nada delo suyo. |
Esto*n*z torno a Muca co*n* gra*n*d gozo. Ahe España, q*ue* estudiera en paz τ |
no*n* co*n*dria del tie*n*po del Uildo,[187] q*ue* fue p*ri*cep, fasta el rey tornado en |
discordia. ¶ Esto*n*z era p*ri*mado en Toledo Sinde*r*do, el q*ue* dixiemos de-
|suso a q*ui* Uatiza por si toliera el arcobispado τ lo diera asu he*r*mano, | [que]
era arçobispo de Yspalis; este q*ue* co*n* miedo delos moros q*ue* uiniero*n* | q*ue*
uido q*ue* todo yua amal τ co*n* pesar delo q*ue*l fiziera, Uatiza delexo | [fol.22v] |
España τ su arçobispadgo τ fue a Roma. Los de Toledo esleyero*n* ot*ro* arço-
|bispo ensu lugar, a do*n* Urba*n*, bo*n* om*ne*, a pesar de do*n* Oppa, arcobispo
de Yspa-|lis, q*ue* selos q*ue*rien amos los arçobispadgos tener, o delexar
Yspalis por | Toledo. ¶ Do*n* Iulia*n* passo co*n* esta p*re*sa la mar τ uino se p*ar*a
Muca τ co*n*tol de | como fiziera; τ[i] Muca fuese ueer sobresto co*n*
Miramomeni en Fire-|ma τ delexo la tie*r*ra a comie*n*da de Taric Abicie*n*t.
Pues acordaro*n* se q*ue* | uiniese Taric el mismo co*n* Iulia*n* τ dioles aiuda xij.
mill cauall*er*os, | τ q*ue* aiudasen a Iulia*n*; τ pasoles a España en sembra*n*ca de
m*er*cadores | τ aribaro*n* a Gibel, en arauigo le dizie*n* "mo*n*t" pues el Mo*n*t de
Taric, esto | fue Lxxxxij°. año delos arabes, enla era de dcccLj. ¶ Qua*n*do
esto oyo el | rey R*od*ri*g*o, enuio co*n*tra Iulia*n* asu sob*ri*no Ene*n*to,[ii] τ lidio
muchas uezes en ca*n*po, | fue ue*n*çido y muerto, y andaua Iulia*n* por Bethica
τ por Lusitania. Los | godos, como era*n* desusados de lidiar, era*n* mal trechos
q*ue* co*n* las paces | q*ue* ouiero*n* ta*n* lue*n*go tie*n*po ni*n* auie*n* armas ni*n* cura
delas. En ta*n*to[188] Taric τ | Iulia*n* tornaro*n* se a Muca en Africa τ uido Muca
q*ue* Iulia*n* bien andaua | enla fazie*n*da, dioles mayor ayuda a Taric *J*ulia*n*, p*er*o
no*n* fiaua au*n* bie*n* en Iulia*n*, | τ retouose en fieldad do*n* Nala, cue*n*de de
Q*ui*ngitania. τ do*n* Iulia*n* τ Taric pasaro*n* | mar, comen*ç*aro*n* de destruyr
Bathica τ Lusitania. Oyolo el rey R*od*ri*g*o τ sa-|liole ala carrera de Xerez, del
ot*ra* p*ar*te qua*n*do fuero*n* al rey Gualafera, | estaua*n* los arabes co*n*el co*n*de
Iulian. Al rey R*od*ri*g*o, segu*n*d costu*n*bre delos godos, | trayero*n* lo en un carro
de boij[189] τ co*n* q*u*atro mulos,[iii] τ el rey co*n* sus[190] p*re*ciosos | paños τ su
corona de oro enla cabesça, come*n*çaro*n* la batalla. τ aturo | la fazie*n*da .viij°.
dias,[191] de do*min*go a do*min*go; asi q*ue* muriero*n* delos arabes | bie*n* xvj. mill; τ
por m*ue*st*r*o peccado[iv] los moros co*n* efuerço de *J*ullia*n* τ delos ch*r*ist*i*a-|nos
q*ue* era*n* co*n* el, ouiero*n* de q*ue*bra*n*tar la haz del rey R*od*ri*g*o. Comen*ç*aro*n* de |
fuyr los ch*r*ist*i*anos, dia de do*min*go. v. idus del mes xaniel, el Lxxxxiij°. delos a-

---

i *DRH*: III.xx
ii *DRH* 'Eneconem'.
iii *DRH*: 'duobus mulis'.
iv *EG* is rather harsher in its attribution of the causes of defeat, *DRH* places the blame on the period
of inactivity beforehand and also directly on Wittiza.

|rabes, enla era de Lij. Los fijos de Autiza q*ue* echara el rey R*o*d*ri*go de t*ie*rra | era*n* co*n* el enla fazie*n*da τ era*n* asi p*ar*tidos q*ue* el uno estudiese ala parte | [fol.23r] | dies*tra* del rey R*o*d*ri*go τ el ot*ro* ala sinies*tra* τ dizie*n* q*ue* estos dos ant*e* noche | ouiero*n* su fabla co*n* Taric q*ue*, ellos no*n* lidia*n*do, se*ri*e el rey R*o*d*ri*go ue*n*çido; τ Taric p*ro*-|metioles gra*n*d algo τ donas, q*ue* les dara el regno desu padre q*ue*l tenie al | rey R*o*d*ri*go,[i] τ asi dizie*n* q*ue* acaesçio. Los q*ue* ganaro*n* Asia τ Europa, en un dia fuero*n* | ue*n*çidos delos moros. P*er*o asi el rey R*o*d*ri*go lidio muy bie*n* τ defe*n*diose q*ua*nto | pudo, en cabo fue ue*n*çido el co*n* los suyos τ delos fuero*n* p*re*sos delos mu-|ertos delos escaparo*n*, en ta*n*to no*n* sopiero*n* q*ue* se fizo el rey R*o*d*ri*go, si no*n* q*ue* fala-|ro*n* sus paños reales τ sus çe*n*dalias τ su corona τ su cauallo Ouel-|la[192] de un tremedal cabo un rio; p*er*o a tie*n*po falaro*n* en Uiseo, una çibdad | de Portugal, un sepulc*ro* τ dizie*n* las letras de epitafio: "Aq*uí* iaze el rey | R*o*d*ri*go, post*ri*mero rey delos godos". τ asi fino la p*ro*fecia del paño de Toledo[ii] | τ la coudiçia τ los fechos del rey R*o*d*ri*go τ la yra τ la crude*n*cia del conde do*n* | Iulia*n*, homiçiero contra Dios τ contra los omnes, que trayo et destruyo la tierra τ la fe *ch*ristiana. ¡El su no*n*bre mal τ cruo por sie*n*pre!

Todos los fechos delos godos, como fueron uençidos[iii]

| ¡A ay Dios! aq*uí* esfeneçe el bie*n* τ | la ondra τ el poderio delos godos, enla era de Lij. ¡Q*ue* cueyta τ q*ue* | dolor! La gente q*ue* ta*n*tas yantes τ ta*n*tos regnos ue*n*çio τ sobiugo, en u*n* | dia fue ue*n*çida τ subiuzgada; esta ge*n*t gotica q*ue* co*n*q*ui*so Sicithia τ Pa*n*to, | Asia τ G*re*cia, Macedonia, Jlirico τ las p*ar*tidas de orie*n*t τ p*ri*so a Tiro, q*ue* era | señor de Babilonia τ de Asiria, de Media τ de Siria τ de Horromana, | τ lo mataro*n* en una odra de sang*re* por q*ue* sie*n*pre se delecto en destruyr | sang*re*; τ esta gent q*ue* subiugo Roma asu s*er*uicio τ ot*ro*si a Uale*n*s el enp*er*a-|dor τ Atila rey delos gunos[193] τ delos alanos τ delos uandalos, ahe qua-|n*t*as cosas fizo, en un dia, por una batalla, de huest de Mafomat, fue ue*n*-|çida τ subiuga[da].[194] ¶ Mucho deue*n* los omes q*uí*tarse del mal τ legar se al bie*n*, | mucho mas los reyes τ los p*ri*ncipes, q*ue*los sus peccados maiamie*n*to | son del pueblo.

---

[i] *EG* passes over the other material causes of defeat.
[ii] The link to the prophecy is not overtly made in *DRH*.
[iii] *DRH*: III.xxi

Delos bienes de España[i]

Maguer todo el mun-|do ganaron, Asia τ Europa τ Galia τ Gerica,[195] que es
Narbona τ Rocoma τ | [fol.23v] | Alba τ Uicoma, que pertenesçie al señorio delos
godos τ ala prouençia de Narbo-|na τ Tingitania, una çibdad que es señora de
diez çibdades en Africa; en | España fizieron su senorio τ su ient τ su
morada. ¶ Esta[196] tierra es que Dios | bendixo τ aquí dio sus donos. A España
tienga .iiij. rios cabdales, como | el parayso: Ebro, Duero, Taio, Anabes;[ii] τ
España ha habondamiento de po-|zos τ de fuentes τ de rios como Sucrar τ
Guadalinar, que nasçe en ter-|ritorio del obispagdo de Çiguença enla
prouinçia de Toledo, menos de otros | rios buenos que omne non podrie
contar. España es abondamiento de bue-|nas mises τ buenos frutos τ
pescados, de leche τ de queso τ de | manteca, de toda caça τ de muchos
ganados; de cauallos τ de mu-|los τ de uillas τ de castiellos, de pan τ de uino τ
de todo metal:[197] oro | τ plata, fierro, arambre, cobre, plomo, estaño, seda τ
paños, lino, | peñas, miel τ olio: omes de buen engeño, sotiles, fuertes, sabios,
lige-|ros, francos, osados, batalerosos, bien usados, fieles, leales a senorio, | de
buen estudio, bien razonados, abastados de palabra, conplidos de | todo bien.
¡Que digamos mucho! España en mundo non a par τ son pocas | tierras que
semeien. Maguera tan leal, tan abastada, en un dia fue sub-|iugada τ uençida,
como si non ouiese y omes por pleyto o por fazien-|da τ por peccado de
señor.

Que mal sufrio España[iii]

| ¡Que dolor! Ya non auie quí alcar la mano a defender España, fizo | la tierra
yerma, _llena_[198] de gentes agenas; renouaron los males de | Hercules τ delos
griegos; renouaron se los males delos alanos τ delos | uandalos, agora
compeço de regnar en España lenguaie ageno; ploro | τ non ouo quí la
conortar nin que fablase del su mal;[iv] el non-|bre de Ihesu Xristo abaxado el τ
del Mahomat alçado, la yglesia quebrantada | la mezquita alcada; asi que non
finquuo eglesia cathedral en España que | non fuese destruyda a suelo, si non
la de Yspalis o de Seuilla τ esta | fizo[199] por que Oppa el arçobispo con los que
y eran por escapar tornose | [fol.24r] | al señorio delos moros por les fazer guerra
τ paz; τ los que fincaron | a este pleyto alli, en tantos lugares fueron dichos τ

---

[i] This is not a formal _DRH_ division. As is frequently the case _EG_ shows a significant reduction of
rhetoric and change of order of elements recounted.
[ii] _DRH_: 'Ana et Bethi' For this detail, see Aengus Ward (ed.), _Cronica de Espayña de Garcia de Eugui_, p.
57.
[iii] _DRH_: III.xxii
[iv] A lengthy rhetorical passage embedded with Biblical quotations (_DRH_: III.xxii.10ff) is replaced by
a 1 line summary.

son mixtarabes, | mecthlados co*n* arabes τ dezimos los nos oy endia
mocarabes. | Esto*nz* fuero*n* todos los tesoros pe*r*didos τ las reliq*u*ias τ los
cuerpos | delos sa*n*tos. ¿*Que* diremos mucho? Qua*n*to mal sufrio Babil*onia* de
Ciros τ Dario, | si no*n* q*ue* sie*n*pre pues fue yerma; qua*n*to mal Alarico fizo a
Ro-|ma τ otrosi Athaulfo τ los godos τ Gase*ri*co τ los ua*n*dalos; τ qua*n*to | mal
sofrio Ihe*rusa*lem; τ qua*n*to mal τ qua*n*to fuego sufrio Cartagena, | de mano de
Scipio, p*r*incep de Roma, ta*n*to o mas sufrio España en | un dia solo por si
mismo, ca Dios no*n* pudo sofrir los. De suso dixi-|emos del Uatiza τ del rey
R*odrig*o τ delos ot*ro*s reyes q*ue* por engaño q*ue* | por muert q*ue* por trayciones
regnaua*n* τ por la he*re*gia de Uale*ns* el | enpe*r*ador, q*ue* regno fasta el tie*n*po del
rey Cheradio.

Que peccados fi- zieron los reyes godos[i]

| Digamos Q*ue* males fiziero*n* los reyes | godos τ sus peccados. Ataulfo fue
muerto en Barçilona, | mataro*n* lo los suyos por trayçio*n*; **otrosi Agagito
mataron lo los suyos**;[ii] otrosi Turismundus por consejo de su h-|ermano
fue muerto en Tolosa; ot*ro*si Eurigio mato asu he*r*mano Thudo-|rico; ot*ro*si
Amalaricus matose en Narbona; ot*ro*si uno q*ue* se fizo como | loco a Thudis
pe*ro* si ma*n*do q*ue* no*n* fiziesen mal aq*ue*l loco,[iii] Q*ue* no*n* lo meres-|çiera, q*ue* el
ya fiziera de tales; ot*ro*si Th*e*odisclo degollaro*n* le los sus | o estaua comie*n*do;
ot*ro*si Atila, los suyos lo mataro*n* en Merida; ot*ro*si | Locuogildo[200] mato asu
fijo por q*ue* no*n* que*r*ie seer he*re*ge asi como el; ot*ro*-|si Uite*r*ino mato a
trayçio*n* a Luyba, fijo de Recaredo; ot*ro*si Ui*n*cte*ri*co ma-|taro*n* lo los suyos o
seye comie*n*do; ot*ro*si el rey R*odrig*o saco los oios | a Uatiza; ot*ro*si Uatiza
ma*n*do casar alos cle*ri*gos τ toliol los p*r*uil-|lieios alas ygle*si*as τ leua*n*tose
co*n*tra la ygle*si*a; otrosi R*odrig*o fizo lo q*ue* | oyestes; ot*ro*si Iulia*n* fizo lo q*ue*
sabedes τ[iv] lo q*ue* es peor aun dize*n* q*ue* | mato el rey Rodrigo por pleyto de su
muge*r*; ot*ro*si do*n* Froyla mato | [fol.24v] | asu he*r*mano Unatromi[201] por sus
manos; ot*ro*si los por se ue*n*gar mataro*n* | Froyla en Canicas. τ por estos
ta*n*tos τ ta*n* gra*n*des[202] males q*ue* Dios sofrir | no*n* pudo τ pesaua ael τ alos
om*ne*s, uino todo este mal ala ti*e*rra d'Espa-|ña, qual se nu*n*qua pudo
eme*n*dar.

---

[i] BN Res/278 text corresponds definitively to 302/N from this point onwards. See above p. 4.
[ii] This reference does not figure in 302/N and appears to correspond to 'Sigericus fuit a suis similiter
interfectus' *DRH*: III.xxii.86–7.
[iii] The mercy of Theudis is drawn from *DRH*: II.xii.35ff.
[iv] *DRH*: 'Rodericus, ut creditur, interfectus'.

Dela conquista de[203] Taric en España[i]

ǀ Fecha la batalla, Taric segudo alos *christianos* fasta Eceia[204] la çibdad τ los ǀ
Q*ue* era*n* y, co*n* los q*ue* fuero*n*, saliero*n* a Taric τ lidiaro*n* bie*n* τ lo q*ue* Dios
q*ui*ere, fu-ǀero*n* ue*n*cidos *christianos*. Esto*n*z se plego Taric a una fue*n*t cerca
del muro τ por este ǀ no*n*bre despues aca la fue*n*t de Taric. Los *christianos*, en
q*ue* oyero*n* q*ue* yentes q*ue* ue*n*çi-ǀero*n* alos godos τ era*n* om*ne*s q*ue* comie*n* los
o*m*es,[ii] descoraznaro*n* τ ouiero*n* miedo, ǀ τ desma*n*paraua*n* uillas τ castillos τ
uinie*n* a Toledo q*ue* era mas fuerte. ǀ Pues Iulia*n* co*n*seio a Taric q*ue* p*ar*tiese
sus huestes por la *tie*rra destruir τ el da-ǀrie delos suyos por ayudar a ganar
por las *tie*rras. Esto*n*z Taric enuio u*n* ǀ so tornadizo q*ue* fuera *christi*ano,
Moieyatro*n*[205] uaslo de Miramomeiñ, co*n* dcc caua*lle*ros ǀ co*n*tra Cordoua;
enuio ot*ra* hueste co*n*tra Malaga τ a G*ra*nada; el co*n* la mayor ui-ǀno contra
Montesa o Matixar, cerca Iahen, et prisola, et destruyola. Mogeyr uino se a
una uilla de Cordoua q*ue*l dezie*n* S*er*deta,[iii] τ mouiose enla noche escu-ǀra q*ue*
fazie nublado τ uino p*ar*a Cordoua, q*ue* oyera dezir q*ue* el poder de Cor-
ǀdoua era ydo en ayuda a defender Toledo. Toda Cordoua era bie*n* cercado
de ǀ muro **si non la puent, que era el muro** flaco τ delo caydo τ por alli
auie entrada al muro τ por una fi-ǀguera q*ue* estaua al muro entraro*n* τ
mataro*n* las uelas, pues echaro*n* es-ǀcaleras τ subio gra*n*d poder, p*ri*siero*n* las
torres desende abriero*n* las pu-ǀertas τ diero*n* les fuego. Al dia claro uido el
p*ri*ncep de Cordoua los mo-ǀros **en**[206] los muros, entrose[207] enla yglesia q*ue*
auie esto*n*z y gra*n*d fortaleza, fue ǀ y cercado tres meses; pues uido q*ue*
escapar no*n* podie fuyose de noch*e* ǀ co*n* pocos. Oyolo Mogeyr τ enuio en
pos el τ traye el caualo ferido τ ca*n*-ǀsado τ fue p*re*so τ aducho al Mogeir τ el
enuiolo a Taric. No*n* fue p*ri*n-ǀçep ningunos de los godos p*re*so si no*n* este,
los ot*ro*s o muriero*n* o fuxiero*n* ǀ o *pleytearon*[208] o redimiero*n* a feudo. Ta*n*to
aturo la c*er*ca q*ue* p*ri*so Cordoua τ poblaro*n* ǀ [fol.25r] ǀ la de moros τ de iudios
q*ue* y fallo. La[iv] ot*ra* hueste p*ri*so a Magalena a Malaga τ los ǀ *christianos* fuero*n*
se ala montaña. La ot*ra* hueste p*ri*so a G*ra*nada τ poblaro*n* la de mo-ǀros τ de
iudios q*ue* auie y, luego fuero*n* se a Oriuela q*ue* es agora dicha Murçia ǀ τ
cercaro*n* la. El señor de Murçia, como sabio τ cuerdo, fizo parar las mug*er*es
ǀ en cabellos en los muros,[v] q*ue* semeiasen omes, q*ue* era*n* y pocos τ pone*r*
sauanas ǀ por señas τ ruecas por armas por los muros; el salio como
me*n*saiero a ǀ la hueste τ dema*n*do treguas fasta un dia, temie*n*do q*ue* era
gra*n*d poder; pues ǀ sopiero*n* q*ue* era*n* pocos repi*n*tiero*n* se delas t*re*guas, p*er*o

---

[i] *DRH*: III.xxiii
[ii] *DRH*: 'licet falso' omitted by translator.
[iii] The source of these details, 'pastore, quem ceperant', is not mentioned by *EG*.
[iv] *DRH*: III.xxiiii
[v] *DRH*: 'fecit mulierum capita circumcidi'.

touiero*n* se. τ fuese la ǀ hueste p*ar*a Toledo τ falaro*n* la **yerma** τ
desemparada[209] delos ch*ri*st*i*anos τ poblaro*n* ǀ la de moros τ de iudios q*ue*
fallo y Taric. Pues uino se p*ar*a Guadalfa-ǀiara τ uino posar al poyo de
Culema, q*ue* dizie*n* esto*n*z Gibel Çulema τ ǀ pusiero*n* le no*n*bre Gibel[210] Taric.
En esa uilla, q*ue* esta acerca del poyo, falla-ǀro*n* una mesa gra*n*d τ redo*n*da de
una piedra ue*r*de τ[i] auie en ella ccc pies ǀ de si misma, el uno era p*re*ciado τ
cu*n*pliero*n* lo de oro; τ puso no*n*bre a esa ǀ misma uilla Medinat Almeyda,
"uilla dela mesa". Pues uino se p*ar*a Admaya, ǀ q*ue* esto*n*z era cibdad τ dizie*n*
le Pat*ri*cia,[ii] q*ue* por fambre q*ue* por coyta ouo de seer p*re*-ǀsa τ p*ri*so los
tesoros; τ deuasto Astorga τ p*ri*so a Gegio*n*, una çibdad de Asturias, ǀ τ puso
omes nobles por cabdiellos enlas t*ie*rras, pues torno en Toledo, el ǀ Lxxxxiij°.
años delos moros. Enta*n*to Muça Fide Acayr, enel año dicho ǀ enel mes de
Ronada*n*, oyo dezir como lidiaua τ era aue*n*turado co*n*tra los ch*ri*sti-ǀanos τ
qua*n*to ganaua delos del Taric, maguer su uasallo τ q*ue* por ael gana-ǀua τ por
su ma*n*dado y uiniera, ouo enuidia τ paso la mar co*n* bie*n* xij. ǀ mill armados τ
aribo en Algezira Tafrada. τ co*n*seiaro*n* le q*ue* se uiniese por o ǀ uiniera T*ari*c τ
q*ue* apartose[211] lo q*ue* el ganara; ot*ro*s dixiero*n* q*ue* no*n* ganarian y p*re*-ǀcio
p*re*nder lo p*re*so de mas q*ue* y podrie nasçer scandalo entrellos, mas q*ue* ǀ se
fuesen p*re*nder lo q*ue* el ot*ro* no*n* pudo p*re*nder q*ue* esto p*re*so no*n* lo podrie
per-ǀder. Este co*n*seio p*ri*so τ uino se p*ar*a Asadia,[212] la qual en arauigo dize*n*
Ab-ǀnaçelin q*ue* **es** entrel mar τ Xeres, q*ue* agora dize*n* Asidona, p*ri*sola por
fuerça. ǀ [fol.25v] Desent uinose p*ar*a Carmona, sopo q*ue* la no*n* podrie p*re*nder,
puso pleyto co*n* ǀ Iulia*n* q*ue*lo no*n* conoscie*n* y q*ue* se fiziese ue*n*çedizo[213] τ
fuydizo τ q*ue*lo cosdrien ǀ enla uilla por ch*ri*st*i*ano τ qua*n*do y fuese, q*ue* de
noche o de dia, q*ue* abriese las ǀ puertas τ **entrarien;**[214] τ asi lo fiziero*n* τ asi
p*ri*siero*n* la uilla por este engaño. ǀ Dese*n*t uino a Yspal*is* o Seuill*a*, esta en
tie*n*po delos selignos τ delos ua*n*-ǀdalos fue muy noble mas los godos
toliero*n* ende el senorio τ ca-ǀmiaro*n* la a Toledo. Çerco la Muçar τ no*n* auia
y omes q*ue*l su poder era ǀ ydo a Beia τ p*ri*so τ poblola de moros τ de iudios
q*ue* fallo y. Desend fue ǀ τ p*ri*so a Beia, pues uino a Mica*n*[215] la çibdad τ
saliero*n* co*n*tra el τ ue*n*ciero*n* ǀ lo ese dia a do*n* Muça; ot*ro* dia ouo su acuerdo,
Muça uio q*ue* era*n* mu-ǀchos τ fortalados, echo les çelada τ ouiero*n* se de
meter entrel mu-ǀro τ los moros; τ los moros saliero*n* ala batalla τ lidia*n*do
saliero*n* al-ǀgunos moros como q*ue* uinie*n* en ayuda τ ouiero*n* miedo τ fuxie-
ǀro*n* los ch*ri*st*i*anos τ q*ue* del **alcanço**[216] τ delos q*ue* estaua*n* alas celadas ma-
ǀtaro*n* τ p*ri*siero*n* muchos ch*ri*st*i*anos τ los q*ue* escaparo*n* pocos τ feridos ǀ τ
ue*n*çidos. Ouiero*n* miedo τ ot*ro* dia p*er*diero*n* el coraço*n* τ dema*n*daro*n* fa-

---

[i] The figure is not given in *DRH* although the same figure appears in various manuscripts of the
Estoria de Espanna, see for example *P.C.G.* I.316.a, n.43.
[ii] *DRH*: 'exinde uenit Amayam, olim patriciam ciuitatem'.

ı bla τ salieron fablar con el señor τ los moros amostraron le un uieio ı en
lugar de Mitaramomanin. [i] τ demandaronle tregua τ dioles quanto pi-ıdieron τ
tornaron se ala uilla con gozo τ acordaron se τ dixieron que Mo-ıromomenin
era uieio τ que morie luego τ ayna τ que se deramarien ı los moros. τ
quebrantaron los christianos la tregua τ los moros demandaron ı fabla, que
dizien que ¿por que quebrantauan las treguas que auien puesto con Mira-
ımomenin? τ dixieron quel uieran uieio a Miramomenin. τ los moros ı
mostraron otro moro niño por Miramomenin τ dixieron: "Engañados ı
andades, que Dios es con nos, que **Miramomeni, quando quiere,**[217] es uieio
τ quando quiere ı niño". Estonzi[ii] perdieron el coraçon los christianos τ lidiaron
τ los moros ı de foradar el muro τ pusieron pleyto que la uaziasen la uilla a
tres ı dias τ que fuesen co[n] lo so, **saluos τ** seguros τ asi fue presa Merita, el
Lxxxxiiijº. ı [fol.26r] ı año delos moros, el postrimero dia del mes de Ramadan.
Aiuntaron ı se los christianos de Beia τ de Lapla τ de otras **partes** τ furtaron las
fortalezas ı de Yspalis τ mataron alos que falaron y de Muça τ alçaron se en
ella. Los ı que escaparon uinieron se a Muca τ a Merita, que prisiera; Muca,
quando lo ı oyo enuio su fijo Abdulaziz τ reconbro Yspalis τ mato quantos y
ı falo τ priso a Lepan τ mato a quantos y fallo. Mientre este aca era, Pela-ıgios
guerreaua en Asturias a moros. Muca con goço τ con ganan-ıçia tornose para
Toledo. Otrosi Taric era muy loçano por quanto fiziera ı τ conqueriera τ salio
a reçebir a Muca a parte de Talauera τ Muça reçibi-ıolo con encubierta buena
τ mal coraçon τ penso de se esquiuar[218] por algu-ına guisa τ dixo que pasara
su mandado de prender christanos **a uida** τ on-ıdrar[219] les las treguas τ
demandol cuenta delos tesoros que falo τ de ı la mesa que falo **en Alcala τ
diol buena cuenta a qui non fallo** en que trauar. Fueron amos a
Caragoça[220] τ prisieron la, ı τ otros muchos castiellos en Carpentania τ en
Celtiberia. Entanto[iii] el ı señor ouo dolor del christianismo τ non quiso que
todos se perdiesen los que a-ıdorauan al su nonbre τ retouo τ manparo a don
Pelayo, el que fuxiera[221] ı a Cantabria por don Eutiza, que lo quisiera çegar.
Este oyo muerte delos ı christianos τ quebrantamiento delos godos τ priso su
hermana τ fuyo con ella ı alas Asturias. Los arabes prisieron toda España si
non pocos omes ı que fincaron enlas montañas, como en Biscaya τ en Alua τ
en Ruchonja, Ypuschu-ıa τ en Tuchama[222] τ Aragon, que Dios retouo por
que el su nonbre non fu-ıese oluidado en España, que azaz auie otro mal.
Enlo preso pusie-ıron los moros porlas tierras sus alcaxdes que ganasen los
tribu-ıtus τ los pechos delos que fincaron en seruiton τ en captiuuerio τ feu-

---

i The ruse involving hair dye employed by Miramomelin is misunderstood by the translator.
ii This incident is recounted at unusually great length by translation.
iii *DRH*: IIII.i. Although this represents a significant *DRH* textual break, the textual priorities of the
EG are different. See above p. 15.

ǀdo; enlas partidas de Gentio²²³ ganaron los moros grand algo τ a-ǀuie y un *christi*ano por nombre **Munuça**²²⁴ τ este era fantar delos mo-ǀros τ **ayudauales.**²²⁵ Este ouo se de pagar dela hermana de Pelayo ǀ por su fermosura τ puso su amor con el τ enuiolo a Cordoua con ǀ [fol.26v] ǀ mensaie a Muca, en uos de mensaiero. Entanto este Munuça priso herma-ǀna de Pelayo τ yogo se con ella τ despues casola con un su criado.ⁱ Quando uino ǀ don Pelayo, que lo sopo, pesol τ toliol su hermana τ que por esto τ que por sabor ǀ de uengar el *christi*anismo,ⁱⁱ començo de guerrear. Sopolo Muca τ enuiolo man-ǀdar prender a trayçion o como quier τ que lo aduxiesen a Cordoua. Fueron ca-ǀualeros [a] Asturias por prender lo τ desenganol uno dela poridad. τ fu-ǀxose **Pelayo** ²²⁶ en un cauallo τ aribo aun rio que dizen Pionia; τ uinie ǀ grand τ diose a nadar τ los otros non osaron pasar nin entrar antel, ǀ τ asi escapo. Estonz legaron se muchos delas montanas que eran escon-ǀdidos τ conortolos τ dixo que esto era mandadura²²⁷ de Dios τ fuesen de ǀ buen coraçon τ fianse en Dios τ el les ayudarie, atodos plogo, iura-ǀron lo por rey τ por señor τ començo de guerrear τ uençer batallas τ ma-ǀtar muchos. Lo quel uinieran por prender tornaron se a Cordoua. Oyo esto Ta-ǀric τ **envio**²²⁸ un su princep de su alcaman τ a don Oppa, arcobispo de Seuilla, ǀ quelo uiniesen conseiar quese tornase su uasallo τ si non quel guerreasen τ ǀ que prisiesen. Oyoⁱⁱⁱ esto Pelayo que uinien sobrel τ ouo miedo, que tenie poca ǀ conpaña τ puso se enlas cueuas de Asueuia, que de plan Dios las fizo ǀ que non temien **cerca**²²⁹ nin batalla. τ entro y bien con mill omes; dela otra parte en-ǀtraron los moros τ destruyeron mucho por Asturias τ uinieron aquellas ǀ cueuas. τ quando no les podien conbater, el arcobispo començol de predicar ǀ a don Pelayo que se tornase uasallo de Taric τ dixo a Pelayo: "Bien sabedes ǀ como los godos uençieron todo el mundo τ su poderio τ su señorio atodo ǀ quanto Dios quiso τ agora pues ellos a quebrantados τ ael plaze, ¿que cuy-ǀdas fazer contra Dios?, prende mi conseio: tornate uasallo de Taric, fazerte ǀ *ha algo que* **escaparas con**²³⁰ *tu conpaña et si non ni tu tendras*²³¹ a dos uasallos ǀ nin ellos a ti". Respuso²³² Pelayo: "Arçobispo, bien sabes que por fe-ǀchos que tu feziste τ tu padre Egica τ tu hermano Eutiza τ Iulian, ǀ fue Dios yrado τ por nuestro peccado se perdio la tierra τ los godos τ la ǀ [fol.27r] ǀ yglesia τ si Dios non era non puede dar y conseio, mas con estos que tengo e fiuzia en ǀ Dios que cobrare España τ Dios sera ende hondrado τ la yglesia alcada τ bien se que tal ǀ conseio daries a tu, *christi*ano como tal como tu". Tornose Oppa τ dixo alos arabes: ǀ "Non ay al aqui sinon *de* lidiarlos a fuerça". Conpecaron de lidiar la cueua con fondas ǀ τ con saetas, mas Dios era con ellos τ fizo y su demuestra

---

ⁱ *DRH*: 'Munnuza, procurante quodam liberto, sibi sororem Pelagii copulavit'.
ⁱⁱ The Christian element is added by the translator.
ⁱⁱⁱ *DRH*: IIII.ii

marauilosa, q*ue* | saetas τ las piedras q*ue* echaua*n* tornaua*n*se τ firie*n* aellos,[233] τ semeiaua q*ue* | lidiaua*n* a Dios qu*an*do co*n*batie*n* logar q*ue* Dios fiziera,[234] a q*ui* no*n* podie*n* nozer. | Asi muriero*n* delos de fuera bie*n* xxij. mill om*es* τ esto*n*z se fuero*n* much*o* | desmagados. Pelayo co*n* su co*n*pana come*n*ço de be*n*dezir a Dios τ los moros | p*ar*tiero*n* se ende muy q*ue*bra*n*tados. Enta*n*to salio **Pelayo** dela cueua co*n* los suyos, | τ come*n*ço de ferir e*n*dellos; los moros al fuyr mato τ p*r*iso muchos sin g*ui*sa, los | ot*r*os fuyendo **muriero*n***[235] se en un rio como los del rey Pharato*n*. **Pelayo**[236] | p*r*iso a do*n* Oppa, arçobispo de Yspalis, unos dize*n* q*ue* Oppa fue fijo de Eutiza, otros que hermano de Julian, mas la verdad fijo fue de Egica, hermano de Eutiza.

| Como leuaron de Toledo [a] Asturias las reliquias[i]

| Pues asi se p*er*dio la t*ie*rra, Urbano, p*r*imado de Toledo, _sucesor_[237] de Side*n*do, q*ue* dixi-|mos q*ue* fue [a] Roma, el co*n* los ot*r*os p*r*isiero*n* el archa delas reliq*ui*as τ delos | p*r*iuileios τ los esc*r*iptos de Sant Illefonso, e de Julian Pamerio et la vestimenta | que Sancta Maria dio a Sant Illefonso, por q*ue* no*n* se p*er*diese leuaro*n* lo todo alas Asturias. | Ahe Toledo no*n* fue destruyda, q*ue* los *chr*ist*i*anos q*ue* y era*n* re*n*diero*n* se por suyos τ por | les obedescer τ pusiero*n* su pleyto q*ue* ouiesen ygl*es*ia τ q*ue* touiesen su ley pa-|ladina τ su oficio c*r*istianiego τ fincaro*n* co*n* la costu*n*bre de Sant Ysidoro τ de | Lea*n*dro; τ oy dia ha*n* en Toledo .vj. parochias q*ue* tiene*n* ese oficio.[ii] Estos q*ue* asi | se diero*n* τ pleytearo*n* τ fincaro*n* en su lugar son dichos moçarabes, mez-|clados co*n* arabes τ de*n*de ouiero*n* este no*n*bre fasta hoy. En ese tie*n*po era | arçidiano de Toledo Ena*n*cio, bue*n* *chr*ist*i*ano τ sabio τ bie*n* razonado τ Fruoda-|rio era obispo de Occitania τ estos sie*n*pre touiero*n* los **yn**stitutos[238] del Eua*n*-|g*e*lio fata el tie*n*po delos almochades, q*ue* come*n*caro*n* en tie*n*po del rey do*n* Alfonso. | [fol.27v] | En este demedio acaescio lo q*ue* dize*n* del obispo de Malaga. Esto*n*z era do*n* **Iulian**[239] | obispo de Seuilla τ dize*n* le los moros Caxe*n*t Almatra*n*, este sopo mucho | de arauigo τ traslado muchos libros *chr*ist*i*anegos alos moros τ fizo Dios | mucho por el. Esto*n*z ouo y un electo Cleme*n*s q*ue*, por miedo delos almoades | uinose a Talau*er*a,[iii] τ alli moro fasta q*ue* murio. Esto*n*z uiniero*n* tres obispos | a Toledo: el de Asidonia τ de Elephe τ el de Marchena τ un arçidiano muy | bue*n* *chr*ist*i*ano τ dize*n* los moros Archiquez; τ alli moraro*n* en Toledo fazie*n*do | su oficio τ el uno dellos iazie enla ygl*es*ia mayor.

---

[i] _DRH_: IIII.iii
[ii] _DRH_: 'et uiguet hodie in VI parrochiis Toletanis'.
[iii] A personal note of Ximénez de Rada, 'cuius contemporaneos memini me uidisse' removed.

Qui leuo las reliquias a Asturias[i]

ı Algunos dize*n* q*ue* las reliq*ui*as fuero*n* leuadas Asturias por ı ma*n*dado²⁴⁰ de do*n* Iulia*n*, p*ri*mado de Toledo τ de Pelayo, lo q*ue* estar no*n* pu-ıede, q*ue* do*n* Iulia*n* tres fue de Illefon*s*o τ de Sidendo, en cuyo tie*m*po se p*er*dio la ı uilla de Toledo τ toda España. Fue .iiij. de Iulia*n* aesta guisa: pues Sant ı Illefon*s*o fue Q*ui*rico,²⁴¹ τ pues el Iulia*n* Pom*er*io, **pues esti Sisberto,** pus este Fe-ılix, pus este Gede*n*cio τ pus este Sind*er*edo, *so* q*ui* fue la çibdad de Toledo p*re*sa ı τ toda España destruyda.

Delos que dizen de la primaçia fue en Yspalis[ii]

ı Otrosi dize*n* algunos q*ue* la p*ri*macia fue **de primero** en Yspalis τ pues q*ue* torno ı a Toledo, lo q*ue* seer no*n* puede τ por esta prueua: el xvj. co*n*cilio q*ue* fue ı en Toledo fue despuesto Siseb*er*to,²⁴² q*ue* era p*ri*mado de Toledo, por su culpa, ı por g*en*e*r*al se*n*te*n*cia del co*n*cilio de arçobispos τ de obispos τ de la cl*er*içia τ no*n* ı q*ui*siero*n* tractar nada enel co*n*cilio fasta q*ue* ouiesen p*ri*mado; τ trasladaro*n* τ ı p*ri*siero*n* por arçobispo τ p*ri*mado de Toledo a do*n* Felix, arçobispo de Seuilla, ı τ en esse mismo co*n*cilio camiaro*n* a do*n* Faustino de Braguena ala ygl*es*ia ı de Yspal*is* τ[iii] a do*n* Felix, obispo de Portugal, ala ygl*es*ia de Braguena τ de-ıspues fiziero*n* su co*n*cilio, pues si mayor fuese el arçobispagdo de ı Seuilla ¿como trasladarie*n* su arçobispo a menor dignidad? lo q*ue* estar ı no*n* puede. Bie*n* ouo y ta*n*to: los ua*n*dalos τ los alanos mient*re* uisq*ui*-ıero*n*, su cabo del regno τ de señorio terrenal en Seuilla lo ouiero*n*, ı mas la p*ri*macia en Toledo; a tie*m*po los godos traslataro*n* la siet τ el ı [fol.28r] ı señorio de Seuilla a Toledo porq*ue* el señorio celestiar dela p*ri*macia τ de ı la ygl*es*ia en uno co*n* el terrenal τ q*ui* lo no*n* sabe olo no*n* cree dema*n*de los ı esc*ri*ptos τ asi lo falara. Esta es la u*er*dad.[iv]

De la muerte del conde don Iulian[v]

ı Tornemos ala estoria de suso. Pues asi ue*n*cio **Pelayo**²⁴³ τ don ı Munuca fue preso τ muerto cerca de un rio q*ue* dize*n* Ona τ cerca un ı burgo q*ue* dize*n* Olalies τ maguer q*ue* la cibdad de Gegio*n* sea destruida ala ı tie*r*ra dize*n* Gerio*n* τ ali es el monest*er*io de Sant Saluador. Oyo Muca de mu-ıerte de Munuca τ cuydo q*ue* fuera co*n*seio de Iulia*n* τ de fijos de Eutiza, ı τ p*ri*so los τ

---

[i] See p. 15 above.
[ii] See p. 15 above.
[iii] Exceptionally, these details, dealing with the primacy of Toledo, are retained in great detail. See above p. 16.
[iv] The appeal to historical writings is, broadly, from the *DRH*, although the final comment appears to be initiative of the translator.
[v] *DRH*: IIII.iiij.

descabecolos. ⁱ Los godos q*ue* fuyera*n* τ q*ue* se escondiera*n* oyero*n* dez*ir* ₁ de
como Dios aun no los auie oluidado et oyeron de como venciera **Pelayo**, ₁ τ
de como Dios diera ue*n*ga*n*ça alos godos de Iulia*n*, acoiero*n*se todos a **Pe-**
₁**layo** por obedecer le por faz*er* cabo del τ morir τ beuir co*n*el; τ desce*n*diero*n*
₁ delas Esturias τ luego p*r*isiero*n* una cibdad Leon, q*ue* era ya de moros τ ma-
₁taro*n* qu*an*tos era*n* y come*n*ço de se alçar la fe. Esto*n*z paso a Esturias do*n* ₁
Alfonso, muy bue*n* *christ*iano, fijo del co*n*de do*n* Pedro de Ca*n*tabria τ diol su
fija por ₁ mug*er* **Pelayo**, q*ue* auie no*n*bre Ormisenda. En cabo τ pues de
mucha bueña ba-₁talla, murio **Pelayo** en Canicas τ uisco enel regno xviij.
años. Murio^ⁱⁱ ₁ **Pelayo** τ regno su fijo do*n* Fafila, era .dcclxx τ regno dos años;
τ era buena ₁ señal, ni*n* fizo bue*n* fecho, si no*n* q*ue* fizo pi*n*tar muy noble
mie*n*tre una ₁ ygl*es*ia de Santa Cruz τ pues lidio co*n* un oso τ el mato al oso τ
el oso ₁ ael^ⁱⁱⁱ q*ue* gano [muerte] **y Fafila**,²⁴⁴ τ regno su cuñado do*n* Alfonso,
fijo ₁ del duc de Ca*n*tabria, era dcc Lxxij τ regno ix. años. Este fue de dicho ₁ τ
de fecho muy catholico, q*ue* amaua ley τ fe τ faziela amostrar bie*n* ₁ tener τ
fue bueno, piadoso asi co*n* sabor de todos fue electo. Este Alfonso ₁ fue fijo
del duc de Ca*n*tabria τ de linage del gl*o*rioso rey Recaredo. ₁ Este lidio co*n*
muchos moros τ ue*n*cio τ p*r*iso uillas τ castiellas, lo q*ue* no*n* ₁ podie retener
destruyelo a suelo, p*er*o retouo en Galliçia estos: Lucho, ₁ Tuda τ Astorga;
qu*an*do desce*n*dio delas Esturias ue*n*cio alos moros ₁ [fol.28v] ₁ τ gano a Leon τ
depus ende aca ouo no*n*bre el rey τ p*r*iso t*ie*rra de Ca*n*pus qu*an*to se encier-
₁ra de Estola τ de Carreo*n* τ de Pisuerga τ de Adricio destos .v. rios, **et**²⁴⁵
gaño en p*ar*-₁tida de Castilla, Siet Ma*n*cas τ Dueñas τ Seldaña τ Amaya τ
Mira*n*da τ Çi*n*-₁soria²⁴⁶ τ Alesanco τ Trasmera τ Suppuerta τ Carraçio*n*; gano
en Alua Orduña ₁ τ Biscaya τ Nauarra τ Ruchonia τ fizo τ labro muchos
castiellos fas-₁ta el Puerto de Aspa τ lib*r*o qu*an*tos *christ*ianos pudo τ poblo τ
enpa-₁ro lo q*ue* gano. τ ta*n*to qu*an*to Dios mayor poder le daua τ lo exaltaua,
ta*n*to ₁ mas homildoso era τ amado delos pobres τ fazedor delas ygl*es*ias; τ ₁
breume*n*t se esforço **de**²⁴⁷ co*n*plir las vij. obras de m*i*s*e*ric*o*rd*i*a asi q*ue* los
*christ*ianos ael ₁ se uenie*n* como a padre. Este do*n* Aldefo*n*so ouo de su mug*er*
Ormisenda, fija de P*elayo*, ₁ dos fijos: Froyla τ Uimarano τ una fija: Odisinda τ
ot*r*a fija²⁴⁸ de gana*n*çia. ₁ τ murio su muert τ prueua de muchos oyero*n* dezir
qu*an*do el murio ₁ una uoz enel çielo τ enel ayre τ^ⁱᵛ dizie: "Uedes como
muere este om*n*e dre-₁chuero²⁴⁹ τ no*n* tenie y mie*n*tes ne*n*guno; tollido es
dela faz de iniq*u*idat τ su ₁ memoria **sera**²⁵⁰ en paz sie*n*pre". τ fue enterrado

---

ⁱ *DRH*: 'et eos pariter pactis et capitibus et uita priuauit', the eloquence of *DRH* is lost on the
translator.
ⁱⁱ *DRH*: IIII.v
ⁱⁱⁱ *DRH*: 'ab eodem urso fuit miserabiliter interfectus'.
ⁱᵛ Although the langauge is very reduced to this point the Biblical allusion is retained.

co*n* su muge*r* Ormisenda enla ₁ ygle*s*ia de Santa M*ari*a, en te*r*mino de Canicas. Murio[i] Alfonso τ regno su fijo do*n* ₁ Froyla, era de **dc**lxxxxj τ regno xiij. años; τ poblo Ouiedo τ fizo y ygle*s*ia ₁ cathedral τ uio q*ue* de tie*m*po del rey Uatiza aq*u*a los cle*ri*gos casaua*n* τ te-₁nie*n* sus muge*r*es τ q*ue* no*n* era co*n*tra derecho, ma*n*do q*ue* dexasen las mugeres ₁ τ desent no*n* casase*n* τ q*ue* touiesen su castidad τ q*ue* por tal como esto τ como ₁ otras cosas muchas se pe*r*diera la *chri*st*i*andad; τ por esto q*ue* fizo bie*n* ala cle*ri*-₁zia τ ot*r*os bienes muchos, maguer fue en si mal, en este mu*n*do diol ₁ Dios por gualardo*n* poder sobre los enemigos. Ue*n*çio τ mato a do*n* Ho-₁mar, duc de Cordoua, bie*n* co*n* Liiij. uezes mill moros q*ue* destruyen Ga-₁llizia τ subiugo algunos q*ue* se **le** alçara*n* en Galliçia q*ue* nol q*ue*rie*n* obedes-₁cer τ ot*r*osi los nauarros τ fizo paz co*n* ellos; τ p*ri*so muge*r* de su li-₁nage doña Moñina τ lexola p*r*enada; τ fue τ subiugo alos uasco-₁nes q*ue*l co*n*trallaua*n*. Qua*n*do torno fallo su muge*r* doña Monina en-₁[fol.29r] ₁ caesçida de fijo τ ouo no*n*bre Alfonso como su abuelo el bueno. Enta*n*to Froyla ₁ oyo τ uio q*ue* su he*r*mano Uimarano salio muy bueno τ cortes τ fra*n*co τ ar-₁dit τ de buenas man*er*as τ q*ue* se pagaua*n* todos del; temio pe*r*der el regno por ₁ el τ matolo por sus manos. τ por emie*n*da de muer*t*e de su he*r*mano afijo τ ₁ p*ri*so por fijo asu sob*ri*no Ue[re]mu*n*do, fijo de Uimarano. En cabo sus uasallos ₁ mismos mataro*n* a do*n* Froyla por q*ue* mato asu he*r*mano en Canicas; murio ₁ Froyla τ fue enterrado en Ouiedo co*n* su muge*r* doña Monina. Murio[ii] Froyla ₁ τ regno su he*r*mano Aurelio, era dccc.iiij; este regno vij. años. Ensus dias ₁ caso asu he*r*mano Silo co*n* Odisinda, he*r*mana del rey Fruela τ por esta ouo Silo ₁ depus el **regno**. Regno Aurelio .vij. anos τ murio de su muer*t*e τ regno Silo por ₁ Odisinada su muge*r*, q*ue* fue he*r*mana de Froyla, era de **dcccx**.[251] Fue Silo[252] alçado rey ₁ en Prauia τ regno viij. años; τ fizo paz co*n* los arabes τ subiugo algu-₁nos q*ue* no*n* q*ue*rie obedescer en Gallizia. Alfonso, fijo de Fruela por mano de ₁ *su tia*[253] Odismada τ ma*n*daua τ goue*r*naua el p*a*l*a*c*i*o τ escusaua en muchas co-₁sas a do*n* Silo su cuñado. Murio Silo su muer*t*e τ fizo se enterrar enla y-₁gle*s*ia de Sant **Iohan**[254] q*ue* el fizo. Muerto Silo, Odisinda co*n* todos los p*ri*ncipes ₁ dela ti*er*ra, acordaro*n* se τ fiziero*n* rey a do*n* Alfonso, fijo de Fruela.

Del rey don Alfonso el casto[iii]

₁ Co*n*peco de regnar Alfonso era de dcccxviij. Ma*u*regatus ₁ su tio, he*r*mano q*ue* fue de su padre de gana*n*çia, pasose a moros por faze*r* ₁ guerra al sob*ri*no,

---

[i] *DRH*: IIII.vi
[ii] *DRH*: IIII.vii *EG* removes *DRH* mention of rebellion by slaves.
[iii] See p. 15 above.

q*ue* p*er*diese el regno τ q*ue* lo ouiese el τ el q*ue* obediçiese ǀ alos moros. Pues co*n* poder de arabes entrole la ti*er*ra τ Alfonso fuxose ǀ a Nauarra τ ad Al*g*ua, Mauregato por ganar se co*n* moros dauales las ǀ ui*r*gines τ las casadas τ las mo*n*ias, por co*n*fonder la ley de Ihe*s*u Xri*st*o τ p*er*o ǀ a ho*n*ta²⁵⁵ de Dios τ dela *chr*i*st*i*a*ndad, ouiese²⁵⁶ el regno v. años τ fino mal τ fue ǀ peor enterrado; τ los sus **años** no*n* lo co*n*tamos ael sino*n* a do*n* Alfonso, q*ue* mag*ue*r ǀ echado de ti*er*ra, el regno suyo era de derecho. Murio Mauregato τ regno ǀ Ueromu*n*do, fijo de Uimarano sob*r*ino del rey Froyla. Este regno .ij. años, ǀ τ mag*ue*r muy grandioso τ uieio, q*ue* tenie mal el regno τ co*n*tra derech*o*, q*ue* era ǀ [fol.29v] ǀ diachano; enuio por do*n* Alfonso τ fizolo recebir por rey obedescer como a señor τ ǀ uisco co*n* el iiij. años τ vi. meses; τ fino τ fue enterrado en Ouiedo co*n* su mug*er* ǀ doña Inula*n*, p*er*o en uida se p*ar*tio dela por la orde*n* q*ue* auie τ lexaro*n* dos fijos chi-ǀcos: Ramiro τ Garçia. Este^i rey do*n* Alfonso, fijo del rey Fruela, salio bueno τ catholi-ǀcho τ piadoso τ ue*n*turoso; τ nu*n*qua ouo q*ue* ueer co*n* mug*er* τ fue dicho el rey casto, ǀ τ regno xl. años. Ensus dias los moros co*n* Mucay su p*r*incep entraro*n* en ǀ Asturias τ salio les ala carrera el rey do*n* Alfonso aun lugar q*ue* dize*n* Luchos τ ǀ uençiolos τ mato delos mas de Lxx mill τ asi los q*ue*bra*n*taro*n* dessa, q*ue* ouiero*n* de ǀ faz*er* paz τ aun treguas. El xjº. año q*ue* regnaua, alcosele el regno τ ouo de ǀ fuyr do*n* Alfonso al monest*er*io de Abilien*se*; τ pues do*n* Thufredo τ sus fieles uasa-ǀlos ouiero*n* lo de tornar al regno τ fue señor como deuie. Digamos sus ǀ bienes τ lo q*ue* fizo por Dios: fizo sus pala*t*ios reales, fuertes, ricos τ fer-ǀmosos en Ouiedo; pues fizo la ygl*es*ia cathedral en uoca*t*io*n* de Sant Salua-ǀdor τ fizo y doze altares en honor delos doze ap*ost*olos; τ cerca dela ygl*es*ia ǀ de Sant Mi*guel*^ii fizo una ygl*es*ia de Santa M*ar*ia, toda de piedra marmol τ puso en ǀ el altar de Sant Mi*guel* la arca delas reliq*u*ias q*ue*l aduxiero*n* de Toledo do*n* Pelagio ǀ τ do*n* Urba*n*, arcobispo de Toledo, enel tie*n*po q*ue* los moros entraro*n* en España; τ ǀ ali faze Dios muchos de miraglo τ dize*n* q*ue* ali es la casula q*ue* Santa M*ar*ia dio ǀ a Sant Illefonso τ dize*n* ot*r*os q*ue* ala *vastacion*²⁵⁷ de Toledo fue esta arca leuada [a] As-ǀturias, desent a Ih*er*u*s*al*e*m τ pues torno a Toledo τ **pues** otra uez [a] Asturias. Un^iii ǀ dia, mira*n*do el rey la obra dela ygl*es*ia, pe*n*so de faz*er* una cruz rica τ estra-ǀña τ p*r*eçiada; τ fizo dema*n*dar buenos maest*r*os τ aparesciero*n* le dos ǀ angeles en sembla*n*te de om*n*es τ maest*r*os. Dixiero*n*: "Rey^iv nos te faremos ǀ obra qual tu dema*n*das τ meior τ mas rica τ ayna". Dioles el rey oro ǀ τ plata τ piedras p*r*eciosas qua*n*tas dema*n*daro*n* τ dioles

i *DRH*: IIII.viii
ii *DRH*: 'sancti Saluatoris'. A lengthy Biblical reference is passed over.
iii *DRH*: IIII.viiii
iv The direct speech does not appear in *DRH* or indeed *EE*. As previously the translator shows an interest in creating a higher degree of immediacy in set piece scenes. See above pp. 23–25.

una casa apar-|tada que les non enbargase ninguno.[i] Ala tarde fueron ueer que
obra fazien; cla-|uero[258] non ouo quien abrir la puerta, entraron por fuerça τ
non auie ninguno, | τ tammaña era la claridad que salie dende que se leuantaua
dela cruz que era |[fol.30r] | ya fecha, que non osaua ninguno estar. Fizieron lo
saber al rey; el rey enbio | por los obispos τ por toda la clerizia τ fizieron su
procession τ con gran deuoscion | entraron ala τ prisieron la cruz τ sacaron la
ende τ uinieron ala yglesia τ o-|freçiola el rey al altar de Sant Saluador. Este
miraglo fue dicho al[259] | papa τ por esto τ por otras cosas enuio el rey acabar
del papa que ouiese y ar-|cobispadgo, o que fuese obispado por si. De
mientre el andaua en esto el [a]caes-|çio que doña Semaña, su hermana, ouose
de casar a escuso con el conde don Sancho, | buen cauallero τ noble τ de
grand guisa τ ouo en ella un fijo que dixieron don Bernal-|dio. El rey, quando
lo sopo, pesol de tal cosa seer fecha menos de su | mandado, priso asu
hermana τ fizola entrar monia en un monesterio; al | conde don Sancho fizolo
echar en fierros τ meter en grandes cárçeles que iogui-|ese y siempre al su
seruiçio;[260] fizolo criar a grand uiçio τ a grand sabor, el ti-|empo este niño salio
bueno τ proz τ cortes τ uencio de maneras a toda | su natura.

De la batalla de Roncas valles[ii]

| En tanto el rey don Alfonso uido que non tenie fijo τ non auie cercaño |
heredero tanto como este fi[jo] de su hermana, el non querie que heredase[iii] por
que | fuera fecho a su pesar τ uio que era uieio penso como diese rey pus de |
sus dias omne que mantouiese[261] bien el regno τ el pueblo τ la fe τ oyo | dezir
del rey _Carlos_[262] τ como era buen catholico τ buen guerrero τ | auenturado con
moros τ enuiol ensu poridad dezir por letras que uini-|ese para el τ aquel darie
el regno d'España. Ca[r]les enuio dezir que lo gra-|desçie τ que lo recibie, mas
por Dios que nol pesase por que luego non | uinie, que quando los moros
ganaran España pasaran los puertos de | Aspa τ quel tolieran Galia τ Gotica τ
Bordel τ Pleyto[263] τ Turan τ fasta to-|da Equitania; auie guerra con moros τ
auia **ayna** todo lo que perdiera cobra-|do τ que uençiera alos moros cerca el
Puerto de Aspa τ la partida de | Celtiberia que dizen oy Catalueña τ quando lo
suyo ouiese conbrado τ los | moros echados aquend el puerto, que luego
uinien para el τ recibrie lo | [fol.30v] | quel daua τ farie quanto el mandase. Dela
otra parte, los españoles, los principes | τ los conseios, sopieron la uerdad[264]
como el rey don Alfonso enuiara por Car-|los por darle España, pesoles; τ

---

[i] Again, the _EG_ expands on legendary material, see above pp. 20–23.
[ii] _DRH_: IIII.x
[iii] The editorial comment on the relationship between Alfonso and Bernardo is not drawn from
DRH.

touiero*n* su acuerdo τ fuero*n* todos al rey. | Dixiero*n*: "Señor,[i] tu τ tus auuelos por nos ganastes la tie*r*ra τ auedes el reg-|no τ agora por honta d'Espana τ deti mismo τ de uos, como si no*n* ouiese | y om*n*es de recabdo, enuieste por Carlos q*ue*l des la tie*r*ra. Fata aq*uí* ouiemos la- | zeria[265] en gañar la tie*r*ra, agora q*u*iere nos dar señor, q*ue* nu*n*qua del ouiemos | ayuda ni*n* co*n*seio ni*n* esfuerço τ subiugar nos a yente, q*ue* no*n* se*r*emos señores | de fijos ni*n* de mug*er*es delos cuerpos τ delos au*er*es. Enuia dezi*r* al Kar-|los q*ue* no*n* y ue*n*ga, q*ue* gelo no*n* p*r*ometist o q*ue* dexiste cosa q*ue* no*n* pudiste[266] con-|plir τ si lo no*n* fazemos τ oyemos q*ue* uiene, cortartemos la cabeça co-|mo a sennor q*ue* tal fecho faze τ daremos la tie*r*ra a moros o tornaremos | sus uasallos; τ almemos se*r*emos señores de n*ues*t*r*as cabescas, maguer | como en cautiuo, mas q*ue*remos de moros q*ue* de ch*ist*ianos como son oy | en Toledo". Qua*n*do el rey uido q*ue* mal fiziera τ q*ue* mal se podrie seguir, | pe*r*o el lo[267] auie fecho a buena parte, enuio dezir a Karlos q*ue* no*n* uini-|ese, **quel no darie España, que no podrie, que fuera hy mal conseiado, et si uiniese** q*ue*l pesarie; τ[ii] demas q*ue* asi era q*ue* ni el ternie pro ael ni el a el. | Kar*l*os, q*ue* auie ya echado los moros aq*ue*nt los puertos τ cobrara lo | suyo τ se guisaua por uenir reçebir España, oyo este ma*n*dado τ pe-|sol de coraço*n* τ touose por maltrech*o* τ por escarnesido, enuio reb-|tar al rey do*n* Alfonso por q*ue* lo p*r*ometiera τ gelo no*n* tenie τ enuiol | menazar τ dezir q*ue* asu pesar entrarie en España τ cobrarie la | tie*r*ra. Guisose Karlos τ uino para aq*uí* a España τ qua*n*do fue alos Pu-|ertos de Aspa fallo en algunos lugares ch*ist*ianos q*ue* se moraua*n* co-|mo en feudo delos moros τ come*n*ço Karlos ende; los ch*ist*ianos q*ue* lo o-|yero*n* ouiero*n* miedo τ q*ue* cuydaro*n* q*ue* Carlos auie fecho amiztad | co*n* moros. Oyolo el rey do*n* Alfonso τ lego sus huestes, los de As-|turias τ de Alba τ de Biscaya τ de Nauarra τ de Ruchonia τ de | [fol.31r] | Aragon τ saliero*n* ala carrera τ todos co*n* acuerdo de ante morir q*ue* a poder | de fra*n*cos beuir. τ era ya legado Karlos alos Puertos d'Aspa τ do*n* Rolda*n*, | p*r*efecto de Bretaña τ el conde Anselino Egiardo, p*r*eposito del palat*i*o del rey | Carlos era ya co*n* la dela*n*tera enel **ual** de Ro*n*casuales τ subiero*n* se al plano | q*ue* les no*n* enbargase la mo*n*tana. τ co*n* aiuda de Dios, ouolos de ue*n*çer | el rey do*n* Alfonso τ murio y Rolda*n* τ ot*r*os muchos q*ue* serien lue*n*go de co*n*-|tar τ dela gra*n*d cueyta q*ue* auie*n* los fra*n*cos ta*n*xiero*n* su cuerno τ Kar-|los oyolo, q*ue* uinie ya enel ual q*ue* dize*n* hoy de Carlos τ oyo la p*er*dida | q*ue* auie fecha τ ouo miedo τ co*n*peço de fuir τ tornar asu tie*r*ra. τ dela ot*r*a | pa*r*te[268] Be*r*nalrt, su sob*r*ino del rey do*n* Alfonso, por pesar

---

[i] These occasions of direct speech are not from *DRH*, this may be from a popular source or indeed the initiative of the translator. *EG* removes the vehemence and ire of Bernardo. See above p. 23–26, and Gómez Redondo, 'La materia'.

[ii] Details of Alfonso's response again are not from *DRH*.

q*ue* ouo q*ue* tenie el co*n*de ¦ do*n* S*ancho* so padre enla carçel, ot*r*osi q*ue* no*n* osaua[269] parar ant*e* su tio, uino ¦ se p*ar*a Caragoça. τ guerreaua a *chr*ist*ia*nos[i] τ fazie mucho mal, era bue*n* ca-¦uall*ero* τ amaua*n* lo mucho los moros; maguer el, qu*an*do oyo q*ue* su tio auie ¦ de au*er* fezie*n*da, pesol τ dema*n*do ayuda alos moros por aiudar a ¦ su tio τ p*er*o co*n*tra *chr*ist*ia*nos, q*ue* por lo uno q*ue* por lo ot*r*o diero*n* gela. Este co*n* ¦ gra*n* poder uino, dio enla caga del rey Karlos τ desbaratola τ ma-¦to τ p*r*iso muchos dellos τ segudolos τ asi torno do*n* Carlos de ¦ España ho*n*drado τ ue*n*çido. El, por g*u*isar se meior, q*ue* tornarie a Espa-¦ña ue*n*garie esta honta, de dia en dia se guisando, ouo de **enfermar** τ morir ¦ en Aq*u*isgra*n*. Algunos τ qua*n*tos ioglares τ dize*n* ensus roma*n*ces[ii] ¦ q*ue* el rey Carlos lidio co*n* moros τ q*ue* ue*n*cio τ p*r*iso muchas uillas τ ¦ castiellos en España τ abrio el camino de Fra*n*cia p*ar*a Santiago. Es-¦to digo[iii] q*ue* ue*r*dad es q*ue* gano en Catalueña, en Barçilona τ Giro*n*da τ Au-¦sune*n*[270] τ Urgel τ dize*n* q*ue* todo esto p*er*tenesçie al señorio de Fra*n*cia; τ ¦ dize el co*n*de de Barçilona q*ue* pasado es el feudo τ q*ue* es ya **suelto**[271] ¦ el omenage. Esto sea como q*u*ier ala selo uea*n*. Esto[iv] gano Carlos τ ¦ co*n*peco de regnar enla era de **d**cccxxv, en tie*n*po del rey do*n* Alfonso ¦ el casto τ despues aca yo no*n* fallo q*ue* ganase el si no*n* lo q*ue* deximos, [fol.31v] ¦ sabemos q*ue* Taragona fue ganada en tie*n*po de do*n* Bern*ard*o, arçobispo τ p*r*imado ¦ de Toledo, asi como dize enel *regist*ro de p*ap*a Urbano, el conde de Barçilona ¦ p*r*iso Lerida τ Tortosa τ Fraga; do*n* Tizo*n* p*r*iso **Mo*n*çon**[272] q*ue* fue muy noble en Ara-¦gon τ despues un su traydor diola al co*n*de de Barçilona. El rey do*n* Pedro de ¦ Aragon p*r*iso Huesca τ Caragosca τ Tarascona τ Calatayub τ Doroca[v] co*n* sus ¦ entradas τ co*n* sus t*er*minos; p*r*isolas el rey do*n* Alfonso de Aragon p*er*o co*n* ayu-¦de do*n* Gasto*n* de Be*a*rt,[vi] q*ue* ouo algo en Aragon τ co*n* ayuda del co*n*de Alperchas. ¦ Este ouo **depues** Tudela τ diola asu fija doña Margelina en casamie*n*to co*n*el rey ¦ do*n* Remiro de Nauarraga.[273] Este rey do*n* Alfonso de Aragon caso co*n* la reyna ¦ doña Urraca de Castiella, madre q*ue* fue del enp*er*ador d'España τ no*n* ouo ¦ en ella fijos; τ este poblo Soria, Almaça*n*, Berla*n*ga, a Uilforado. τ p*er*o en ¦ t*er*mino de Castiella el rey do*n* Alfonso su suegro q*ue* p*r*iso Toledo et priso Tala-¦uera, Maqueda τ Sant Ollaia, et poblo Escalona et priso Madrit τ Cana-¦les τ Olmos, Talama*n*ca τ Uzeda τ Guadalfaiara, Fita, Almogera τ po-¦blo Buytrago. Estonz p*r*iso Alcala co*n* Bern*ard*o, arcobispo de Toledo τ poblo Se-¦gouia, Auilla,

---

[i] Much of this, familiar, detail has been added to the *DRH* narrative, and may be indicative of an epic influence. See above p. 20.
[ii] *DRH*: 'Non nulli histrionum fabulis inherentes...'. See Gómez Redondo, 'La materia', p. 281.
[iii] The first person is that of the translator, not *DRH*.
[iv] *DRH*: IIII.xi
[v] The translator has run together the conquests of Alfons and Pere.
[vi] *EG* maintains *DRH* interest in noble lineage, particularly in Aragon.

Salamanca con sus terminos τ con sus obispados, que eran yer-|mos delos moros aqua; Medina Çelin, que fue dicha Ciguenca τ Atiença | τ Lariba τ Fendaluz, el los suyos lo ganaron. Osma τ Sant Esteuan de | Gormaz, en tienpo delos condes, fueron de christianos; Huebte, Oreia, Cauria, | prisolas el enperador; su fijo don Sancho priso Uales;[274] el rey don Alfonso el bue-|no, nieto del enperador,[i] gano **Cuenca**, Alarcon, Moya, Plazencia, Beiar, Alcaraz τ | Calatraua τ Caguey,[275] Que fueron perdidos en tienpo; el rey don Ferrando, padre | del rey don Alfonso que gano Toledo, priso Coynbria. Don Alfonso, que primado ouo | nonbre en Portugal, priso Ulisbona, Santaren τ Elbora τ Sintria, los otros | castiellos desus obispados el pueblo los unos τ su fijo don [Sancho][276] los | otros. Delos que pues fue ganado, dezir lo emos ensu lugar, pues uea-|mos si es mas de creer alos romançes[ii] o a la uerdad, que sabemos que es | asi, que en todo esto non ueo de Carlos co[n]quista ninguna; τ demas estos | [fol.32r] | poblatones τ estas conquistas fueron de cc. años aqua τ de muerte de Karlos | aca[iii] son bien cccc años. Pues ¿que gano? o ¿quando lo gano? si dizen que lidio con | moros, uerdad es que quando torno uencido d'España que nol dexaron pasar el puerto | aca, elos non quisieron dezir que los uençieron christianos si non moros, pues ¿como | puede seer que abriese caminos a Sant Iague?, que non ouo poder del puerto | pasar, que ante que Carlos fuese era y grand el camino a Sant Iayme.[iv] Pero tanto | pudo seer quando era niño que y uiniese en romeria que lo echo[277] su padre | el rey Pepino de tierra de Françia por que se leuantaua contra el τ su man-|damiento τ ouo de uenir en Toledo. Estonz ouo de uenir discordia en-|tre Galafre,[v] rey de Toledo τ Marfil de Caragoça; τ Karlos touo con Gala-|fre τ lidio τ uencio muchas uezes con los de Marfil. A tienpo oyo muerte | de su padre el rey Pepino τ torno a Françia con Galliana, fija del rey Ga-|lafre τ dizen Que la torno christiana τ caso con ella τ dizen quel fizo palatios muy | ricos τ buenos en Bordel.

Aqui torna al rey don Alfonso el casto[vi]

| Tornemos al rey don Alfonso el casto: al año .xxxº. que regnauan, dos prin-|cipes de moros, Albobez τ Elhy,[278] con sus huestes entraron en Gal-|liçia; τ uenciolos don Alfonso τ mato τ priso muchos dellos. El un princep | fino en

---

[i] *EG* demonstrates an early interest in Alfonso VII, see Martin, *Les Juges de Castille*, esp. p. 140 ff. and 176 ff.
[ii] *DRH*: 'fabulosis narrationibus'.
[iii] *DRH*: 'cum ab eius morte anni pene efluxerunt CCCC'.
[iv] *EG* interpretation of *DRH* rebuttal of Carlos's importance is rather more vehement in its demonstration of Spanish independence.
[v] Mainete details are drawn directly from *DRH*.
[vi] *DRH*: IIII.xii

un lugar q*ue* dize*n* Nato*n*, el ot*ro* fino en un rio q*ue* dize*n* Aceia. | Ot*ro*si al
xxxvij°. año q*ue* regnaua do*n* Alfonso, Mahomat, un p*r*incep | moro,
leua*n*tose co*n*tra su señor en Me*r*ita τ fue echado de *tie*rra. Este uino | se a
merçed del rey do*n* Alfonso por faz*er* le se*r*uicio, q*ue* oyo dezir sus bie-|nes τ
fue bie*n* recebido τ moro y. vij. años. Al viij°. leua*n*tose co*n*tra | el rey do*n*
Alfonso en *un* castiello Q*ue* dize*n* Santa Ch*r*ist*i*ana, co*n* los Q*ue* tenie | en fiuza
de moros, q*ue*l uinie*n* en ayuda. τ do*n* Alfonso uino τ p*r*iso el | castiello τ
p*r*iso a do*n* Mahomat τ cortol la cabeca τ co*n* el mas de | L mill moros. Pues
torno do*n* Alfonso a Ouiedo, sano τ co*n* uictoria τ ga-|na*n*cia. Fazemos
cue*n*ta q*ue* regno el rey do*n* Alfonso Lij. años, mas por | si no*n* mas de
quare*n*ta τ uno, q*ue* los q*u*at*ro* regno co*n* Sillo τ los ot*ro*s v. | [fol.32v] | qua*n*do lo
echo de *tie*rra Mauregato v. τ regno co*n* Uetemu*n*do .ij años τ caso; τ | en esos
xLi. no*n* ouo q*ue* ueer co*n* mug*er* τ fue casto τ ma*n*touo bie*n* su regno. τ |
murio τ fue enterrado en Sa*n*ta M*ar*ia la q*ue* **el** ouo edificado.

Del rey Ueremundo[i]

| Muerto el rey do*n* Alfonso el casto, regno Remiro, fijo del rey Uermu*n*do
Q*ue* | fue diachono q*ue* do*n* Alfonso se [lo] ma*n*dara en uida. E come*n*co de
regnar era | de **dccc**lxxvij,[ii] τ fue **casar** en Bardulia. De mie*n*tre el **tard**aua[279]
ala, alçose gra*n*d | p*ar*tida de su *tie*rra co*n* el co*n*de Neposciano, q*ue* era su
uasallo. Oyolo el rey do*n* Re-|miro, tornose p*ar*a su hueste en Lugo,[280] una
çibdad de Gallizia τ p*r*iso Astires | τ Asturias Q*ue* era*n* co*n* el, pues ouiero*n*
fazie*n*da, ue*n*çio el rey do*n* Remiro τ | fuxo Nepociano τ p*r*isiero*n* lo dos
co*n*des Sape*m*e τ Cipio τ p*r*esentaro*n* lo al rey | Remiro; τ p*r*isolo τ çegolo τ
pusolo en un moneste*r*io de mo*n*ges τ asi cobro su *tie*rra.·

Como legaron paganos[iii]

| Esto*n*z paganos de Normania, mu-|uie cruda gent, aribaro*n* co*n* muchas
naues al Faro de Gallizia. El | rey Remi*ro* ouo su co*n*seio τ lidio co*n* ellos;
mato τ p*r*iso muchos τ ue*n*ciolos | τ q*ue*mo las[281] naues. Los q*ue* pudiero*n*
escapar por mar en naues corri-|ero*n* τ fiziero*n* gra*n*d daño en Seuilla τ asi
co*n* p*er*dida tornaro*n* asu *tie*rra. | τ acabo del año alçaro*n* se co*n*tra el rey
Remiro un su co*n*de Aldarico τ do*n* Pi-|molo, el meior om*n*e de su cort, co*n*
viij. fijos q*ue* auie. Ouolos el rey de p*r*end*er* | τ çegolos todos. Pues el rey
come*n*ço de guerrear co*n* moros τ destruyo | qua*n*to fallo dellos. Esto*n*z uino
sobre el rey gra*n*d poder de moros, el Rey | temiose que era grand poder τ

---

[i] *DRH*: IIII.xiii
[ii] *DRH*: 'DCCCLVIIII'.
[iii] See above, p. 15.

alçose con su poder en un castiello Flauio; | τ de noche como en uision como
en sueño aparescio al rey Remiro Santia-|gue en senblança de cauallero τ
dixol: "Non temas, yo so el apostol, | lidia τ uenceras".[i] Otro dia conto esta
uision alos obispos τ ouieron grand go-|zo. Entraron enla fazienda τ ala
mayor priesa aparescioles Santiago | uesiblemientre con poder en cauallo
blanco, armas blancas τ seña blan-|ca; τ desent aqua es costunbre hoy en dia
dezir en fazienda "Dios ayu-|da [et] Santiago". Plogo a Dios, uencio el rey
don Remiro; priso muchos τ | [fol.33r] | mato delos mas de lxx. mill. Estonz
priso el rey Flauio τ Albaydan τ Cala-|gurra. El dio τ establesçio[ii] que
Santiague ouiese una caualleria ensus caual-|gadas que fue por costunbre τ asi
es oy en dia en algunas fronteras. El rey auie | y consigo un hermano don
Garcia τ por que era menor τ nasciera pues muert de su pa-|dre el **Rey** don
Ueremundo que fue diachono, amaualo τ daual toda su casa a mandar | τ todo
su regno como asi mismo. τ doña Vrraca, muger que fue del rey de Casti-
|ella, era **muyt** buena christiana τ daua sus presentes alas yglesias; el rey fizo
estonz | de obra τ de adriello Santa Maria; a dos milleros[282] de Ouiedo. Regno
don Remiro .vj. | años τ fino τ fue enterrado τ delexo un fijo Ordoño.
Muerto[iii] el rey don Re-|miro regno su fijo Ordoño enla era de
[d]cccL[x]v,[283] τ regno x años τ fue muy | bueno. Caso con doña Monina τ
ouo en ella fijos Alfonso, Uermundo, Remiro, | Ordoño, [iv] Froyla, que pues
fue dicho Aragontus; este poblo Tudan τ Leon la çib-|dad τ[284] Astorga τ
Amaya τ Patricia, que fincaron yermas pues que lo gano el rey | don Alfonso
de moros. El primer año que començo de regnar conquiso los uascones | que
se leuantaron contra el; otrosi uino grand poder de moros τ uenciolos τ gaño
| mucho dellos. Estonz un godo que fue tornadizo, princep delos moros,
leuanto | se contra el rey de Cordoua τ priso muchos castiellos τ dizen le en
arauigo | por nonbre Bencaçim; τ gano Çaragoça τ Osca τ Tudela τ Toledo τ
dioles por se-|ñor so el su fijo Lop. τ despues uino en Catalueña τ en tierra de
Campos; τ | fizo y mucho mal τ uencio dos duques de franceses, Sancho τ
Pulion τ prisolos | τ echolos en carçel. Pues Muca, rey de Cordoua, uino τ
uencio a Lop, | fijo de Bencaçin τ prisol dos principes moros Ynbencaniça τ
Al Poz τ su fijo | Azech. Estonz Carlos, mas non el mayor, su fijo uio que los
non podien uen-|cer por armas nin por poder, dioles sus presentes τ firmo
con ellos tre-|guas τ paz. Muca, quando esto oyo, ouo grand sabor τ mandose
lamar | rey d'España. Pues Muca uino contra Ordoño loçanament; el rey don

---

[i] As previously, *EG* presents a more immediate scene in direct speech not drawn from the source.
See above pp. 23–25.
[ii] This detail is not in *DRH*, the present tense reference is that of the translator.
[iii] *DRH*: IIII.xiiii
[iv] *DRH*: 'Nunium, Odoarium'.

Or-|doño salio adela*n*t co*n* su hueste τ co*n* Albayda, q*ue* aun poco ouiera q*ue* la | gaño Muca de *chr*ist*i*anos τ la **en**fortalesçiera de muros τ de omes τ de ar-| [fol.33v] | mas. Muca, en q*ue* oyo esto del rey do*n* Ordono, uino por **correr**[285] Albayda, | τ aribo aun mo*n*t q*ue* dize*n* Laturio τ fizo[286] y sus tie*n*das. El rey do*n* Ordoño p*ar*-|tio su hueste, la meatad fizo[287] enla cerca, la co*n* otra meatad uino τ lidio co*n* | Muca τ ue*n*ciolo τ menos delos ot*r*os mato de caualle*r*os mas de x. mill. | Muca escapo co*n* tres plagas τ p*er*dio lo q*ue* traye τ las ioyas τ los p*re*sentes | q*ue*l diera Karlos fincaro*n* al rey do*n* Ordoño; τ torno asu hueste τ de*n*t a vij. | dias ouo p*re*sa la çibdad τ destruyola a suelo τ mato qua*n*tos y fallo. Pues | Muca co*n* qua*n*to ouo tornos su uasallo τ fizo por muchas batallas co*n* | moros τ ue*n*cio. El rey do*n* Ordoño co*n*q*ui*so Cauria co*n* su rey **Zeyt** τ **Salamanca con su rey** Muygeres τ | mato muchos, delos q*ue* fincaro*n* fuero*n* ue*n*didos. Esto*n*z uiniero*n* de Nor-|ma*n*dia corredores por mar τ fiziero*n* gra*n*d daño enla**s** puertas[288] co*n* armas | τ co*n* fuego, pues [pa]saro*n* alie*n*t mar en Maure*n*tania[289] τ destruyero*n* la çibdad | Uachor τ mataro*n* y muchos moros. Pues desgastaro*n* Mayorga τ Minor-|ga τ Iuica τ Forme*n*taria τ las ysllas Beleares τ mataro*n* y muchos mo-|ros; pus uiniero*n* en G*re*çia τ co*n* sus naues tornaro*n* asu t*ie*rra. El rey do*n* Ordo-|ño fino de dolor delos pies,[i] unos dize*n* q*ue* el xº. año q*ue* regnara, ot*r*os | dizie*n* q*ue* el xvjº. τ fue enterrado en S*an*ta M*ari*a de Ouiedo co*n* los ot*r*os reyes.

Del rey don Alfonso[ii]

| Muerto el rey do*n* Ordoño regno su fijo | Alfonso τ era esto*n*z de xiiij. años; co*n*pesco de regnar era de **dccc**. | Lxxv. τ regno xLvj. años. Qua*n*do fino el padre el no*n* era y τ oyolo τ sa-|lio a Ouiedo τ soterrolo asu padre ondradame*n*t τ alcaro*n* lo luego rey. | Mientre ordenaua su regno τ maguer niño, Froyla fijo de Ueramu*n*do, | de p*ar*te de Galliçia, co*n* gra*n*d poder començo de entrar la t*ie*rra τ de subiu*g*ar | τ de regnar; el rey do*n* Alfonso e*n*q*ue* lo oyo uiño en Alaua por guisar se | τ yr cont*ra* Froyla. Enta*n*to Froyla uino a Ouiedo τ el comu*n* dela uilla[290] | [m]a[t]o[lo][291] por q*ue* se leuaua cruda mie*n*tre; oyolo do*n* Alfonso τ plogol. τ en-|de **finco en**[292] paz τ co*n*pesco de poblar los yermos; poblo Sabla*n*ca τ Ceya, | τ fizo y fortalezas. Esto*n*z do*n* Ayla, co*n*de de Alua, leua*n*tose co*n*tra do*n* | [fol.34r] | Alfonso; τ el rey fue cont*ra* el τ pusolo en fierros τ enuiolo a | Ouiedo; τ los de Alua fiziero*n* omenage al rey por seer sie*n*pre leales | ensu s*er*uit*i*o τ asi subiugo Alaua asu señorio. Esto*n*z uiniero*n* co*n*tra el rey | Ymu*n*dar τ Alcanatar co*n* gra*n*d poder de moros; τ ue*n*ciolos el rey do*n* | Alfonso τ puso su amiztad co*n* los nauarros τ

---

[i] *DRH*: '...expleto anno Xº, quidam dicunt XVIº regni sui, morbo podagrico interceptus...'.
[ii] *DRH*: IIII.xv

con los galos. Caso este | rey don Alfonso en Francia con una dueña que ouo nonbre Amelina, pus le di-|xieron Remena; desta ouo fijos .iiij°: don Garçia, don Ordoño, don Froyla τ don | Gonçalo, que fue arçidiano de Ouiedo. Este rey don Alfonso fue bueno τ piadoso, | τ comenco destruyr lo que los arabes tenien τ deuasto Lençia pero con ayuda de | uascones τ de nauarros; de mas partio a pobres τ alas yglesias el te-|soro que dexo su padre τ fizo la yglesia de Santiago de marmor τ de piedra, | que ante de tierra era; τ fizo muchas yglesias en obispado de Ouiedo; en-|fortalescio **palacios**²⁹³ τ castiellos. Estonz poder de moros de Toledo ui-|nieron contra el τ uenciolos τ gano mucho dellos. Bernaldo, el que dixie-|mos, era buen gerero,²⁹⁴ τ fizo un castiello Carpinium en termino de Sala-|manca; τ pasose a moros τⁱ fizo grand daño al rey don Alfonso fata que | solto asu padre, que iazie preso τ çiego en Cordoua; τ pues torno τ ayu-|do al rey don Alfonso. Pues los moros uinieron contra don Alfonso τ fi-|zieron se dos huestes τ uencio la una Bernaldo en Ualmoriella τ la | otro uencio el rey que yua a Paluoraria τ los moros tornaron se asi co-|fondidos. τⁱⁱ pues los moros cercaron Camora τ el rey entro ante | enla uilla τ mando atodos sus uasallos quel uiniesen acorrer; dela | otra parte uino Bernalt τ uencio alos moros τ mato a don Althama, que an-|daua y como por propheta delos moros.

De Roncasvalles

| Estonz dizien unos que ouieron moros fazienda en Ronças ual-|les con Carlos Marçel; τ por que fueron .iij. Carlos: Karlos Magno | τ Karlos Caluo τ Karlos Marcel τ los escriptos ançianos τ la fama | publica se acuerdan a uno, dizen que aquella batalla fizo Carlos Magno, | [fol.34v] | pero si alguno meior lo sabe plaze me a mi τ otorgogelo; mas yoⁱⁱⁱ ten-|go que non fue sinon Carlos Marce. Estonz Froyla, su hermano del rey, con los otros | quatro fizieron fabla por matar asu hermano τ fueron descubiertos τ prisolos | el rey a don Muño τ a don Ordario²⁹⁵ τ Froyla τ cegolos. Ueremundo fuyo en As-|torga τ guerreo vij. años; τ pus el rey cerçolo en Garciliareⁱᵛ τ priso la uil-|la τ destruyola τ priso asu hermano que era con grand poder de moros τ cegolo; | asi lo enuio a moros. τ fue el rey τ castigolos de Uentosa τ de Astorga | por que reçibieran a don Ueremundo; τ despues [fue]²⁹⁶ contra Coybria τ prisolo. Estonz comenca-|ron poblar los christianos las cibdades de Portugal: Uiseo, Flauio fata Taio. | Estonz un duc delos moros Abohaly fue preso τ presentado al rey

---

ⁱ Bernardo el Carpio legend recurs at this point in different manner to that of the source. See above p. 20.
ⁱⁱ *DRH*: IIII.xvi. *EG* again demonstrates significantly different priorities in textual organisation.
ⁱⁱⁱ *DRH*: 'tempore Magni Caroli dicimus accidisse'.
ⁱᵛ *DRH*: 'Graliare'.

τ redi-|miose por c. mill m*a*τ*auedi*s. Este rey poblo Sietma*n*cas τ Dueñas τ
otras | buenas uillas en t*ie*rra de Ca*m*pos, pues co*n*q*ui*so τ destruyo algunos
loga-|res çerca de Toledo; e diero*n* le parias por treguas de tres años τ tor-
|no asu t*ie*rra. Pues Addamus, un su c*n*iado, pe*n*so por matar al rey τ fizolo |
luego rastrar. Pues fizo el rey la ygl*e*sia de Sant Iague τ de Sant Fa-|gu*n*do τ de
Sant P*ri*mitiuo τ pues las destruyero*n* los arabes. τ gano un | castiello Gozon
en la marisma de Asturias τ poblo bie*n* Çamora τ di-|reuos^i como ouo este
no*n*bre: Mie*n*tre la poblaua*n* **el rey** subio en un ot*er*o por | mirar la puebla τ
la t*ie*rra, e un so moço²⁹⁷ fallo una uaca τ por escarnio di-|xol: "¡Camora!" τ
oyolo el rey τ rixose²⁹⁸ desta palaura τ fue dizie*n*do el τ los | otros "he çamora
he çamora" τ otorgogelos el rey q*ue* sin falla oy dia; suele*n* | dezir alas uacas
negras "moras" en algunos logares. Pues el rey, | co*n* sabor de ta*n*ta uictoria,
enuio a Roma al p*a*p*a* Iohañ, q*ue* era esto*n*z, [do]s²⁹⁹ | cap*e*llanos suyos: do*n*
Sueuio τ do*n* Deside*ri*o, q*ue* loasen³⁰⁰ como ganara gra*n*d | t*ie*rra τ acrecie la fe
τ q*ue* los gradesciesen; τ el ot*r*osi q*ue* era p*r*esto por | sie*m*pre seer obedie*n*te
ala ygl*e*sia de Roma^ii τ morir por la fe τ por el al-|camie*n*to³⁰¹ de *christi*anos τ
q*ue* rogaua q*ue* otorgase Ouiedo seer metropolitana, | τ no*n* seer subiecta si
no*n* ala ygl*e*sia de Roma. Fuero*n* estos co*n* letras del | [fol.35r] | rey τ recabdaro*n*
τ tornaro*n* co*n* letras del p*a*p*a* τ co*n* un su me*n*saiero Reynal-|do co*n* tal letra:
"Ioha*n*, ^iii obispo sieruo delos sieruos de Dios, al hondrado τ | noble fijo do*n*
Alfonso rey de Asturias τ atodos los obispos τ los abbades | τ los caua*ller*os
de toda la *christi*andad, sal*u*t τ apostolical bendicion. Por q*ue* nos | Dios dio
poder anos de amonestar todos los fieles *christi*anos por el poder | q*ue* n*u*est*r*o
señor Ih*es*u *Christ*o q*ui*so otorgar a Sant Pedro τ a Sant Paulo τ asus
antecesor-|res, dizie*n*do "Lo q*ue* ligares sobre t*ie*rra s*er*a ligado en t*ie*rra τ lo
q*ue* soluieres | enla t*ie*rra s*er*a suelto enel cielo"; τ dixo ot*r*a uez enla pasio*n*:
"yo ruego por ti, | p*er*o q*ue* no*n* falesca tu fe", por q*ue* la u*u*est*r*a bueña fama
fue a nos demostrada | por **Seuerino** τ Deside*ri*o, p*r*estes, roga*n*do nos,
amonestamos τ ma*n*damos, de a-|q*ue*l poder q*ue* nos auemos q*ue*
p*er*seueredes en este bie*n* q*ue* auedes come*n*cado;³⁰² | τ otorgamos^iv nos esta
lazeria en remisio*n* de u*u*est*r*os peccados; ot*r*osi, si al-|guna cosa auedes
menest*er* de n*u*est*r*o señorio aiudar uos hemos de g*r*a-|do τ recebir uos
hemos como a h*er*manos τ como electos de Dios | asu s*er*uiti*o*; τ por q*ue*
todos de un acuerdo τ de un coraço*n* rogastes τ | dema*n*distes cosa

---

^i The first person narrative voice here is not that of *DRH*.
^ii All of these details are extrapolated from the surrounding text in *DRH* which shows a significantly
less fervent religious outlook than that of the translation.
^iii *DRH*: IIII.xvii
^iv The content of this letter is quite different in rhetoric, although the details regarding Oviedo and
the messengers are the same. The quotations from Matthew 16 and Luke 22 are maintained.

derechura, estableçemos Ouiedo çibdat metro-|polita τ ma*n*damos q*ue* qua*n*to los reyes diero*n* o da*n* o dara*n* q*ue* sea firm*e*, | τ ma*n*damos a uos q*ue* lo obedescades τ lo reconoscades por metropo-|litana; τ ma*n*do uos q*ue* ayades en comie*n*da τ en guarda al portador | dela letr*a*s. Bene ualete." "Ioha*n*[i] obispo, delos sieruos de Dios, al rey | de Gallizia, sal*u*t τ apostoligal bendicio*n*. Recibimos u*uest*ras letras τ | gr*a*desiemos uos mucho, por q*ue* ta*n* bie*n* uos auedes leuado co*n*tra la | romanal ygl*e*sia; τ rogamos a Dios q*ue* uos de uictoria sobre los ene-|migos de la fe τ uos de uida τ sal*u*t τ cresça **Dios** el regno τ u*uest*ro se-|norio. E roga*n*do uos ma*n*damos q*ue* fagades alos obispos co*n*sagrar | la ygl*e*sia de Sant Iague el apostol τ fazed y co*n*çilio. τ sepades q*ue* nos ot*r*o-|si auemos muy cruda guerra co*n* moros τ loado a Dios, auemos | su uictoria sobrellos; onde uos rogamos q*ue* nos enuiedes algunos | [fol.35v] | cauallos moriscos delos q*ue* dize*n* alfarazes co*n* q*ue* nos enparemos τ | fagamos a Dios seruit*i*o τ uos ayamos q*ue* gradescer τ ayades bie*n* τ | gualardo*n* de Dios τ de **los** gl*o*riosos apostoles Pedro τ Paulo τ de nos, cuyo po-|der tenemos en t*ie*rra, maguer no*n* somos ende dignos. Ualete". El[ii] rey | do*n* Alfonso ouo gra*n*d gozo qua*n*do uido las letras del p*a*pa τ ma*n*do su cort | τ su co*n*cilio a dia sabido, ricos om*e*s, duques, caua*ll*eros, obispos, cl*e*rigos | τ q*ue* uiniesen co*n*segrar la ygl*e*sia de Sa*n*tiague. Fueron y obispos do*n* Uice*n*t, | obispo[iii] de Leon, do*n* Gomelo de Asturias, do*n* H*er*megilo de Ouiedo, do*n* Diago | **Tudensso**,[303] do*n* Egica, obispo de Cauia, do*n* Sisenado, obispo de Yerena, do*n* Re-|caredo, obispo de **Lucena, don Tehodosindo, obispo de** Bretaña; todas las cibdades destos era*n* ya de *chr*ist*i*anos. | τ fuero*n* y ot*r*os q*ue* son obispados, delos era*n* yermos τ delos tenie*n* | moros: do*n* Iuha*n*, obispo de Aucena, do*n* Dulcidio de Salama*n*tina, do*n* Ia-|cob de Caucia,[304] do*n* Faust*i*no de Coynbr*i*a, do*n* Ardimiro de Lametena,[305] do*n* Toude-|miro,[306] obispo de Uiseo, do*n* Gomaro, obispo de Portugal, do*n* Angemiro | obispo de Bragena, do*n* Eleta obispo de Çaragoça; las çibdades destos, | ya si las tenie*n* los reyes de Asturias, o si era*n* yermas, o en poder | de moros, asi fincaro*n* fasta tie*m*po q*ue* regno el rey do*n* Alfonso q*ue* gano | Toledo; τ los obispos destas cibdades fueron a Ouiedo τ alli uinie*n* | delos enla cibdad delos enel t*er*mino τ por ende en algunos li-|bros es lamada Ouiedo, cibdad delos obispos. A cabo delos xj. | meses pasados, el rey, co*n* su mug*er* τ co*n* sus fijos τ co*n* los obis-|pos τ sus ricos omes, uino faz*er* co*n*cilio a Ouiedo; por ma*n*damiento | del p*a*pa τ otorgamie*n*to de todos fiziero*n* Ouiedo metropolitana τ else-|yero*n* a do*n* H*er*me*n̄e*gilo por arcobispo por q*ue* todas

---

[i] *DRH*: IIII.xviii
[ii] *DRH*: IIII.xviiii
[iii] As in the case of Councils of Toledo, the lengthy list of bishops is preserved all but intact.

las v. prouincias de Es-|paña era*n* en poder de moros,[i] ala las auie*n* destruydo;
τ ali falaro*n* | de su ordinat*io*n τ delas ygle*s*ias τ del regno, pues cada uno
regno | asu lugar. Pues[ii] el **rey** do*n* Alfonso p*r*iso asu fijo do*n* G*ar*c*i*a, q*ue*
deuie regnar τ | echolo en fierros en Gozame*n*, q*ue* auie miedo q*ue* aiudarie a
do*n* Nuño | [fol.36r] | *Ferrandes* su sueg*r*o, o q*ue*rie auer guerra co*n* el. τ la reyna
doña Semana q*ue* ante fue-|ra dicha Amelina, ya como q*ue* era, no*n* se pagaua
del rey, osi por q*ue* era enfer-|mo o uieio e lazrado, mouio todos sus fijos,
q*ue* les pesase de como fizie-|ra su padre asu he*r*mano mayor τ fizolos iurar
co*n* do*n* Nuño Ferrande*s* q*ue* saca-|sen a do*n* Garcia dela p*r*ision τ q*ue*
echasen al padre del reygno τ asi lo fiziero*n*. Come*n*-|caro*n* guerra τ echaro*n*
al padre de t*ie*rra τ sacaro*n* su **hermano**[307] dela p*r*isio*n*; el rey fuyo **a** |
Asturias τ pusose en una uilla q*ue* dezie*n* Boydes τ mal su gr*a*do ouo de | dar
el regno asu fijo do*n* Garcia; otorgogelo ante sus fijos τ ante sus ricos omes | τ
sus co*n*ceios. Pues el rey do*n* Alfonso fue a Sa*n*tiague, al torno rogo asu fijo
q*ue*l di-|ese poder τ yrie sobre moros; otorgogelo τ diol poder τ fue τ ue*n*cio τ
mato | τ p*r*iso mucho τ torno co*n* gana*n*cia a Camora τ como bie*n* come*n*çara
bie*n* fino, | τ maguer ue*n*çio alos estraños τ asu fijo no*n* pudo. Alla enfermo τ
fino τ | fue enterrado en Astorga, pues fue leuado ende a Sa*n*ta M*ar*ia de
Ouiedo τ fue | y enterrado co*n* su mug*er* doña Semaña. Fino[iii] el rey do*n*
Alfonso era dccccxxj., e pues el regno su fijo do*n* Garcia tres años. Este
guerreo co*n* moros τ fizo | les daños τ **quemoles τ destruyoles muchos**
castiellos τ ue*n*cio ad Axolas, rey delos aragabes τ p*r*isolos co*n* otros
muchos, | τ ribo co*n* gra*n*d gana*n*cia aun lugar q*ue* es dicho el Tr*en*blo τ de alli
fuyo A-|yolas τ torno alos suyos. Fino el rey do*n* Garcia acabo de tres años τ
| fue enterrado en Ouiedo co*n* los ot*r*os reyes. Pues[iv] el dize*n* q*ue* regno su |
he*r*mano de Ordoño, era dccccxxiiij. Este regno viij. años τ vj. meses, | el rey
do*n* Alfonso auielo en su uida adela*n*tado en Galazia. Es-|te retouo las
man*er*as del padre, amaua a Dios τ pobres τ engle*s*ias, | τ q*ue*bra*n*taua moros;
otrosi en tie*n*po desu padre fizo batallas co*n* mo-|ros τ ue*n*cio muchas uezes.
τ de pues q*ue* regno ce*r*co Talau*er*a τ uinie | co*n* moros en acorro τ ue*n*ciolos τ
p*r*iso Talau*er*a τ asi co*n* uictoria co*n* hon-|dra torno asu t*ie*rra τ p*r*iso al
p*r*incep dela hueste de Cordoua q*ue* uiniera | y. Pues q*ue* ouiero*n* los reyes
moros ta*n* mal t*r*echos de ch*r*ist*i*anos, ouiero*n* | su fabla co*n* Abderabe*n*, rey de
Cordoua τ co*n* Almotahpo,[308] **rey** de Ti*n*gitania τ | [fol.36v] | demanda*r*o*n* ayuda
aestos dos reyes; τ ellos seyendo en dubda, ma*n*daro*n* | gelas so peña delas

---

[i] *DRH*, '...et ut tanta angustias tolerabat antiqua Toletani concilii instituta sollicite contuentes,
Ouetensem ecclesiam et ceteras...'.
[ii] *DRH*: IIII.xx
[iii] *DRH*: IIII.xxi
[iv] *DRH*: IIII.xxii, 'legitur'.

cabescas τ dela ley τ Aluos Alpaz,[309] aly de Cordoua, con | hueste τ con
Amotanip,[310] rey de Tingitania, uinieron a Sant Esteuan, ribera de | Duero.
Estonz uino el rey don Ordo[ño] τ mato Al[311] Hulit τ Almaholep τ otros |
principes τ luego mouio su hueste contra Merita τ destruyeron fasta toda |
Lusitania; τ priso un castiello Colubri, agora le dizen Alanz τ asi torno con |
uictoria τ con ganancia. τ torno a Leon faziendo a Dios gracias τ fizo su cort |
de ricos omnes τ de obispos τ de clerigos; τ con otorgamiento deles, mu-
|do[312] la yglesia de Sant Pedro τ Sant Paulo enla uilla dentro, por seer | mas
seguro τ fizieron la yglesia o eran ante los baños moriscos τ ala fue | la yglesia
cathedral. Estonz era obispo de Leon don Frumino. τ ali auie | tres casas τ en
la[313] una fizieron el altar de Santa Maria τ la otra de Sant | Saluador τ delos
sanctos τ enla otra de Sant Iuhan Bautista τ delos | martires τ delos confesores
τ delas uirgines τ adobo[314] bien la yglesia | τ fizo la consagrar alos obispos, que
fueron y xij. Estonz, por otorgami-|ento de todos, fue el rey coronado a
tiempo. Esto[i] pasado, el rey de | Cordoua, con pesar delas gentes que perdiera,
mouio su guerra τ uino | fata Mindona; τ salio ael el rey don Ordoño τ
murieron muchos de | cada parte; este dia non se pudieron uencer. Pues esto
oyo Abderaben, | τ con un grand hueste uino τ entro en Nauarra τ lego aun
lugar | que oy dia dizen Muez; esto peso al rey don Garcia, que era fijo del rey
don | Sancho τ enuio demandar ayuda al rey don Ordoño; τ el uino con su po-
|der τ quando fue en Ual Iuquera[315] τ lidiaron y τ plogo a Dios τ murieron | y
muchos christianos τ fueron y presos dos obispos: don Dulcidio de Sa-
|lamanca τ don Hermogio de Tudena;[316] τ por Hermogio dieron en reenes[317]
asu | sobrino don Pelayo, que pues fue martiriado por Dios τ por Dulcidio |
dieron otros reenes τ asi escaparon. Pues esto el rey don Ordoño | mouio su
hueste sobre moros τ uino fasta Sintilla; mato τ pri- [fol.37r] so muchos τ
destruyo[318] uillas τ castiellos muchos: Sarmalayan, Helip, | Plamacio τ
Casteion τ Magnacia τ otros muchos. τ pus torno τ fallo asu muger | doña
Monina, que ante fuera dicha Eluira, finada; pero ouo en ela dos fijos: |
Alfonso τ Remiro; τ pues caso con doña Redegada,[319] que fue de Galliçia τ
depues | la dexo, por sospecha que ouo dela. Estonz enuio por los condes que
gouernauan | Castiella τ dizien que non fazien asu guisa; τ uinieron a corte aun
lugar que di-|zen Regular, en riba del rio que dizen Carreon τ ouo y su fabla τ
uinieron[320] y Mu-|ño Ferrandes τ Almondor Blanco τ su fijo don Diago τ
Ferrand Osuero; τ asi | seyendo en fabla fizolos prender τ echar en fierros τ
enuiolos a Leon | τ echolos en carçel, pues fizolos descabecar τ alli gaño mal
precio. Pues | puso su amiztad con don Garcia Enegez Arista, princep de
Nauarra τ caso con | su fija doña Sancha τ despues priso Nagera τ Uicaria,

este no*n*bre ouo por ⎸ q*ue* alli iugaro*n* los godos, pues al tornado asu regno enfermo en Ca-⎸mora τ fino τ fue enterrado en Leon ala ygle*s*ia cathedral.

Froyla[i321]

⎸ Muerto el rey do*n* Ordoño, regno su he*r*mano do*n* Froyla en la era de ⎸ ccccxxxij. τ regno un año τ dos meses τ casara co*n* doña Moni-⎸na τ ouo en ella tres fijos: do*n* Alfonso τ do*n* Ordoño τ do*n* Remiro τ otro ⎸ de su amiga, do*n* Aznar. Este rey ot*r*o bie*n* no*n* fizo, si no*n* q*ue* mato los fijos ⎸ de un noble uaro*n* suyo do*n* Alismu*n*do τ a tuerto τ sin culpa. Ot*r*osi ech*o* ⎸ de t*ie*rra asu he*r*mano do*n* Fronino, obispo de Leon. τ por estos buenos o-⎸bras[ii] diol Dios enfermedad τ lepra τ iagio[322] un año τ dos meses. τ ⎸ fino τ fue enterrado cerca su he*r*mano do*n* Ordoño τ el obispo do*n* Froniño ⎸ torno a Leon.

Delos godos alcaldes de Castiella, onde se leuantaron los condes τ los reyes[iii]

⎸ A la sazo*n* los om*n*es nobles de Bardulia, q*ue* agora ⎸ es dicha Castiella, ate*n*die*n* sus co*n*des, q*ue* los matara el rey de Leon ⎸ a tuerto; Muño Ferrand*es*, Almo*n*dar Aluo τ do*n* Diago su fijo, matolos por ⎸ auer la t*ie*rra mas asu ma*n*dar. Pues uiero*n* los **bardulianos** q*ue*, qua*n*do yuan a cort, q*ue* ⎸ fazie*n* delos escarnio τ fazie*n*les tuerto e*n*sus iudiçios τ fazienles ⎸ [fol.37v] despe*n*der lo suyo en cortes τ q*ue* los mataro*n*. Asi sus co*n*des ouiero*n* su ⎸ acuerdo pora si τ los q*ue* auie*n* por uenir, esleyen[323] dos cauall*er*os los mas ⎸ cuerdos, los mas poderosos,[iv] τ fiziero*n* los alcaldes q*ue* lis iudgasen. ⎸ Estos fuero*n* Nuño Rasuera, fijo q*ue* fue de Nuño Blachides τ Falauio[324] ⎸ Caluo. Este Falauio poco estaua en iudicio,[325] porque se ensañaua ayna ⎸ τ usaua mas de armas q*ue* de caua*ll*e*r*ia τ de caça; pe*r*o de su linage saliero*n* ⎸ nobles om*e*s de Castiella. Este Flauio ouo dos fijos, Ferrand Flauio[v] ⎸ τ Uelemu*n*do Flauio; do*n* Ferrand ouo fijo a Flauio Ferrand*es*, do*n* Flauio ouo ⎸ fijo a Nuño Flauio, do*n* Nuño[326] caso co*n* doña Egilona τ ouo ⎸ en ella a Flauio Nuñez, do*n* Flauio ouo a Diago Flauio, do*n* Diago ⎸ caso co*n* la fija de un muy noble om*n*e de Asturias do*n* R*o*d*rig*o, este o-⎸uo fijo a do*n* Ruy Diaz, q*ue* fue dicho Ca*n*peador; el ot*r*o he*r*mano Uere-⎸mu*n*do Flauio ouo fijo a R*o*d*rig*o

---

[i] *DRH*: V.i
[ii] The sarcasm is the initiative of the translator and does not reflect *DRH*.
[iii] This is not a separate *DRH* chapter, see Martin, *Les juges*, and above p. 15.
[iv] *DRH*: 'non de potencioribus', *EG* misses the point by omitting the negative.
[v] The translation of proper names appears unduly influenced by the Latin at this point..

Ueremu*n*doz,³²⁷ τ do*n* R*odrig*o ouo fijo a Fera*n*d | Royz, do*n* Ferrand ouo fijo a do*n* Pedro Ferrand*ez*, mas no*n* el q*ue* dixiero*n* el Castellano.ⁱ

De Muño Rasueraⁱⁱ

| El ot*ro* alcalde, do*n* Muño Rasuera, fue bu-|eno τ piadoso τ derechurero, pe*ro* todos los demas pleytos | traye a co*n*posicio*n* por amor de paz τ era mucho amado [τ] sobeio. | Este ouo un fijo, G*onçal*o Nuñez, de chiq*uí*nez come*n*ço de seer bueno | τ fra*n*co τ ardit τ de bue*n* reçebir τ salio guerrero τ defendedor | delos pobres τ delos pueblos. Su padre do*n* Nuño cr*í*aua los | fijos τ las fijas delos nobles om*es* dela t*ie*rra τ todos ael ca-|taua*n* como por padre τ señor. τ fino Muño Rasuera τ q*ue* por la | bo*n*dat del τ q*ue* por su fijo, fiziero*n* a G*onçal*o Nuñez alc*al*de de toda Castiel-|la. Este caso co*n* doña Semaña,³²⁸ fija de Nuño Ferrand*es* τ ouo en ella | un fijo, Ferrand Gon*çal*ez;³²⁹ si bueno fue el auu*el*o Muño Rasuera, | meior fue el fijo G*onçal*o Nuñez τ el meior delos el nieto Ferrand | Go*n*çales. Murio el padre τ todos acordaro*n* en faz*er* alc*al*de a F*erran Gonçales.*| Este salio ardit τ de bue*n* sentido τ fue de bueña acuçia asi | [fol.38r] | q*ue* sopo sacar Castiella de señorio de Leon τ q*ue* no*n* fuese ala cort; τ | q*ue* por esto, q*ue* por su bo*n*dat τ del padre τ de auuelo, ouieron su a-|cuerdo castellanos q*ue* lo lamasen co*n*de τ **deu**inieron *sus* uasallos | τ besaro*n* lo la mano, dende aca fue Castiella por si τ los reyes **et los concilios** | de Asturias no*n* ouiero*n* q*ue* ueer de Pisuerga aca. Este guerreo mu-|cho co*n* moros τ gano delos, este edifico la ygl*es*ia de Sant Pedro enla | rib*er*a de Ralo*n*ça τ dotola bie*n* τ a tie*n*po fino τ fizose ali enterrar. | Fino el co*n*de Ferrand Go*n*caluez τ fizo³³⁰ su fijo el co*n*de do*n* Garcia Ferrandez τ | fue bueno τ ardit τ fra*n*co τ lidio mucho co*n* moros τ co*n* los reyes | de Asturias q*ue* q*ue*rien destruyr Castiella τ no*n* pudiero*n*, ante la enpa-|raro*n* bie*n*. Esteⁱⁱⁱ poblo muchos castiellos en rib*er*a de Duero τ acreçio | ensu señorio fata el rio de Carreo*n*. Este edifico el monasterio de Sant | Cosma τ Sant Damia*n* enla rib*er*a del rio d'Arla*n*ça enla uilla q*ue* dize*n* | Cueuas **R**uuias,³³¹ τ dio al monest*er*io muchas her*e*dades τ ma*n*do lo la-|mar el ifantadgo por q*ue* si alguna dueña fija de rey o de | linage τ casar no*n* q*uí*siese, [uisquiesse], sacando ende la uida dela mo*n*ges, on-|drada.³³² Fino el co*n*de do*n* Garcia Ferrandes τ fue enter-|rado en Sant Pedro de Cardeña, puesⁱᵛ fizo su fijo do*n* Sancho conde; fue bu-|eno, leal τ piadoso τ sabio. Este gano Peñafiel τ Pa*n*pliga τ Monte-|lio τ Mo*n*te Leon τ Gormaz τ Osma τ

ⁱ The 'judges' section is particularly closely translated, see Martin *Les juges*.
ⁱⁱ *DRH:* V.ii, the approbatory description of Nuño Rasuera is cut short. The rubric in 302 is embedded in the line of text.
ⁱⁱⁱ *EG* shows a detailed interest in various Counts of Castile. See Martin, *Les juges*.
ⁱᵛ *DRH*: V.iii

Santesteua*n*, q*ue* era de moros. Este ⸗ dio los buenos fueros de Sepuluega τ dio fuero alos fijos d'algo ⸗ q*ue* no*n* fuesen en hueste si les algo no*n* diesen. Este ouo un fijo, Garcia ⸗ Sanchez, enuiolo casar a Leon co*n* fija del rey τ fue ali muerto a tra-⸗yçio*n* por cuydar q*ue* como el co*n*de era uieio^i τ no*n* auie mas de aq*ue*l ⸗ fijo, q*ue* tornarie Castiella a señorio de Leon. τ despues caso su fija, ⸗ doña Eluira, co*n* el rey do*n* Sanc*h*o el mayor, Q*ue* era rey de Aragon τ de Nauar-⸗ra τ deste diremos^ii pues en su lugar. Este co*n*de do*n* Sancho finco ⸗ niño qua*n*do murio su padre τ la madre ouo amor co*n* un moro q*ue* ⸗ [fol.38v] ⸗ dizie*n* Almazorre τ puso co*n*el q*ue*l matarie el fijo a yerbas τ q*ue*l darie ⸗ la ti*er*ra; τ una couige*r*a^333 q*ue* lo sopo mesturolo τ ala tarde enuio la mad*r*e ⸗ por do*n* Sanc*h*o τ diol q*ue* beuiese el baso delas yerbas τ fizo el beuer a ⸗ su madre p*r*ime*r*o por fuerca τ murio luego; τ alli parescio lo q*ue* q*ui*-⸗siera fazer. τ en Portugal dize*n* Oña por madre,^iii τ fizo un monaste*r*io τ ⸗ dixol Mioña τ ali enterro asu madre τ dio mucha buena he*r*edad al ⸗ monaste*r*io. Almonzorre cuydo q*ue* era muerto do*n* Sancho τ q*ue* auie la madre ⸗ la ti*er*ra, no*n* fue asi;^iv salio do*n* Sanc*h*o ael τ uençiol τ gano mucho *de* el τ enpa-⸗ro bie*n* su ti*er*ra. A tie*n*po murio do*n* Sanc*h*o su muert τ fue enterrado en On-⸗dra co*n* su madre.

Delos reyes de Asturias^v

⸗ Agora tornemos alos reyes de Asturias. Muerto Froyla, regno ⸗ do*n* Alfonso, fijo del rey do*n* Ordoño, era de **d**ccccxxxiij τ regno v. años ⸗ τ vij. meses contado el un año de meses. Este ouo muger a doña Semaña_τ ouo fijo al yfant*e* do*n* Ordoño q*ue* fue malo τ mataro*n* lo cer-⸗ca de Cordoua. Este rey do*n* Alfonso fue libiano de coraço*n* τ q*ui*so fazer ⸗ **penitencia**^334 delos peccados q*ue* auie por faz*er* τ fizo τ uaco^335 τ lexo el regno, ⸗ entrose mo*n*ge en Sant Fagu*n*d, ^vi sobre la rib*er*a del rio q*ue* dize*n* Ceya τ dio ⸗ el regno asu he*r*mano do*n* Remiro, q*ue* uiniera de Camora. Fue^vii do*n* Remiro ⸗ alcado rey era de **d**ccccxxxix, co*n*tado un año τ regno och*o* años τ dos ⸗ meses. E **a**^336 pocco de tie*n*po do*n* Remiro Q*ue* era sobre moros co*n* ⸗ su hueste, su hermano don Alfon fue repuso τ salio dela mongia τ ⸗ fuese p*a*ra Leon τ come*n*ço de entrar el regno; oyolo el rey do*n* Remiro ⸗ τ salio ala ti*er*ra τ çerco asu he*r*mano en Leon τ acabo de dos años p*r*isolo ⸗ τ echolo en una carcel. Dela ot*r*a p*a*rte do*n* Alfonso τ Remiro τ Ordoño, fijos ⸗ de Froyla el q*ue* suso

---

^i This editorial comment is not from *DRH*.
^ii *DRH*: 'de quo, si Deus dederit, postea prosequemur'.
^iii *DRH*: 'more Hispanico'.
^iv This sentence is the translator's gloss on the aftermath of the anecdote.
^v *DRH*: V.iiii
^vi *DRH*: 'dominos sanctos,' *EG* correctly recognises the alternative toponym for Sahagún.
^vii *DRH*: V.v

dixiemos, co*n* co*n*seio delos asturianos q*ue* se te-|nie*n* por mal trechos q*ue* non fuera*n* lamados al co*n*seio qua*n*do do*n* Alfonso | se entro mo*n*ge τ dio el regno asu he*r*mano, co*n*pescaro*n* de guerrear | contr*a* do*n* Remiro; puñaua*n* por qual guisa se q*u*iere pon*er* en poder de | [fol.39r] | do*n* Alfonso, fijo de Froyla, al rey do*n* Remiro. Fue do*n* Remiro co*n* poder en Astu-|rias τ q*ue*bra*n*tolos τ p*r*iso alos fijos de Froyla τ echolos enla carcel co*n* su | he*r*mano do*n* Alfonso. A pocos dias el rey cego asu he*r*mano τ alos ot*r*os τ fizo | un moneste*r*io de Sant Iulia*n*, cabo Leon τ ali les dio qua*n*to ouiero*n* menest*er*| mient*r*e uisq*u*iero*n*. Murio ali do*n* Alfonso τ fue y enterrado co*n* su muge*r* doña | Semaña;³³⁷ este do*n* Alfonso regno ci*n*co años τ .vj. meses, al sieteⁱ fue cegado, | τ uisco çiego dos años τ vij. meses. Puesⁱⁱ el rey do*n* Remiro entro el | regno de Toledo τ p*r*iso Madrid τ destruyo los m*o*ros τ p*r*iso los q*ue* era*n* y de | la ot*r*a p*ar*te. El co*n*de Ferrand Go*n*caluez enuio dema*n*dar ayuda al rey don | Remiro, q*ue* moros entraua*n* por Castiella τ uino el rey τ aiu*n*taro*n* se las | huestes de Castiella τ de Leon en Osma; τ lidiaro*n* co*n* los moros τ uen-|çiolos τ mataro*n* τ p*r*isiero*n* muchos τ tornaro*n* *christ*ianos co*n* gana*n*cia. Puesⁱⁱⁱ | fuero*n* el rey τ el co*n*de co*n* su poder *contr*a Caragoça; τ Abenaya, q*ue* era rey | dend, ouo miedo τ tornose uasallo del rey Remiro. τ torno amistad **con** Ab-|derame*n*, rey de Cordoua, q*ue* era su señor τ aiudaro*n* le a co*n*q*ue*rir castiel-|los q*ue* era*n* en el regno de Caragoça co*n*tra el τ torno el rey co*n* ondra | por Asturias. τ do*n* Abenaya, rey de Caragoça, mi*n*tio la postura del | rey Remiro τ tornose ad Aberame*n* τ amos uiniero*n* co*n*tra el rey τ | co*n*tr*a* Ferrand Goncaluez τ legaro*n* *fata* Siet Ma*n*cas; oyolo el rey τ el | conde, saliero*n* τ lidiaro*n* co*n* ellos τ ue*n*ciero*n* *christ*ianos τ fue p*r*iso Abenaya. | Los q*ue* escaparo*n* metiero*n* se enel Alfondiga, uino en pos ellos el rey; p*r*iso | Alfondega τ qua*n*tos era*n* y aq*u*a τ ala muriero*n* mas de Lxxx mill moros; | τ asi torno³³⁸ co*n* gana*n*cia τ el co*n*de Ferrand Go*n*zalez co*n* su traydor Abenaya τ **con** gra*n*d | gana*n*cia τ uictoria; Aderame*n* escapo co*n* pocos, fuyo a Cordoua. Esto*n*z fue | eclipsi del sol q*ue* aturo una hora del dia. Esto*n*zⁱᵛ un p*r*incep delos moros A-|ceypha, co*n* gra*n* poder τ do*n* Diago Nuñez τ Ferrand Go*n*zalez, mas no*n* el co*n*de,ᵛ con | poder de *christ*ianos τ entro por la t*ie*rra τ come*n*ço de poblar Salama*n*ca τ Le-|desma τ Ribas τ Baños τ Alfondega τ Peña τ ot*r*os castiellos. Esto*n*z | [fol.39v] | poblo el co*n*de do*n* R[odrigo] Amaya τ fizo gra*n*d daño en Asturias enlas p*ar*ti-|das de S*an*ta

---

ⁱ *DRH*: 'in Vᵒ anno', *EG* has 'siete' in all three manuscripts.
ⁱⁱ *DRH*: V.vi
ⁱⁱⁱ *DRH*: V.vii
ⁱᵛ *DRH*: V.viii
ᵛ *DRH* subsequently comments 'non illum comitem Castelle', and *EG* follows this, although factually incorrect, in a attempt to absolve Fernán González of collaborating with the infidel.

Illana; salio aellos el rey do*n* Remiro τ ue*n*ciolos τ p*r*iso a Fer-|ra*n*d Go*nz*alez τ a Diago Munez, enuiolos a Leon τ echolos en carcel; pues | co*n*seio³³⁹ se a tie*n*po τ por q*ue* era*n* om*n*es nobles, sacolos dela p*r*isio*n* τ fizie-|ro*n* le omenage τ fuero*n* sus uasallos. Esto*n*z caso su fijo del rey don | Remiro co*n* doña Vitarica, fija del co*n*de Ferrand Go*nz*alez de Castiella. Este | rey do*n* Remiro caso la segunda uegada co*n* doña Teresa, sobre no*n*bre Flore*n*-|tina, fija q*ue* fue del rey do*n* Garcia el Te*n*bloso q*ue* fue de Nauarra τ ouo en ella | el yfant do*n* Sa*n*cho τ doña Eluira; τ fizo un monaste*r*io en Leon cerca del pala-|tio del rey τ dixiero*n* lo Sant Saluador τ ali ofrecio su fijo a Dios el xix | año q*ue* regnaua. Pues cerco Talaue*r*a, q*ue* p*r*ime*r*o fue dicha Auis, enla p*ro*uen-|çia de Toledo τ uiniero*n* moros en acorro τ ue*n*ciolos τ mato bie*n* doze | mill τ p*r*iso mas vij. mill τ torno asu tie*r*ra. Pe*r*o por co*n*seio de su muge*r* | doña Teresa, fizo un monaste*r*io de Santa Ma*r*ia en ribe*r*a de Duero τ fizo ot*r*o | de Sant Andres τ de Sant X*r*is*t*oual sobre Ceya τ fizo ot*r*o de Sant Migu*e*l en | Ual de Orna, q*ue* es agora dicha Distriana τ diol muchas buenas he*r*e-|dades. τ uino en romeria a Ouiedo τ enfermo ali τ aduxiero*n* lo a | Leon τ ali fizo su co*n*fesion e[n]la uig*i*lia de Epi*p*ha*n*ia τ ante los obispos τ | los abades τ dizie*n*do: "Desnudo sal del uie*n*tre de mi madre, desnu-|do tornare alla; Dios es mi aiudador,[i] no*n* temo q*ue* me faga mal o*m*e. | Señor, en tus manos comie*n*do mi alma". Saliol el sp*i*ri*t*u del cuerpo, | enterrado enel moneste*r*io de Sant Saluador, el q*ue* fiziera pa*r*a so fija. | Muerto[ii] el rey do*n* Remiro, regno su fijo do*n* Ordoño, azac cuerdo. | Esto*n*z so he*r*mano do*n* Sa*n*cho de padre, co*n* co*n*seio desu auu*e*lo, rey de Nau-|arra τ por co*n*seio del co*n*de Ferrand Go*nz*alez de Castiella, entrose por Leon | por echar del regno al rey do*n* Ordoño, su he*r*mano. El rey, en q*ue* lo | sopo, guarescio sus fortalezas de armas τ de co*n*ducho τ defe*n*-|dio bie*n* su regno τ por esta saña desecho la muge*r*, fija q*ue* era del co*n*-|[fol.40r] | de Ferra*n* Go*nz*alez τ caso co*n* doña Eluira τ ouo en ella un fijo, do*n* Ueremu-|do, q*ue* fue potarico. Los gallegos, q*ue* sopiero*n* la discordia de leoneses τ de | castellanos τ alcaro*n* se ot*r*osi; el rey do*n* Ordoño fue sobrellos τ lego fata | Uilixbona τ q*ue*mo τ p*r*iso τ mato τ ue*n*cio τ castigo τ domo τ tornos co*n* | hondra. τ enta*n*to adobaro*n* el rey τ Ferrand Go*nz*alez. Esto*n*z uiniero*n* poder de mo-|ros τ entraro*n* Castiella fasta Sant Esteua*n*, ribe*r*a de Duero. τ el co*n*de Fer-|ra*n*d Go*nz*alez, co*n* poder de Castiella τ s[a]lio³⁴⁰ τ q*ue*bra*n*to los τ ue*n*ciolos τ gano | muchos dellos. Enta*n*to el rey, q*ue* ma*n*dara hueste sobre moros, adoles-|cio mal τ fino en Çamora τ fue enterrado en Sant Saluador de Leon | co*n* su padre.[iii]

---

[i] The allusions to the Psalms and the Book of Job are maintained by the translator.
[ii] *DRH*: V.viiii
[iii] *DRH*: 'quod pater suus condiderat'.

Muerto[i] el rey do*n* Ordoño, regno su he*r*mano do*n* Sancho, nieto ¡ del rey do*n*
Garcia de Nauarra, era de ccccLxxij. τ regno xij. años. Pues ¡ sus ricos omes
q*u*isiero*n* lo matar τ fuxo asu auu*g*lo a Nauarra.[ii] Dela otra ¡ p*ar*te, el co*n*de
Ferrand Go*n*ç*a*lez τ los leoneses alcaro*n* rey a do*n* Ordoño el Malo, ¡ q*ue* fue
fijo de do*n* Alfonso, el q*ue* entro mo*n*ge τ despues fue cegado τ reg-¡no τ diol
por mug*er* a doña Uitana, la q*ue* fue mug*er* del rey don ¡ Ordoño. En Castiella
auie un niño[iii] muy noble, do*n* Uella τ no*n* q*u*erie ¡ obedescer al co*n*de;
Ferrand Go*n*ç*a*lez co*n* el poder echo lo de t*ie*rra τ fuese a mo-¡ros, [a]
Abderame, rey de Cordoua. El rey do*n* Sancho, q*ue* era echado de Leon, fizi-
¡erase muy grueso τ por co*n*seio del rey do*n* Garcia de Nauarra su auuelo,
fue ¡ p*ar*a Cordoua τ dema*n*do co*n*seio [a] Abderame de aq*ue*la grosura; τ diol
a toma*r*[341] ¡ una yerba τ ma*n*dol q*ue* se trauase τ torno qual q*u*iso. Esto*n*z co*n*
poder ¡ de moros τ co*n* do*n* Uella, q*ue* echara F*er*ra*n* Go*n*ç*a*lez de t*ie*rra, dela
ot*ra* p*ar*te co*n* poder ¡ de nauarros, co*n*bro el regno de Leon τ de Galliçia; τ
daño sus en-¡emigos τ al co*n*de F*er*ra*n* Go*n*ç*a*lez; τ do*n* Ordoño Malo fuyo
por enpararse en ¡ las Asturias. El co*n*de toliol la fija τ diola a ot*r*o do*n*
Ordoño τ fuyo se ¡ a moros τ murio ala como astroso[iv] *d*el regno qua*n*do
caso doña Tere-¡sa τ ouo un fijo do*n* Ramiro. Esto*n*z, por ruego de su mug*er*
τ dela he*r*ma-¡na doña Eluira la monina, enuio firmar paz **por** ensus dias co*n*
Ab-¡[fol.40v] ¡ derame, q*ue*l enuiase el *cuerpo*[342] de Sant Pelagio τ enuio por el al
obispo do*n* Blasco de ¡ Leon τ ot*r*os me*n*sag*er*os τ fizo g*u*isar o pusiesen el
cuerpo τ qua*n*do lo aduxiesen. En ta*n*-¡to cayo discordia τ come*n*çaro*n* de
guerrear entresi los gallegos τ el rey fue ¡ p*ar*a ala τ **domo**[343] los malos.
Esto*n*z p*ar*tio Gallizia,[344] τ do*n* Garcia q*ue* era p*r*incep de de*n*-¡de[345] Duero
uino co*n* su hueste fata rib*er*a del rio τ pe*n*so muert de su señor; ¡ diol una
ma*n*çana τ empozonada; τ uido luego el rey q*ue* era de muert τ tor-¡nose a
Leon τ fino acabo de q*u*atro dias;[346] τ fue enterrado enel monest*er*io de ¡ Sant
Saluador cabo su padre τ su he*r*mano.[v] Murio[vi] el rey do*n* Sancho τ regno ¡ su
fijo do*n* Remiro τ era de hedad de v años, era de dccccLxxv τ regno **xxv.** ¡
años. Este, por co*n*seio de su madre doña Teresa τ de doña Eluira su tia ¡ la
monina, firmo paz τ treguas por q*ue*l diesen el cuerpo de Sant Pelayo, ¡ como
lo dema*n*dara el padre τ diero*n* gelo τ pusolo enel monest*er*io q*ue* fizo ¡ su
padre. El ij°. año q*ue* regnaua, los normados co*n* su rey Gu*n*diredo riba-¡ro*n*
en Gallizia τ destruyendo lo q*ue* falaua*n* legaro*n* fasta un lugar q*ue* es dich*o* ¡

---

[i] *DRH*: V.x
[ii] The deatils of Sancho's obesity and treatment for it are included below by *EG*.
[iii] *DRH*: 'nobilis adolescens'.
[iv] This detail does not appear in *DRH* or *EE*.
[v] *DRH*: 'iuxta patrem in sancti Saluatoris'.
[vi] *DRH*: V.xi

Onagro τ mataron a don Sisenando, obispo de Santiague. Al tercer año,
quando qui-|sieron tornar asu tierra con ganancia, el conde Gonzalo Sanchez
firio en ellos en | nonbre de Santiague; τ uenciolos τ desbaratolos τ mato al
rey τ toda su con-|paña τ quemo todas sus naues. Entanto[i] los moros eran
seguros dela | tregua del rey Remiro τ entraron se por Castiella τ nolos pudo
enparar **el conde Fferand Gonçaluez** | τ perdio Sietmancas τ Dueñas τ
Sepuluega τ Gormas τ muchas uillas | τ muchos castiellos; τ eran con los
moros don Uella, el que echara de tierra | Ferrand Gonzalez τ los moros con
aquesta soberuia quebrantaron las treguas que pusi-|eran con el rey Remiro τ
degastaron a Camora. Ferrand Gonzalez uio tanto daño de | lo que ganara
murio de cordoio,[ii] τ fue enterrado enel monesterio que el fizo | de Sant
Pedro. El rey don Remiro caso con doña Urraca; pues, como era ni-|ño de
dias τ de seso, non precio el conseio de la madre ni dela tia τ comenco | de
mal traher los principes de Galliçia. Los gallegos non gelo pudieron sofrir | τ
fizieron rey asu parte a don Ueremundo, fijo del rey don Ordoño, en la | [fol.41r]
| yglesia de Santiague. Oyolo don Remiro τ fue contra el τ lidiaron dos dias en
Porti-|lo de Areyas; τ murieron sin guisa τ non uencio ninguno τ asi partieron
se. τ pues | fino el rey don Remiro en Leon τ fue enterrado en[347] Distriana.
Entretanto Al-|morexi, rey delos moros, destruyo **de** parte de Gallizia fasta
Santiague; τ | Dios, a ondra del apostol, dioles enfermedad asi que sin armas
murieron | todos τ marauila si escapo quien dixiese el mensaie. Murio[iii] don
Remiro, | regno don Ueremundo τ los leoneses recibieron los de grado por
que murio | el rey don Sancho su tio τ don Remiro su sobrino, ael pertenesçie
el regno. Començo | de regnar era mil τ regno xvij. años. Este fizo las lees
delos godos | τ delos santos padres bien guardar τ maguer en otra manera
fuese bue-|no, de grado oyo lezongeros τ mestureros; τ acasçio que tres
criados de | la yglesia de Santiague, Çadon τ Cadon τ Ansilon, pensaron muert
asu señor | Atualpho, arcobispo de Santiague τ dixieron al rey quel arcobispo
auie | puesto de recebir la ley de Mahomat τ de predicarla τ de dar la tierra | a
moros. El rey crouolo[348] por que era fijo del que diera la mançana enpoz-
|nada al rey don Sancho τ ouo su conseio τ enuio por el **que uinjesse a fabla**
con poca conpaña. Uino | el arcobispo ante de Pasqua τ dixo que ante uerie al
rey celestial que al | terrenar τ dixo su missa.[349] Entanto el toro, que era
aducho brauo para ras-|trar el arcobispo, uino se para la yglesia τ puso los
cuernos en las manos | del arcobispo τ lexo los y τ fuyo se al mont. El
arcobispo fizo gracias a Dios | τ maldixo aquelos quelo mesturaran, que non
falescies en su natura lisiado **ni** |**mesielo**,[350] τ asi fue. El rey, en que uido este

---

[i] *DRH*: V.xii
[ii] This detail is not from *DRH*.
[iii] *DRH*: V.xiii

miraglo, pidio merçed al arcobis-|po q*ue*l pe*r*donase; τ el pe*r*donolo mas no*n*
lo q*u*iso ueer; τ salio ende τ uino | se al segu*n*do dia pus de Pasqua ala ygle*s*ia
de Santa Eulalia τ fino ali a pocos | dias; τ nolo pudiero*n* aduçir al cuerpo ala
ygle*s*ia de Sa*n*tiague τ ente-|raro*n* lo y en Santa Eulalia. El[i] rey [don
Ueremudo][351] ouiera dos nobles amigas, | τ amas he*r*manas, q*ue* era om*n*e sin
Dios; τ ouo enla una al yfant do*n* | Ordoño τ dela ot*ra* la yfañt doña Eluira.
Este ifant do*n* Ordoño ouo a tie*n*po |[fol.41v]| enla ifant doña Fromilda fijos
do*n* Alde*fon*s*o*, Pelayo, do*n* Sancho, doña Semaña. Este | rey do*n* Remiro ouo
dos mug*er*es de Leon: doña Blasq*u*ita τ, ella uisq*u*iendo, | caso co*n* doña
Eluira τ ouo fijos de amos; de doña Eluira ouo do*n* Al-|fonso τ doña Teresa,
de doña Belasq*u*ita ouo ifant doñ*a* Xp*ris*t*i*na. Esta doña | Xp*ris*t*i*na caso co*n*
do*n* Ordoño el Çiego, fijo del rey Remiro, e ouo en ella do*n* | Alfonso τ do*n*
Pelayo τ la co*n*desa doña Aldue*n*za. Esa doña Alduenca caso co*n* | do*n*
Pelayo, fijo de do*n* Fruela el Diachono τ ouo en ella al co*n*de do*n* Pelayo | τ
do*n* Ordoño τ do*n* Pedro τ a do*n* Nuño τ ala madre del co*n*de do*n* Suero τ su
her-|mano τ la co*n*desa doña Teresa; τ por q*ue* la madre fue señora de Cario*n*
| fizo y la ygle*s*ia de Sant Zoyl, aca dice*n* en Toledo de Sant Soles, [ii] pe*ro* asi
de*n*de | fuero*n* dichos ifantes de Cario*n*.

De batallas de Almonzorre[iii]

| Esto*n*z Agip,[352] rey delos Arabes, ma*n*dose lamar Alma*n*çor τ q*u*iere | ta*n*to
dezir como defendedor,[iv] por q*ue* uençiera otras uezes *chris*t*i*anos, | τ esto por
peccado del rey Ueremu*n*do. Esto*n*z do*n* Uela, el q*ue* dixiemos, co*n* | ot*ro*s
*chris*t*i*anos τ **unio ael τ dixol quel darie toda la tierra de xristianos τ
mouio su hueste con**[v] su fijo Abdemalit τ come*n*co de degastar τ des-|truyr
Castiella τ Leon τ Nauarra; τ aiudauale much*o* a cofonder q*ue* los | ricos omes
del regno estaua*n* mal entresi τ mal co*n* el rey. Almacorre | **acogie**[353] bie*n*
alos *chris*t*i*anos τ fazieles algo τ pro τ asi aiudaua*n*le τ ga-|naua*n* co*n* ellos; asi
q*ue* uino ala ribe*ra* de Duero q*ue* era moio*n* entre *chris*t*i*anos | τ moros τ finco
y sus tie*n*das τ uino cont*ra* el co*n* su poder el rey Ue-|remu*n*do;[354] τ dio salto
en la alugada[355] de Almacorre τ mato y mucho no-|ble om*n*e de arabes. El
rey Almazorre de duello tolio los paños τ | fizo su duelo por la muert de sus
uasallos τ los suyos co*n*braro*n* | coraço*n* por este duelo τ tornaro*n* τ leuaro*n*

---

[i] *DRH*: V.xiiii
[ii] This comment is not from *DRH*, and may therefore indicate local knowledge on the part of the
translator.
[iii] See p. 15 above.
[iv] The etymology of the name 'Almanzor' and lengthy details of his life suppressed by a translator
interested only in Christian Spain.
[v] This detail appears only in BN Res/278.

uencido al rey Ueremundo ₁ fata los puertos de Leon τ destruyeron quanto falaron. Enbargolos la ₁ ybernada τ maguerra con daño, tornaron con uencida τ con hondra asu ₁ tierra. Los christianos ouieron miedo que tornarien los moros al otro año, prisi-₁eron los cuerpos santos τ delos reyes que eran por toda Leon τ leuaron ₁ [fol.42r] ₁ los [a] Asturias, a Ouiedo τ soterraron los enla yglesia de Santa Maria; unos de Leon ₁ leuauan el cuerpo de Sant Froylano, obispo τ soterraron lo³⁵⁶ en Sant Iohan ₁ Apostol, en un ual que dizen de Casar. El[i] otro año uino Almoncor con su hu-₁este, entro enla tierra del rey Ueremundo, fuese a Ouiedo, non oso atender; ₁ Almançor çerco Leon τ priso la a tiempo τ destruyola toda a suelo si non una tor-₁re que fizo por remenbrança alos que auien de uenir; τ pus refizolo todo de nue-₁uo τ puso enlas puertas mucho buen marmor τ las torres τ los mu-₁ros de piedra picada. τ despues priso Astorga τ quebranto los somizos **de**³⁵⁷ las ₁ torres τ priso Cayanca, que agora dizen Ualencia τ Sant Fagund τ destruyo otros ₁ muchos castiellos; τ asi por peccado delos christianos[ii] renouose la del rey ₁ Rodrigo, la tierra destruyda τ dela presa τ las reliquias leuadas, las yglesias deson-₁dradas τ con todo esto uencio toda uia Almancor. Al[iii] xiij. año entro Alman-₁cor por Portugal, destruyendo quanto falaua τ propuso de quebrantar la yglesia ₁ de Santiague el Apostol; τ quando fue ali o estaua el cuerpo fizo grandes tru-₁enos τ re[lam]pagos en dia claro τ ouo miedo τ fuxo dende, pero leuanto las ₁ campanas τ señal τ leuolas a Cordoua τ pusolas enla mesquita por lampa-₁das τ ali souieron muy gran tiempo.[iv] En tanto plogo a Nuestro Señor τ cayo en-₁fermedad enlos moros τ murieron muchos dellos por muerte sobitan-₁na; pus uido Almancor que enfermauan las gentes τ quelas perdie, començo de ₁ salir dela tierra. Quando lo oyo el rey Ueremudo, enuio ala grand poder de pe-₁ones τ como los falauan flacos τ enfermos fizieron en ellos grand da-₁ño; τ asi maltrechos fue echado Almancor de toda la tierra. El rey don Uere-₁mudo, pus se uido tan grand cueyta, enuio sus mensaieros al rey don Garcia el ₁ Tenbloso, al conde Garcia Ferrandez, rogol[es][v] quel perdonasen si erarra contra ellos τ por Dios τ ₁ por la fe enparar quel uiniesen aiudar τ asi lo fizieron. Mouieron sus po-₁deres τ otrosi aquel rey Ueremudo, maguera auie enlos pies podraga, le-₁uantolo en andas τ todos en uno aiunntaron se en un lugar que dizen Ca-₁latonacor τ salioles ala carrera τ Almancor, que andaua por la tierra como ₁ [fol.42v] ₁ de yda τ lidiaron con el todo un dia τ non se pudieron uençer; partiolos la noche. ₁ Almancor uio daño de

---

[i] *DRH*: V.xv
[ii] The editorial comment of Ximénez de Rada is kept to a minimum in the translation.
[iii] *DRH*: V.xvi
[iv] *DRH*: 'que longo tempore ibi fuerunt'.
[v] The Vermudo of *EG* is rather more penitent than that of *DRH*. Compare V.xvi.17 ff.

su compaña, delos muertos τ delos feridos τ delos | enfermos τ non oso
atender τ fuxo de noche; τ quando fue en un ual que dizen Bo-|riecorixi³⁵⁸
uido se mal trecho τ con grand dolor murio alli τ leuaron lo a Medi-|na
Çelim. Aca los christianos, quando cuydaron lidiar, non ouieron con quien; τ
falaron las | tiendas paradas τ bazias τ robaron el campo; pero el conde Garcia
Ferrandez fue enpos elos | τ mato τ priso quantos el pudo conseguir. Luego,ⁱ
al otro año, leuantose Abdema-|lic, fijo de Almancor τ por uengar asu padre
mouio su hueste τ entro por | la tierra τ uino a Leon; cercola τ prisola τ
destruyo los muros τ quanto su padre y³⁵⁹ | fiziera todo a suelo. Oyolo el
conde don Garcia τ saliol ala carrera o andaua τ li-|dio conel τ uenciolo τ
echolo de tierra τ loado a Dios, despues aca fizo la tierra | toda en paz.
Estonz el rey Uermudo τ el rey don Garcia de Nauarra τ el conde Garcia
Ferrandez | ouieron su acuerdo τ cada uno delos tornaron asus ricos omes τ
asus | caualleros τ las heredades τ lo que les tenie forçado, por que non ouiesen
razon | de se pasar a moros. Estonz el rey Ueremudo, por conseieros malos,
o-|uo de prender³⁶⁰ a don Gudesteno, obispo de Ouiedo; τ unos monges, ya
que uieron | en sueño, fueronse para el rey τ monestaron le que dexase aquel
obispo si-|no que grand daño uinie ala tierra, el nolo crouo.ⁱⁱ Estonz cayo
grand sequedat en | la tierra, que nin louie, nin arauan, nin senbrauan, pues el
rey a tiempo solto a-|quel obispo τ luego al dia luuio mucho τ crescieron los
frutos que algunos | auenturaron se a senbrar; τ el rey iuro mandamiento de
yglesia τ mandaron le | que refiziese la yglesia de Santiague τ las otras yglesias
que moros destruyeron τ a-|si lo fizo. τ pus a pocos dias enfermo τ murio en
una uilla que dizen Bo-|rizo τ asi fue soterrado. Pues su fijo don Alfonso, que
fuera rey, lo saco dend, | τ leuolo a Leon τ lo enterro con su muger doña
Eluira. Muertoⁱⁱⁱ el rey don | Ueremudo, era de mill τ xvij, fue alçado rey su
fijo don Alfonso, era de v. | años; este regno xxvij. años. Su madre ouo
nonbre doña Eluira τ fue | dado a criar al conde don Melendo Gonçaluez de
Gallizia τ ala condesa doña |[fol.43r] | Mayor, su muger. Crescio este rey don
Alfonso τ despues caso con doña Eluira, | fija deste conde quelo crio τ ouo
desta muger fijo τ fija, don Ueremudo τ doña Sancha. | Esta doña Sancha caso
despues con el rey don Ferrando de Castiella, fijo del rey don | Sancho de
Nauarra τ doña Eluira, fija del conde don Sancho. Este rey don Alfonso, de
mientre e-|ra moco de poco sentido, dio una hermana que auie, doña Teresa,
por muger a don | Abdalla, rey de Cordoua, en tal conuenencia quelo ayudase
de guerra contra el rey | de Cordoua. Este pleyto nunqua plogo a ella, nin
consentir lo que quiso, ante le dixo | asi: "Cata que yo christiana so τ curiate³⁶¹

ⁱ DRH: V.xvii
ⁱⁱ EG narration is more immediate. See above pp. 23–25.
ⁱⁱⁱ DRH: V.xviii

q*ue* Dios en q*ue* yo creo, matarte a por esto". El | no*n* dio nada por ello τ por fuerca yogo co*n* ella τ luego fue ferido de muert | del angel p*re*cucie*nt* τ ma*n*dola p*re*nder τ leuar asu t*ie*rra co*n* mucho oro τ co*n* mucha | plata; τ lego a Leon τ pus p*ri*so abito de mo*n*ge τ fizo su uida enel monest*e*rio | de Sant Pelayo τ ali fino. Esto*n*z naçio discordia entrel co*n*de Garcia Ferrandez | τ su fijo, el co*n*de do*n* S*an*ch*o* τ asi q*ue* amos en sus guerras[i] despoblaro*n* Auilla τ ot*ro*s **muchos castillos** τ | muchos logares τ Sant Estaua*n* ot*ro*si. El conde Garcia Ferrande*z*, como era de gra*n*d co-|raço*n*, maguerra auie co*n* su fijo guerra ouo fazie*n*da co*n* moros τ fue y preso | τ lagado muy mal τ murio a pocos dias τ despues redimiero*n* el cuerpo; | troxiero*n* lo a Sant Pedro de Cardeña. Muerto[ii] el co*n*de do*n* Ferrand, **finco**[362] co*n*dado a su | fijo do*n* S*an*ch*o* τ salio muy bueno τ dio muy buenos fueros τ tolio los ma-|los q*ue* falo; τ firmo su amor co*n* el rey de Leon τ[iii] co*n* el de Nauarra como fi-|ziera su padre τ co*n* ayuda delos mouio sus huestes τ paso por Toledo, | q*ue*ma*n*do τ destruyendo τ por Cordoua ot*ro*si. Pues diero*n* le gra*n*d auer τ | fincaro*n* q*ue*bra*n*tados τ asi ue*n*go asu padre. Aca el rey do*n* Alfonso fizo co*n*cilio | τ poblo Leon ot*ra* uez, la q*ue* Alma*n*cor τ su fijo destruyero*n* como de suso es co*n*-|tado; **con**firmo las lees goticas τ anadio ot*ra*s q*ue* usa oy en Leon τ lego los hu-|esos[363] delos reyes q*ue* era*n* deramados por las t*ie*rras τ aduxolos ala y-|gle*s*ia de Sant Iuh*an*. Ot*ro*si recibio a co*n*seio τ a ruego **del cuende don Sancho a** los fijos de do*n* Uela, q*ue* | era*n* co*n* los moros τ fezie*n* τ podrie*n* faze*r* gra*n*d daño τ p*er*donolos τ dioles | su h*er*edad τ gra*n*d señorio ala enlas mo*n*tanas τ cabo las mo*n*tanas. Pues | [fol.43v] | esto el rey do*n* Alfonso ce*r*co a Uiseo τ anda*n*do aderedor la uilla mira*n*do andaua | se desarmado, fue ferido[364] de saeta por las espaldas, sintio el | golpe τ fizo su penete*n*cia τ comulgo τ murio; desterraro*n* la uilla τ a-|duxiero*n* lo a Leon τ enterraro*n* lo co*n* su padre. Muerto[iv] el rey do*n* Alfonso, | regno su fijo do*n* Ueremudo, era de mill xLiij. τ regno q*ua*tro años. E co-|me*n*ço lo del padre, refaze*r* las ygle*s*ias, dar buenos **fueros** τ ma*n*tener los pue-|blos τ los poderes.[365] Este caso co*n* doña Teresa, fija del co*n*de do*n* S*an*ch*o*. Ot*ro*si, | este do*n* S*an*ch*o* ouo una fija, unos le dizie*n* doña Mayor, ot*ro*s do*n*a Eluira, como | q*u*ier q*ue*l diga*n* esta caso co*n* el rey do*n* S*an*ch*o* de Nauarra, q*ue* dizie*n* el Mayor; τ ouo | desta muge*r* al rey do*n* Garcia **et el rey don Ferrando**.[366] Po*r*[v] q*ue* linage delos reyes de Leon τ delos | co*n*des de Castiella no*n* auie*n*do fijos, torno en

---

[i] *DRH* mention of 'sarraceni' cut.
[ii] *DRH*: V.xviiii
[iii] Compare V.xviiii.5 ff. *EG* presents an abbreviated version of what are essentially the same details.
[iv] *DRH*: V.xx, *EG* search for a language presents a rather different rhetoric to that of *DRH*.
[v] *DRH*: V.xxi, *EG* chapter structure is more logical in this instance. *EG* also shows considerable interest in the fate of the other Christian kingdoms of the Peninsula.

las fijas **del tiempo** del rey do*n* Uere-|mudo τ del co*n*de do*n* Sanc*h*o; aca
ueamos como desce*n*diero*n* de Nauarra τ como | casaro*n* τ q*ue* ouiero*n* de
alla.

Delos reyes de Nauarra

| Demie*n*tre Leon τ Castiella τ Nauarra andaua*n* maltrechos de moros, |
leua*n*tose uno q*ue* dizie*n* Enego,[i] τ por q*ue* era agudo, aspe*ro* τ guerrero, di-
|xol uno: "Por buena fe, ni*n* el atista no*n* acie*n*de mas el fuego q*ue* este faz*er*|
la guerra". Dixo el otro: "Arista p*ar*a el fuego, Enego p*ar*a los moros".[ii] Asi
flabi*n*-|do³⁶⁷ crescio *esta* famadia τ pues dizie*n* le Enego Arista τ moraua en |
las mo*n*tanas de Nauarra τ de Aragon τ pues desce*n*dio al plano de | Nauarra
τ alli fizo muchas batallas co*n* moros τ ue*n*cio muchas | uezes; τ ali lo alcaro*n*
por rey, ca era bueno τ aue*n*turado τ amado | de todos. Este ouo fijo a do*n*
Garcia Eneges τ diol mug*er* de natu*r*a de reyes. | Muerto[iii] Enego Arista,
regno su fijo do*n* Garcia τ salio muy bueno τ fazie | granados males a moros.
Por aue*n*tura, un dia q*ue* seye en un bur-|go q*ue* dizie*n* Lapu*n*be τ la reyna
doña Uraca su mug*er* co*n* el, legaro*n* | moros adesora esco*n*didos, co*n*batiero*n*
al³⁶⁸ burgo τ mataro*n* al rey τ diero*n* | ala reyna una la*n*çada enel costado; pues
acorieron las ge*n*tes τ fu-|xiero*n* los moros. La reyna era p*re*nada τ uisco
poco, pe*ro* pario ante | [fol.44r] | τ salio el fijo segu*n*d esto*n*z fue dicho τ uisto τ
oydo τ asi es oy la | famadia, naçio por la la*n*çada; τ aun pus a dias fino la
madre, q*ue* lo iuro τ | lo testimonio τ lo dio p*ro*uado. Este ouo no*n*bre
Sancho Garcia. La reyna finada, | un noble om*n*e delas mo*n*tanas, q*ue* fuera
c*r*iado de do*n* Enego Arista, p*r*iso | al niño τ c*r*iolo bie*n* como deuie τ
demostrol buenas man*er*as fasta q*ue*l | fizo co*n*brar el regno; τ diol mug*er*
doña Theuda de natura de reyes, | τ ouo desta mug*er* un fijo q*ue*l dixiero*n* do*n*
Garcia el Tebloson;³⁶⁹ ouo ot*ro*si iiij. | fijas: doña Semana, doña M*ar*ia, doña
Teresa, doña Blasqu*i*ta, esta caso co*n* | do*n* Nuño, co*n*de de Biscaya. Este rey
do*n* Sanc*h*o aforçaua mucho alos moros, | gano mucho delos elos corrie*n* fata
Mo*n*t d'Oca τ a Pa*n*plona. τ el rey, | lo uno por q*ue* a uegadas asaltaua*n* por las
mo*n*tanas τ q*ue* no*n* auie*n* to-|dos bestias, fizo faz*er* auarcas como los ot*ro*s τ
andaua*n* por los fue-|rtes logares todos a pie; τ dende le dixiero*n* el rey do*n*
Sanc*h*o Auarca. τ | auie ot*r*a manera, q*ue* si caual*er*o o escud*ero* o om*n*e tal ueye
ca*n*sado[iv] daual su | cauallo τ el andaua a pie. Este gano fasta Mo*n*t d'Oca τ
fasta Didela τ fata la Hues-|ta*n* τ la mo*n*tana de Aragon; τ fizo algunos

---

[i] *DRH*: 'ex Bigorrie', compare Eugui, *Crónica*, p. 380.
[ii] This detail in direct speech is not *DRH*, although such immediacy is typical elsewhere of *EG*.
[iii] *DRH*: V.xxii
[iv] These details correspond only loosely to the more extensive description provided by *DRH*.

castiellos enlos **oteros**³⁷⁰ q*ue* hoy | dia dize*n* S*anch*o Auarca.ⁱ Pues los moros ouiero*n* co*n* el fazie*n*da τ ue*n*cio los | muy mal, asi³⁷¹ q*ue* apenas escapo q*ui* lo co*n*tase dellos. Este regno xxv | años, murio este rey era de dccccxLiij. años. Muertoⁱⁱ el rey do*n* S*anch*o, | regno su fijo el rey do*n* Garcia, q*ue* pues le dixiero*n* el Te*n*bloson por esto que | qua*n*do oye nueuas de p*ar*te de moros luego tremie; p*er*o era bue*n* uarraga*n* | τ mucho esforçado τ el q*ui* ant*e* cometie o ferie ala fazie*n*da el era mas | uezes. Este ot*r*osi siguio la man*er*a del padre de andar **en**³⁷² la guerra si q*ui*er a | pie si q*ui*er a cauallo τ ot*r*osi dixiero*n* le Garcia Auarca. Regno xxv años τ mu-|rio era de dcccclxviij. Ot*r*osiⁱⁱⁱ **este muerto, regno su fijo don Sancho que pues fue dicho el Mayor,**³⁷³ [caso con Eluira], fija [que] fue del *con*de do*n* S*anch*o de Castiella τ ouo en ella dos fijos, do*n* Garcia τ do*n* Fernando. Do*n* | Garcia fue fijo mayor τ iurado por seer pus su padreⁱᵛ τ asi lo fue; este ouo| [fol.44v] | dos do*n* S*anch*o τ do*n* S*anch*o el mayor auie de regnar en pus su padre τ fino en Pe-|nale*n*, el ot*r*o fijo do*n* S*anch*o mataro*n* lo en Rueda a traycio*n*, p*er*o este ouo un fijo | do*n* Remiro q*ue* pus a tie*n*po como diremos adela*n*t caso co*n* fija de Mio Çit | Ruy Diasᵛ qua*n*do era poderoso en Uale*n*çia; τ ouo en ella un fijo Garcia Remirez | q*ue* despues fue rey de Nauarra, asi q*ue* por ue*n*tura salio del regno del po-|der de Aragon, q*ue* era ya como enagenado como diremos de iuso,ᵛⁱ p*er*o con-|bro lo su**yo**. Muert el rey do*n* Pedro de Aragon sin fijos τ ot*r*osi su h*er*mano el rey | do*n* Alfonso q*ue* fino en Fraga sin fijos, aragones**es** no*n* auiendo rey de natu*r*a, | ouiero*n* su acuerdo co*n* nauarros τ acordaro*n* todos en do*n* Pedro T**ares** q*ue* era o*m*e | noble en Aragon q*ue* fue rey; τ fuero*n* por el. La cort fue en Mo*n*ço*n*. Sopolo | do*n* Pedro Tares,ᵛⁱⁱ τ fue mal co*n*seiado q*ue* se touiese en carto, asi fue q*ue* los ricos | om*n*es q*ue* uiniero*n* por el no*n* lo uiero*n* por tres uezes q*ue* fuero*n* | ael; los ricos omes touiero*n* se **por** maltrechos,³⁷⁴ q*ue* los no*n* reçibie. Agora ¿q*ue* farie qua*n*do fue-|se rey? Pusiero*n* ent*r*esi q*ue* nu*n*q*u*a a este reçibiesen por rey τ asi q*ui*taro*n* se q*ue* **non** lo | uiero*n*. **Aca** los nauarros, do*n* Aznar de Oyteca τ do*n* Fortu*n* Enegones de Leet, | uiero*n* q*ue* andaua*n* en dubda τ no*n* auie*n* rey de natu*r*a de Aragon, enuiaro*n* | por Garcia Remirez, nieto de Ruy Diaz **et** del ifañt do*n* S*anch*o, q*ue*

ⁱ The translator's attempts to abbreviate *DRH* run into significant difficulties. Compare V.xxi.24 ff.
ⁱⁱ *DRH*: V.xxiii
ⁱⁱⁱ *DRH*: V.xxiiii
ⁱᵛ This is an editorial comment by the translator.
ᵛ *DRH*: 'Roderici Didaci'.
ᵛⁱ Translator's comment.
ᵛⁱⁱ The section in *DRH* dealing with this exchange appears in the chapters dealing with Aragón (esp. VI.ii) although the scene is rather more vivid in *EG*.

dixiemos q*ue* mu-|rio en Rueda, q*ue* era de natura delos reyes de Nauarra.[i] τ
leuaro*n* lo a Pa*n*-|plona τ alcaro*n* lo rey, asi salio Nauarra de poder τ de
señorio de Ara-|go*n*. Este caso co*n* doña Margelina, fija del co*n*de de
Alpe*r*ches, q*ue* pasaua por | Castiella, del exadiza del *con*de do*n* R*odr*i*g*o de
Castiella. [ii] Este ouo en esta re-|yna al rey do*n* San*ch*o q*ue* fue muy bueno τ
sabio τ ouo dos fijas, doña Bla*n*ca | q*ue* caso co*n* el rey do*n* San*ch*o de
Castiella, fijo del enp*er*ador,[iii] τ ouo en ella al | rey do*n* Alfonso de Castiella
q*ue* ue*n*cio la de Ubeda; la ot*ra* fija fue doña Mar-|garita, q*ue* caso conel rey
Rogel de Cecilia τ ouo en ella al rey Guille*n* q*ue* | fue abastado de gra*n*des
riq*ue*zas. Este Guille*n* caso co*n* doña Iuaña, fija | del rey Enric de Anglat*ie*rra τ
no*n* ouo en ella fijos; pues, el muerto, | doña Iuhaña caso *con* el co*n*de Remo*n*
de Tolosa τ fizo en ella al *con*de |[fol.45r] | do*n* Remo*n* de Tolosa[iv] q*ue* pues fino
sin fijos uaro*n* τ h*er*edo su fija q*ue* caso co*n* Alfonso, | fijo del rey de Fra*n*çia
dela reyna doña Bla*n*ca, fija q*ue* fue del Rey do*n* Alfonso[v] | de Castiella.
Ot*r*osi, este mismo rey do*n* Garcia Remirez, pues q*ue* murio doña Mar-
|gelina, caso ot*ra* uez co*n* doña Urraca, fija del enp*er*ador τ ouola en doña
Co*n*true-|da, h*er*mana de do*n* Diago Abteganis τ ouo desta una fija doña
San*ch*a q*ue* pues ca-|so co*n* do*n* Gasto*n*, uizco*n*de de Beart τ fino do*n* Gasto*n*
sin fijos τ pues caso doña | San*ch*a ot*ra* uez co*n* el *con*de do*n* Pedro de Molina
τ ouo en ella un fijo, do*n* Rodrigo, pues le | dixiero*n* do*n* Al*m*eric. Este fue
bizco*n*de τ h*er*edo Narbona, por q*ue* el *con*de do*n* Pedro fue | fijo de do*n*
Ormisenda τ Narbona p*er*tenescie a ella de h*er*edar. Muerto el rey | do*n*
Garcia Remirez, su mug*er* doña Urraca, fija del enp*er*ador, caso co*n* Aluar
Ruyz.[vi] | El rey do*n* San*ch*o, q*ue* dixiemos de suso, fijo q*ue* fue de do*n* Garcia
Remirez, caso co*n* doña | Baeça, fija del enp*er*ador de Castiella τ ouo en ella
dos fijos, el rey do*n* San*ch*o | de Nauarra τ al ifañt do*n* Ferrando τ ot*ras* tres
fijas. Do*n* San*ch*o *el que* fue en la d'Ubeda τ des-|pues ouo una enfermedad[vii]
q*ue* no*n* podie caualgar, e por se encobrir no*n* | se dexaua ueer si no*n* asus
p*r*iuados τ pusose en el castiello de Tudela | τ ali moro τ ali fino; τ aq*ue*l
dixiero*n* rey do*n* San*ch*o el Encerrado. El ot*r*o fijo, do*n* Ferrando, | salio muy
bueno τ muy ardit τ por su ue*n*tura corrie*n*do un cauallo cayo τ | murio ende.

---

[i] See Martin, *Les juges*, for the possible motivations behind the legend of the Judges.
[ii] This detail is added by the translator.
[iii] The figure of Alfonso VII, and his title, take on an added importance in *EG*. See Martin, *Les juges*,
esp. p. 140 ff. and 176 ff.
[iv] *DRH*: 'qui Tolose adhuc hodie principatur', Raymond died in 1249. This is an example of *EG*
interest in the respective genealogies of the Iberian kingdoms, developed further in subsequent
cases.
[v] This detail is added to the *DRH* text.
[vi] Personal note of Ximénez de Rada, 'et me sua tempora inuenerunt', taken out.
[vii] This detail does not appear in *DRH*.

La una fija fue doña Bele*n*guera, esta caso co*n* el rey Recardo ⎸ de Anglat*ie*rra τ murio el rey sin fijo; τ la reyna uisco en un moneste*ri*o τ ⎸ sie*m*pre de bueña uida τ ali fino; τ la ot*ra* fija, doña Gosta*n*ça, q*ue* murio qua*n*do ⎸ auie a casar. La te*r*cera fija, doña Bla*n*ca, caso co*n* Tibaldo, co*n*de de Cha*m*paña, ⎸ τ ouo en ella a do*n* Tibaldo. Este Tibaldo caso co*n* fija del co*n*de delas Marchas ⎸ τ despues partiero*n* se por ygle*s*ia a gra*n*d pesar della; pues este do*n* Tibaldo ⎸ caso co*n* fija de do*n* Guisart de Belioc τ de doña Sebilia,[i] fija de Felip, co*n*de ⎸ de Fra*n*dria; τ desta muge*r* ouo una fija doña Bla*n*ca, q*ue* despues caso co*n* ⎸ do*n* Iuha*n*, duc de Bretaña. Pues este Thobaldo caso otra uez co*n* doña ⎸ Margarita, fija de un noble p*r*incep Arche*n*bad, e ouo en esta dos fijos, ⎸ do*n* Thobaldo τ do*n* Ped*r*o[ii] τ ot*r*os. Este do*n* Tibaldo, por faz*er* se*r*uit*i*o a Dios, pasose ⎸ [fol.45v] ⎸ a ultra **mar et** en aiuda de la t*ie*rra sa*n*ta τ gano ala uillas τ castiellos q*ue* dio ⎸ a c*hr*ist*i*anos, fizo mucho bie*n* a caual*er*os me*n*guados τ pues torno asu ⎸ t*ie*rra. Este heredo Nauarra.[iii]

Delos reyes de Castiella[iv]

⎸ Dixiemos delos reyes de Nauarra, tornemos en lo de Castiella, co-⎸mo descendiero*n* de Nauarra. Muerto el co*n*de do*n* Sanc*h*o **de** Castiella h*e*redo su ⎸ fijo el co*n*de do*n* Garcia τ los ricos omes de Castiella andidiero*n* le casamie*n*to ⎸ co*n* doña Sanc*h*a, fija del rey de Leon; asi q*ue* este ifant do*n* Garcia τ su cuñado, el rey ⎸ do*n* Sanc*h*o de Nauarra el Meior, guisaro*n* τ uiniero*n* se a Sant Fagu*n*do por faz*er* ⎸ las bodas. Este[v] ifañt Garcia furtuse de noche τ fue ueer su esposa τ q*ue* fa-⎸blase co*n* ella. Esto*n*z eran en Leon tres fijos del co*n*de do*n* Uela, do*n* Rod*r*igo τ do*n* Dia-⎸go τ do*n* Enego, echolos de t*ie*rra su padre el co*n*de do*n* Sanc*h*o. τ pues no*n* pudiero*n* ⎸ esq*ua*ntra el τ tornaro*n* se al fijo. Asi fue q*ue* uido asu esposa τ fablo co*n* ella ⎸ τ p*a*rtiero*n* se muy pagados. Aq*ua* saliero*n* fijos del co*n*de do*n* Uela τ otros caua-⎸leros echados de t*ie*rra τ mataro*n* lo τ fuyero*n* se; τ los q*ue* fuero*n* falados fu-⎸ero*n* **todos** destorpados. Leuaro*n* lo a enterrar o iaçie su padre τ la esposa fizo ⎸ gra*n*d duelo sin g*ui*sa τ q*ui*so se echar muchas uezes co*n*el en la fuesa q*ue* ⎸ mucho lo amaua. Aca el rey do*n* Sanc*h*o el Mayor entro Castiella por razo*n* de ⎸ la muge*r*, este ganara mucho de ante τ acreciera el regno. Esto*n*z Na-⎸guera era cabo del regno de Nauarra, aeste tie*m*po el co*n*de do*n* Diago Porcel ⎸

---

[i] Once more *EG* retains detailed genealogical information.

[ii] Reference to, and comment on, his daughter Leonor is removed. This reference to Teobaldo without mention of his status as king (1253) has led some scholars to believe that *EG* must therefore date from before 1253. See above p. 8.

[iii] *DRH*: 'Dominus dirigat uias eius', the present tense of *DRH* is not retained.

[iv] *DRH*: V.xxv

[v] The *EG*'s account, broadly similar in detail contains less anecdotal information than that of *DRH*.

poblo Burgos e [de] otros muchos burgos que auie en el camino fiço un bueno, esta | Burgos q*ue* oy es τ fue poblada en la era de ccccxxij. τ mudo el | camino q*ue* por miedo de moros solie yr por Al*au*a τ por Asturias τ por | fuera de Carrera τ q*ue* fuese por Naguerra τ por Briuiesca τ por Amaya | τ por ce*r*ca de Carrio*n*, fata q*ue* uiniese om*n*e [a] Astorga τ a Leon.

Del primero rey del Castiella[i]

| Aqui digamos como el rey do*n* S*anch*o, seyendo rey de Naua-|rra τ señor de Aragon τ de Castiella, como heredo su fijo do*n* Fernando el | menor Castiella por la madre τ fizo y cabesca de regno o era ant*e* co*n*dado; | τ como ot*ro* su fijo, Remiro, ouo Aragon τ fizo y cabesca de regno; τ como | [fol.46r] | lo pe*r*dio esto do*n* Garcia, rey de Nauarra, q*ue*lo deuie todo he*r*edar como fijo | mayor.[ii] Este rey do*n* S*anch*o el Mayor, padre destos, auie un cauallo muy | bueno en q*ue* sienp*re* fuera aue*n*turado τ amaualo much*o*; una uez fue | ala mo*n*tana τ come*n*do este cauallo ala reyna en Naguerra,[375] Q*ue* lo ma*n*-|dase guardar bie*n* asi q*ue* no*n* caualgase ni*n*guno en el.[iii] Ydo, el yfant | do*n* Garcia rogo asu madre Q*ue* gelo diese p*ar*a caualgar, ella otorgogelo. So-|polo un caual*er*o su uasallo τ natural de Castiella τ dixo:[iv] "Señora, no*n* | me semeia seso de dar a u*ues*t*ro* fijo el cauallo Q*ue* uos el rey asi come*n*-|do, si q*ui*er por no*n* caer del ni*n* seer ocasionado el ifa*n*t, si q*ui*ere por dar-|gelo alguno τ pesarie al rey q*ue* al no*n* fuese. Pasar ma*n*damie*n*to del | rey no*n* es bien, como en esto poco τ en lo demas". La reyna touose | por **bien** co*n*seiada, qua*n*do lo dema*n*do el ifa*n*t no*n* q*ui*so dar. Sopo q*ui*[376] gelo co*n*seia-|ra τ pe*n*so pe*n*samie*n*to malo, q*ue* este caual*er*o q*ue* ta*n*to pode*r*io ouo de la destor-|uar co*n* su madre, q*ue* auie de ueer co*n* ella el.[377] Fue asu h*er*mano do*n* Ferrand*o*, | q*ue* por ruego τ mas por menazas de muert*e* como de h*er*mano mayor, | fizol[v] q*ue* otorgase co*n* el q*ue* falaro*n* asu madre co*n* aq*ue*l caual*er*o τ demas q*ue* fa-|blaua*n* en su muert*e*; τ asi deste g*ui*sado mezclaro*n* lo co*n* el rey. Qua*n*do | uino, **el fiando** en[378] sus fijos, creolos τ fue iudgada por q*ue*mar τ no*n* la | auie q*ui*[379] salvar. El rey do*n* S*anch*o por ue*n*tura auie un fijo, do*n* Remiro,[vi] en | una noble dueña de Aiuuar, este leua*n*tose τ desmi*n*tio q*ue* no*n* era uer-|dad τ saluarie ala reyna su madrastra, segu*n* fuero era τ derecho. | Lidio co*n* q*ua*tro uno a uno τ ue*n*cio τ saluola asi. Ela p*r*iso a este do*n* Remi-|ro τ afijolo τ dixo q*ue* este era

---

[i] *DRH*: V.xxvi, there is a clearer justification for inclusion of this passage in *EG* than in *DRH*.
[ii] This is an editorial comment by the translator.
[iii] A lengthy explanation of the positioning of stables in Navarrese houses is left out.
[iv] There is no equivalent direct speech in *DRH*. As previously the stuff of legend is recounted more vividly in *EG*. See above pp. 20–23.
[v] In a reversal of previous practice, the direct speech is left out here.
[vi] This version is substantially different to that of *DRH* as the Latin has no duel and 'monje de Najera' saving Eluira from flames, and Ramiro is not so prominent. See above p. 20 ff.

su fijo τ los otros no; andaua por que here-|dase Castiella aca. Los fijos uieron que erraran τ dixieron la uerdad τ pi-|dieron merçed al rey τ ala reyna; τ falaron que don Ferrando quelo otorgaua a fuerça. | La³⁸⁰ madre perdonolos, mas iuro que don Garcia non heredarie Castiella; τ querie | la dar asu antenado, pues, a ruego del rey τ delos castellanos otor-|go Castiella a don Fernando, por tal pleyto que Aragon, que eran sus arras, que las otor-| [fol.46v] | gase a don Remiro por heredad τ quelo otrogaua ella τ asi fue τ asi se parti-|o la tierra.ⁱ τ fino el rey don Sancho τ don Garcia fico rey de Nauarra, don Fernando lamose | rey de Castiella τ don Remiro rey de Sobarbe τ de Aragon.

Delos reyes de Aragonⁱⁱ

| Digamos delos reyes de Aragon. El primero fue don Remiro que | dixiemos τ aquese primero **se** lamo rey de Aragon. Este ouo fijo al rey don | Sancho. Este ouo iij. fijos, don Pedro τ don Alfonso τ don Remiro el monge τ todos fueron | reyes de Aragon atemporadas desta manera. El rey don Sancho su padre cerco a Hu-|esca τ touola grand tiempo çercada; τ un dia andando deridor la uilla fue fe-|rido de una saeta τ nolo uido ninguno. El rey encubriose τ fue asu tienda | τ fizo iurar asu fijo don Pedro por muert o por uidaⁱⁱⁱ que non dexase³⁸¹ Huesca fata que | fuese presa τ asi lo fizo. Pus fizo su confesion τ caualgo τ pus demostro la feri-|da τ asi murio τ leuaron el cuerpo al monesterio de Sant Uictorian. τ su fijo | Pedro Sanchez fico enla çerca, a pocos dias priso la çibdad de Huesca τ torno asu | señorio. Este rey fue el que priso Ruy Dias Mio Çit τ touol pocos dias preso, | τ despues solto **lo** a tiempo. Este rey don Pedro ganara mucho de moros τ murio | sin fijos; τ regno pus el su hermano don Alfonso, que murio enla de Fraga.ⁱᵛ Este ca-|sara con doña Urraca, madre **que fue** del enperador τ murio sin fijo. Estoncesᵛ fizo el | regno de Aragon como ante dixiemos **sin heredor de natura**³⁸² de Nauarra τ esleyeron a don Pedro | Tares por rey τ perdiolo por mal conseio. Estons nauarros fizieron rey a don Garcia | Ramirez τ aragoneses sacaron al yfañt don Remiro dela mongia, con otor-|gamiento del papa, por curiar el regno de dampno; τ alcaron lo rey en Hues-|ca τ caso con hermana del conde de Preyus; τ fue bueno τ muy guerrero³⁸³ τ here-|do caualeros τ ricos omes de uillas τ de castiellos τ ouo en esa muger una | fija, doña Petronela, de pues ouo

---

ⁱ This is an editorial comment by the translator.
ⁱⁱ *DRH*: VI.i. For the rubrics of *DRH* see Fernández-Ordóñez, 'La técnica'.
ⁱⁱⁱ Much of the genealogy of the kings of Aragón is recounted at great length and with additional detail, see Jerez, 'La Historia', and above, p. 29 ff.
ⁱᵛ *DRH* makes no reference to Fraga here.
ᵛ *DRH*: VI.ii

no*n*bre doña Urraca;ⁱ esta caso *con* el *con*de do*n* Re-|mo*n* de Barcilona q*ue*
dixiero*n* Cab d'Estopa,³⁸⁴ por q*ue* auie los cau**i**elos sorros | τ bla*n*cos. Pues
torno el rey asu mo*n*gia τ fico el co*n*de por señor τ doña Urra-|ca por reyna.
Esto*n*ze plego al co*n*dado de Barçilona al señorio de Aragon. Este | do*n*
Remiro enreq*ue*çio su monaste*r*io seyendo rey, asi como paresce hoy el | [fol.47r]
| abat de Mo*n*t Aragon. Esta doña Urraca, no*n* se acordaua[n] aragoneses
q*ue*la c*r*iarie, | τ diero*n* la asu tio el enp*er*ador de Castiella*ii* q*ue* la c*r*iase; τ c*r*iola
τ pusol no*n*bre Ur-|raca, no*n*bre de su madre, q*ue* an*te* le dezie*n* Petonela τ
los ricos omes de Aragon | diero*n*le casamie*n*to co*n* do*n* Remo*n*, como
diximos suso. Doña Urraca, por reco-|noscimie*n*to dela c*r*iazo*n* ante q*ue*
uiniese **ad** Aragon, fizo omenage por si τ por | sus fijos uenir a cort del
enp*er*ador; asi aturo fata la ce*r*ca de Que*n*ca q*ue* la a-|plazo un noble om*n*e τ
el rey de Castiella, por destouar q*ue* la no*n* ouiesen, | auie*n*do guerra co*n*
moros τ *con* sus uezinos, los reyes, no*n* **pudo** des-|çerca*r*la τ **solto**³⁸⁵ pleyto
alos aragoneses por tal q*ue* la descercarie*n* τ asi fue. | Pues*iii* esta doña Urraca
q*ue* diximos ouo [con] este co*n*de dos fijos τ una fija: | τ do*n* Alfonso τ do*n*
Sanc*h*o τ doña Dolça,³⁸⁶ caso co*n* el rey do*n* Sanc*h*o de Portugal τ pus dire-
|mos de su linag*e*. Do*n* Sanc*h*o caso co*n* doña Sancha, fijo del *con*de do*n*
Nuño de Casti-|ella τ*iv* ouo en ella a do*n* Nuño Sanchez; este caso *con* **fija de**
do*n* Lop Dias τ partiero*n* | se por pare*n*tesco τ asi fino sus fijos. Do*n* Alfonso
regno pus dias desu pad*r*e | τ dela reyna doña Urraca τ ouo los *con*dados; este
gaño mucho de moros | τ fue bueno τ fra*n*c. Ensus dias se poblo Teruel el a
pesar de moros; | otrosi este rey poblo ot*r*os castiellos. Este caso *con* doña
Sanc*h*a, fija del enp*er*ador | de Castiella τ ouola en su mug*er* la enp*er*adriz doña
Rica, q*ue* fue fija | del duc de Polloño³⁸⁷ τ he*r*mana del enp*er*ador de
Co*n*sta*n*tinopla. Este [rey]³⁸⁸ do*n* | Alfonso ouo tres fijos: do*n* Ped*r*o, do*n*
Alfonso τ do*n* Fernando; τ ot*r*osi tres fijas: doña Costa*n*ça, | doña Leonor τ
doña Sanc*h*a. Diero*n* el co*n*dado de P*r*oue*n*ca a do*n* Alfonso; este fue | bueno
τ cuerdo τ caso co*n* nieta del co*n*de de Fuisa τ ouo en ella a do*n* | Alfonso,
*con*de de P*r*oue*n*ca.*v* Este gano muchos castiellos del *con*dado d'Alp*er*chas, |
este caso co*n* doña Beat*r*iz, fija del *con*de Horila*n*dia τ ouo en ella q*ua*tro fijas.
| Destas la una caso co*n* do*n* Loys, rey de Fra*n*çia, la ot*r*a co*n* Herico, rey de
An-|glati*er*ra, la*vi* ot*r*a *con* su he*r*mano el *con*de Ricart, la ot*r*a *con* Carlos,

ⁱ Many of these details are not drawn from *DRH*. See above, p. 29 ff.
ⁱⁱ None of these details from *DRH*. There is particular emphasis here on Alfonso VII.
ⁱⁱⁱ *DRH*: VI.iii
ⁱᵛ The daughter of Lope Díaz is not mentioned in *DRH*. See above, p. 29 ff.
ᵛ *DRH*: 'qui nunc Prouincie principatur', the present tense reference is removed as a consequence of
the following lines.
ᵛⁱ These last two daughters are not mentioned in *DRH*. Reference to Beatriz as countess suggests
that the knowledge of the translator extends past her wedding to Charles of Anjou in 1248 but not

hermano del rey ¡ de Françia que dixiemos. Fino este conde sin fijo³⁸⁹ uaron τ heredo Prouençia esta ¡ fija menor que caso con Carlos. La otra fija doña Gostança caso con el rey de ¡ [fol.47v] ¡ Ungria τ fino el sin fijos; torno **ad** Aragon τ su hermano el rey don Pedro ca-¡sola con Frederico, rey de Ceçilia, que pues fue enperador τ pues fue despues-¡to por yglesia; τ quando fue leuada a Ceçilia³⁹⁰ τ al torno perecio una nab con ri-¡cos omnes de Aragon que la leuauan. Este Frederico ouo en esta muger al rey ¡ Henrico, esteⁱ caso con fija del duc de Austria τ ouo en ella fijos. Pues Fre-¡derico temiose de Henrico, que ternie con la yglesia τ **en la guerra**³⁹¹ prisolo τ pusol en ¡ una torre τ ali fizo su uida fata que murio en Apalia. Don Ferrando, **el otro fijo**, era a-¡bad de Mont Aragon. La otra fija doña [Sancha]ⁱⁱ caso con el conde Remon de To-¡losa τ ouo en ella una fija doña Juhaña que caso con Alfonso, conde de Pey-¡cho,³⁹² hermano de Loys, rey de Françia, que pus heredo Tolosa por la muger, que ¡ fino el conde sin fijo. **Et el otro fijo deste cuende mismo, que dixieron Remon, caso con la otra fija del dicho rey don Alfonsso que dixieron dona Sancha.** Elⁱⁱⁱ otro hermano don Pedro fue rey bueno τ franc τ cor-¡tes τ daua quanto auer podie τ por dar a dueñas τ a caualeros, enpe-¡ñaua uillas τ castiellos. Este ouo su amiztad con el rey don Alfonso ¡ de Castiella, pues adibaron τ uino le **en** aiuda ala batalla de Ubeda, ¡ τ desta batalla diremos pus en su lugar. Este rey don Pedro priso Castil τ A-¡dimuz; este caso con doña Maria, fija de don Guillen, señor de Montpeller, ¡ τ dela fija del enperador de Costantinopla τ ouo en ella un fijo don ¡ Iayme; estonz se aiunto el señorio de Montpeller al regno de Aragon. ¡ τ aeste rey don Pedro ouo coronado papa Innocencio enla yglesia de Sant ¡ Pancracio. Pus quando el arcobispo de Narbona, don Arnalt, mouio gue-¡rra contra los hereges de Tolosa, este rey don Pedro uino en aiuda del conde ¡ de Tolosa, non contra la ley mas por defender tierra desu cuñado; τ ¡ uino con pocos aragoneses τ muchos franceses τ con el conde de Fox ¡ τ fue asi como Dios quiso cerca de Moriello, e fue τ murio el rey don Pedro ¡ τ muchos nobles omnes **de** Aragon: don Aznar Pardo τ don Pedro Pardo, su fijo τ ¡ don Martin de Hulesa³⁹³ τ don Gomez de Luna; τ los condes fuxieron a Tolosa. El rey ¡ don Pedro fue soterrado enel monesterio de Sexena que fiziera su madre do-

---

to her death in 1267, when Charles inherited Provence. The third daughter, Sancha, married Richard of Cornwall in 1243.

ⁱ EG returns to close translation of DRH.

ⁱⁱ 302: 'Iuhana'. These details are not from DRH. 302 confuses mother and daughter, while BN Res/278 assumes that the daughter in question is Leonor, when in fact it is Sancha who is being described. For this reason, BN Res/278 adds a sentence to account for the existence of the third daughter of Alfonso not realising that Sancha's matrimonial career has just been outlined. Alphonse of Poitiers inherited Toulouse from his wife in 1249.

ⁱⁱⁱ DRH: VI.iiii

ǀña reyna Sancha τ lo enriqʋiçio de dueñas τ de riqʋezas. Murio el rey era ǀ
[fol.48r] ǀ m.cclij. Muertoⁱ el rey don Pedro, su fijo don Iayme fico³⁹⁴ chico τ
criaualo el conde ǀ Simon de Monfort τ desposaralo con su fija. Pues
aragoneses, temiendo qʋelo ǀ non podien auer et, si lo ouiese, qʋe aurien por
señora fija de qʋi fue en fecho τ ǀ en conseio dela muert del rey, entro la tierra
en discordia; τ los unos ricos ǀ omnes τ los demas alçaron se contra la tierra por
la dar³⁹⁵ al ifañt don Fernando de Montara-ǀgon, hermano de su padre. Los
otros τ los pueblos, con el señor de Albaraçin, contra-ǀdizien fata qʋe ouiese a
don Iayme τ estando el regno asi en grand rebuelta. Entre ǀ tanto, don
España, obispo de Santa Maria de Albarraçin, en sus despensas propias,ⁱⁱ con
aiuda ǀ del señor de Aluarazin τ fue a Roma τ procuro departamiento de aqʋel
esposalicio, ǀ asi qʋe don Pedro de Benauent, diacono τ cardenal de Santa
Maria τ por mandamiento del ǀ papa uino, departio este casamiento τ pus
rendieron este ifañt don Jayme asus ua-ǀsalos. τ pus entro por la tierra como
lo yuan iurando sus uillas yua el entrando ǀ fasta andido todo el regno τ los
qʋe se qʋisieron alçar non ouieron o yr pues fueron ǀ en Teruel;³⁹⁶ el rey yua
para ala, salieron ende τ delos fueron a Ualençia, qʋe era de moros, ǀ τ delos a
Castiella. Pues perdonolo el rey τ tornaron ala tierra. El Rey estonz, ǀ por
conseio de sus vasallos que era niño para gobernar la tierra, partiola fasta
fuese ǀ de edat τ fizo tres gouernadores: el uno de Catalueña τ el otro de
Ebro ǀ aqua, el tercero de Ebro alla; estos fueron los qʋe touieron siempre con
el a tiempo ǀ por conseio τ por ruego destos perdono alos echados del regno τ
quando fueron ǀ y fueron bien uenidos τ los gouernadores fueron mezclados τ
fueles muy ǀ mal gradescido, como qʋien sirue a niño qʋe non a edade. Pues a
tiempo crescio ǀ τⁱⁱⁱ caso con doña Leonor, fija del rey don Alfonso de
Castiella; τ ouo en ella ǀ un fijo don Alfonso,³⁹⁷ τ pues uino el cardenal don
Iuhan τ partioles por manda-ǀmiento de papa, por qʋe eran parientes; pero el
fijo fue legitimado al regno τ alo ǀ qʋe fijo deue heredar de padre. Pues desto
compeço guerra³⁹⁸ con moros τ gano ǀ Mayorga τ Minorga τ Euiça τ delexo y
sus uarones por defender; τ ǀ torno a España τ gano Ualencia con todo su
reysmo.³⁹⁹ Pues como diximos qʋes ǀ partio de doña Leonor, caso con doña
Uiolant fija del rey Andres de Ungria, ǀ [fol.48v] ǀ τ fija dela reyna Yales,⁴⁰⁰ qʋe
fue fija del enperador don Pedro τ de doña Uiolant, ǀ enperatriz de
Costantinopla, qʋe fue de linage de Françia; τ desta ouo fijos don ǀ Pedro τ

ⁱ DRH: VI.v
ⁱⁱ The events surrounding the succession of Jaume are dealt with in greater detail by EG. Of
particular interest is the emphasis on Albarracín, nowhere mentioned in DRH. See above, p. 29 ff.
The references to governors and the difficulty of regency arrangements does not appear anywhere in
DRH.
ⁱⁱⁱ Note this is repeat of what appeared earlier in the chapter.

do*n* Iayme τ do*n* S*anch*o τ doña Yoles,[401] q*ue* caso *con* do*n* Alfonso rey de Castiella,[i] fijo | del rey do*n* Fernando.

Delos reyes de Nauarra[ii]

|Tornemos al rey do*n* S*anch*o el Mayor: pues ouo su t*ie*rra p*a*rtida τ ordenada,[iii] | do*n* Garcia p*a*ra Nauarra, do*n* Ferrando p*a*ra Castiella, do*n* Remiro p*a*ra Aragon, mouio | guerra *con*t*ra* el rey de Leon. Acaescio un dia q*ue* andaua este rey do*n* S*anch*o a caça | en un uillar antigo o ouiera uilla τ fue por ferir un puerco τ puso se | en un escriçio; τ alço el benablo por darle τ nol dio, q*ue* Dios no*n* q*ui*so τ torcio | sele el braço. τ el rey, de gra*n* dolor, desce*n*dio τ cataro*n* aq*ue*l lugar τ auie | y un altar uieio[iv] esc*ri*pto de Sant Antoli*n* τ fizo su oraçio*n* τ touo su uig*i*lia | τ asi guaresçio; τ ali poblo Pale*n*çia τ dio la cibdad ala yg*le*sia de Sant An-|tolin, como oy paresce. Aca el rey de Leon uino *con* pocos τ p*ro*puso amiztad | *con* el rey do*n* S*anch*o, asi q*ue* caso su fijo do*n* Ferrand*o con* doña S*anch*a, fija del rey de Leon τ dio el | rey do*n* S*anch*o asu nuera *con* su fijo qu*a*nto ganara de Pisuerga alla, *con* plaze*r* del | rey de Leon. Aca el ifant do*n* S*anch*o Garcia, q*ue* auie de regnar en Nauarra, fue en | rom*er*ia a Roma, a Sant Pedro τ a Sant Paulo. Enta*n*to fino su padre, el rey | do*n* S*anch*o, era m.iij. este **regno** xxxv. años τ enterrolo su fijo el rey do*n* Ferrando | en Oña. Otros*i*[v] este do*n* Garcia de Nauarra, de mie*n*tre era en su rom*er*ia, su | h*er*mano do*n* Remiro, rey de Aragon, sobre los t*er*minos come*n*co[402] de guerre-|ar el regno; τ segu*n* dize*n* puso amiztad *con* moros, *con* el rey de Hues-|ca τ co*n* el rey de Çaragoça τ entro por Nauarra τ c*er*co Tafalla. En esto do*n* | Garcia, q*ue* uinie de rom*er*ia q*ue* lo oyo, *con* poca de *con*paña τ gra*n*d sonido de tro*n*-|pas dio salto al aluor del dia enla hueste; desbaratolos τ ue*n*ciolos | **asi** τ fuxo el rey do*n* Remiro,[vi] τ por esto do*n* Garcia[403] toliol qu*a*nto le auia da-|do su padre si no*n* fue Sob*r*arbe τ Ribagorca.

Como el rey don Ferrand de Castiella ouo Leon[vii]

|Entre ta*n*to cayo discordia ent*r*e el rey do*n* Ferrand de Castiella τ el | rey do*n* Ueremudo de Leon, q*ue*l uino emie*n*te de como su padre el rey | [fol.49r] | do*n*

---

[i] This is the first reference to Alfonso X as king, therefore placing the date of composition after 1252.
[ii] *DRH*: VI.vi
[iii] *DRH*: 'pace inter filios ordinata'.
[iv] Although the same details are given *EG* is considerably more laconic.
[v] *DRH*: VI.vii
[vi] The extensive details of Ramiro's flight are reduced to one verb.
[vii] *DRH*: VI.viii

Sancho le prisiera grand tierra τ fue repiso por que la diera asu fija en casamiento con don ⎸ Ferrando. Alegaron sus poderes leoneses el rey don Ferrando[i] con su hermano, el rey don ⎸ Garcia de Nauarra τ con don Remiro de Aragon, aiuntaron se enel Ual de Famaion, que es çer-⎸ca del rio[404] de Carion. τ el rey don Ueremudo **dellino por si mismo**[405] matar a don Ferrand. τ el sopo bien ⎸ desuiar[406] el golpe τ el rey don Ueremudo fue ali deribado τ muerto τ muchos ⎸ ricos omes de Leon con el. Leuaron lo muerto para Leon τ enterraron lo con su muger doña ⎸ Teresa, esto fue era de mLiiij. Muerto[ii] el rey de Leon sin fijo uaron, el rey don ⎸ Ferrando mouio su hueste por entrar el regno quel pertenesçie por la muger; τ maguer ⎸ que lo non querien recebir por la muert del rey, ouieron **lo de recebir et ouieron** mucha guerra, en la fin ⎸ reçibieron lo xº. kalendas iunio τ pusol la corona en la cabesça don Fernando,[407] obispo ⎸ de Leon. Este rey don Fernando uisco xxxx años τ seyes meses τ afirmo las leyes ⎸ goticas τ añadio otras que eran menester alos pueblos. Este ouo fijos enla rey-⎸na doña Sancha, hermana del rey[408] don Remiro de Leon, a don Sancho τ a don Garcia τ a don Alfonso ⎸ τ doña Eluira τ ouo ante que Leon ganase a doña Urraca τ fizo alas fijas leer[iii] ⎸ τ alos fijos usar en caueria.[409]

De como el rey don Ferrando de Castiella mato al rey don Garcia de Nauarra[iv]

⎸ El rey don Garcia de Nauarra ouo enuidia ⎸ desque asi puiaua el poderio desu hermano don Ferrando τ temio que atodo querie pa-⎸sar. Acaescio que don Garcia enfermo en Naguerra τ don Ferrando uinolo ueer. τ ouo su con-⎸seio don Garcia que lo prisiese a don Ferrando τ el sopolo τ fuyo τ asi escapo. Otrosi a pocos dias ⎸ enfermo don Ferrando, uinolo ueer don Garcia τ fue y preso τ enuiolo a Ceya. τ don Garcia prometio ⎸ τ dio a los que guardauan τ fuyo τ uino a Nauarra, asi escapo. Pues don Garcia ⎸ mouio la guerra τ ouo de uenir con nauarros τ con gascones; τ aiuntaron se ⎸ en Atapuerca τ don Ferrando **dela otra parte** enuio merçed a don Garcia como a hermano mayor quel ⎸ perdonase τ que non ouiese y mas mal. Don Garcia era buen cauallero de armas τ de grand ⎸ coracon τ non quiso, que lo preçiaua nada. Otrosi cuaalleros de Nauarra que eran y desere-⎸dados rogaron a don Garcia que les tornase lo suyo, el non quiso nin solament oyrlo, ⎸ diziendo que lo non farie τ elos despidieron se del τ desnaturaron se[410] del por cort, ⎸ τ

---

[i] *EG* follows a group of *DRH* manuscripts which incorporate a later correction from 'plantata' to 'Tamaronis'. See Valverde, p. 229, Jerez, 'La Historia' and above p. 8.
[ii] *DRH*: VI.ix
[iii] *DRH*: 'studiis feminarum'.
[iv] *DRH*: VI.x

pasaro*n* se al rey do*n* Ferrand*o*. El amo q*ue* cr*i*aua a do*n* Garcia dixo: "Señor,
ueo q*ue* oy morredes | [fol.49v] | uos aq*u*í, mas yo no*n* uere u*uest*ra muert";
tolliose todas las guarnizones τ | pr*i*so un capilo de fierro enla cabesça τ la*n*ça
τ escudo τ fuellos ferir τ mu-|rio y. Luego dos cau*alle*ros q*ue* fuero*n* del rey
Ueremudo de Leon uiniero*n* de tr*a*ujes-|so[411] una cuesta ayuso, las la*n*ças
te*n*didas, mataro*n* al rey do*n* Garcia, muchos | nobles om*e*s ali co*n* el. Luego
ma*n*do do*n* Ferrand*o* q*ue* fi*n*case la fazie*n*da τ no*n* matase*n* | a ni*n*gun
*chr*is*ti*ano; mas delos moros q*ue* y uiniero*n*, pocos escaparo*n* q*ue* muertos q*ue* |
pr*e*sos τ do*n* Ferrand*o* ma*n*do enterrar asu he*r*mano do*n* Garcia enel
monest*e*rio de Santa M*ar*ia de | Naguera q*ue* el fiziera. Asi[ii] do*n* Fernando
gano la t*ier*ra del he*r*mano τ fue señor de | Castiella τ de Leon τ de Gallizia τ
de Asturias τ de Naguerra τ de Ebro aca; | τ ma*n*do q*ue* Ebro fuese moio*n*
ent*r*e Castiella τ Nauarra τ fico Nauarra al ifa*n*t | do*n* S*an*cho, fijo del rey do*n*
Garcia q*ue* murio en Peñale*n*; Aragon co*n* Ribagorça **a** do*n* Remiro, | su
he*r*mano. Pues fue la t*ier*ra toda en paz, do*n* Ferrand*o* enuio su hueste sobre
moros | a Portugal τ defendiero*n* se por suyos asi q*ue* fincase*n* los moros enla
t*ier*ra; τ çe*r*co | a Uiseo τ auie y muchos balesteros q*ue* fazie*n* y gra*n*d daño,
entrellos auie | un balest*e*ro q*ue* su balesta pasaua q*ua*tro escudos τ los om*n*es
armados τ fa-|çie*n* de fuera su adargas de tablas dobladas; τ fue ce*r*cada gra*n*d
tie*n*po, en | cabo fue pr*e*sa τ falaro*n* al balest*e*ro q*ue* mataua al rey do*n* Alfonso
su sueg*r*o, q*u*el fi-|riera por las espaldas τ cortaro*n* le las manos τ el un pie τ
sacaro*n* le | los oios; los ot*r*os todos entraro*n* a espada. Pues ce*r*co a Lam*e*do τ
co*n*batiola co*n* | engenios τ pr*i*sola τ delos mato τ delos retouo p*ar*a las ygl*e*sias
labrar q*ue* | era*n* derribadas. Pues puso de ce*r*car Coy*m*bria, q*ue* era cabo del
regno τ en acha-|que de rom*e*ria q*ue* yua a S*an*tiague fue dema*n*dar aiuda del
apostol; τ uelo y τ tor-|no τ[ii] çe*r*cola τ defendiese bie*n* q*ue* auie much*o*
co*n*ducho τ muchas armas. | Esto*n*z auie y mo*n*ges q*ue* moraua*n* entrelos
moros en un lugar much*o* | estrecho q*ue* oy dia le dize*n* Louorno,[412] τ
sufrie*n*do mucha fa*n*bre τ alcaro*n* se, | τ tenie*n* mucho pa*n* de tr*i*go τ çeuada τ
mijo q*ue* no*n* sabie*n* los moros. Pues | uio q*ue* el rey do*n* Ferrand*o* no*n* auie
co*n*ducho τ q*ue*rie deste*r*rar Coymbria, acoriero*n* le | los mo*n*ges co*n* este pa*n* τ
fico la hueste. A dias pletearo*n*, asi q*ue* diesen |[fol.50r] | la uilla τ q*ue* saliesen co*n*
sus cuerpos en saluo τ asi fue pr*e*sa Coy*m*bria. Acaescio ento*n*z q*ue* un |
om*n*e de Greçia andaua en rom*e*rias τ[iii] uinie de Ih*er*usal*e*m τ yua a S*an*tiague *z*
dixo[413] "No*n* fue | cau*alle*ro maguer asi lo pintaua sino*n* pescador", e uio en
sueños el dia q*ue* pr*i*siero*n* a | Coymbria como q*ue* era[414] τ la çe*r*ca de

---

[i] *DRH*: VI.xi

[ii] This passage provides a fine example of the *EG*'s search for a style. The language employed is considerably more concise and unpolished than that of *DRH*.

[iii] The confusion of *EG* mirrors that of *DRH*, VI.xi.60 ff.

Coy*m*bria τ uido q*ue* dio un cauallo bla*n*co bie*n* ｜guisado **al** apostol S*an*tiague
τ uiol q*ue* lidiaua *con* los moros q*ue* entrara en Coynb*n*a. ｜ Este ouo gra*n* gozo
qua*n*do desp*er*to, dixolo a todo el pueblo q*ue* Coy*m*bria era p*r*esa ｜ τ
con toles[415] aq*ue*la uisio*n* τ contaro*n*[416] el dia τ la hora τ falaro*n* q*ue* asi fue
como el ｜ dixo. τ asi p*r*iso el rey do*n* Ferrand*o*, delexo toda aq*ue*la t*ie*rra en
comie*n*da **a** Sisenado, q*ue* se pa-｜sara a moros, era uasalo de Amenadab, rey
delos moros τ fiziera mu-｜cho mal a *ch*r*is*t*ianos τ despues se reco*n*çilio; fico
ali por goue*r*nador τ por ua-｜sallo del rey. Do*n* Ferrand*o* asi torno ala t*ie*rra,
fue a S*an*tiague τ fizo y sus uigilias ｜ τ sus oblat*i*ones τ pus torno a Castiella τ
fizo muchos bienes.

Del rey don Ferrando que partio los regnos[i]

｜Pues, como era bue*n* rey τ bue*n* *ch*r*is*t*iano, ｜ temie*n*do q*ue* los fijos baraiarie*n*
despues sobre los regnos, partio**ge**los en ｜ su uida: a do*n* S*an*ch*o*, q*ue* era mayor,
del rio de Pisuerga toda Castiella τ Naguera ｜ τ como a Taia fata Ebro; a do*n*
Alfonso Leon τ Asturias τ Trasmera, fata el ｜ rio q*ue* dize*n* Ona τ Astorga τ
una p*ar*tida de Ca*m*pos τ Beriza fata uilla Uy[417] en ｜ un mo*n*t q*ue* dize*n*
Ezebredo; alas fijas, a doña Urraca Camora; a doña El-｜uira Toro; a do*n*
Garcia Galliçia co*n* aq*ue*la p*ar*tida q*ue* dize*n* Portugal. Qua*n*do[ii] esta cort ｜ fue
fecha, mouio la hueste sobre moros τ p*r*iso Gormaz τ Uado del Rey ｜ que
dizen **et Aguillera et Berlanga,** ｜ q*ue* estonces dizie*n* Ualeranica[418] e[n]la
rib*er*a de Sant Iusto τ S*an*ta Emereçiana [τ] Gormezes, ｜ τ otr*as* muchas torres
τ athalayas donde ueye la entrada enel Ual ｜ de Burge Coxi, q*ue* agora dize*n*
Caracena τ fata Medina Celim, todas las ｜ deribo. Pues fue a **Cantabria,**[419] τ
echo ende los moros τ gano las mo*n*ta-｜nas de Ocar τ de Onna. Pues torno
*con*tra Toledo τ talo toda la t*ie*rra Tala-｜u*er*a τ Talama*n*ca, Guadalfaiara, Alcala,
Madrid τ todo lo ot*r*o cabo Toledo; ｜ asi Q*ue* el rey de Toledo p*r*ometiol q*ue*l
darie cadaño gra*n*des parias. Esto*n*z ｜ acabo **d**el rey de Seuilla el cuerpo de
Sant Ysidoro τ fuero*n* por el τ a-｜[fol.50v] ｜duxiero*n* lo obispo de Leon, do*n*
Alnido,[420] τ do*n* Ordoño, obispo de Astorga. Otrosi este ｜ do*n* Ferrando fizo
ende leuar al monest*er*io de Santa M*ar*ia de Burgos los cuerpos de Santa ｜
Iusta τ de Santa Rufina,[iii] q*ue* segu*n*d dize*n* se demostraro*n* en aq*ue*l lugar.
Este do*n* Ferrando ｜ fizo la ygl*es*ia de Sant Ysidoro τ enriq*ue*çiola de oro τ de
plata τ **de seda** τ[421] de he*r*e-｜dades; el auie p*r*ometido por se ente*r*rar en Sant
Pedr*o* de Arla*n*ça, pues a ruego de ｜ su mug*er* la reyña doña Sancha camio su
p*er*missio*n* ala ygl*es*ia de Ysidoro q*ue* el ｜ fiziera τ ot*r*osi fizo sacar τ leuar ala el

---

[i] See p. 15 above.
[ii] *DRH*: VI.xii
[iii] *DRH* details of monastery and *DRH* comment 'ego nolo set diffiniat qui presumit' removed.

cuerpo desu padre, el rey do*n* S*anc*ho, q*ue* ǀ iazie en Onna. Ot*r*osi, por ruego dela poblo Camora, q*uela* destruyera Alma*n*-ǀcor;ⁱ ot*r*osi dize*n* q*ue*, por q*ue* Auilla fue lue*n*ga mie*n*tre destruyda, q*ue* leuaro*n* ende ǀ los cuerpos destos sa*n*tos: Uice*n*t, Sabina, C*h*rist*e*te, ot*r*os dize*n* q*ue* son y, ot*r*os dize*n* ǀ q*ue* son enel moneste*r*io de Arla*n*ça, ot*r*os dize*n* q*ue* el cuerpo de Sant Uice*n*t es ǀ en Leon e el de Santa Xp*r*ist*e*te en Pale*n*çia; q*ui* mas sabe diga.ⁱⁱ Ma*n*do ot*r*osi este ǀ rey do*n* Ferrand*o* q*ue* touiesen en Leon las lees goticas. Este̊ⁱⁱⁱ fue sie*m*pre de buena ǀ uida τ fizo algo alas ygl*e*sias τ mayor mie*n*tre ala de Sant Saluador ǀ τ ala de Sant Ysidoro Q*ue* fiziera; τ fizo gra*n*des bienes alos moneste*r*ios pobres. ǀ Acaescio un dia q*ue* oyo misa enla ygl*e*sia mayor de Leon τ uido q*ue* de pobreza q*ue* ǀ dizie*n* sus horas descalcos τ dioles por sie*m*pre re*n*ta sabida p*ar*a los q*ue* an de mi-ǀnistrar. Otrosi comie*n* un dia enel moneste*r*io de Sant Fagu*n*do τ diero*n* le un ǀ uaso de uidrio Q*ue* era del abat co*n* q*ue* beuiese τ cayol dela mano **sobre la mesa**⁴²² ǀ τ pe*r*eçio τ dema*n*do **ende** p*er*don τ dio al abat un uaso muy rico de oro co*n* piedras ǀ p*r*eciosas.ⁱᵛ Establescio al moneste*r*io de Clun*i*ego cada año mill ma*r*aued*i*s en ǀ los pechos del rey; ot*r*osi la reyna fizo mucho de bie*n* τ sienpre. Pues en-ǀfermo τ uido en uision a Sant Isidoro τ dixol como⁴²³ deuie mo-ǀrir; fizo se leuar a Leon τ maguer **en**fermo fue la noche de Nauidad τ ǀ oyo enla ygl*e*sias sus matines τ sus misas τ dizie*n* el ofiço toleda-ǀno. La misa mayor dicha, fizo su *con*fession ant*e* los obispos τ todo el ǀ pueblo τ dema*n*do p*er*do*n* a Dios τ a todo el pueblo q*ue* rogasen a Dios **Nuestro Señor** por ǀ el τ pus comulgo. τ otrosi uino un dia τ puso la corona τ los paños ǀ [fol.51r] ǀ del rey sobre los cuerpos sa*n*tas τ dixo: "Ih*es*u Xp*r*ist*o* señor, cuyo el poder **es** τ el ǀ señorio τ el regno ue*r*dade*r*o, tu eres sobre todas las ge*n*tes del mu*n*do; esto q*ue* ǀ tenia, p*ar*a ti lo tenia, aq*u*i lo delexo, faz delo como señor τ com*i*e*n*do te mi al-ǀma". Toliose los paños:ᵛ "Desnudo sali del uie*n*tre de mi madre, desnudo tor-ǀnare ala". Uistiose luego de celiçio τ de lana τ echose en la ceniza τ ali ǀ estido ese dia τ al ot*r*o dia de Sant Iuh*an*, a ora de medio dia, fino τ fue y ǀ enterrado. τ regno *con* su padre xij. años, sin su madre, **xij** en Castiella τ en ǀ Leon xvj. años; por todo regno xL. años τ vj. meses xij. dias. Entro en Leon ǀ och*o* dias por andar de decie*n*bre τ fino te*r*cer dia pus de Nauidad, era de mill ǀ Lxxxxv. La reyna uisco sobrel ij. años τ fino vj. dias de nobie*n*bre τ ǀ fue ali enterrada; τᵛⁱ fincaro*n* los fijos⁴²⁴ do*n* S*anc*ho τ do*n* Garcia τ do*n* Alfonso τ

ⁱ *DRH*: 'Zemoram'.
ⁱⁱ This is the comment of the translator, compare *DRH* 'asserere non presumo'.
ⁱⁱⁱ *DRH*: VI.xiii
ⁱᵛ Lengthy comment on Moors removed.
ᵛ Although *EG* remains close to *DRH* the Job allusion is not from the source. Compare folio 39v above.
ᵛⁱ *DRH*: VI.xiiii

doña | Urraca τ doña Eluira ensus particiones; mas el rey don Sancho, como
era ma-|yor, nol plazie dela particion.

**Delos bienes de Castiella. Como el rey don Sancho echo sus
hermanos de tierra τ como murio el[i]**

|El rey don Sancho non se touo | por pagado de fincar con Castiella τ con
Nauarra τ començo de guerre-|ar con los hermanos τ con las hermanas por
ganar lo todo τ seer señor, | esta[ii] costumbre **heredo** delos godos, que non
catauan los mayores alos menores | nin menores alos mayores. El rey don
Fernando uido la bondad de don Alfonso | τ ouole comendado las hermanas
doña Urraca τ doña Eluira τ don Alfonso | **guiauase**[425] por doña Urraca que
era muy cuerda τ muy sabidor. Don Sancho regno | era de mill Lxxxxv τ uisco
vj. años. Este[iii] començo luego guerra con don Alfonso, | legaron sus poderes τ
lidiaron y murieron y muchos τ fue uençido don Alfonso | τ fuyo a Leon.
Pues otra uez pusieron dia, legaron en un logar que dizen Golpe-|gera[426] en
tal postura que qui uençiese diese el regno al otro. Lidiaron τ fue uençi-|do el
rey don Sancho τ murieron y muchos, cada uno tornaua asu logar. El | rey don
Sancho auie un caualero Ruy Dias,[iv] τ conseiol que tornasen con los que pudiese
| τ que fallarie el rey don Alfonso su hermano sin compaña, lo uno por que
eran | cansados del uençer τ delos durmien τ delos non podien lidiar τ delos
|[fol.51v] | yrien derramados con sabor dela uençida τ non se podien aiuntar delos,
que ya se-|rien ydos. Dixieran otros que non era bien yr a escuso τ campo
uençudo. Dixo[v] Ruy Dias | que noche τ dia entraua por dia, nin batalla non
auie tiempo sabido nin hora; si-|guieron su conseio τ fue uençido τ
desbaratado don Alfonso sin sospecha τ ouo | de ser presa en Santa Maria de
Carrion. τ asi fueron uençidos leoneses τ gallegos, | τ don Alfonso fue preso
en Burgos.[427] Pues por conseio desu hermana doña | Urraca τ don Pedro
Ansures, prometio de palaura mas non de coraçon que entra-|rie monge **en el
monesterio de Sant Ffagundo τ assi escapo τ fue monie.** Pues con
conseio de Pedro Ansures τ de Gonçalo Ansures τ de Ferrand Ansu-|rez,
todos tres hermanos quel aguardauan por mandado de doña Urraca, | salio
dela mongia τ uino se para Toledo. El rey Almenun de Toledo diol sus |
casas cabo el alcacar para el τ asus christianos por non fazer enoio alos moros,
| plogol mucho con el. Don Alfonso començo de guerrear τ fazer mucho mal

---

[i] *DRH*: VI.xv
[ii] *EG* alters the order of *DRH* elements and returns to end of VI.xiiii.
[iii] *EG* resumes narration of *DRH* VI.xv.
[iv] *DRH* 'campiator'.
[v] The version given by *DRH* is rather more approving of the Cid and contains a deprecatory
reference to Galician and Leonese knights.

a ⎢ moros, los q*ue* era*n* co*n*trarios de Almenu*n*. Qua*n*do no*n* guerreaua andaua ⎢ todauia a caça. Anda*n*doⁱ un dia a caça, lego a B*r*iuega τ uido pueblo poco ⎢ enlas cueuas delas peñas τ uido bue*n* lugar de toda caça τ plo-⎢gol co*n* aq*ue*l lugar; sopolo Almenu*n* τ diogelo p*ar*a sus caças τ poblol ⎢ de sus mo*n*teros *chr*ist*i*anos q*ue* traye cuyo linag fico y **fasta**⁴²⁸ el tie*m*po del ⎢ arçobispo do*n* Iulia*n*, el q*ue* pobla la collaçio*n* de Sant Pedro. Acaesçio un dia ⎢ q*ue* Almenu*n* fue ueer su huerta τ yua fabla*n*do *con* sus uieios: "Uilla ⎢ ta*n* fuert*e*, ¿q*ue* tenie?"ⁱⁱ Dixiero*n* los uieios: "Fa*n*bre". Dixo el: "¿qual?" Dixiero*n* le: ⎢ "Toler el pa*n* uit⁴²⁹ años mas la fruta, q*ue* ta*n* gra*n*d pueblo q*ue* no*n* puede seer ⎢ sin comer". Oyo esto do*n* Alfonso τ calo τ touolo ensu coraço*n* p*ar*a tie*m*po si pu-⎢dier o azmo ouiese. Ot*r*osi acaescio un dia q*ue* seye do*n* Alfonso cabo Alme-⎢nu*n* τ leua*n*taua*n* sele los cabellos τ el rey aplanaua los *con* la mano τ ⎢ qua*n*to mas aplanaua mas se alçaua*n*; τ los uieios q*ue* lo uiero*n* τ los ⎢ q*ue*lo oyero*n* uiero*n* q*ue* era señal q*ue* este deuie ganar Toledo τ dixiero*n* ⎢ por co*n*seio al rey q*ue* lo matasen. Al rey uinol en mie*n*te q*ue*l segurara ⎢ τ q*ue* p*r*ometiera bie*n* τ el q*ue*l fazie se*r*uit*i*o, no*n* los q*ui*so creer ni*n* q*ui*so fazer ⎢ [fol.52r] ⎢ *con*t*r*a lo q*ue* Dios q*ue*rie faz*er*, p*er*o ta*n*to rogol q*ue* si Dios *con*seiol diese q*ue* uinie-⎢se emie*n*t*e* como le recibiera τ puso *con* el pleyto q*ue* no*n* guerease ael ⎢ ni asu fijo ni*n* corriese su t*i*e*r*ra a Toledo ni*n* a su regno τ asi lo **uino.**⁴³⁰ Doña ⎢ Urraca uio q*ue* do*n* S*an*cho andaua enpus deseredala delo suyo τ ella *con* los ça-⎢moranos fiziero*n* cabdiello a do*n* Arias Go*n*z*a*lez su amo por se defender, ⎢ ca uie mala señal τ pesauales dello do*n* Alfonso. Entreta*n*toⁱⁱⁱ do*n* S*an*cho entro ⎢ por Leon τ gano lo p*er*o *con* lazeria. Aca el rey do*n* Garcia co*n*pesçose de leuar mal ⎢ co*n* las ge*n*tes ca se guiaua por un su c*r*iazon uil om*n*e Uermudo,^{iv} τ rogaro*n* ⎢ al rey q*ue* lo q*ui*tasen de si q*ue* mal le co*n*seiaua; τ no*n* q*ui*so, q*ue* ante fazie peor. ⎢ Pus no*n* lo pudiero*n* sofir τ mataro*n* gelo dela*n*t τ sopolo⁴³¹ el rey τ co-⎢me*n*çolos de aterrar τ echar de t*i*e*r*ra τ menazar τ ellos uno a uno ⎢ q*ui*taua[n]se del τ yua*n* se a do*n* S*an*cho; asi q*ue* qua*n*do fue entrado por la t*i*e*r*ra fa-⎢lola en discordia τ falesçie*n* le los⁴³² uasalos a do*n* Garcia τ yua la toda gana*n*do ⎢ do*n* S*an*cho. Do*n* Garcia uido q*ue* mal sele ponie su pleyto salio dela t*i*e*r*ra *con* cccc. ⎢ caual*er*os τ fuese a moros τ dema*n*doles ayuda cont*r*a su he*r*mano τ ⎢ p*r*ometioles Q*ue* les darie su regno τ *el* de su he*r*mano. Dixiero*n* los mo-⎢ros: "No*n* ouieste seso por retener tus uasallos, menos rete*r*nas a nos ⎢ ni*n* auernies co*n* nos, ot*r*osi p*r*omete[s]nos lo ageno, tu p*er*diste lo tuyo ¿co-⎢mo nos daras lo de tu he*r*mano q*ue* el no*n*

ⁱ *DRH*: VI.xvi
ⁱⁱ It is notable that all details relating to the city of Toledo here are faithfully retained.
ⁱⁱⁱ *DRH*: VI.xvii
^{iv} This name is a translation error of *DRH* 'Habebat autem quendam uernulum causa familiaris secreti plus debito sibi carum,...', BN Res/278 has Vermillo.

querra?; non andas con recabdo, de-|manda otro conseio, nos enpararemos lo nuestro a quien nos lo demandare". | Dieron le sus ioas τ sus presentes τ asi con grand uerguença tornose a Por-|tugal τ priso algunos castiellos; pues ouo guerra⁴³³ con su hermano don | Sancho τ fue uençido don Garcia τ preso τ leuado a Luna,ⁱ τ alli adolesçio τ fino en | las prisiones; τ hoy dia asi iaze.ⁱⁱ Puesⁱⁱⁱ don Sancho ouo ganado amos los | regnos delos hermanos, quiso auer lo delas hermanas τ mucho mas | por que sabie que amauan a don Alfonso τ que les pesaua desu malandança. | τ uino τ çerco a Çamora τ don Arias Gonzalez con sus fijos dentro τ defendi-|ese bien en su castiello,ⁱᵛ τ sufrien mucha de malandança τ de lazeria. |[fol.52v]| Pues un caualero Uelido Ataulpo, por cuydarᵛ fazer seruitio a doña Urraca τ | por desterar Camora, salio en un cauallo como que yua fuyendo de parte del | agua mientre conbatie la uilla aderredor; τ firio a don Sancho de una lança τ don Ruy | Diaz fue enpus el fasta las puertas dela uilla por ferirlo τ entro don | Uelido, Ruy Dias quiso entrar τ çerraron le la puerta τ firio en ella. Muerto | el rey don Sancho, castellanos τ nauarros fueron en cuyta τ dellos lidiauan τ de-|los fuyen τ fueron muy mal trechos; τ con grand duello leuaron lo a enterrar | a Oña. Enteradoᵛⁱ el rey don Sancho, castellanos τ nauarros legaron se en Burgos | τ esleyeron por rey a don Alfonso que era en Toledo, pero asi que se saluase que non fuera | en conseio de muerte de don Sancho τ enuiaron sus mensaieros escondidos. Otrosi | doña Urraca, señora de Leon τ de Castiella, ouo su conseio que enuiase por su | hermano don Alfonso que uiniese prender los regnos τ esto en grand poridad, quele | non uiniese algun destoruo. Entre tanto algunos christianosᵛⁱⁱ por fazer plazer al rey | de Toledo yuan le con nueuas dela muert; acaescio que Pedro Ansurez andando co-|mo solie cadadia en uoz de trebeio auna legua τ mas de Toledo todauia | por saber nueuas de Castiella, delos **que** uinien τ el era bien algarabiado; fa-|lo uno que uinie por dezir al rey Almenun desta muerte. Pedro Asures sacol | a fabla dela carreraᵛⁱⁱⁱ τ descabeçol, asi fizo a otros tres por que lo non sopiese ante | el rey que don Alfonso el que tornaua; lego uno de su hermana dona Urraca τ yua | este τ entrose⁴³⁴ con el τ oydas las nueuas τ las cartas guisauan se por | yr de

---

ⁱ *EG* follows *DRH* error, see Valverde, p. 241, n.68.

ⁱⁱ This is a possible reference to VI.xxxiiii, although it is not clear quite when 'oy dia' refers to.

ⁱⁱⁱ *DRH*: VI.xviii

ⁱᵛ The apparent sympathy with the defenders of Zamora does not reflect the outlook of *DRH*.

ᵛ As above, the translator's sympathies appear to lie with Urraca and the defenders. Much of the detail of what follows is not *DRH* and may, in the light of the translator's use of epic sources elsewhere, be drawn from epic sources. See above, p. 20 ff.

ᵛⁱ *DRH*: VI.xviiii, 'Castellani et Nauarri', the reference to the Jura de Santa Gadea is drawn from *DRH*.

ᵛⁱⁱ *DRH*: 'Set uiri diabolici, qui nunc dicuntur iniciati...'.

ᵛⁱⁱⁱ *DRH*: 'duxit eum quasi causa colloquii extra uiam'.

noche a escuso. Otro dia lego el mensaie que enuiauan por el castellanos, ¡ pus don Alfonso non quiso uenir a escuso sin conseio τ mandamiento de Almenun que lo criara ¡ τ quel fiziera mucho bien τ mucha ondra, esto fizo al pesar delos suyos. Fablo ¡ con Almenun, dixol como enuiauan por el τ quel gradescie lo quel fiziera τ quel manda-¡se que asi farie. Respuso el rey: "Mal te conseiauan yr sin mio conseio, que viij. dias[i] ¡ a que sope muert de tu hermano τ faziete guardar por ueer que faries, si fueses ¡ de muert o de presion non podries estorcer; agora ueo que seras qual deues. Promete ¡ me en dias mios τ deste mi fijo seas amigo de amigos τ yo tuyo,[ii] τ ¡[fol.53r]¡ prende oro τ plata τ ue a bueña uentura τ si as[435] menester mi aiuda enuia por ¡ ella τ yo otrosi enuiare por la tuya". Asi fue puesto τ non pusieron en la tregua ¡ un fijo chico que estaua y τ asi uino don Alfonso a Castiella con mucho oro τ mucha ¡ plata τ grand riqueza.

Quando torno don Alfonso en Castiella, muerto don Sancho[iii]

¡ Era m.c.i. don Alfonso entro la tierra en edat de xxx años τ vij meses, ¡ τ primero uino a Leon a doña Urraca su hermana, que era muy cuerda τ de buen ¡ conseio. Luego uinieron ael castellanos por darle la tierra, pero que se saluase que non ¡ fuera en **conseio de** la muert de don Sancho. El fue presto por saluarse τ por iurar τ non ouo ¡ y qui lo quisiese reçebir; τ mas adelantose Ruy Diaz τ recibiolo. Esto peso al ¡ rey que se adelantaua, auiendo y meiores[iv] que el, pues alçaron lo rey. Este reg-¡no xLiij años como agora diremos. Este ouo v. mugeres ueladas, una pues ¡ otra leal ment τ segund la ley: la primera doña Agnes; la ij doña Gostança; la ter-¡çera doña Berta; la iiij. doña Helisabet; la v. doña Beatrix. De doña Ignes non ¡ ouo nada; de doña Gostança ouo a doña Urraca, que fue muger del conde don Re-¡mon, este don Remon ouo en ella una fija doña Sancha τ don Alfonso que pues fue enperador[v] ¡ dicho de Castiella; de doña Berta que fue de Toscana non ouo nada; de doña ¡ Helisabet ouo a doña Sancha, que fue muger del conde don Remon[vi] τ ouo a doña Eluira, ¡ que fue muger de don Roger, rey de Ceçilia, este fue hermano de don Robert Guis-¡gard τ fijo de Nuquedo de Altauila, este uenie de Normandia τ priso Çeçilia ¡ τ Paulia τ Capua; de doña Beatrix, que fue de parte de Françia, non ouo nada. ¡ Menos destas mugeres ouo dos muy nobles amigas: a doña Xeme-¡ma Gomez τ ouo en ella a doña Eluira

[i] This detail is not from DRH.
[ii] DRH once more is less immediate, and characterised by reported speech.
[iii] DRH: VI.xx
[iv] DRH does not justify Alfonso's anger in the same way.
[v] EG again places emphasis on the emperor.
[vi] In fact, Count Rodrigo González de Lara.

que caso con el conde don Remon de To-｜losa τ el conde don Remon ouo en
ella a don Alfonso Iordan, el sobre nonbre por que ｜ nascio alla andando el
conde en la tierra santa de Iherusalem[i] por la predicacion τ ella mo-｜nestança
que papa Urbano fazie en França, este estableçio que los que fuesen en ｜
acorro de la tierra santa leuasen cruz enel ombro diestro; desa misma doña
Se-｜mena Gomez ouo el rey una fija doña Teresa, que caso con el conde don
En-｜ric, cormano del conde don Remon padre del enperador,[ii] este don Enric
ouo en ｜[fol.53v]｜ ella a don Alfonso que pues fue rey de Portugal. Tornemos al
rey don Alfonso de ｜ Castiella, este salio bueno, esforçado, catolico, fazedor
de bien a pobres, ordenes, ｜ clerigos τ yglesia. Entanto[iii] don Alfonso oyo que
Almenun rey de Toledo auie crua guer-｜ra con el rey de Cordoua τ mouio su
hueste τ uinolo [a]iu[d]ar,[436] τ plogol Alme-｜nun τ diol olmos τ canales para
las conpañas quel enfermauan; τ pues amos ｜ fueron sienpre en uno τ fueron a
Cordoua asu guisa τ pues tornaron con ondra ｜ τ con ganançia ala tierra. Estonz
murio doña Agnes la que dixiemos τ caso con doña Gostança. ｜

Como fue ganada Toledo[iv]

Murio Almenun τ regno ｜ su fijo Hysem τ uisco poco pues su padre τ regno
su hermano Hyahya ｜ que non fue en la iura. Este salio muy malo de maneras τ
non salio al padre ｜ nin al hermano; los moros non lo pudieron sofir enuiaron
dezir en pori-｜dad los mayores **de Toledo** al rey don Alfonso que guerrease,[v]
pues pasado era su pla-｜zo, que uiniese cercar Toledo τ que guisarien que la
ouiese. Asi que começo la guer-｜ra[437] τ tolio el pan **a Toledo** por quatro
años τ taio las huertas τ los moros podero-｜sos dauan le pasada porel mal
señorio, pues cercola τ partio sus huestes ｜ en quatro partidas τ prisola enla
era de mill cxxj, dia de Sant Urban, viij ｜ kalendas de iunio al xx. año[vi] que
regnaua, so tal conuencia que fincasen y los moros ｜ en sus heredades et quel
diese su pecho como Almenun et que les fincase su ｜ mecuyta la mayor. τ por
que la retenençia era en dubda non quiso esleer y ar-｜cobispo fata otro año τ
estonz quelo farie cabo de su regno quando fue to-｜do apagado; pues gano
Medina Çelim, Talauera τ Coymbria τ ｜ Auilla τ Segouia, Salamanca,
Sepuluega, Coria, Coca, Cuellar, Yscar, Me-｜dina, Canales, Olmos, Olmedo,
Madrid, Atiença, la Riba, Osma, Berlanga, ｜ Maqueda, Escalona, Fita,
Consuegra, Buytrago; todo esto con sus terminos. ｜ Pues uido que Dios era

---

[i] The details of the (extra-peninsular) crusade are reduced.
[ii] As previously, reference to Alfonso VII is emphasised.
[iii] *DRH* VI.xxi.22 ff.
[iv] *DRH*: VI.xxii, 302 rubric embedded in first line.
[v] This reasoning is drawn from *DRH*.
[vi] No attempt is made to keep *DRH* verse, and details are reduced to a minimum.

co*n* el τ guiaua sus fechos, lego su cort τ fizo ⎮ cabesça de regno **a** Toledo τ[i] lamo sus obispos τ esleyero*n* por arco-⎮bispo a do*n* Be*r*nald q*ue* era **muyt** bue*n* om*n*e τ bue*n* ch*ri*st*i*ano τ dio ala ygle*si*a por ⎮ aras Briuga τ Barciles τ Cabañas dela Sag*ra* τ Couexa τ Rodielas ⎮ [fol.54r] ⎮ τ Alcolea so Talaue*ra*,[438] τ Melgar q*ue* dize*n* Aceuh, Almonaçir τ Alpuebrega τ ⎮ mesones τ tie*n*das τ molinos τ fornos τ uiñas τ huertas τ muchos ⎮ buenos p*ri*uilegios por q*ue* faze*n* su aniuersario.[ii]

Como perdieron en España la costunbre gotica[iii]

⎮ Esto*n*z tenie*n* en España la costu*n*bre delos moça-⎮raues τ **el officio**[439] segu*n* la costu*n*bre de Sant Ysidoro τ de Sant ⎮ Lea*n*dre τ la letra godica, q*ue* oy dia dize*n* toledana; τ por ruego dela rey-⎮na enuio[iv] al rey rogar al p*a*p*a* G*re*gorio el vij.[e] q*ue* les camiase esta cos-⎮tu*n*bre τ q*ue*les otorgase la romana ala fra*n*çesa. El p*a*p*a* al *ruego*[440] del rey ⎮ q*ue*l dema*n*do τ[v] enuio a do*n* Ricardo, el abat de Sant Uictor[441] de Marçella, ⎮ q*ue* ordenase las ygle*si*as de España τ uino τ no*n* fizo ta*n* bie*n* como deuie; ⎮ τ do*n* Bernaldo fuese p*ar*a Roma τ fallo muerto al p*a*p*a* Gregorio τ auie*n* ya ⎮ fecho ot*ro* p*a*p*a*, Urbano el i. Reçibiolo muy bie*n* τ co*n*segolo τ diol el palio τ ⎮ su p*ri*uilegio τ otorgolo la p*ri*maçia delas Españas.[vi] Salio dela cort τ ⎮ uino a Tolosa τ fizo y concilio co*n* los obispos de Gallia Totica τ co*n* el ar-⎮çobispo de Narbona τ p*us* uino asu ygle*si*a, **y llegaron el dia que mando et consagro la eglesia** a honor de Santa M*ari*a τ de Sant ⎮ Pedro τ de Sant Paulo τ de Sant Esteua*n* τ nel dia C*ri*spini τ C*ri*spiniani, ⎮ τ puso enel altar mayor muchas reliq*ui*as q*ue*l diero*n* enla cort de Ro-⎮ma τ otras muchas q*ue*l dio el rey τ la reyna desus tesoros. Pues ⎮ qua*n*do **uieron**[442] espanoles q*ue* los camiaua*n* su ofit*i*o τ la letra toledana, ⎮ leua*n*tose el pueblo τ la caualeria τ la cle*ri*zia τ dixiero*n* q*ue* ni*n* lo rece-⎮bie*n*, ante morie*n* τ q*ue* ante aurie*n* ot*ro* rey q*ue*les touiese ala costu*n*bre ⎮ que fue**ra** sie*n*pre. τ en esto andaro*n* co*n*pusit*i*o*n* q*ue* lidiasen dos caua*ller*os, uno ⎮ por la costu*n*bre toledana τ ot*ra* por la fra*n*cesa τ el q*ue* ue*n*çiese q*ue* touie-⎮se su costu*n*bre. **Lidiaron**, el q*ue* era por la toledana era de linage q*ue* dize*n* oy dia ⎮ delos dela Ma*n*tança, cerça de Pisurga τ ue*n*çio. Esto plogo a españoles[vii] ⎮ τ peso ala reyna q*ue* era fra*n*çesa τ pusose co*n* el rey τ dixo q*ue*l[443] y no*n* ⎮ deuie seer iudgada por armas mas q*ue* p*ri*siese dos libros, uno

[i] *DRH*: VI.xxiii.
[ii] *DRH*: 'pro quibus hodie eius memoriam et exequias ueneratur ecclesia Toletana...'.
[iii] *DRH*: VI.xxiiii
[iv] *EG* suppresses mention of Bernard de Sauvetat and his French origins.
[v] *DRH*: VI.xxv.
[vi] *DRH*: 'et primas institutus Hispaniarum et apostolice sedis benedictione suscepta...' *EG* preserves the insistence on the primacy of Toledo.
[vii] *DRH*: 'populus tocis Hispanie'.

toleda-|no τ otro fra*n*ces τ q*u*elos echasen en una fuguera; el q*ue* saliese q*ue* se
no*n* | [fol.54v] | q*u*emose era señal de Dios τ q*ue* mas se pagaua τ q*ue* aq*u*el
ualiese. τ asi lo fizi-|ero*n*: q*u*emose y el fra*n*ces τ salio dende el toledano. Esto
peso ala reyna τ pu-|so se co*n* el rey τ pidiol en doño τ por me*r*çed q*ue*
touiese la costu*n*bre fra*n*çesa, | τ el rey ma*n*dolo asi a cle*r*igos τ legos so pena
delos cuerpos τ delos aue*r*es. | Asi fiziero*n*. Por ende fue dicho el p*r*ouerbio:
"O q*u*isiere*n* los reyes, ala ua*n* las ley-|es". Pe*r*o fincaro*n* en Toledo algunas
ygle*s*ias por testimo*n*io q*ue* dize*n* aq*u*el ofit*i*o, | τ fizo ot*r*osi el psalte*r*io
toledano en muchos logares.

De don Bernaldo, que fue arçobispo[i]

| Digamos del arcobispo, q*ue* fue τ como **cobro**[444] la mezq*u*ita τ la fizo | el
ygle*s*ia τ q*u*ebra*n*to la co*n*ue*nen*çia del rey τ delos moros. Este arçobis-|po do*n*
Be*r*nalt fue de te*r*mino Agenesi de un castiello q*ue* dize*n* Saluedad; este | Leo,
mie*n*tre era **niño**,[445] p*us* çerro la corrona τ diose a cauale*r*ia. P*us* ouo de en-
|fermar τ p*r*ometio seer mo*n*ge en Sant Aurenoio,[446] τ asi lo fue. Pues don |
Ugo, abat de Cunego, sacolo ende τ leuolo co*n*si. Pues el rey do*n* Alfonso |
enuiol por un bue*n* om*n*e por el abad de Sant Fagu*n*d, enuiol a do*n* Be*r*nalt |
co*n* ot*r*os mo*n*ges p*r*ouo y bie*n*. A pocos dias p*r*iso el rey Toledo τ fizolo
eleyto | **dende** como dixiemos desuso.[447] Pues el rey do*n* Alfonso p*r*iso
Toledo τ, sosegada, |fuese p*ar*a Leon. Aca el arçobispo, co*n* co*n*seio dela
reyna τ co*n* poder de cauall*er*os, | pusose al alua d*e*l dia enla mezq*u*ita mayor; τ
qua*n*do los moros fuero*n* aper-|cebidos el ouo fecho y altar τ ca*n*to y misa.
Los moros ouiero*n* pesar del | creba*n*tar la postura, enuiaro*n* se q*u*erellar al
rey τ dema*n*dar si era el | en co*n*seio.[448] El rey, qua*n*do lo oyo, pesol de
coraço*n* τ uino de Sant Fagu*n*d a Toledo | en tres dias, temie*n*do q*ue* pe*r*derie
Toledo, co*n* ardit de cemar ala reyna τ al ar-|çobispo, q*ue* pasara*n* so iura τ su
iura τ su postura. Los moros ente*n*diero*n* q*ue* pe-|saua al rey τ no*n* fuera en
co*n*seio τ q*ue* cuydaua faz*er*, uiero*n* como sabios q*ue* les | podrie uenir mayor
daño[449] por esta iusticia co*n* todos los *ch*ri*sti*anos τ salie-|ro*n* chicos τ gra*n*des
almenos fata Olias recebir al rey co*n* duelo τ pedile | me*r*çed. El rey, qua*n*do
los uio, descendio de su cauallo τ co*n*peco de lorar co*n* | ellos. Dellos dixiero*n*
su q*u*erella τ dema*n*daro*n* le un do*n* y el otorgolo. "Señor", | [fol.55r]| dixiero*n*,
"lo fech*o* sea pe*r*donado,[ii] pues ueemos q*ue* atti pesa; de lo q*ue* finca, guarda |
tu p*r*omesa". Peso al rey porel ruego τ por q*u*eles otorgo, si no lo q*ue* el q*u*erie
co*n*plir; | pe*r*o fue apaziguado τ ent*r*o en Toledo bie*n* y en paz.

---

[i] *DRH*: VI.xxiiii
[ii] The equivalent passage of direct speech in *DRH* shows a healthy instinct for self-preservation on
the part of the Islamic Toledans and is, implicitly, less complimentary to Alfonso VI.

Como don Bernaldo fue a Roma τ en Toledo fizieron otro obispo[i]

| Aese tienpo predico la cruzada papa Urbano para | ultramar τ el arçobispo
don Bernald, por auer los perdones, guisose τ espidiose de sus | canonigos por
yr ala. El ydo, a .iiij. iornadas sus canonigos, como eran auene-|dizos, en mal
bien auenidos, asmaron que don Bernald que nunqua tornarie al arço-|bispado,
esleyeron otro arçobispo τ desampararon sus ofiçiales τ sus mayordomos. |
Fue el mensaie al arçobispo τ dio tornada por Sant Fagund τ truxo ende
monges | τ uino a Toledo; τ priuo al electo τ alos electores τ sacolos dela
yglesia τ co-|mendola alos⁴⁵⁰ monges fata o el uiniese; τ dend aca fincaron
algunas | costunbres de horas dezir en Toledo. El arçobispo fuese paral papa
τ sopolo | quel fizieran sus canonigos τ soltol el uoto τ diol el perdon que
tornase asu tierra | τ ordenase su yglesia, ante que mayor mal y uiniese, como
era conquista. Torno-|se el arçobispo τ uino por Guascueña τ troxo buenos
omes τ fijos de bue-|mos omes, specialment troxo de Moxac a Sant Guiralt,
que fue primero capiscol | de Toledo τ pues arçobispo de Bragana; de
Beorges traxo a Sant Pedro, el primero | arçidiano de Toledo τ de pues fue
obispo de Osma; de Agigno aduxo a don | Bernalt, el segundo capiscol de
Toledo τ de pues fue obispo de Osma τ ar-|cobispo de Santiague τ de
Compostela; troxo niño a don Pedro que de pues fue arçi-|diano de Toledo τ
depues fue obispo de Segouia; τ otro don Pedro que de pues | fue obispo de
Palencia; τ otro don Remon de Saluedad, que depues fue obispo | de Osma
pus San Pedro; de Petro aduxo a don Ieronimo niño, este fue de pues |
obispo de Ualençia en dias de Ruy Diaz el Canpeador,[ii] mas duro poco a |
christianos τ pues tornose a Toledo τ el arçobispo don Bernalt enuiolo | que
ministrase a Çamora τ este fue primero proprio τ asegurado obispo de
Çamora; | de[iii] Lemosin aduxo a don Burdino, que depues fue arçidiano de
Toledo τ de pues | obispo de Coybria τ depues fue arçobispo de Bragana τ
depues que fue obispo |[fol.55v] | fizo se lamar Mauriz, digamos deste. Fino papa
Urbano τ de pues el fue | y⁴⁵¹ papa Pascual segundo τ este Burdino Mauriz
priso grand auer τ seruio al | papa τ pidiol que despusiesen al arçobispo don
Bernalt de Toledo que lo criara, que | dizie que era uieio τ que fiziese ael; el
papa τ la corte prisieron su seruicio mas | non cunplieron su demanda, ca era
mala, el touose por escarnido. τ estonz | acaesçio mal τ discordia entre papa
Pasqual τ Oto el enperador; tenie el | enperador al papa τ alos cardenales
presos τ don Burdino pasose al enper-|ador e ya amos descomulgados

i *DRH*: VI.xxvi
ii *EG* translates closely these *DRH* passages.
iii *DRH*: VI.xxvii

tractaro*n* de faze*r* p*a*p*a* τ fiziero*n* a do*n* Bur-|dino τ fizo se lamar G*r*egorio viij°; τ co*n* el poder del enpe*r*ador entro en Ro-|ma τ asentose en la siella de Sant P*ed*ro. Entreta*n*to libro Dios a p*a*p*a* P*a*scu*a*l dela | p*r*ision τ alos cardenales τ uino en Apulla τ moro y much*o* desterra-|do τ asi murio en cueyta.[i] τ despues fue el p*a*p*a* Gelasio, este enuio let*r*as | al arçobispo desta man*e*ra: "Gelasio, ob*i*spo sie*r*uo delos sieruos de Dios, al a-|mado h*er*mano B*er*nalt, arçobispo de Toledo τ p*r*imado delos obispos d'Espa-|ña, salut τ apostoligal be*n*diçio*n*. Bie*n* sabedes como Burdino, arçob*i*spo | de Sa*n*tiague,[ii] delexo su ygl*esi*a τ pasose al enpe*r*ador q*ue* es descomulgado, | τ sabedes como p*a*p*a* Pascual n*ue*st*r*o antecesor lo descomulgo τ ma*n*do q*ue* | esleyesen ot*r*o arcob*i*spo; agora es fecho p*a*p*a* co*n*tra derech*o* τ co*n*tra ley, co*n* poder | del enpe*r*ador, onde uos ma*n*damos *que* p*r*oueades ala ygl*esi*a de Bragana | de arçobispo τ denu*n*çiat por descomulgado a Mauriçio. Dat*a* en Gayeta, | viij° k*a*l*endas* ap*r*iles". Ese mismo p*a*p*a* uino a Leon sobre Ruedaño τ ali fino τ | no*n* cu*n*plio el año τ despues fue p*a*p*a* Calixto ij°, q*ue* era ob*i*spo de Uiana, | h*er*mano del co*n*de do*n* Remo*n*, padre q*ue* fue del enpe*r*ador de Castiella;[iii] este | fizo paz co*n* Oto τ torno a Roma τ do*n* Burdino fue p*r*eso τ encarcelado | en Calab*r*ia, enel monest*er*io de Santa T*r*inidad de Capua τ ali uisco fasta | el tie*n*po de p*a*p*a* Eugenio iij°, q*ue* fue q*ua*rto de Alexa*n*dre p*a*p*a* τ ali fino a-|si como dicho es. τ de tales omes ordeno do*n* B*er*nald su ygl*esi*a τ de | pues delos fizo ob*i*spos τ delos arçobispos enlas ygl*esi*as q*ue* ua-|[fol.56r]| caua*n*. Depues[iv] do*n* B*er*nalt ouo su ygl*esi*a bie*n* ordenada, cerço Alcala τ fizo y | su bastida q*uel* oy paresce τ p*r*isola por fambre. Ot*r*osi el rey do*n* Alfonso ouo bie*n* | puesto a Toledo, mouio su hueste τ uino sobre los moros q*ue* era*n* ce*r*ça de | Duero τ p*r*iso las fortalezas τ los planos τ echolos todos a mal por | q*ue* lo ganaua[452] asi q*ue* Dios en todo bie*n*, en p*r*iuilegios q*ue* daua a cauall*er*os τ a or-|denes, lamauase enpe*r*ador d'España.[v]

De Ruy Diaz

| Esto*n*z Ruy Dias era mal q*u*isto del rey do*n* Alfonso τ echolo de ti*er*ra, lo uno | por su co*n*seio[vi] se guiaua el rey do*n* Sanch*o* co*n*tra desere*d*ar sus h*er*manos τ por | q*uel* agutio ta*n*to la iura. τ ali ente*n*dio q*ue* nol plazie co*n*el τ salio dela ti*er*ra co*n* parien-|tes τ co*n* amigos τ acostados τ fue guerrear ala

---

[i] *DRH*: 'Gayete'.
[ii] *DRH*: 'bracarensis'.
[iii] *DRH*: 'Aldefonsi imperatoris Hispani'.
[iv] *DRH*: VI.xxviii
[v] *DRH*: 'imperatorem Hisperie'.
[vi] The view of the translator is rather different to that of Ximénez de Rada as this comment is not from *DRH*.

fro*n*tera de Aragon a moros ┆ τ ouo fazie*n*da *con* el rey do*n* Ped*r*o de Aragon, he*r*mano del rey do*n* Alfonso q*ue* fino en ┆ Fraga τ fue ue*n*çido τ p*r*eso; τ pues q*u*itaro*n* se por amigos d'amigos. Depues ┆ Ruy Diaz p*r*iso Uale*n*çia τ uino sobrel Bucar *con* gra*n*des pode*r*es τ Ruy Diaz ┆ enuio dema*n*dar aiuda al rey d'Aragon; τ uino el mismo *con* su poder τ ue*n*çie-┆ro*n* a Bucar, y el escapo a pies de cauallo fasta el mar, q*ue* se puso en una gal-┆*e*a; los ot*r*os fuero*n* todos muertos τ p*r*esos τ fue muy gra*n*d la gana*n*çia del ┆ ca*n*po. τ asi fi*n*co Uale*n*çia asu ma*n*dar τ como dixemos fizo y ob*i*spo a Ie-┆ronimo. A pocos dias fino Ruy Diaz τ sacaro*n* el cuerpo de Uale*n*çia con ┆ mucha lazeria; τ cobraro*n* moros la çiudad τ aduxiero*n* a do*n* Ruy a Sant ┆ Pedro de Cardeña τ alli lo enterraro*n* τ alli iaze.

De su linage[i]

┆ Digamos de Mio Çit, como uino de linage. Layn Caluo, q*ue* fue alcalde ┆ de Castiella τ fue co*m*pañe*r*o de Nuño Rasuera el alcalde, do*n*de uiniero*n* ┆ los reyes de Castiella, Layn Caluo ouo fijo a Ferrand Laynez; este ouo a ┆ Layn Ferrandez τ a Nuño Laynez τ a Layn Nuñez τ a Diago Laynez;[453] ┆ este caso *con* fija de Ruy Aluarez de Asturias, bue*n* om*n*e τ bue*n* caualle*r*o, ┆ τ ouo en ella a Ruy Diaz. Depues[ii] q*ue* fino su padre c*r*iolo el rey do*n* Ferra*n*-┆do. Qua*n*do el rey do*n* Ferrand*o* uino a muert come*n*dolo a s*u*s fijos, de pues el dio ┆ se mas al rey do*n* S*a*nch*o* τ fizolo cauale*r*o τ fue muy bueno enla fazie*n*da ┆[fol.56v] ┆ q*ue* ouo el rey do*n* S*a*nch*o* *con* el rey do*n* Ramiro en Gad*a*s;[iii] ot*r*osi qua*n*do lidio *con* su he*r*ma-┆no do*n* Gar*ç*ia en Sant Are*n* fue muy bueno; ot*r*osi qua*n*do lidio *con* su he*r*mano do*n* ┆ Alfonso en Golpige*r*a;[454] ot*r*osi muy bueno en la cerça de Çamora, e bueno qua*n*do fue en ┆ p*u*s Uela de Adolfos[455] fasta las puertas de Çamora τ no*n* pudo entrar τ firio ┆ enla puerta; τ bueno qua*n*do lidio por el rey do*n* Alfonso *con* Seme*n* Garçiez de ┆ Torrellas; τ bueno qua*n*do lidio *con* un moro Hariz en Medina Çelim; τ bue-┆no qua*n*do lidio *con* el rey d'Aragon en Toruar; τ bueno enla p*r*ision de Uale*n*çia; ┆ e bueno qua*n*do fue Bucar ue*n*çido. Ruy Diaz caso *con* doña Simeña, fija ┆ del *con*de do*n* Diago de Asturias τ ouo en ella a Diago Royz τ mataro*n* lo ┆ moros en *Con*suegra; τ ouo dos fijas, doña X*r*ist*i*na τ X*r*ist*i*ana,[456] q*ue* caso *con* el ifa*n*te ┆ do*n* Ramiro de Nauarra en Uale*n*çia, onde uiene*n* rey de Nauarra τ de Cas-

---

[i] *DRH*: V.i This returns to the Judges section, and places it in a role more conducive to highlighting the importance and lineage of the Cid.

[ii] These details are not from *DRH* although they would have been readily available from the epic tradition.

[iii] As above, such references are not drawn from *DRH* but must have been commonly held to be true.

ｊtiellaⁱ como suso dixiemos; τ ouo a doña Marina q*ue* caso *con* el *con*de de Barcilona.

Del rey de Castiella ⁱⁱ

ｊ Tornemos alos reyes de Castiella. ｊ Esto*nz* enfermo el rey do*n* Garcia, q*ue* iazie p*re*so en Luna τ do*n* Alfonso bie*n* lo sol-ｊtarie mas temiese q*ue*l pornie la t*ie*rra en rebuelta; τ *con* todo eso el rey ｊ do*n* Alfonso bie*n* auie en coraço*n*, pues q*ue* no*n* auie fijos ni*n* los esp*er*aua au*er*, ｊ delexar la t*ie*rra a do*n* Garcia de pues de s*us* dias. Enta*n*to adolescio de muert ｊ τ ma*n*daua lo soltar τ do*n* Garcia no*n* q*ui*so, ante rogo al hermano τ alos obis-ｊpos τ asus uasallos q*ue* pues q*ue* lo no*n* soltara*n* en uida, q*ue* lo no*n* soltasen ｊ enla muert τ q*ue* asi lo enterrasen por ensie*m*plo d'España.ⁱⁱⁱ τ fino en era ｊ de mill. τ cxvij, al xvj° el año q*ue* regnaua do*n* Alfonso; τ acercaro*n*se ｊ asu muert do*n* Raner, q*ue* era legado de Roma; τ do*n* Ber*n*ald, q*ue* era p*ri*mado d'Es-ｊpaña, q*ue* dixo la misa. A pocos de dias fino doña Urraca τ despues do*ña* El-ｊuira τ enterraro*n* las con su padre el rey do*n* Ferrand*o*. Muertas^{iv} las mug*er*es d*e*l ｊ rey do*n* Alfonso, una enpos ot*r*a, doña Ynes τ doña Costa*n*ça τ doña Alberta ｊ τ doña Helisabed, caso despues **con** la Çaeda, fija de Abenabet τ tornola *chr*isti-ｊana τ ouo no*m*bre doña M*ari*a. Este dio a do*n* Alfonso lo q*ue*l diera su padre: ｊ Caracuel, Alarço*n*, *Con*suegra, Mora, Ocaña, Oreia, Ucles, Uepte, Amasa, ｊ[fol.57r] ｊ T*ri*go τ Cue*n*ca. Desta ouo al yfañt do*n* S*an*ch*o* τ diol a c*ri*ar al *con*de do*n* Garcia de Cabra. τ de-ｊpues por *con*seio de Amenadab enuio por los moros de Africa τ lamolos por ｊ no*m*bre Almorauedes, por q*ue*l aiudasen; τ^v ellos pasaro*n* τ fiziero*n* al: mataro*n* ｊ Amenadab, por q*ue* diera su fija τ los castiellos al rey do*n* Alfonso. Dend aca ｊ los del Andaluzia no*n* q*ui*siero*n* obedeçer a *chr*ist*i*anos, ni*n* auer mas de un señor, ｊ τ todos obedeciero*n* al Miramomeni*n*. De pues legaro*n* se moros *con* gra*n*d po-ｊder en un logar q*ue* dize*n* Roda τ lidiaro*n* *con* el *con*de do*n* Rodrigo τ *con* el *con*de do*n* ｊ Garcia τ fuero*n* ue*n*çidos los *chr*ist*i*anos. De^{vi} pues el rey do*n* Alfonso, por esto ue*n*gar, le-ｊgo su poder τ lidio *con* Miramomelin en un lugar q*ue* dize*n* Sagriella τ murie-ｊro*n* y muchos p*er*o fuero*n* ue*n*cidos *chr*ist*i*anos. Ese año salio do*n* Alfonso τ corrio ｊ Cordoua τ Seuilla; τ Miramomelin, maguer tenie gra*n*d poder τ q*ue* era ｊ *con* el *con*de do*n* Garcia Ordonez, no*n* oso salir ael τ asi torno hondrado. El^{vii} rey ｊ

ⁱ See Martin, *Les juges*. The translation is more impressed with Rodrigo's doings than is the Navarrese archbishop...
ⁱⁱ *DRH*: VI.xxviiii
ⁱⁱⁱ The comment on exemplarity is not from *DRH*.
^{iv} *DRH*: VI.xxx
^v *DRH* scathing comments about andaluces removed.
^{vi} *DRH*: VI.xxxi
^{vii} *DRH*: VI.xxxii

do*n* Alfonso era ya uieio, e uino Miramomelin τ ce*r*co Ucles. El rey do*n* Alfon | enuio alla su fijo do*n* S*ancho*, con el *con*de do*n* Garcia su amo τ *con* poder de castellanos. | Lidiaro*n* τ mataro*n* el cauallo al ifant do*n* Sancho τ depues lidiaro*n*[457] a pie τ lama*n*-|do "¡Castiella!", cortaro*n* el pie al co*n*de; τ no*n* ouiero*n* acorro τ depues uio q*ue* no*n* | podie*n* escapar, exose sobre su c*ri*ado por no*n* ueer su muerte τ mataro*n* al *con*-|de do*n* Garcia τ depues al ifañt do*n* S*ancho* τ asi fuxiero*n* castellanos. τ el *con*de Garcia | Fernandez τ el *con*de do*n* Ma*rti*n τ ot*ro*s *con*des τ om*ne*s fuyendo, *con*siguiero*n* lo los moros[458] | τ mataro*n* los en un lugar q*ue*l pusiero*n* no*n*bre vij Puertos τ depues do*n* | Pedro Fra*n*co, come*n*dador de Ucles, le camio el no*n*bre τ dixo les vij *Con*des. | Los ot*ro*s *con*des τ los q*ue* escaparo*n* uiniero*n* a Toledo con gra*n*d bergue*n*ça τ dixo | les el rey: "*Con*des, ¿do es mi fijo?". Respuso el *con*de do*n* Gomez: "Dema*n*dad lo a | q*ui*lo come*n*daste". Dixo el: "Aq*ui*lo come*n*de recabdo me dara, q*ue* nu*n*q*ua* uerna | sin el; mas uos q*ue* fuestes por faze*r*le se*r*uit*i*o, ¿como uiniestes o q*ue* q*ui*sies-|tes aq*ui*?" Respuso Aluar Hañes:[i] "Señor, nos no*n* pudiemos de foyr la ue*n*-|tura q*ue* Dios q*ui*so dar a u*uest*ro fijo de asi morir τ bie*n* ueyemos q*ue* razo*n* | era derecha de morir y todos con el τ fuera meior p*ar*a nos; mas era |[fol.57v] | mayor daño p*ar*a uos; pues no*n* pudiemos ael acorrer uiniemos acor-|er auos, q*ue* erades ya ca*n*sado, q*ue* no*n* pe*r*diesedes la t*ie*rra q*ue* auedes con mucha | lazeria ganada τ por q*ue* no*n* fuesedes desondrado en u*uestra* uegez lo q*ue* no*n* fu-|estes en ma*n*çebez. Agora fazed lo q*ue* q*ue*rades de nos a u*uestr*a uolu*n*tad". [ii] El rey, | esto dizie*n*do τ lora*n*do, nu*n*qua amanso su yra. Esto*n*z pe*r*dio Ucles τ Cue*n*ca | τ Amasa, T*ri*go, Uepte, Oresa, Ocaña, Co*n*suegra. Despues[iii] los *con*des τ los ricos | om*ne*s de Castiella uiero*n* el rey uieio τ maltrecho τ no*n* auie fijo uaro*n*, | τ pe*r*die el seso q*ue* por sus dias q*ue* por muerte del su fijo; aiu*n*taro*n* se todos | en Maga*n* τ acordaro*n* se por q*ue* la t*ie*rra fincase en paz, si el rey muriese, | q*ue* fablasen casamie*n*to de uno dellos con doña Urraca, fija del rey, mad*r*e | q*ue* fue del enp*er*ador,[iv] asi q*ue* todos acordaro*n* q*ue* la dema*n*dasen p*or*al *con*de don | Gomez. τ no*n* oso yr ne*n*guno al rey con estas nueuas τ rogaro*n* a don | Çidiello, q*ue* era su alfaq*ui*m τ su p*ri*uado, q*ue* lo fablase. Qua*n*do lo oyo el rey, | pesol de coraço*n* τ dixo: "¡Yo so en culpa qua*n*do **iudio**[459] ata*n*to q*ue* ueer con mi | en fablar casamie*n*to de mi fija τ q*ue* tal melo no*n* osan dezir mis ua-|sallos!". Echol luego de t*ie*rra a do*n* Çidiello τ ma*n*do q*ue* nu*n*q*ua* mas se p*ar*ase | antel τ asi los *con*des τ el iudio fuero*n* mal pagados.[460] Do*ña* Urraca

---

[i] Compare *DRH*: VI.xxxii.33ff, *EG* rhetoric is considerably reduced by comparison with the source.
[ii] As previously, *EG* direct speech expands upon the laconic *DRH* narration.
[iii] *DRH*: VI.xxxiii
[iv] *EG* takes every opportunity to mention Alfonso VII.

aui-|e estonz un fijo Alfonso τ por que non amaua asu padre nin nunqua se |
allego al rey ca lo criara el conde don Pedro de Traua, don Alfonso non auie |
cura del. τ depues, con conseio de su corte τ de su pueblo τ de sus | obispos,
despusola τ diola por muger al rey don Alfonso de Aragon; τ le-|uola consigo
aca el rey don Alfonso mientre pudo τ uisco, gouerno su | tierra en paz τ bien
asi que todos andauan seguros de noche τ de dia. Entanto[i] | el rey don
Alfonso adolesçio de una enfermedat de que iago un año τ daquela | murio,
pero los fisicos fazien le cadadia algun poco caualgar. Entonz acaescio | un
miraglo en Toledo que las piedras del altar de Sant Ieronimo manauan | agua
τ era y don Pedro, obispo de Leon τ don Pelayo, obispo de Ouiedo; estos
conla clerizia | τ conel pueblo mouieron de Santa Maria con procession τ fueron
fasta su altar τ dixieron |[fol.58r] | y misa τ fizieron y sermon τ todos beuieron
daquel agua, pero non sabien que **era** este | miraglo. Fino a pocos de dias el
rey τ creyeron que esto podrie seer. Murio | el rey el primer dia de julio,
iueues amanesçiente, ese dia murio paz τ | nasçio guerra. El obispo don
Bernald canto xx dias sobrel misa τ por que se dub-|dauan dela retenençia de
Toledo leuaron le a Sant Fagund o iazien sus mugeres. | Regno, pus salio
Toledo de mano de Almenun, xL años vj meses xij dias.

Del rey d'Aragon como ouo Castiella τ Leon[ii]

| Muerto el rey don Alfonso de | Castiella, el rey don Alfonso de Aragon, con
su muger doña Urraca, entro por | la tierra; τ maguer algunos se quisieron
alçar non pudieron τ cobraron toda la | tierra. El rey que, con miedo dela reyna
que la auie sospechosa τ que de castellanos, | todas las de mas fortalezas dio a
tener alos aragoneses, e he uos[iii] los | señores de toda España. Este firmo
bien la tierra, cerço las uillas, poblo el suelo | de Castiella: Uilforado, Uerlanga,
Soria, Almaçan. Pero parientes casaron asi: don Sancho | el Mayor ouo fijos a
don Ferrando τ a don Ramiro, don Ferrando ouo a don Alfonso τ el a doña
Ur- |raca; don Ramiro ouo a don Pedro τ el a don Alfonso; τ asi eran
segundos cormanos τ | non quiso Dios que ouiesen fijos. El conde don Pedro
Ansures ouo criado de niñez | a doña Urraca τ ella depues que regno cogio
mal querençia con el τ tollio le | la tierra; τ el rey d'Aragon uio quel
gualardonaua mal la criazon y el seruitio, tor-|nole la tierra τ desque de aqui
compeço a querer mal al rey. Depues que gelo entendio | el rey, faziela guardar
τ pesaua a ella. De pues uio el rey que non era seso | guardar muger, de mas
que tenie oio a mal, aduxola fasta Soria, que el po-|blara τ alli delexola asu

---

[i] *DRH*: VI.xxxiiii
[ii] *DRH*: VII.i
[iii] The address to the readers is that of the translator.

g*u*isa q*ue* fuese o fincase o q*u*isiese asu g*u*isa. Ella q*u*ito ǀ se del rey τ uinose p*ar*a Castiella τ fizo corte en Burgos[i] τ dema*n*dola ǀ t*ie*rra desu padre a Pedro Ansurez. Diogela toda, p*er*o q*ue* la tenie **toda** de mano del rey. ǀ Ot*r*osi gela diero*n* los ot*r*os. Esto*n*z Pedro Ansurez fizo paños d'escarlata τ bie*n* ǀ g*u*isado del dia q*ue* mouio leuo una soga ala garga*n*ta fasta q*ue* lego al rey d'A-ǀrago*n* al Castellar τ dixol: "Señor, la t*ie*rra di ami señor natural, el cuerpo ǀ τ la lengua q*ue* te fizo omenage trayo atu poder; faz de mi qua*n*to q*u*isieres." ǀ [fol.58v] ǀ El rey, maguer yrado, ente*n*dio q*ue* fiziera τ fazie τ co*m*plie derecho τ p*er*donol τ ǀ diol sus ioas τ asi lo enuio. Este iuyzio es oy en España.[ii] Castellanos[iii] come*n*çaro*n* ǀ auer discordia entre si, el co*n*de do*n* Gomez cuydaua casar co*n* doña Urraca τ el ǀ co*n*de do*n* Pedro ot*r*osi τ ella tenielos amos pagados. Pero el conde don Gomez quisiera casar con ella en uida del padre τ a escuso fiziera*n* un fijo q*ue* ouo no*n*bre Furtado τ do*n* ǀ Gomez como en uez de marido co*n*peço de enparar la t*ie*rra τ de yr co*n*tra los a-ǀragoneses, el co*n*de do*n* Ped*r*o ot*r*osi acabo co*n* ella lo q*ue* q*u*iso, como fue despues p*r*ouado. El rey ǀ de Aragon, q*ue* aun tenie las mayores fortalezas q*ue* come*n*dara alos aragoneses, ǀ mouio su hueste τ ent*r*o por Castiella. Aca el co*n*de do*n* Gomez τ el co*n*de do*n* Pedro, con ǀ blueços fuero*n* co*n* castellanos co*n*tra el τ aiuntaro*n* se en Ca*n*po d'Espino. El co*n*de ǀ don Pedro[461] tenie la seña, do*n* Gomez tenie la çaga, lidiaro*n* como q*ue* fue la seña fue ǀ abatida τ fuxo el co*n*de do*n* Pedro. Do*n* Gomez fino y τ asi ue*n*cio el rey ǀ de Aragon. τ el co*n*de do*n* **Pedro**[462] uinose p*ar*a la reyna a Burgos. Desende el rey ǀ fuese p*ar*a Leon τ falleçio le el auer p*ar*a dar alos caualle*r*os τ puso mano a ǀ los tesoros delas ygl*e*sias q*ue* diera*n* los reyes; esto peso a Dios τ alos om*n*es. ǀ Esto*n*z leoneses τ gallegos, con do*n* Alfonso, fijo della reyna, saliero*n* co*n*tra el rey; ǀ τ fuero*n* ue*n*çidos leoneses τ asi torno el rey ondrado de sus enemigos, ǀ τ mato al co*n*de do*n* Gomez τ q*u*ebra*n*to alos q*ue* tenie*n* con el co*n*de do*n* Pedro. Con todo eso el ǀ co*n*de non p*r*eçiaua nada el q*u*ebra*n*to, q*ue* cuydaua casar co*n* doña Urraca τ ma*n*daua ǀ ya como rey. Los castellanos tenie*n* se por mal trechos por muchas cosas, ǀ τ lo de mas por su señora, q*ue* delexara su marido τ andaua asi en adulter*i*o*s*, ǀ co*n*pecaro*n* de co*n*tra dezir su razo*n* alo q*ue* ma*n*daua el co*n*de.

---

[i] The place of meeting is not mentioned in *DRH*.
[ii] *DRH*: 'cuius factum Hispani adhunc hodie inmitantur', the figure of the king is more honourable in the *EG* version.
[iii] *DRH*: VII.ii

Como alçaron rey al que fue enperador[i]

| Castellanos todos,[463] mayor mie*n*tre el *con*de do*n* Gomez de Maçane-|do τ do*n* Gutierre Ferrandez de Cast*r*o, temie*n*do este casamie*n*to, esleyero*n* | por rey a do*n* Alfonso, fijo de do*na Vrraca*[464] τ del *con*de do*n* Remo*n*, q*ue* fuera c*r*iado en Gal-|lizia τ enuiaro*n* porel *con* co*n*seio dela madre[ii] τ del *con*de do*n* Pedro. Este ce*r*ço ala | madre enlas torres de Leon; despues ouiero*n* abene*n*çia, diero*n* ala reyna | lo q*ue* q*u*iso en q*ue* uiuiese, lo ot*r*o finco asu fijo. El *con*de do*n* Pedro fuese p*ar*al *con*de de | [fol.59r] | Barçilona. Aca el rey do*n* Alfonso de Castiella *con*peço de guerrear las fortalezas | q*ue* tenie el rey d'Aragon. El rey uino *con* poder de Aragon τ de Nauarra τ qua*n*do fuero*n* | iu*n*tados por lidiar ouo y ob*i*spos τ arçobispos τ omes de orde*n* τ ricos om*ne*s τ uie-|ro*n* q*ue* aiu*n*tando se q*ue* se*r*ie mal τ q*ue* podrie nasçer discordia por se pe*r*der la ti*er*ra como | al tie*n*po del rey R*od*r*i*go. Por su *con*seio dellos ouo fabla *con* el rey de Aragon τ demos-|trole el derecho q*ue* el auie enel regno τ pusolo en su mano τ rogol q*ue* to-|mase lo q*ue* q*u*isiese τ q*ue*l diese lo q*ue* q*u*isiese como padre, q*ue* todo lo q*ue*rie p*ar*a el | fazer se*r*uiti*o* τ hondra. De pues el rey de Aragon uio q*ue* ta*n* bie*n* y uinie τ no*n* | lo q*ue*rie por guerra, touo lo por bie*n* *con*seiado τ gradesciol lo q*ue* dixo τ ma*n*-|dol tornar τ dar todo lo suyo, ca era bue*n* *chr*is*t*iano τ rogol τ *con*seiol como fu-|ese bueno τ como se ma*n*touiese el τ s*us* uasallos bie*n*; τ asi firmaro*n* su | paz τ tornaro*n* en sus logares amigos de amigos. Conpeço[iii] de regnar es-|te do*n* Alfonso, fijo de doña Urraca, en Castiella era mill ccxlvj τ regno L años et su madre regnara, des- | pues que fino don Alfonso, quatro años.

| Dela batalla de Fraga que se perdio el rey d'Aragon[iv]

| Fecho el adobo entre los reyes, oyo el rey de Aragon q*ue*l entraua*n* mo-|ros la ti*er*ra τ fue en acor*r*o τ ouo fazie*n*da *con* ellos en Fraga τ el, q*ue* sie*n*pre | ue*n*çiera, ali fue ue*n*çido, asi q*ue* nu*n*qua pareçio. Unos dize*n* q*ue* fue p*r*eso τ rede-|mido τ aduxo a Mo*n*t Aragon τ dalli se[465] fue pe*r*der de ue*r*guença; ot*r*os dize*n* q*ue* | escapo dela fazie*n*da τ no*n* fue p*r*eso τ de ue*r*guença no*n* oso tornar ala ti*er*ra; | ot*r*os dize*n* q*ue* a tie*n*po uino en Aragon τ fablo *con* algunos q*ue* sopiero*n* de | s*us* poridades; ot*r*os dize*n* q*ue* ali se pe*r*dio τ q*ue* no*n* fue coñosçido.

---

[i] *DRH*: VII.iii
[ii] This contradicts (in error?) *DRH*: '...resistente nichilominus sibi matre et comite Petro de Lara'. This is the beginning of the reign of Alfonso VII, a key figure in *EG*.
[iii] *DRH*: VII.iiii, the addition of the reference to Alfonso VII, once more highlighting the importance of this figure, is drawn from the beginning of the following chapter.
[iv] What follows here returns to *DRH* VI.iii.

Del enpera-dor de Castiella[i]

| Tornemos a do*n* Alfonso de Castiella. Este fue muy | bueno, ardid τ fra*n*co τ ouo buenos uasallos τ gano much*o* de | moros. Este gano Coria τ fizo y obispo. Do*n* Be*r*naldo, arçob*i*spo de Toledo, or-|denada su ygle*s*ia fino[ii] iij nonas ap*r*il*es*, el xiij. año q*ue* regnaua el enpe*ra*-|dor τ fue enterrado en Santa Ma*r*ia de Toledo la q*ua*l saco de poder de moros. | De pues del fue arçob*i*spo do*n* Remo*n*d de Osma. Despues el enpe*ra*-|[fol.59v] | dor çerco Calatr*a*ua, q*ue*l fazie gra*n*d guerra τ p*r*isola τ otorgo la ygle*s*ia co*n* s*u*s | derechos ala ygle*s*ia de Toledo; *et* delos castiellos τ delos logares q*ue* era*n* | de Calatr*a*ua, delos retouo τ delos estruyo como Alacuris, Caracuy, Sa*n*ta | Eufemia, Mesta*n*ça, Alcudia τ Almodouar, q*ue* fazie*n* gra*n*d mal. τ por q*ue* a-|si lo guiaua Dios, lamauase enpe*ra*dor.[iii]

Delos reyes de Portugal[iv]

| Digamos aq*u*i la genealogia delos reyes de Portugal. El *con*de don | Enric, q*ue* caso *con* doña Teresa, fija del rey do*n* Alfonso q*ue* gano Toledo, fue | muy bueno τ cuerdo τ redro mucho los moros de Portugal. Este uinie | toda uia a corte del rey de Castiella fasta ento*nz* τ el rey como a uazi-|no daual auegadas pasada de no*n* uenir,[v] τ asi poco a poco se pe*r*dio el | señorio. Este Enric torno las siedes cathedrales a Uiseo τ Lo*n*geio[466] en | Portugal τ fizo y ob*i*spo el arçob*i*spo do*n* Be*r*nald τ poblo Braguena, q*ue* era y-|erma. Do*n* Enric[vi] se lamaua *con*de por su linage, doña Teresa reyna por | su padre. Do*n* Enric, a ruego dela reyna, dio atodos los obispos de Por-|tugal sus p*r*iuilegios muy buenos τ s*u*s franq*ue*zas, este Enric ouo a | doña Teresa τ a do*n* Alfonso, q*ue* depues del fue señor de Portugal. Este | caso *con* doña Mofalta, fija del *con*de Maurie*n*sis τ ouo en ella a do*n* Sanc*h*o | τ a do*ñ*a Urraca, esta doña Urraca caso *con* do*n* Ferrand*o*, q*ue* depues fue rey de Leon τ | ouo en ella a do*n* Alfonso, de q*u*i diremos depues; ot*r*osi ouo a doña Teresa | q*ue* caso *con* Phelipo, *con*de de Fla*n*dria τ fino sin fijos. Do*n* Sanc*h*o, fijo de do*n* Alfonso, ca-|so co*n* doña Dolça, fija del *con*de de Barçilona de do*n* Remo*n* τ dela reyna doña | Urraca de Aragon τ ouo en ella fijos a do*n* Alfonso, q*ue* depues fue rey de | Portugal, este caso *con* doña Urraca, fija del rey do*n* Alfonso de Castiella τ o-|uo en ella al rey do*n* Sanc*h*o q*ue* depues fue rey τ despues despuesto

[i] *DRH*: VI.iiii
[ii] *EG* reduces the Latin rhetoric to a minimum and cuts the quotation of Bernard's epitaph.
[iii] *DRH*: 'hispaniarum regem'.
[iv] *DRH*: VII.v. *EG* groups all the non-Castilian genealogies, thereby departing from *DRH* practice.
[v] Once more, when dealing with genealogies, *EG* departs from close translation of *DRH*.
[vi] *EG* resumes *DRH* narration.

como ⏐ diremos adela*n*te;ⁱ τ ot*r*o fijo do*n* Alfonso, q*ue* caso en Fra*n*çia *con*
doña Matiel-⏐la, *con*desa de Boloñaⁱⁱ q*ue* despues regno de su he*r*mano como
diremos a-⏐dela*n*t; τ ot*r*o fijo do*n* Ferrand*o*, q*ue* caso en Castiella *con* la fija del
*con*de do*n* Ferrand*o con* doña ⏐ Sanch*a*; τ ouo en ella una fija, doña Leonor, q*ue*
caso *con* el rey [de] Daçia τ fino ⏐ [fol.60r] ⏐ sin fijos. El rey do*n* S*an*ch*o*, **de** q*ui*
dixiemos, menos de do*n* Alfonso, q*ue* regno, ouo en ⏐ la fija del *con*de ot*r*o
fijo, el yfañt do*n* Pedro, q*ue* caso *con* la fija de do*n* Armi*n*got, *con*-⏐de de Urgel
τ fino sin fijos, deste diremos depues q*ue* fue del.ⁱⁱⁱ Ouo este ⏐ mismo do*n*
S*an*ch*o* ot*r*o fijo do*n* Ferrand, q*ue* caso *con* la *con*desa de Fla*n*dria τ fino sin
fijos; ouo ⏐ ot*r*osi una fija ese do*n* S*an*ch*o* q*ue* caso *con* do*n* Alfonso, rey de
Leon, auie*n*do su mug*er* doña ⏐ Bele*n*guera, fija del rey de Castiella τ ouo en
ella al ynfañt do*n* Ferrand τ a doña S*an*ch*a* ⏐ τ doña Dolça,^{iv} τ estos todos
muriero*n* sin fijos. Tornemos^v a do*n* Alfonso, rey, ⏐ su fijo del conde do*n*
Enric τ dela reyña doña Teresa q*ue* se **llamo** p*r*ime*r*o rey de Portu-⏐gal por la
mad*r*e, q*ue* el padre p*r*ime*r*o se lamo duc, depues *con*de. Este acabo mu-⏐cho
bue*n* p*r*iuilegio dela corte de Papa Eugenio iij°. Et fecieronle muchas gracias.
⏐ Fizo el regno tributario ala corte. Este fizo el moneste*r*io de Sa*n*ta Cruz en
Co-⏐ynb*r*ia τ fizo el moneste*r*io de Alcobaça τ enriq*ue*çiolo de riq*ue*zas τ de
he*r*edades ⏐ τ de p*r*euilegios. Este gano Sa*n*ta Iusta de Lixbona, Elboro τ
Alanq*ue*llo τ poblo ⏐ ot*r*os logares yermos. Este lidio *con* el rey do*n* Ferrand
de Leon τ fue ue*n*çido τ p*r*eso τ de-⏐pues a pocos dias q*ue* lo saco el rey de
Leon finose en Portugal τ enterraro*n* ⏐ lo en Coynbria enel moneste*r*io q*ue*
fizo de Sa*n*ta Cruz. Depues del regno su fijo ⏐ do*n* S*an*ch*o*, bueno τ sabio τ
ue*n*çiol muchas uezes alos moros e p*r*iso a la Selua, ⏐ muy rica cibdat τ fizo y
ob*i*spo, mas de pues la cobraro*n* los moros. Este ⏐ poblo muchos de logares
q*ue* iazie*n* yerm*o*s: la Cueua de Santa Yllana, q*ue* dize*n* ⏐ oy Gauillana, la
Guardia, Mo*n*t Sacro, Puerto de Malos, Torres Nueuas ⏐ τ ot*r*os muchos
buenos logares. De pues adolesçio τ fino τ regno su fijo ⏐ do*n* Alfonso.
Luego fue muy bue*n* ch*r*ist*i*ano τ de pues om*n*e de su uolu*n*tad, duro ⏐ poco τ
fino τ regno su fijo do*n* S*an*ch*o*, q*ue* p*er*dio el regno. El yfañt do*n* Pedro, q*ue*
dixiemos, ⏐ q*ue* caso *con* fija del *con*de d[e]⁴⁶⁷ Urgel, no*n* ouo fijos; la mug*er*
ouo de morir τ delexo ⏐ el *con*dado a do*n* Pedro en q*ue* uisq*u*iese,^{vi} depues q*ue*

ⁱ *DRH*: 'qui etiam adhuc regnat', Sancho's reign ended in 1248.
ⁱⁱ *DRH*: 'et per eam habet hodie comitatem'. *EG* is aware Afonso became king in 1248.
ⁱⁱⁱ These details are not from *DRH*. See above p. 8.
^{iv} *DRH*: 'Dulcis remanit', the date of composition of *EG* may therefore be after the death of
Aldonza in 1267, see Julio González, *Alfonso IX*. There is also reference to Alfonso IX's children in
VII.xxiiii.17 ff. See above, p. 8 for possible dating of the translation.
^v *DRH*: VII.vi
^{vi} The reference to the doings of Pedro, his descent and loss of kingdom is not from from *DRH*. For
this, and *EG* interest in kings of Mallorca and Aragon, see above p. 29ff.

tornase as*us* he*r*ederos; el rey do*n* ₁ Iayme de Aragon, muerta la *con*desa, por
q*ue* ael pe*r*tenesçie el *con*dado, temie*n*do ₁ q*ue* sele malmet*g*ñe, fizo co*n*pusiçio*n*
co*n* el yfañt do*n* Pedro q*uel* diese el regno de ₁ Mayorga *con* su *con*q*u*ísta por
s*us* dias τ q*uel* dexase Urgel τ asi fue. Des- ₁[fol.60v] ₁pues el yfañt enoiose de
mar pasar a tie*n*po τ fizo co*n*posiçio*n* q*uel* diese Mur-₁uiedro τ Sogorue τ
Moriella τ ot*r*os logares por s*us* dias τ q*ue* delex*g*se Mayor-₁ga τ asi fue.[i] Pues
los dio al yfañt do*n* Alfonso, fijo del rey de Aragon, q*ue* las ₁ touiese por el.
Otrosi digamos como pe*r*dio el regno el rey do*n* Sanc*h*o τ como lo ouo ₁ su
he*r*mano el *con*de de Boloña.

Delos reyes de Castiella τ del enperador[ii]

₁ Tornemos al enpe*r*ador de Castiella, fijo de doña Urraca. Este ouo dos ₁
mug*er*es, doña Bele*n*guera τ doña Richa. De doña Bele*n*guera ouo a do*n*
Sanc*h*o ₁ τ a do*n* Fernand τ a doña Helisbet τ doña Baeça; doña Helisabet
caso *con* el rey Lo-₁ys de Fra*n*çia τ ouo en ella a doña Adelez, q*ue* caso *con* el
*con*de do*n* Po*n*tiz τ aq*u*ella ₁ *con*desa ouo a doña M*ar*ia, mad*r*e dela reyna doña
Iuhaña,[468] q*ue* caso co*n* el rey do*n* ₁ Ferrand de Castiella q*ue* p*r*iso Cordoua τ
Seuilla;[iii] la ot*r*a fija doña Baeça caso *con* el rey ₁ do*n* Sanc*h*o de Nauarra τ ouo
dela dos fijos τ dos fijas de q*ue* ya deximos de su-₁so. De pues, el enpe*r*ador,
por *con*seio del *con*de do*n* Malric de Lara τ del *con*de do*n* Ferrand ₁ de
Trastamari,[469] p*ar*tio los regnos alos dos fijos: dio a do*n* Sanc*h*o, q*ue* era fijo
mayor, ₁ Castiella fasta Sant Fagu*n*d τ Moro dela Reyna, Euter de Fumos τ
Orama ₁ τ Couiellas τ Medina τ Arenal τ el te*r*mino de Auilla τ desent como
cor-₁re calçada q*ue* dize*n* Gurnea τ en Asturias como p*ar*te Riba de Ona;
todo lo ot*r*o ₁ *con*tra el mar τ *con*tra Portugal dio al fijo menor do*n* Ferrand.
Depues desta diuisio*n* ₁ mouio su hueste el enpe*r*ador τ[iv] fue *con*tra Cordoua; τ
Aue*n*garia, señor de Cor-₁doua, *con* miedo delo no*n* podie*n* enparar, dio las
laues dela uilla al enpe*r*a-₁dor τ desi fizo se su uasallo τ besol la mano. Esto*n*z
el arçob*i*spo do*n* Remo*n*d ₁ de Toledo entro en la uilla τ ca*n*to y misa. El
enpe*r*ador no traye yent ₁ por la poblar τ come*n*do la çibdad al moro q*ue* gela
dio: Aue*n*gania; τ fizol ₁ omenage sobrel Alcora*n* por el τ por su fijo el rey
do*n* Sanc*h*o, q*ue* gela diese, yra-₁do τ pagado.

---

[i] The *EG* interest in Portugal and Aragon continues, compare *DRH*: VII.vii.
[ii] *DRH*: VII.vii, Alfonso VII is considered sufficiently important to merit a chapter on his own.
[iii] *DRH* obviously does not contain this detail.
[iv] *DRH*: VII.viii

Como uino el rey de França en España[i470]

El rey Loyz de ¦ França oyo por algunos mezcladores que doña Helisabet era de uil[471] li-¦nage dela madre τ por esto prouar uino como en romería a Santiague τ ¦ uino con el[472] rey de Nauarra. Sopolo el enperador τ fizo corte en Toledo τ ¦ [fol.61r] ¦ fueron espanoles bien guisados τ otrosi el conde de Barçilona que uino y bien guisa-¦do. τ fue y el rey Loys τ dixo el enperador: "Rey yo case con fija deste conde τ oue en ¦ ella estos dos fijos don Sancho τ don Ferrand τ doña Blanca, muger deste rey de Nauarra τ doña ¦ Helisabet, uuestra muger, quiero que sepades que muger tomastes". El rey Loys touose por ¦ pagado τ uio quel mintieran τ gradesciolo al enperador mucho; depues dixo que nunqua ¦ uiera tan fermosa caualeria, nin tan bien guisada,[ii] τ que agora ueye que en mundo ¦ non auie mayor nin mas limpia caualleria. Quitaron se muy pagados τ non quiso ¦ prender el rey nada del enperador si non una carbonçela que leuo τ puso la enla ¦ corona de Nuestro Señor τ[iii] ali es oy dia. Depues[iv] el enperador fue τ çerco Baeça, ¦ τ dubdo de la non poder prender por el grand poder de moros, e uio de noche ¦ en uision a Sant Ysidoro quel prometio aiuda; τ cobro coraçon τ otro dia[473] lidio ¦ τ uençio τ priso la çibdat τ fizo y la yglesia de Sant Ysidoro τ dio y buenas ¦ ioyas τ los moros que y fincaron fueron por catiuos. τ desende fue τ cerço Almaria, ¦ τ el conde de Barçilona τ grand nauio de Iegua[474] uinieron le en aiuda τ prisola por ¦ fuerça τ dio alos ienuezes[475] todo quanto falaron enla uilla; ellos non quisieron ¦ si non una escudiella grand que fallaron y d'esmerelda, al non leuaron.[476] El enperador ¦ τ el conde de Barçilona uinieronse a Baeça τ delexo y por guarda asu fijo don ¦ Sancho τ que enparase Anduiar τ Quesada. Depues tornose el enperador τ al Puerto de ¦ Muradal, a rayz de una enzina, prisol grand mal τ fino ali. El yfañt don Ferrand ¦ so fijo temiese de Leon por su hermano τ delexo y al padre τ uinose con los ri-¦cos omnes que eran y de Leon. Don Sancho[v] delexo quanto tenie alend el puerto τ uino con ¦ el arçobispo don Iohannes τ enterro su padre en Toledo. τ compeço de regnar era m τ ¦ cxc τ vi. τ regno i año. Don Sancho casara en uida del padre con doña Blanca, fija ¦ del rey don Garcia de Nauarra τ de doña Margelina, fija del conde d'Alperches; τ ¦ en uida del enperador auie un fijo don Alfonso τ finco de tres años quando fi-¦no el enperador. Començo de regnar don Sancho τ fazer todos bienes que fazer los pudi-¦ese omne del mundo a Dios[477] τ a omnes.

---

[i] DRH: VII.viiii
[ii] The emphasis on the brilliance of Spanish knights is not made to the same extent in DRH.
[iii] DRH: 'quem etiam memini me uidesse'.
[iv] DRH: VII.xi. EG, interested only in the Christian kingdoms, and demonstrating a narrower view of history, passes over Ximénez de Rada's account of the origins of the Almohads.
[v] DRH: VII.xii

Del rey don Ferrando de Leon[i]

| Aca el rey do*n* Ferrand de Leon su he*r*mano, maguer bueno, creye losengeros[478] |[fol.61v] | τ deseredaua caualle*r*os τ **escuderos**[479] de he*r*edades τ yua se q*ue*rellar al rey do*n* | Sanc*h*o; e mouio su hueste τ uino fasta Sant Fagu*n*d. Oyolo do*n* Ferrando τ ouo mie-|do τ co*n* iiij° cauall*er*os solos τ desarmados uino a do*n* Sanc*h*o adesora o estaua sobre | la mesa. Recibiolo bie*n* τ uiol todo maltrecho τ no*n* q*u*iso comer fasta o lo fizo | bañar τ lauar la cabeça τ dar bueños paños τ asi lo esp*er*o ala mesa. τ | despues comiero*n* τ dema*n*dol como uiniera. Dixo do*n* Ferrand*o*: "Ue*n*go por fazer qua*n*to | ma*n*dedes, por dar uos el regno o por seer u*ues*t*r*o uasallo τ **fazer**[480] uos del | omenage". Dixo do*n* Sanc*h*o: "No*n* mande Dios he*r*mano q*ue* fijo de mi padre τ de mi | madre ami cate señorio, ni a ot*r*o, si no*n* a Dios. El regno q*u*iero p*ar*a uos τ mas | p*er*o ta*n*to uos ruego q*ue* tornades lo suyo alos caualle*r*os τ al *con*de do*n* Ponç | de Muñua,[481] τ alos ot*r*os τ asi ganar uos a Dios τ amar uos ha*n* los om*n*es, | τ yo mas". Otorgogelo τ fizo lo, asi p*ar*tiero*n* por amigos.

Delos freyres de Calatraua[ii]

| Luego desto, pues legaro*n* le freyres de Te*m*ple, q*ue* tenie*n* | Calatra*u*a, q*ue* lo no*n* podie*n* retener ant*e* gra*n*d poder de moros; ot*r*osi do*n* Sanc*h*o non | fallaua ric om*n*e q*ue* gela touiese. Era y ento*n*ze un do*n* Remo*n*d, abad de Fit*er*o, co*n* | ot*r*os mo*n*ges τ auie *con*sigo un freyre, Diago Blasq*u*iz, natural de Buruena, | q*ue* fuera c*r*iado del rey do*n* Sanc*h*o. Este uio al rey en cuyta τ *con*seiol al abad q*u*el diese | Calatraua, q*ue* el gela ma*n*pararie de moros. Dema*n*dola τ touiero*n* lo a locura por | q*ue* era*n* mo*n*ges, p*er*o otorgogela por he*r*adamie*n*to de **Fitero**.[482] Mouiero*n* se el abad τ do*n* | Diago τ dio s*u*s p*er*dones el arçob*is*po do*n* Ioha*n*n*es* τ fuero*n* co*n* ellos gra*n*des yentes, | τ pusiero*n* se en Calatraua τ no*n* uiniero*n* los moros q*ue* cuydaua*n*. Estonz | p*r*isiero*n* y muchos el abito de mano del abat por faz*er* y s*er*uiti*o* τ finco y | do*n* Diago por alcayet. Aca el abbat p*r*iso de todo ganado de su orde*n*, bie*n* fas-|ta xx mill cabeças τ muchos m*ar*auedis,[iii] ca ue*n*dio **muchas heredades** τ dio co*n* todo en Calatra*u*a por **retener.** | A pocos dias fino este abbat τ ent*er*arro*n* lo en Ceruilos, cabo Toledo τ fi-|zo Dios ali mucho por el. Diago Belasq*ue*z uisco depues mucho τ fino τ | fue enterrado en Sant Ped*r*o de Gomiel. El rey do*n* Sanc*h*o depues dio a Calatra*u*a a Fi-|de*r*o, uisco poco τ

---

[i] *DRH*: VII.xiii
[ii] *DRH*: VII.xiiii
[iii] Personal note of Ximénez de Rada 'et ut audiui...' removed.

fue enterrado *con* su pad*r*e en Toledo .ij. k*a*l*endas* septe*n*bris τ regno i año |[fol.62r]| τ xij dias.

Quando regno el rey don Alfonso[i]

| Muerto el rey do*n* S*a*nc*h*o, regno su fijo do*n* Alfonso, era mill cxc viij, en edat | de q*ua*tro años. Este fue fijo dela reyna doña Bla*n*ca, fija del rey do*n* Garcia de | Nauarra τ de niñez fasta q*ue* murio, sie*m*pre puño en todo bie*n*, pe*r*o nu*n*q*ua* le me*n*-|guo laze*r*ia, maguer todo lo ue*n*cio. Luego su tio do*n* Ferrand*o* p*r*isole algunos castiellos. | Qua*n*do fino do*n* S*a*nc*h*o, otorgo la ti*er*ra alos ricos om*n*es τ q*ue* lo ma*n*touiesen fasta el | rey do*n* Alfonso fuese de xv. años, esto*n*z q*ue* gela diesen asu g*u*isa; ot*r*osi asu mu-|erte come*n*dolo el yfañt a do*n* Gutierre Ferrandez de Cast*r*o, q*ue* lo c*r*iase como c*r*iara | ael. Esta comie*n*da peso mucho alos de Lara, al *con*de do*n* Alu*a*ro τ a do*n* Malriq*ue* τ a do*n* | Nuño, fijos del *con*de do*n* Pedro de Lara τ dela co*n*desa do*ñ*a Eua τ a do*n* Garcia Garçiez, q*ue* era | su he*r*mano mayor de madre, fijo de *con*de do*n* Garcia de Cabra q*ue* fino *con*el yfañt do*n* | Sanc*h*o en Uelez.[483] Estos fiziero*n* se *con*seieros a do*n* Gutier Ferrandez q*ue* diese fasta un tie*n*-|po asu he*r*mano do*n* Garcia Garçiez d'Asça[ii] q*ue* c*r*iase al rey τ como era poderoso *con* sus her-|manos en Estremadura q*ue* tenie la ti*er*ra en paz τ a tie*n*po q*ue* gela darie*n*. Crouo los | τ dio gelas *con* pleyto q*ue* lo aguardasen por mayor. Qua*n*do lo touo do*n* Garcia Garçiez, | dixiero*n* los he*r*manos menores q*ue* era*n* de padre τ de mad*r*e: "Dat el yfañt a do*n* | Malric τ todos aguardemos a uos" τ c*r*iolo el τ crouo los como a he*r*manos.[iii] | Qua*n*do lo touiero*n* no*n* diero*n* porel un dine*r*o τ menos por Gutier Ferrandez τ to-|uiero*n* se por señores de Castiella τ *con*pescaro*n* de faze*r* asu g*u*isa.

De la discordia entre los de Lara τ de Castro[iv]

| Esto*n*z uio Gutier Ferrandez q*ue* era mal iugado, | dema*n*do el yfañt como era puesto τ no*n* gelo q*u*isiero*n* dar. D'alli come*n*ço la guerra | ent*r*e los de Cast*r*o τ de Lara τ g*ra*ndes muertes τ por esta discordia ent*r*o el rey | do*n* Ferrand*o* la ti*er*ra τ gano bie*n* fasta Duero. Enta*n*to fino Gutier Ferrandez τ ma*n*do a | s*u*s nietos q*ue* no*n* diesen la ti*er*ra fasta q*ue* ouiese el rey xv años, como ma*n*-|dara el rey do*n* Sanc*h*o. Los de Lara, por q*ue* no*n* q*ue*rie*n* dar les la ti*er*ra, reptaua*n* a do*n* Gutier | Ferrandez τ alos suyos, ellos saluaro*n* se *con* lo q*ue* ma*n*do el rey do*n* Sanc*h*o τ enter-|raro*n* lo en Sant X*r*ist*o*ual de Enis. El

---

[i] *DRH*: VII.xv, once more the *EG* interest in genealogy comes to the fore.
[ii] *EG* suppresses the list of Lara family members which follows.
[iii] *EG* again employs direct speech not used by *DRH*.
[iv] *DRH*: VII.xvi

*con*de do*n* Malriq*ue* come*n*do el yfañt al co*n*çeio | de **Soria** bie*n* a c*ri*ar τ a guardar. El e s*us* hermanos co*n*peçaro*n* de echar la t*ie*rra a mal, | [fol.62v] | τ por esta discordia ent*ro* el rey do*n* Ferrand*o* τ gano el rey toda Estremadura τ fascas | toda Castiella τ fasta Toledo, asi q*ue* xij años fue señor τ poderoso del regno τ | delas rendas τ delos pechos; enta*n*to cost*ri*no a castellanos q*ue* do*n* Malriq*ue* ouo de | faz*er* omenaie por el yfañt τ por toda Castiella, q*ue* fuesen s*us* uasallos. De pues | fuero*n* a Soria por firmar este pleyto τ qua*n*do aduxiero*n* al yfañt q*ue* iurase | seer uasallo del rey do*n* Ferrand*o*, co*n*pesço de lorar τ dixiero*n* q*ue* q*ue*rie comer; aparta-|ro*n* lo por comer τ Pedro Nuñez de Fue*n* Almexir, por curiar lo de errar,[484] p*ri*so | lo so el ma*n*to τ caualgo un cauallo τ fuxo con el τ uino se a Sant Esteua*n*. | Qua*n*do lo sopo el rey ot*ro* dia, touo se por mal escarnido; el co*n*de do*n* Nuño, en | uoz de lo dema*n*dar, uino a Sant Esteua*n* τ p*ri*solo τ uino co*n*el [a] Atiença τ asi co*n*-|pescaro*n* todos a derramar. Do*n* Fe*rr*a*n*do enuio reptar a do*n* Alfonso τ a do*n* Malric | por si τ por el τ por castellanos, q*ue* fiziera omenage. El respuso τ saluose: | "Si iure por mi, fue a fuerça; por mi señor no*n* pud iurar, q*ue* no*n* era de edad | τ[i] no*n* es el tenido; por castellanos no*n* so tenido, q*ue* ni melo ma*n*daro*n* ni son | mis uasallos τ no*n* son en culpa. Yo no*n* se si faz mal o no*n*, mas libre al me-|ior q*ue* pud mi señor de mal pleyto". Depues[ii] p*ri*so el rey do*n* Ferrand*o* todas las | uillas τ los castiellos si no*n* alli o se **a**cogie el yfañt. Enta*n*to fue creçie*n*-|do do*n* Alfonso, **et** fue anda*n*do por la t*ie*rra con do*n* Nuño τ con do*n* Malric τ fuese le tor-|na*n*do la t*ie*rra[485] como yua anda*n*do como a señor natural τ co*n*bro Toledo q*ue* la | no*n* ouiera bie*n* auie xij años τ todo el yfa*n*tadgo q*ue* ant*e* era en dubda entre | los regnos.[iii]

Del rey don Ferando de Leon[iv]

| Este rey do*n* Ferrand*o*, maguer fue asp*er*o co*n*tral sob*ri*no, qua*n*to ensi bueno fue | τ ardit τ fazedor de bie*n*; τ maguer caso con doña Urraca, fija del rey de | Portugal, nu*n*q*ua* estido en paz con el, como q*ue* poblo Çiudat R*o*d*ri*go τ Ledesma en | territorio de Salama*n*ca τ Granada en t*er*mino de Coria τ Benaue*n*t τ Coy-|anca, q*ue* agora dize*n* Uale*n*çia, en t*er*mino de Ouiedo τ Uillalpa*n*do τ Mansiel-|la τ Mayorga en t*er*mino de Leon τ Cast*ro*taraf en t*er*mino de Camora. | Los[v] de Salama*n*ca, como era*n* poderosos, pesoles por q*ue* les poblaua*n* los | [fol.63r] | t*er*minos τ con aiuda de s*us* uezinos fiziero*n* cabo

---

[i] *EG* tendency to employ direct speech sees these exchanges greatly expanded.
[ii] *DRH*: VII.xvii
[iii] *EG* removes a chapter of philosophical musings by Ximénez de Rada and maintains the narrative flow.
[iv] *DRH*: VII.xviiii, *EG* maintains its interest in genealogy and toponyms.
[v] *DRH*: VII.xx

de si a Muño Rauia τ sallie-|ro*n* a cabo a Ual de Muça; τ ue*n*çioles el rey do*n* Ferrand*o* τ p*r*iso a Muño Rauia τ | ma*n*dol cortar la cabeça τ a ruego delos suyos pe*r*dono atodos los ot*r*os. Esto*n*z | p*r*iso el cuerpo del rey do*n* Remiro τ traxiero*n* lo τ enterraro*n* lo en Astorga enla | igle*s*ia cathedral. Esto*n*z[i] era Ferrand*o* Royz el castellano; este qua*n*do ouo dado al | rey lo q*ue* tenie por el, pasose a moros τ de pues uino por furtar τ destruyr | Çibdat R*o*drig*o*; τ como dize*n*, Sant Ysid*o*ro en uision appareçio enla ygle*s*ia alos | que la guardaua*n*, como uinie*n* y moros τ fuero*n* todos ape*r*cebidos τ pusiero*n* | derredor la uilla archas τ corral*es*, ca no*n* era cerçada. τ entro el rey do*n* Ferrand*o*, de | pues uiniero*n* moros ue*n*çidos τ mal ap*r*esos. De[ii] pues el rey do*n* Ferrand*o* enuio | por Ferrand*o* Royz q*ue*l farie algo τ el no*n* q*u*iso delexar de guerrear a castellanos, | τ ouo fazie*n*da *con* ellos en Lubrigal,[486] τ mato asu sueg*r*o do*n* Suero q*ue* esto*n*z | uiuie en Castiella τ murio Aluar Gutierres, he*r*mano de Roy Gutier-|rez,[487] τ muchos ot*r*os τ fuero*n* y p*r*esos el *con*de do*n* Gomez τ Ruy Gutierrez. Es-|tos pleytearo*n* asi τ fiziero*n* omenage a do*n* R*o*drig*o* q*ue* tornase*n*[488] a dias sabidos | qua*n*do ouiese su he*r*mano enterrado; τ retouolo por enterrar fasta q*ue* mu-|rio Ferrand*o* Royz. Do*n* Nuño uino al plazo *con* d*e* caual*le*ros τ dixo do*n* Ferrand*o*: "Ma*n*dat | me p*r*ender". El no*n* tenie tal *con*paña τ asi tornose. Asi escaparo*n* estos d*e*l | pleyto. Muerto do*n* Suero, delexo su fija a Ferrand*o* Ruyz τ caso despues ella co*n* Pedro | Arias τ ouo en ella a R*o*drig*o* P*er*ez de Uilla de Porcos. De pues el rey do*n* Ferrand*o* diol | su he*r*mana de padre, doña Esteuania, a Ferrand Royz τ ouo en ella a do*n* Pedro Fer-|ra*n*dez, el castellano.

De la guerra entre Leon τ Portugal[iii]

| Aca el rey do*n* Alfonso de Portugal *con*peço de guerrear al rey do*n* Ferrand*o*, por | q*ue* poblara en su te*r*mino τ enuio *con*tra el su fijo do*n* Sanc*h*o co*n* su poder. Oyo | lo do*n* Ferrand*o*, q*ue* auie guerra *con* castellanos τ p*ar*tiose **su poder, los unos**[489] *con*tra | castellanos τ los ot*r*os lidiaro*n* τ ue*n*ciero*n* a do*n* Sanc*h*o en Arganal τ mataro*n* | muchos delos sin guisa. El rey de Portugal ouo ende pesar τ no*n* dexo | la guerra; mouio su hueste τ p*r*iso Lauia τ Turo*n* τ ot*r*os lugares τ cerço | [fol.63v] | Badaioz, q*ue* era *con*q*u*ista de Leon τ p*r*iso bie*n* las dos p*ar*tes dela uilla τ los mo-|ros estaua*n* enel alcaçar. Aca uino el rey do*n* Ferrand*o* cabo la uilla; do*n* Alfonso | entrara enla uilla τ no*n* oso y fincar, q*ue* auie de*n*tro moros, fueras ene-|migos. Al salie*n*te dela puerta creba*n*to se la pierna τ asi fue τ adu-|xo al rey do*n* Ferrand*o* τ reconosçio q*ue*l guerreara a

---

[i] *DRH*: VII.xxi
[ii] *DRH*: VII.xxii
[iii] *DRH*: VII.xxiii

tuerto τ re*n*diol el cuerpo ⌈ τ el regno asu ma*n*dar. Do*n* Ferrand*o* ouo del duelo τ per*d*onolo τⁱ no*n* q*u*iso p*r*ender ⌈ nada, si no*n* q*ue* dexase lo q*ue*l p*r*isiera τ asi se q*u*itaro*n* por amigos. τ do*n* Al-⌈fonso nu*n*q*u*a mas pudo caualgar. Esto*n*z p*r*iso do*n* Ferrand*o* Badaioz τ delexola ⌈ en fialdad aun moro Abenabel. Apocos dias denego la postura ⌈ τ obedesçio al Miramomeli*n* τ fizo ende despues mucho mal a *ch*r*i*sti*a*-⌈nos. Los moros oyero*n* q*ue* no*n* podie caualgar el rey de Portugal, ⌈ uiniero*n* τ c*e*rcaro*n* lo en Sant Are*n*. El rey do*n* Ferrand*o* oyolo τ uinolo aiudar, ⌈ los moros no*n* osaro*n* ate*n*der el rey. Do*n* Alfonso gradesciolo a do*n* Ferrand*o*, q*ue* cuyda-⌈ua q*ue*l uinie entrar la ti*e*rra. El rey do*n* Ferrand*o* delexo esto*n*z su mug*e*r doña ⌈ Urraca, q*ue* era su terçera cormana τ caso *con* doña Teresa, fija del *con*de ⌈ do*n* Ferrand*o* τ fino sin fijos. Depues caso *con* hermana del *con*de do*n* Lop de Na-⌈guera, *con* doña Urraca τ ouo en ella dos fijos: do*n* Sanc*h*o τ do*n* Garcia τ muriero*n* ⌈ sin fijos derechos.ⁱⁱ El rey do*n* Ferrand*o* regno xxxj año τ murio en Beña-⌈ue*n*t, era mill cc.xxviij τ fue enterrado en Sant Yague, cerça su ⌈ auuelo el *con*de do*n* Remo*n*d τ cerça su mad*r*e doña Bele*n*guera la enp*e*radriz.

Del rey de Leon, como guerreo τ adobo con Castiellaⁱⁱⁱ

⌈ Muerto el rey do*n* Ferrand*o*, ⌈ regno su fijo do*n* Alfonso τ maguer fue bueno, creye los*en*geros ⌈ τ *con*peço de guerrear *con*tra el rey de Castiella. De pues uiose en ⌈ ta*n*ta coyta q*ue* ouo de uenir a corte al rey de Castiella a Carrio*n* τ ⌈ besol la mano τ deuino su uasallo τ p*r*iso caualle*r*ia del. Ot*r*osi la y p*r*i-⌈so Co*n*rrado, fijo del enp*e*rador de Alemaña τ fue desposado *con* doña ⌈ Bele*n*gueyella, ca era fija mayor τ hered*e*ra, q*ue* no*n* auie do*n* Alfonso fijo ⌈ uaro*n* ni*n* lo cuydaua auer. Despues Co*n*rrado torno en Te*u*tonia ya, ⌈ [fol.64r] ⌈ como fue, p*a*rtiose el casamie*n*to por mano de do*n* Go*n*za*l*o, p*r*imado d'España τ arçob*i*spo ⌈ de Toledo τ por el cardenal do*n* Gregorio de Sant Migu*e*l, τ caso⁴⁹⁰ doña B*e*le*n*guera ⌈ *con* el rey de Leon. Depues q*u*itaro*n* se τ denego la caualle*r*ia del rey τ caso ⌈ *con* fija del rey de Portugal τ ouo en ella dos fijas;^{iv} τ de pues ouiero*n* ⌈ entresi muchas guerras. El rey de Leon ouo en doña Bele*n*guera al rey ⌈ do*n* Ferrand*o*, q*ue* despues her*e*do Leon τ Castiella τ a do*n* Alfonso, q*ue* heredo Molina dello por ⌈ casamie*n*to delo por *com*pra τ a doña Costança, q*ue* fino en Burgos monia, ⌈ τ a doña Bele*nn*guera,^v q*ue* caso *con* doña Iuh*an* de Brena, q*ue* era rey de Ih*er*usal*e*m ⌈ de padre de una mug*e*r

ⁱ *DRH* praise of Fernando is greatly reduced.
ⁱⁱ *EG* maintains its interest in genealogy above all other information.
ⁱⁱⁱ *DRH*: VII.xxiiii
^{iv} *EG* removes detail of Alfonso's children, note particularly 'et aliam filiam, que Dulcis dicitur et adhuc uiuit'. See above p. 9.
^v As always *EG* preserves genealogical detail.

q*ue* ouiera τ ouo en ella una fija, q*ue* caso *con* don ׀ Baldouino, enp*er*ador de Costa*n*tinopla. Este Baldouino, como era niño, ׀ no*n* podie enparar el regno ante s*us* enemigos τ por ma*n*damiento ׀ del p*a*p*a* reçibio el rey Io*ha*n su suegr*o* el inp*er*io en comie*n*da τ asi doña Be-׀le*n*guera finco enp*er*adriz. De pues murio el Rey Io*ha*n τ doña Bele*n*guera ׀ finco el inp*er*io en doñ Baldouino τ en doña M*ar*ia. Depues doña Bele*n*-׀guera p*ar*tiose del rey de Leon por ma*n*damie*n*to del p*a*p*a*, q*ue* era*n* parie*n*tes, ׀ τ despues ouiero*n* mucha guerra τ ganaro*n* mucho del el rey de ׀ Castiella; en cabo torno todo asu fijo do*n* Ferrand*o*. Depues[i] el rey de Leon, ca*n*-׀sado de guerrear a[491] *chri*st*i*anos, guerreo a moros τ gaño dellos Mo*n*ta*n*ges τ ׀ Merida τ Badaioz τ Alca*n*tara τ Cac*er*ez,[492] τ poblo Sebia τ Leon τ Saluat*i*e*r*ra τ ׀ Sabugal τ ot*r*os logares. τ[ii] fino en Benaue*n*t, era mill τ ccLxviij τ fue ׀ enterrado en Sa*n*tiague. Delexo el regno τ las fortalezas as*us* fijas doña ׀ S*an*cha τ doña Dolça. Aca la reyna doña Bele*n*guera, *con* su fijo do*n* Ferrand*o* a q*ui*en fiziera*n* ׀ omenage τ *con* don R*o*dr*i*go, arçob*is*po de Toledo q*ue* yua delant *con* castellanos a-׀monestar los *con*seios, entro por la t*i*e*r*ra τ ouo toda Leon; alas h*er*manas ׀ diero*n* en q*ue* uisq*ui*ero*n* ho*n*dradamie*n*tre.

Del rey don Alfonso como gaño tierra del rey de Leon τ de Nauarra τ d'Aragon[iii]

Tornemos al rey ׀ do*n* Alfonso de Castiella. Ganada la t*i*e*r*ra q*ue* tenie su tio el rey do*n* Ferrand*o*, ׀ depues ouo guerra *con* el rey de Nauarra su tio τ cobro qua*n*to le ׀fol.64v׀׀ p*r*isiera mie*n*tre era niño bie*n* fasta Burgos. De pues gano del rey de Aragon ׀ Fariza, ca lo furto Muño Sancho τ dio lo a do*n* Alfonso. Depues ç*e*rço Cue*n*ca τ no*n* ׀ ouiero*n* acoro τ p*r*iso la τ murola τ enfortalesciola τ diol t*er*minos gra*n*des ׀ τ buenos fueros τ fizo la obispado, q*ue* ante no*n* era. Depues[iv] p*r*iso Alarco*n* τ ׀ diol buenos t*er*minos τ buenos fueros τ poblo la bie*n*; fallo Uepte yer-׀ma τ poblo la τ gano todas sus aldeas; τ p*r*iso ot*r*osi Ucles, depues la oui-׀ero*n* los freyres de Ucles; τ poblo Rib*er*a de Taio, p*r*iso Occaña τ diola co*n* ׀ su t*er*mino alos freyres[493] τ ot*r*osi Oreia; saco depues Calatr*a*ua de poder ׀ de furto τ fizo y *con*ue*n*to[494] de cauall*er*ia delos τ dioles Çorita τ Almogue-׀ra τ Maq*ue*da τ Açeca τ Cocolludo; tololes pobreza τ dioles riq*ue*za por Dios. ׀ Depues[v] poblo Plaze*n*cia τ fizo y obispo; de pues *con*peço guerra *con* moros τ ׀ por *con*seio del arçobispo do*n* M*ar*tin,

---

[i] *DRH*: VII.xxv, *DRH* editorial comment 'verum in senectute positus...' is removed.
[ii] This follows *DRH* MSS I, (and related codices of the first redaction of *DRH*). See Valverde, *Historia*, pp. 30–32 and p. 295, n.146; Jerez, 'La Historia'.
[iii] *DRH*: VII.xxvi
[iv] *DRH*: VII.xxvii
[v] *DRH*: VII.xxviii

q*ue* fue muy bue*n* om*n*e τ q*ue* fue *con* el, paso Gua-|dalq*ue*uir destruyendo qua*n*to fallaua τ no*n* fallo *con*tra*s*tro τ asi torno bie*n* *con* ond*r*a | ala t*ie*rra. Los⁴⁹⁵ moros oyero*n* como *con*peçaua bie*n* do*n* Alfonso τ ouiero*n* miedo τ | leua*n*to^i se un moro Yoseph Maçanudo, rey de Africa de linage delos | almohades τ *con* su poder τ *con* portos τ *con* arabes τ fios τ ethiopos τ *con* el | poder de toda Andaluzia τ uino a ca*n*pos de Alarchos. El rey do*n* Alfonso | salio ael τ fue uolu*n*tad de Dios Q*ue* fue y ue*n*çido el rey do*n* Alfonso τ los *chr*is*ti*a-|nos τ por el bie*n* q*ue* se siguio semeia q*ue* fue fecho de Dios τ q*ue* uiesen q*ue* to-|do uiene por Dios τ lo q*ue* El Q*ui*ere es. El rey mas q*ui*siera y morir, mas *con*-|seiaro*n* le: "Señor,^ii Dios uos tiene mayor ho*n*dra apareiada τ pues el | lo q*ui*ere τ uos por su fe lazrades, guaresçet, Q*ue* buena ue*n*gança auredes". | Esta batalla de Alarcos fue era mill ccxxxiij, xv k*a*lendas aug*usti*, ^iii p*a*p*a* en | Roma Celestino terçio.

De Alarcos, como guerreaua a Castiella christianos^iv

| El rey de Leon τ de Nauarra q*ue*l uinie*n* por aiudar, maguer ni*n* rogados | ni dema*n*dados, tornaro*n* se. El rey de Nauarra torno asu t*ie*rra, el | rey de Leon uino ael a Toledo, depues tornose a Leon. A poco tie*n*po el rey | de Leon τ el rey de Nauarra, como lo uiero*n* creba*n*tado, *con*peçaro*n* le de | [fol.65r] | guerrear. El rey de Leon fizo se *con* moros τ uino por Ca*n*pos fasta Burgos, | todo destruyendo aca; el rey de Nauarra ot*r*osi fasta Soria τ Almaça*n* todo e-|chando amal; dela ot*r*a p*ar*te *con*tra Toledo Yuçef, al segu*n*do año cerco Toledo, | depues Madrid τ depues Alcala depues Uepte depues Cue*n*ca de pues | Ucles depues torno [a] Alcaraz. En todas estas ce*r*cas fue dent*r*o Ferrand Ruyz,^v | senor de Albarazi*n*, no*n* por su uasallo mas por ruego de su muger doña Te-|resa, q*ue* era de Castiella *con* cc caualle*r*os asu costa τ asu mision. Depues | el rey do*n* Alfonso amigo bie*n* *con* su primo cormano el rey do*n* Pedro de Aragon, | τ amos en uno entraro*n* por Leon τ ganaro*n* Ballanios τ Castro τ Coyança, | q*ue* dize*n* Uale*n*çia el Carpio τ ot*r*as uillas τ echaro*n* amal los moros q*ue* era*n* | co*n* el rey de Leon τ asi tornaro*n* amos as*us* regnos ho*n*drados. Al te*r*çio año | adela*n*t ese mismo rey delos almohades uino τ ce*r*ço Toledo τ Maq*ue*da | τ Talau*e*ra τ no*n* pudo p*r*ender nada, mas astrago toda S*an*ta Ollalia, q*ue* no*n* | auie muros τ p*r*iso y S*an*ta + τ Plaze*n*çia τ Mo*n*ta*n*ges τ Trugiello τ asi | tornose. Esto*n*z el rey do*n* Alfonso τ el rey do*n*

---

^i *DRH*: VII.xxviiii
^ii The direct speech again is the initiative of the translator.
^iii The date is kept in the Latin format.
^iv *DRH*: VII.xxx, 'uenire in eius auxilium…simulassent', the *EG* stance is more balanced and less Castilian-centred than that of *DRH*.
^v This detail is not from *DRH*, see above p. 29.

Pedro de Aragon morauan enla sierra de ¡ Sant Uiçent,[i] τ cerça de Auila; quando Miramomelin fue ydo, amos los reyes des-¡cendieron τ fueron τ prisieron Castro de Leon τ Arden τ Castro de Gonzalo τ Castiel de Tierra τ Alua ¡ de Alif τ destruyeron todo fasta Astorga τ tornaron por Alba τ por Salamanca ¡ τ prisieron Mont Real τ otro noble castiello τ con esto tornaron asus regnos. El rey don ¡ Alfonso, por se uengar de sus enemigos, fizo paz con moros τ[ii] dioles alli reenos ¡ un so sobrino Semen Gomez, fijo de su hermana de padre, fijo de Gonzalo Royz de Aça- ¡ gra, este nunqua mas torno a christianos; pasaron lo la mar, a tienpo boluieron se las ¡ guerras τ retouieron alla el moço. Depues[iii] don Alfonso quiso otra uez tornar en ¡ Leon por se meior uengar τ andidieron pleyto que casase el rey de Leon con su fijo ¡ doña Belenguera, por auer paz. El rey non querie, por se uengar τ por que eran parien-¡tes, pero fizo lo a ruego de su muger la reyna doña Leonor τ don Alfonso tornol ¡ quantol prisiera. Depues[iv] don Alfonso τ el rey don Pedro de Aragon entraron por Nauarra, ¡ τ prisieron Ruconia τ Aiuuar, que ouo el rey de Aragon τ Incurra τ Miranda, ¡ [fol.65v] ¡ que ouo el rey don Alfonso. Depues don Alfonso priso Ibida τ Alaua τ aturo mucho la ¡ guerra. Aca el rey de Nauarra desenparo la tierra τ con pocos paso a Ma-¡rruecos.[v] El rey don Alfonso cerço Uictoria grand tienpo τ fueron y sienpre bu-¡enos τ leales; el obispo don Garcia de Panplona enuio letras al rey de Nauar-¡ra que Uictoria non auie acorro τ non fincaua por ellos, que ouiese ende pe-¡sar. El enuio les dezir que se diesen al rey don Alfonso τ asi fue que ya to-¡dos murien de fanbre τ comien unos a otros. Estonz priso Ibida, Alaua, ¡ Gujpuscua, con todos sus castiellos τ sus fortalezas, si non Treuino que pu-¡es la ouo por camio de Incayre τ Miranda por Portiello; τ gaño Sant ¡ Sabastian τ Fuenterauia τ Cegurchaghy[496] τ[vi] Aslucca, Athaun, Irruata τ ¡ Sant Uicent. De pues torno el rey de Nauarra de Marruecos con mu-¡cha riqueza, mas aca perdio esto. A[vii] poco tienpo don Diago Lopez de Faro des-¡auinose con el rey don Alfonso τ delexol su tierra τ paso a moros τ uino ¡ ende grand daño a castellanos. El rey don Alfonso, con su yerno el rey de ¡ Leon, entro en Nauarra τ cerço Estella por que acogieron y a don Diago Lopez ¡ quando salio de tierra. Estonz seyendo y los reyes corrio el rey de Nauar-¡ra fasta Burgos τ

---

[i] This detail is not from DRH.
[ii] The remainder of this sentence is additional detail provided by the translator. Once more EG makes reference to the Azagra family, adding to the DRH text. See above p. 29ff.
[iii] DRH: VII.xxxi
[iv] DRH: VII.xxxii
[v] The details of king's flight (and dishonour) are removed.
[vi] The translator encounters serious difficulty with Navarese toponyms.
[vii] DRH: VI.xxxiii.

por señal dio de la espada en un olmo; τ traya gra*n*d | presaⁱ τ pasaua por Sant Pedro de Cardeña τ oyo dezir q*ue* ali iazie Ruy Diaz, | τ por ho*n*dra del dexo la p*re*sa q*ue* traye. El Rey do*n* Alfonso no*n* pudo al fazer | en Estella q*ue* es muy fuerte τ tornaro*n* se alos regnos. De pues tor-|no a Burgos, fizo y noble moneste*ri*o q*ue* oy dize*n* s*us* Uelgas por a dueñas, | τⁱⁱ fizo ot*ro*si y ot*ro* moneste*ri*o q*ue* dize*n* el Ospital p*ara* enfermos τ p*ara* ro-|meros τ dioles he*re*dades τ gra*n*des riq*ue*zas. Depues estables*ç*io es-|cuelas en Pale*n*çia, ca enuio por maest*ro*s a Fra*n*çia τ a Lo*n*bardia. De pues | gano fascas toda Gascueña por razo*n* de su muge*r* doña Leonorⁱⁱⁱ Q*ue* la deuie | he*re*dar por su madre.

Dela batalla de Ubeda^{iv}

| Enta*n*to salliero*n* las treguas delos moros τ no*n* q*ui*so auer paz co*n* | ellos, por se ue*n*gar delo de Alarchos. Corriero*n* ch*ri*st*i*anos τ fiziero*n* |[fol.66r]| gra*n* daño en Ubeda τ en Baeça τ en Iahe*n* τ en Anduiar. De pues leua*n*to | se Mahomat, fijo del q*ue* ue*n*çio la de Alarchos, *con* poder de moros; cerço | Saluat*i*e*r*ra τ *con* engeñios τ co*n* lue*n*ga cerça τ q*ue* no*n* auie acorro p*ri*sola τ^v co*n* | fanbre, era mill ccxlix enel mes de setie*n*bre. Aca el rey do*n* Alfonso | lego su poder sobre Talau*e*ra por dar lid a Mahomat co*n* el esfuerço de su fijo, | el yfant do*n* Ferrand*o*. Despues ouo su *con*seio mas sosegado q*ue* fuese una τ bue-|na τ no*n* reuatarse τ q*ue*l prometiese dia sabido atodo poder de Mahomat, | τ asi fue. Entre ta*n*to tornose el moro τ retouose Saluat*i*e*r*ra.

Del conseio sobre la batalla^{vi}

| El rey do*n* Alfonso ouo su *con*seio *con* el arçobispo de Tole-|do τ los ot*ro*s obispos τ los ricos om*ne*s τ dixo q*ue* mas q*ue*rie una | uez morir q*ue* sie*n*pre andar en *rebatar*. Ma*n*do por toda la t*i*erra p*re*nder la plata, ua-|sos τ soritgas τ oregeras, ce*n*dales, porpolas, piedras, τ todo esto demas | ue*n*der lo τ faz*er* armas p*ara* la batalla. Los p*re*lados començaro*n* de p*re*dicar | la cruzada. Enta*n*to fino el yfa*n*t do*n* Ferrand*o* en Madrid, era mill ccclix τ | fue enterrado en Burgos. Fizo el rey gra*n*d duelo por el,^{vii} ca era fijo ma-|yor τ de

---

ⁱ These Navarrese details do not figure in *DRH*, although they do appear in subsequent narrations (e.g. *Arreglo Toledano de la Crónica de 1344*).
ⁱⁱ *DRH*: VI.xxxiiii
ⁱⁱⁱ The reason for Alfonso's acquisition of Gascony is not given by *DRH*.
^{iv} *DRH*: VII.xxxv
^v The dramatic tension of *DRH* account is passed over almost completely by *EG*.
^{vi} *DRH*: VII.xxxvi
^{vii} There is no reference to crusading in *DRH*, which concentrates on a lament for Fernando and a description of his death and funeral.

gra*n*d coraço*n*. El[i] arçobispo do*n* Rodrigo fue ala cort τ gano endulge-|çias, e uino predica*n*do por Fra*n*çia τ da*n*do perdones; por la tierra puso paz τ | amor entrelos reyes de Castiella τ de Nauarra τ de Aragon, q*u*elos tenie | esforcados do*n* Alfonso τ puesto q*u*e al torno q*u*e les tornase lo suyo uiniero*n* | le aiudar. Mie*n*tre se alegaro*n* las ge*n*tes, do*n* Alfonso entro por ribera de Chu-|car τ[ii] priso Alcala τ Cucarra τ Garra τ asi torno co*n* gana*n*çia. Uino el año q*u*e | deuie seer la batalla τ de mediano febrero adela*n*t começo de legar | en Toledo muchas ge*n*tes τ de muchos le*n*guiaes, q*u*e los no*n* podie o*m*e | saber, asi q*u*e no*n* cabie*n* enla çibdad, era marauilla q*u*e pa*n* o q*u*e co*n*ducho les a-|bastaua. Pues el rey, por co*n*seio del arçobispo, por q*u*e no*n* baraiase ni*n* bolui-|ese la uilla, sacolos ende en uoz de sermo*n* q*u*e q*u*erie fazer enla huerta | τ pues fuero*n* todos fuera; no*n* los q*u*isiero*n* de*n*tro acoier si no*n* pocos | q*u*e les sacase sus cosas q*u*e y tenie*n*.

Como uino el rey d'Aragon ala batalla[iii]

| [fol.66v] | Al octauo dia de Pe*n*tacosta, dia de Trinidat, lego el rey do*n* Pedro de Aragon a | Toledo τ fue reçibido del rey τ dela clerizia τ del pueblo co*n* gra*n*d procesio*n* τ po-|so enla huerta del rey τ ali ate*n*dio s*u*s ge*n*tes. De[iv] parte de Fra*n*çia τ de aq*u*ella tierra, | come*n*caro*n* de uenir el arçobispo de Bordel τ otros obispos, ricos om*n*es τ nobles | caualleros τ muchos peones; τ do*n* Arnalt, prouisor dela ygle*s*ia de Narbona, | este predicara la cruzada sobre los ereges τ destruyo Cortases τ Uederres[497] | en el era de mill ccxLvij τ oyo esta cruzada τ uino co*n* muchas de ge*n*tes, | τ recibiolo muy bie*n* el rey en Toledo. Otrosi uiniero*n* muchos de Portugal, a-|ragoneses[v] uiniero*n* guisados de todo, uino do*n* Garcia Romero τ Semen Cornel | τ Miguel de Luesia τ Aznar Pardo τ do*n* Guille*n* de Çeruera τ el co*n*de de Purrias do*n* | Remon Fulcoque,[498] Guille*n* de Cardona τ otros ricos om*n*es, poderosos caualeros τ | muchos peones de Castiella,[vi] τ arcob*i*spo de Toledo do*n* Rodrigo, ob*i*spos do*n* Tello | de Pale*n*cia, do*n* Rodrigo de Cigue*n*ça, do*n* Mele*n*do de Osma, do*n* Pedro de Auilla; de Aragon: do*n* | Garcia de Taraçona, do*n* Berenguel de Barçilona, electo; ricos om*n*es de Castiella: | do*n* Diago Lopez de Haro, el co*n*de do*n* Ferrando de Lara, el co*n*de do*n* Aluaro, el co*n*de do*n* | Garcia, todos tres hermanos, Lop Diaz de Haro, Ruy Diaz delos Cameros, Go*n*çalo Rujz |

---

[i] DRH: VIII.i EG creates an altered perspective on these events.
[ii] DRH: VII.xxxvi.38 ff.
[iii] The chapter structure of EG follows its own logic at this point, see above p. 15.
[iv] DRH: VIII.ii, EG provides a greatly abbreviated account of the same details.
[v] DRH: VIII.iii
[vi] EG deletes a lengthy description of the troops and retains only the names of the principal actors.

Giron τ sus hermanos τ otros ricos omes τ nobles τ muchos peones con los |
freyres de Calatraua con su maestro Rodrigo Diaz; los freyres del Tenple con su
| maestro Gomez Remirez, este fino[i] la batalla uençida en su lecho; los fray-
|res del Espital[499] con su prior Gutier Ermildez; los frayres de Sant Yague |
con su maestro don Pedro Arias. Tanto fue el gentio que si non quelo Dios
quiso non deuie | seer cabdelados por omne carnal, nin los deuie conplir
conducho. Los[ii] ultra-|montanos eran mas de xx mill a cauallo τ bien c. mill
peones; τ dauan | cada dia al cauallero .xx sueldos., al peon τ ala muger τ al niño
cada v. sueldos. de pipio-|nes; demas a qui non auie tiendas o seye armas
dauangelo. Estas gentes | bien adobadas, el[iii] dia se fue çercando del plazo,
mouieron se las huestes | de Toledo xj dias para andar de iunio. Los
ultramontanos mouieron | por si τ prisieron por cabdiello a don Lop Diaz. El
rey de Aragon mouio su hues-|[fol.67r]| te con los suyos, el de Castiella con los
suyos τ non se alongauan unos d'o-|tros, asi que en tres dias fueron fasta
Guadalferça τ cerçaron Malagon τ pri-|sieron la. Otro dia legaron los reyes τ
falescio el conducho τ acorio el rey | don Alfonso. Otro[iv] dia uinieron a
Calatraua. Los moros fizieron clauos de | iiij. pies menudos, echaron lo enel
rio muchos sin conta por o auien | de pasar los omnes τ las bestias; asi plogo
a Dios que non finco mal a | ningunos. Era en Calatraua un moro Alcayet,
muy poderoso almohat, | con grand caualeria τ otrosi Auencalez, buen
cauallero. Ouieron su conseio los reyes | que non fincase en Calatraua. En
nonbre [de] Dios fue conbatida τ presa, los moros | echados ende, presos,
muertos τ catiuos; tornaron la alos freyres | que la non tenien.[v]

Como se tornaron los ultramontanos[vi]

| Los ultramontanos, ya que uieron, tornaron se todos de alli, que los non
pudieron | retener si non que fico y don Arnalt, obispo de Narbona, con los
suyos τ con los | que pudo retener, que fueron fata cxx caualeros menos delos
peones. Finco otro-|si con algunos de Pecto don Tibalt de Bleçon, dela una
parte castellano, muy buen | cauallero. El rey de Aragon sienpre fizo fata
tornar[500] con los suyos. Tornaron los ultra-|montanos τ los españoles cada dia
meiorando, fata que legaron Alarcos τ | prisieron la τ otros castiellos
aderredor. Ali lego el rey de Nauarra, quel non | consintio la uoluntad que non

---

[i] *DRH*: 'feliciter expirauit'.
[ii] *DRH*: VIII.iiii a lengthy paean of praise to Alfonso is cut, *EG* maintains its interest in facts alone.
[iii] *DRH*: VIII.v
[iv] *DRH*: VIII.vi 'peruenimus calatrauam'.
[v] The insertion of 'non' is an error in the *EG*.
[vi] See above p. 15.

uiniese a correr a la fe τ al cormano, maguer q*ue* lo ｜ tenie deseredado; τ de ali adela*n*t fuero*n* tres reyes p*r*imos cormanos. ｜ Desende mouiero*n* el p*r*imer dia a Salua T*ie*rra; el domi*n*go adela*n*t touiero*n* los ｜ reyes por bie*n* como p*a*ra batalla τ q*ue* fuese ya mas ape*r*cebidos τ asi fizie-｜ro*n* asi q*ue* el te*r*çer dia fue a pie del puerto de Muradal, q*ue* dize*n* Guadalfa-｜iar. Entre[i] ta*n*to, Mahomat, rey delos moros, legara sus poderes en Iahe*n*, ｜ τ dubdauase ya de lidiar co*n* los *chr*ist*i*anos, temie*n*do q*ue* era*n* muchos τ[501] puso de ｜ no*n* salir aellos, mas q*ue* andase por la t*ie*rra qua*n*do tornase, q*ue* yua*n* ca*n*sados τ se-｜gurados, q*ue* los asaltease. Enta*n*to, algunos ladrones *chr*ist*i*anos, por algo ga-｜nar, dixiero*n* le q*ue*los ultramotanos q*ue* se era*n* tornados q*ue* era*n* gra*n*d poder; ｜ [fol.67v] ｜ los q*ue* fincaro*n* no*n* auie*n* co*n*ducho. Qua*n*do esto oyo, cobro coraco*n* por ue-｜nir ala batalla τ desce*n*dio al plano co*n* sus huestes delas mo*n*tanas de Ia-｜he*n* τ dellos enuio a Baeça τ delos alas Naues[502] de Tolosa, q*ue* enbargasen alos ｜ *chr*ist*i*anos q*ue* no*n* pudiese pasar al puerto de la losa, asi no*n* q*ue* p*r*isiese el puerto, ｜ asi como lo pues co*n*taro*n* los catibos. Mas plogo a Dios q*ue* do*n* Diago Lopes, ｜ q*ue* tenie la dela*n*tera τ enuio adela*n*t asu fijo do*n* Lop τ asus sob*r*inos de S*an*c*h*o ｜ Ferrande*z* τ do*n* M*a*rtin Muñoz τ p*r*isiero*n* el somo del puerto τ echaro*n* τ ue*n*çiero*n* ｜ alos moros q*ue* falaro*n* y τ fincaro*n* y s*u*s tie*n*das. El iueues adela*n*t lega-｜ro*n* los reyes τ las huestes a pie del puerto τ fincaro*n* cabo el rio ｜ q*ue* dize*n* Guadalfaiar. El uiernes mañana mouiero*n* se[503] τ subiero*n* al ｜ puerto; este dia p*r*isiero*n* Ferral, en Castiella çe*r*ca dela losa, alli auie ｜ mal logar la losa q*ue* aun al om*n*e *desarmado* era mala de pasar. Este ｜ dia ouiero*n* fazie*n*da los *chr*ist*i*anos co*n* los moros q*ue* guardaua*n* los puer-｜tos, p*er*o ouo daño de cada p*a*rte; ue*n*çiero*n* los *chr*ist*i*anos. Los reyes ouiero*n* ｜ a oio las tie*n*das delos moros τ ueye*n* el paso malo, temie*n*se de da-｜ño τ no*n* osaua*n* yr a çaga por dema*n*dar ot*r*o camino plano; auie*n* miedo ｜ q*ue*las ge*n*tes, si tornase*n* a çaga, cuydarie*n* q*ue* fuyrie*n* o q*ue* no*n* q*ue*rie*n* lidiar, ｜ τ q*ue* **derramarie*n***[504] τ q*ue*los no*n* podrie*n* tornar ni*n* cabdelar; adela*n*t no*n* podrie*n* ｜ pasar. Entre ta*n*to, uino un pastor o coneiero q*ue* fue, mas semeio an-｜gel o **menssaiero**[505] de Dios τ demostroles y luego bue*n* paso a oio delos ｜ moros τ q*ue* se no*n* tornase a çaga. Los[ii] reyes dubdaro*n* del pastor, p*er*o en-｜uiaro*n* a do*n* Diago Lopez τ a do*n* Garcia Remo*n* q*ue*la fuesen ueer; fuero*n* τ fallaro*n* ｜ lo por ue*r*dad τ p*r*isiero*n* el puerto suso τ fincaro*n* las tie*n*das τ enuiaro*n* ｜ lo dezir alos reyes q*ue* Dios era co*n* ellos τ q*ue* subiese a osadas. Los *chr*ist*i*a-｜nos dexaro*n* el Feral como destruyda τ sabado mañana, oyda la misa, ｜ comulgaro*n* τ recibiero*n* s*u*s pe*r*dones τ armaro*n* se τ fuero*n* por o amos-｜tro el pastor. Los moros, q*ue* uiero*n* q*ue* desma*n*paraua*n* a Ferral

[i] *DRH*: VIII.vii
[ii] *DRH*: VIII.viii

τ delexa-|ua*n* el puerto dela losa τ q*ue* desuiaua*n*, cuydaro*n* q*ue* no*n* q*ue*rie*n* lidiar, | [fol.68r] | τ⁵⁰⁶ poblaro*n* luego otra uez Ferral; ellos cuydaua*n*⁵⁰⁷ q*ue* fuyen los | *chri*st*i*anos. Qua*n*do cataro*n*, **uieron** s*us* señas τ s*us* tie*n*das **suso** cabo dellos τ fuero*n* mal es-|pa*n*tados, enuiaro*n* cau*all*e*r*os q*ue*les fuesen enbargar el paso; τ maguer | co*n* trabaio ouiero*n* de pasar asu pesar. El rey moro ouo pesar q*ue* ta*n* | mal curiaua*n* los puertos τ mudo sus tie*n*das τ s*us* façes al ca*m*po, e l-|a mayor puso en un otero^i q*ue* auie fuerte subida τ las ot*ra*s a diestro; | τ asi amost*r*o τ ate*n*diero*n* de medio dia fata uiesp*ra*s, por cuydar q*ue* li-|diarie*n* ese dia; τ los *chri*st*i*anos no*n* q*ui*siero*n* ese dia. Este rey moro, en q*ue* lo uido, | cuydo q*ue* no*n* osaua*n* lidiar; τ enuio letras a Baeça τ a Iahe*n* q*ue* tenie tres reyes | *chri*st*i*anos ue*n*çidos τ cerçados. Los uieios ente*n*die*n* la ue*r*dat, q*ue* lo fazie*n* *chri*st*i*anos | por ate*n*der s*us* co*m*pañas, q*ue* uinie*n* ca*n*sados, faze*r* lo co*n* seso. Ot*r*o dia domi*n*go, | salio el rey moro τ fincaro*n* su tie*n*da ue*r*meia espera*n*do los *chri*st*i*anos; τ los | *chri*st*i*anos no*n* q*ui*siero*n* fata ot*r*o dia. Ese dia fizo el rey de Aragon cuale*r*o | a do*n* Nuño Sanches, su sobrino. Ese dia andidiero*n* los p*re*gones τ los pe*r*dones | p*ara* ot*r*o dia. Ese dia cometiero*n* los moros alos *chri*st*i*anos τ ellos souiero*n* en | paz τ sin daño ni*n*guno.

Como ue*n*çieron christianos^ii

| Otro dia amanescie*n*t, lunes a media noche, diero*n* p*re*gon por el alu*n*-|gada,⁵⁰⁸ q*ue* se armase ala batala; p*us* oyda la misa τ las co*n*fesiones τ | comulgados, saliero*n* ala batalla, todos de bue*n* coraço*n*. Delos castellanos | do*n* Diago Lopez ouo las p*ri*me*ra*s feridas co*n* los suyos, el az de medio el | co*n*de do*n* Sancho^iii co*n*los te*m*pleros τ ot*r*os nobles om*n*es co*n*el Espital τ Huches⁵⁰⁹ τ | Calatraua; la ot*ra* az de costado Ruy Diaz delos Came*r*os τ Aluar Diaz, | su he*r*mano τ Iuha*n* Gomez de Uze*r*o τ ot*r*os ricos om*n*es; τ la post*ri*mera az | el rey do*n* Alfonso τ el arçb*i*spo do*n* Rod*ri*go τ los ot*r*os obispos; ricos om*n*es, Roy | Gomez τ s*us* he*r*manos τ Ruy Pe*r*ez de Uilla Lobos τ Suor Tellez τ Ferrand | Garcia τ ot*r*os. Menos destos, cada una azez auie s*us* co*n*cei*e*ros, como era*n* | ordenados. El rey de Aragon ordeno **los suyos:**⁵¹⁰ la p*ri*mera az do*n* Garcia, tomo la | ij. Seme*n* Cornel, Aznar Pa*r*do; τ la post*ri*mera el co*n* s*us* ricos omes; ala cos-|[fol.68v]|tane*r*a ot*r*os ricos om*n*es de Aragon; el rey do*n* Sancho de Nauarra, **con sus ricos hombres τ caualleros de Nauarra** co*n* los co*n*seios de | Segouia τ de Auila τ de Medina. Puestas las azes, enel no*m*bre de Dios co-|meçaro*n* la batalla τ come*n*çaro*n* de ferir. Los moros fiziero*n* toda su forta**leza** | en un ote*r*o de arcos de saetas, o estaua los

---

^i As previously *EG* preserves basic details of *DRH* narration, although in much abbreviated fashion.
^ii *DRH*: VIII.viiii
^iii *DRH*: 'Gunsaluus Nunii'.

peones puestas τ armados | τ ligados unos *con* ot*r*os, q*ue* no*n* **pudieron**[511]
fuyr τ ala estaua el rey moro; τ | uistie una capa negra q*ue* fuera de Abdeli
Mumi, q*ue* fue come*n*çamie*n*to | delos almoades τ tenia ant*e* si el Alcora*n*,[512]
el libro q*ue* fizo Mahomat.[i] | Ot*r*osi, fuera del alu*n*gada, estaba*n* azes de
peones *con* s*us* la*n*ças te*n*didas, | elos atados alas piernas q*ue* no*n* podie*n* fuyr;
ante ellos estaua*n* ca-|uall*er*os sin co*n*ta τ sin mesura; a diest*r*o τ a siniest*r*o
estaua*n* caual*er*os sin | co*n*ta τ p*ar*tes[513] q*ue* suele*n* ue*n*çer fuyendo τ nu*n*q*ua*
esta*n* en azes. Om*n*e asmar | no*n* puede, tamaño poder fue de moros; bie*n*
ap*r*isiero*n* ta*n*to *christ*ianos de | algunos catibos dela casa del rey moro, q*ue* de
cauall*er*os soldadados | de señor τ de fijos dalgo sin caud*er*os τ om*n*es de
uilla, era*n* por co*n*to en | carta de Miramomeni*n* de Lxxx mill asuso; delos
peones no*n* era | cue*n*ta ni*n* mesura. Menos destos ouo y un gra*n*d **home**
moro rico de Maru-|ecos q*ue* auie ira del rey τ por faz*er* le s*er*ui*t*io τ ganar su
amor,[ii] sedie a | pie *con* su iente por mas fiel mie*n*tre lo aguardar τ morir o
beuir *con* el.

Los golpes[iii]

| Los *christ*ianos come*n*çaro*n* de subir por fuert*e* logar τ los mo-|ros fiziero*n*
los tornar mucho a çaga. Esto*n*z algunos *christ*ianos dela fa-|zes de Castiella τ
de Aragon aiuntaro*n* se ala p*r*im*er*a az. Los castellanos[514] li-|diaua*n* bie*n*
ot*r*osi, p*er*o asi semeio q*ue* algunos q*u*isiero*n* fuyr; τ dixo el rey do*n* | Alfonso:
"Arçobispo do*n* Rod*r*igo, uos ot*r*os obispos, mal dia es hoy p*ar*a mi τ p*ar*a la |
*christ*iandad. Nu*n*q*ua* fuese yo naçido q*ue* yo s*er*e ue*n*çido; oy se pierde toda
España". | Todos come*n*çaro*n* a lorar[iv] co*n*el τ p*ar*a conortalo τ dixoles:
"Uarones, oy | aq*u*i muramos todos, no*n* ueamos p*er*dida España. No*n* se de
ni*n*guno a | p*r*ision, ante se mate; si no*n* ouiere q*u*i lo matar, q*ue* yo asi fare
amigos | τ uasalos". Entre todos dixo el arçobispo: "Señor, si a morir fuere, |
[fol.69r] | todos yra*n* *con* uos a parayso,[v] q*ue* ni*n* q*ue*remos morir ni*n* beuir si no*n*
con uos τ por | esso son todos estos aq*u*i; mas seet seguro τ no*n* temades, q*ue*
este dia es n*ues*t*r*o | τ hoy ue*n*credes τ ganeredes p*re*cio τ ue*n*garedes u*ues*t*r*a
honta τ Dios es *con* uos". Los | golpes era*n* gra*n*des, los ata*n*bores *sonaban*,[515]
las tro*n*pas semeiaua q*ue* el | mu*n*do se trastornaua. El rey do*n* Alfonso

---

[i] *DRH*: 'librum…secte nepharie'.
[ii] The description of Islamic forces is much abbreviated, while that of the Christian armies is
characterised by careful enumeration of the principal figures.
[iii] *DRH*: VIII.x
[iv] *EG* maintains its vivid expansion of direct speech, see Aengus Ward 'Rodrigo', and above pp. 23–
25.
[v] This version of Rodrigo's speech is significantly expanded, see above p. 25.

q*ue*bro su coraçó*n* τ lorando por los oios[i] | dixo: "Castellanos, hoy es u*uest*ro dia; ¡catad la de Alarcos!". Pues dixo: "Arago-|neses τ nauarros: ¡catad quales fuestes sie*n*pre, q*ue* hoy es u*uest*ro dia!". Uido | los *ch*r*ist*ianos maltrechos τ q*u*iso desce*n*der del cauallo τ lora*n*do τ q*ue*rela*n*do se a | Dios q*ue*l fiziera rey τ que naçiera **en** fuerte pu*n*to τ diçie*n*do: "Dios, ii si no*n* ueyes | ami, acorre atu ley q*ue* se pierde; si tu eres u*er*dade*ro* Dios q*ue* p*ri*siste carne de | Sa*n*ta Ma*ri*a τ tomeste y muert*e* por nos peccadores, q*ue* aq*u*i[516] esp*er*amos muerte por | ti, aiudanos; q*ue* sin ti no*n* ualdremos[517] nada". Enta*n*to fuero*n* co*n*bra*n*do *ch*r*ist*anos, | τ[iii] dixo el rey do*n* Alfonso: "¡A por Dios uayan aiudar ala dela*n*tera". Salio do*n* Garcia | Royz co*n* sus h*er*manos τ fuelos aiudar; do*n* Garcia Remo*n* q*u*iso yr τ retouolo el | rey asu fabla por q*ue* fuese despues meior aiudar. τ dixo ot*r*a uez el rey: | "Arçobispo amigo τ uos ot*ro*s obi*s*pos, aq*u*i morit comigo". Dixiero*n*: "Señor, mo-|rir o beuir[518] *con* uos, mas hoy ue*n*çredes τ biu*e*redes τ gozaremos co*n*uus-|co".iv Enta*n*to, el ma*n*do mouer las señas adela*n*t τ el capiscol do*n* Domi*n*go | Pasqual de Toledo,v q*ue* despues fue dea*n*, leuaua la cruz del arcobispo τ fue | y muy bueno τ puso la cruz *con* los p*ri*mero*s* en somo *con* las señas τ las | señas delos reyes; era la ymage*n* de Sa*n*ta Ma*ri*a de Toledo *con* q*ue* sie*n*pre ue*n*ciero*n*. | τ dizie*n*do: "Dios aiuda τ Sa*n*tiague", los ot*ro*s "Castiella, Castiella", ot*ro*s "Ara-|go*n*, Aragon" τ ot*ro*s "Nauarra", firiero*n* todos de coracon. Gran p*ar*tida delos | moros come*n*çaro*n* de tornar las espaldas,vi dizie*n*do do*n* Alfonso: "Ih*es*u *christo*, | acorre alos q*ue* creemos por ti" τ los obispos dizie*n*do la letania[519] τ el rey | *con*ellos. Asi plogo a Dios q*ue* el rey moro p*us* los no*n* pudo sofrir ni*n* | cabdellar s*us* ie*n*tes τ fuyen; por *con*seio desu h*er*mano Eye*n*t Abazceri[520] ca-|¡ualgo una yegua de muchos colores τ p*ri*so qu*at*ro cauallero*s*vii τ fuxo; τ | [fol.69v] | uino a poder a Baeça. Pregu*n*taro*n* los de Baeça: "¿Como uienes τ q*ue* faremos?" | Dixoles: "No*n* se, el c*ri*ador uos aiude, q*ue* yo no*n* puedo". Caualgo ot*r*a yegua τ uino | se *l*echa noche a Iahe*n*. Aca los *ch*r*ist*anos mataro*n* moros sin co*n*ta. Esto*n*ze dixo | el arçobi*s*po al rey do*n* Alfonso: "Señor, gradeçed a Dios esta m*er*çed q*ue* uos ha | fecho". El rey deçe*n*dio del cauallo lora*n*do τ echose en ti*er*ra. Esto*n*z el arco-|bispo, todos los obispos

---

i It is tempting to see an echo of the *Cantar de Mio Cid*. For epic influences on *EG* see Gómez Redondo, 'La materia'. BN Res/278 'de los oios'.

ii See above p. 25.

iii This is a second version of the previous exchange, thereby providing added tension in *EG* not seen in *DRH*.

iv The figure of Alfonso VIII, and indeed that of Ximénez de Rada himself, is rather different here by comparison with *DRH*. For a detailed analysis, see above p. 27.

v 'preferente eam Dominico Pascasii canonico Toletano', the *EG* reference is not, therefore, original.

vi *EG* narration differs considerably throughout this section.

vii The echo of Hannibal after the battle of Zama is that (perhaps consciously?) of *DRH*.

con el a pie, començaro*n* de ca*n*tar "Te Deu*m* laudam*us*". ¡ Asi era*n* los ca*m*pos leños de muertos, q*ue* apeñas podie*n* pasar de ca-¡ualo sobre los muertos; τ suso o estaua el rey falaro*n* muy fermo-¡sos moros muertos τ ya desnodos,⁵²¹ q*ue*los desnudaro*n* robadores q*ue* y-¡ua*n* dela*n*t. τ fata la noche no*n* les diero*n* uagar delos segudar a cada ¡ pa*r*te τ asma*n* q*ue* muriero*n* y moros de dozie*n*tas uezes mill asuso τ ¡ ch*r*ist*i*anos no*n* de xxv adela*n*t. No*n*ⁱ uos podrie om*n*e *con*tar, no*n* auie*n* ni*n*gu-¡nos uagar de mirar como bie*n* lidiaro*n* castellanos τ aragoneses ¡ τ nauarros τ qua*n*tos y se ace*r*taro*n* cada uno por si τ todos en uno. ¡ Ala noche mudaro*n* se los ch*r*ist*i*anos alas tie*n*das delos moros, asi ¡ q*ue* ni*n*gunos no*n* tornaro*n* as*us* tie*n*das si no*n* los açenbleros q*ue* torna-¡ua*n* por el *con*ducho; τ ta*n*ta fue la muchedu*n*bre delos moros q*ue*los ¡ ch*r*ist*i*anos no*n* pudiero*n* co*n*plir el q*ua*rto logar del alu*n*gada delos moros,ⁱⁱ ¡ τ q*ui* q*ui*so oro τ plata τ seda alli lo fallo; τ pe*r*o ante dia descomulgaro*n* ¡ atodo aq*ue*l q*ue*el ca*m*po robase, mal peccado *con* la cobdiçia. Algunos o-¡uo y pe*n*iuros. Pe*r*o no*n* fue co*n*ta de camelos⁵²² τ de bestias τ de *con*ducho ¡ q*ue* y fallaro*n*. Alli moraro*n* ese dia τ ot*r*os ca*n*sados τ no*n* q*ue*maro*n* to-¡das las huestes si no*n* la*n*ças τ saetas q*ue* fuera*n* delos moros τ ape-¡ñas las acabaro*n*, maguer q*ue* las q*ue*mauan a mal faze*r*. Alguñosⁱⁱⁱ apartaro*n* ¡ se τ ce*r*caro*n* Bilches; al te*r*çer dia mouiero*n* se las ie*n*tes⁵²³ τ p*r*isiero*n* Bilches ¡ τ Tolosa τ Baños τ Ferral, q*ue* cobraro*n* q*ue* la fallaro*n* yerma. Ot*r*osi al-¡gunos fuero*n* a Baeça τ fallaro*n* la yerma τ fuero*n* todos a Ubeda, ¡ si no*n* los uieios τ los enfermos q*ue* fincaro*n* enla mezq*ui*ta τ ali ¡ [fol.70r] ¡ les diero*n* fuego. Qua*n*do esto oyero*n*, los ch*r*ist*i*anos fuero*n*⁵²⁴ τ çe*r*caro*n* Ubeda al ¡ vjº dia p*us* la batalla τ luego a dos dias fue p*r*esa, asi q*ue* do*n* Lop Ferrandez ¡ de Luna τ Aragon subio enel muro, los moros q*ue* lo uiero*n* re*n*diero*n* se ¡ al rey τ asi entraro*n* la uilla. τ los moros diero*n*, por q*ue* **escaparon** a ui-¡da,⁵²⁵ mil mill m*a*rauedis; pues aruego delos p*r*elados destruyero*n* toda Ubeda, ¡ q*ue* no*n* pudiese moro y fincar. Pe*r*o escaparo*n* los moros, mas no*n* lo p*r*isi-¡ero*n* lo q*ue* p*r*ometiera*n*. Pues los ch*r*ist*i*anos començaro*n* de robar τ furtar en-¡tre si τ dioles Dios una enfermedat tal q*ue* un co*n*pane*r*o a ot*r*o no*n* po-¡die ayudar, ni*n* uasallo a señor. Pues tornaro*n* a Calatraua τ fallaro*n* ¡ el duc de Austria q*ue* uinie muy bie*n* guisado pa*r*a aiudar ala batalla. ¡ Desende torno se⁵²⁶ *con* el rey **de** Aragon, q*ue* era su sob*r*ino. El rey do*n* Alfonso, ¡ *con* el arçobispo τ *con* los suyos, uino a Toledo τ fue reçebido *con* p*r*ocession. ¡ Asi tornaro*n* todos as*us* tie*r*ras alegres τ fue la batalla era mill ccl, ¡ lunes xv dias por andar de iulio.

ⁱ *DRH*: VIII.xi
ⁱⁱ Broadly similar details are given by *EG*, however the intimate first person narrative voice is removed.
ⁱⁱⁱ *DRH*: VIII.xii

Quando fue fecha la batalla[i]

| Al otro año luego el rey *con* los suyos p*ri*so Castil de Dueñas τ dio | lo alos freyres de Calatr*a*ua cuyo fue τ Eznauexoro,[527] q*ue* dio a | los freyres τ p*ri*so Alcaçaz τ p*ri*so Riopal. Pues torno τ touo la Pe*n*-|tecosta en S*an*to Torcat, cabo Alcala τ Guadalfaiara,[ii] *con* su muger **la reyna** do*ñ*a | Leonor τ su fijo do*n* Enric τ su fija doña Bele*n*guera τ s*us* **nietos**,[528] do*n* | Ferrand*o* τ do*n* Alfonso. Este año come*n*ço el año malo de fanbre, q*ue* murie*n* | las ge*n*tes de fa*n*bre por la t*ie*rra τ por las cales; pe*ro* el rey τ los p*re*-|lados acorie*n* qua*n*to podie*n*. Esto*n*z renouo su amiztad *con* el rey | de Leon, Q*ue* cada uno fuese de su parte *contra* los moros τ tornol | qua*n*to p*ri*siera, El Carpio τ Mo*n*t Real τ diol por aiuda a do*n* Diago | Lopez. Desi gano el rey de Leon Alca*n*tara, q*ue* dio alos freyres de Cala-|traua τ[iii] luego tornose *con* el rey; do*n* Alfonso mouio su hueste τ entr*o* | en Toledo era de mill ccLj, vij dias por andar de agosto. Pues salio | de*n*de τ paso por C*on*suegra τ Calatr*a*ua τ ce*r*ço Baeça τ fallo y a do*n* Diago | [fol.70v] | Lopez *con* gra*n*d caual*er*ia. Pues uieron q*ue* los ch*ri*st*i*anos murie*n* de fanbre, pusiero*n* tre-|guas co*n* los moros τ tornaro*n* a Calatraua τ falaro*n* los freyres q*ue* murie*n* | de fanbre τ este era dono malo, q*ue* maguer q*ue* algunos mucho comie*n* no*n* per-|die*n* la fanbre, q*ue* no*n* auie*n* fuerça **con** los *con*duchos. El arçobispo do*n* R*odrigo* p*ar*tio co*n* | **ellos** lo q*ue* touo, q*ue* les dio toda su plata τ torno todo com*er* τ beuer en ma*n*da; me-|nos desto cu*m*plidos de *con*ducho desde Epip*ha*nia[iv] fata las oct*auas* de Sant Iuha*n*. | Esto*n*z poblo[529] el Miraglo, q*ue* fazie gra*n*d daño a ch*ri*st*i*anos. Esto*n*z fizo se*r*mon | sobre los pobres τ los ricos om*n*es p*ri*siero*n* q*uien* dos q*uien* mas asi q*ue* no*n* falaua*n* ape-|nas pobre Q*ue* pidiese enla uilla. Esto*n*z dio el rey do*n* Alfonso, a ruego del arco-|bispo, xx aldeias por h*er*edat a S*an*ta M*ar*ia de Toledo. Alos[v] liij. años q*ue* regno do*n* | Alfonso fue ueer asu yerno el rey de Portugal; qua*n*do fue en Plaze*n*cia, la postr*i*-|mera cibdad de su regno, en una aldeia q*ue* dize*n* Arenado, adolescio τ fizo su *con*-|fesion ant el arzobispo don Rodrigo et otros obispos et su fija doña Belenguera et sus nietos τ comulgo; τ[vi] fino e*ra* mill cclij., dia de S*an*ta Fe, lunes vj dias anda-|dos de ochubre τ fue aducho a Burgos. Enterraro*n* le en **el monasterio de** las Huelgas de Bur-|gos q*ue* el fiziera.

---

[i] *DRH*: VIII.xiii
[ii] 'in uilla ecclesie Toletane que Sanctus Torquatus dicitur...'. This additional detail perhaps indicates familiarity with the geography of the Archbishopric of Toledo on the part of the translator.
[iii] *DRH*: VIII.xiiii
[iv] As previously, *EG* removes Biblical citations and allusions, thereby perhaps indicating the extent of knowledge of the expected audience?
[v] *DRH*: VIII.xv
[vi] A *DRH* lengthy passage of praise for Alfonso VIII is cut.

Muerto el rey don Alfonso fino[530] **don Endric**[i]

| Enterrado el rey don Alfonso, Enric su fijo fue luego alçado[ii] rey, en edat |
de xj años τ regno dos años τ x meses. Acabo de xxv dias que fino | don
Alfonso, fino su muger la reyna doña Leonor, fija del rey de Anglatierra τ |
fue enterrada con el rey, **finco** el regno τ el rey don Enric en comienda dela
reyna | doña Berenguela. Estonz los condes, fijos del conde don Muño, don
Aluaro τ don | Ferrando τ don **Gonçaluo**, por tener la tierra en poder τ
uengar se de sus enemigos como fizie-|ra su padre con el rey don Alfonso,
andaua por que criase el rey don Enric τ al-|gunos en que fiaua la reyna eran
en este conseio, especialment don Garcia Lo-|renz, un cauallero de Plazencia
que lo daua de mandado de[531] la Reyna τ la guardaua. En | tanto el conde
don Aluaro prometio a don Garcia Lozen una uilla que dizen Tabla, por |
heredat, por tal que conseiase a don Enric que se diese a criar lo el conde.
Entendio | lo la reyna como sabidor τ otorgogelo; τ uiolo por bien pero con |
[fol.71r] | segurança atal: iuro el conde en mano del arcobispo que lo criase
lealment τ touie-|se la tierra en paz τ non fiziese mal a caualeros nin a ordenes
nin yglesias nin alos | pueblos. τ asi lo reçibio el τ sus hermanos τ salieron con el
de Burgos. Comen-|caron de apremiar τ de quebrantar los ricos omnes τ
andar por la tierra asu guisa. | Estonz priso algunas cosas τ forco dela yglesia
de Santa Maria de Toledo; τ **el dean** don Rodrigo, que tenie | las uezes del
arçobispo τ descomulgol τ fizol iurar mandamiento de yglesia que | nunqua
mas pusiese mano enlo de Santa Maria de Toledo.[iii] Los ricos omnes, en[iv] |
que uieron esta destruyçion, legaron se todos en uno: don Lop Diaz de Haro,
Gonzalo | Royz Giron τ sus hermanos Ruy Diaz τ Aluar Diaz delos Cameros τ
don Alfonso | Telez τ otros muchos fizieron cort en Ualladolit τ pidieron
merçed ala Re-|yna que ouiese duelo dela tierra, que yua amal. Dixieron lo al
conde τ non dio por to-|dos nada, ante començo toller ala reyna su conducho
en la[532] tierra τ lo quel delexara su | padre en que uisquiese τ mandaua la salir
del regno, que se fuese asus **arras**[533] a Leon con | sus fijos, que Castiella non
podie sofrir tantos señores. Estonz la reyna uido se | en coyta τ priso su
hermana doña Leonor, que pues caso con el rey de Aragon, | τ puso se en
Oriello, un castiello de don Garcia Ruyz Giron τ ali moro fata que murio | el
rey don Enric. Los otros ricos omes fezien seruitio al rey como a señor
natural, | τ guardauan[534] τ ondrauan a doña Berenguela como a fija de su
señor na-|tural τ maguer con su conseio τ conseio dela, refrenauan mucho a don
[Aluaro].[535] El | yfant yua ya creçiendo,[536] τ de grado querie ya tornar asu

---

[i] DRH: VIIII.i
[ii] DRH: 'eleuatur'
[iii] EG notably maintains all details provided by DRH at this point, see above p. 18 ff.
[iv] DRH: VIIII.ii

hermana, mas non lo ⌐ podie faz*er* q*ue* lo aguardaua el *con*de; τ el por auer lo
mas en poder andaua ⌐ le casmie*n*to *con* la fija del rey de Portugal τ no*n* plogo
a Dios q*ue* fuese,[537] ca ⌐ era*n* parie*n*tes. τ p*er*o caso *dona*[538] Amafalta *con* el, era
niño pues los p*ar*tio p*ap*a Inno-⌐*cen*tio iij° τ asi fue ella engañada. P*us* q*ui*so
casar *con* **ella** el *con*de do*n* Alfonso τ no*n* q*ui*so ⌐ ela τ tornose asu t*ie*rra. P*us*ⁱ
dela cort de Ualadolit el *con*de *con* s*us* ueladores paso ⌐ se a Estremadura de
Duero τ sopo auer **antes algunos**[539] delos mayores ensu ⌐ ayuda; pues paso
la sierra τ uiño a Maq*ue*da. La reyna doña Bere*n*guela ⌐ sabie q*ue* no*n*
guardarie*n* **tan bien como deurien,** q*ue* el *con*de no*n* era om*n*e asi *a*gutioso,
enuio ala un ⌐ [fol.71v] ⌐ om*n*e asco*n*didame*n*t saber q*ue* fazie*n* o q*ue* dizie*n*.
Fallaro*n* este om*n*e dela reyna, fue ⌐ barru*n*ta*n*do por meter mayor mal entre
el ifañt τ su h*er*mana, doña Bele*n*g*ue*-⌐ra; asacaro*n* q*ue* traye letras dela reyna
doña B*e*leng*ue*ra p*ar*a unos de Ca*n*pos τ q*ue* mata-⌐sen al rey co*n* yerbas; ante
q*ue* uiniese la cosa a pr*ue*ua, enforcaro*n* lo τ ro*n*piero*n* ⌐ una carta. Pues la
falsedat no*n* se puede encubrir; sopiero*n* q*ue* fue asaca-⌐do τ mi*n*tira. Enta*n*to
el *con*de do*n* **Aluaro**[540] uido q*ue* murmuriaua*n* los pueblos ⌐ τ los caual*er*os τ
los ricos om*e*s τ no*n* oso entrar en Toledo ni*n* fincar ⌐ en su t*er*mino τ uino a
Uepte. Esto*n*z do*n* Ruy Gomez de Ual U*er*de, om*n*e ⌐ muy noble de Castiella,
q*ue* era mucho amado del yfañt, q*ui*so se uenir ⌐ a la reyna; **ouolo de saber**
don Ferrand Muñoz, sobrino del conde don Aluaro que tenie *con* ⌐ el priso
lo,[541] τ aduxo lo [a] Alarco*n* τ p*ri*so τ [el conde fizo guerra a][542] los q*ue*
sopiero*n* τ q*ue* se otorgaua*n* co*n* ⌐ la reyna. Uino el *con*de *con* el ifañt a
Ualadolit τ fizo y cort *con* s*us* ue-⌐ladores τ *con* los estremadanos de cabo de
Duero τ pasada la Pasqua ⌐ de resuretio*n*, come*n*ço de astragar los delas casas
q*ue* tenie*n* *con* la reyna. ⌐ Pues c*er*co a do*n* Suer Tellez en un castiello q*ue* dize*n*
Mo*n*t Alegre; do*n* Garcia Royz ⌐ τ s*us* h*er*manos τ Alfonso Tellez, q*ue* lo oyo τ
uiniero*n* lo aiudar; τ pues ⌐ q*ue* uiero*n* y la seña del rey, no*n* osaro*n* y entrar.
Enta*n*to Suer Tellez ouo ⌐ de dar el castiello al rey. Dende fuero*n* por Ca*n*pos
astraga*n*do alos dela ⌐ reyna τ moraro*n* algunos dias en Carrio*n*. Desende
mouiero*n* se *con*tra Uil-⌐lalua de Alcor *con*tra do*n* Alfonso Tellez. τ caual*er*os
q*ue* fuero*n* delant fallaro*n* ⌐ un caual*er*o τ robaro*n* lo τ firiero*n* lo τ p*er*o escapo
se delos τ puso se en el ⌐ castiello τⁱⁱ defendiose bie*n*. El *con*de q*ui*tose dela
c*er*ça, uinose a Pale*n*çia. Doña ⌐ B*e*le*n*guera *con* s*us* ueladores pusose en
Oriello τ en Castro Sinc*er*o,[543] τ seyen en ⌐ cueyta, ca el rey uinie*n*do aellos,
no*n* osarie*n* lidiar ni*n* se podrie*n* defender, si non ⌐ tornase a España a
honta.[544]

ⁱ *DRH*: VIIII.iii
ⁱⁱ *DRH*: VIIII.iiii, *EG* follows the text of *DRH* closely.

De muerte del rey Enric[i]

ꞁ Morando en Palençia, poso el yfañt en casa del obispo, começaron ro-ꞁbar τ prender lo suyo de su yglesia como de urtos.[545] El yfañt non era ꞁ bien guardado; acaesçio que un donzel echo un teiuelo de una torre ꞁ [fol.72r] ꞁ ayuso τ firio al ifant, apocos dias murio de aquel golpe. Mas ante ꞁ que fuese sabido la reyna doña Belenguera enuio a don Lop Diaz et a don Garçi ꞁ Royz por su fijo, don Ferrando, que era con el rey de Leon su padre en Toro τ ellos uinie-ꞁran. Oyeron dezir paladino la muerte del rey don Enric τ non lo quisieron [dezir] ꞁ al rey de Leon mas, como pudieron aduzir[546] al infañt ala madre. Estonz ꞁ salio el conde de Palençia τ uino a Castro **d'Arjego** Que encubriese la muert del ꞁ rey; mas non lo pudieron encubrir; asi Que la reyna τ los ricos omnes ꞁ **entraron**[547] en palatio con duelo τ recibio los el obispo don Tello con su proce-ꞁsion. Pues uinieron a castiello de Dueñas τ ali fablaron con el conde de ꞁ adobo τ non los quiso oyr sinol diesen a criar el ifañt don Ferrando que auie ꞁ de regnar. La reyna τ los ricos omnes, como eran escarmentados delo ꞁ que fiziera teniendo asu tio don Enric, non quisieron; τ auido su conseio sa-ꞁlieron de Ualadolit τ uinieron a Estremadura τ non la quisieron coger ꞁ en ningun lugar. Otrosi reçibio letras de Segouia que lo reçibien, asi ꞁ pues torno a Ualadolit τ ali oyo dezir que don Sancho Ferrandez, hermano del ꞁ rey de Leon, uinie con poder contra la reyna τ contra su fijo. Alli[iii] enbio las ꞁ letras porla tierra alos conceios que touiesen[548] fieldad τ uerdad τ ela _naturaleza_[549]ꞁ tanto que otorgaron uenir a cort a Ualladolit. τ alli ouieron su conseio τ fal-ꞁlaron la por fija mayor τ heredera τ fallaron como el rey don Alfonso ꞁ la fiziera iurar quando lo desposo con cuydado que era desfiuzado de fijo ua-ꞁron. Et iurada por señora quiso retener su regno. Pues salieron alos canpos, ꞁ que non cabien enlos palaçios τ demandaron le su fijo por señor τ ella otor-ꞁgolo τ reçibieron asu fijo don Ferrando τ fizieron le omenaie τ aduxieron lo a ꞁ Santa Maria τ alçaron lo rey en edat de diziocho años τ cantando la clerizia "Te ꞁ Deum laudamus".

Como alçaron rey a don Ferrando[iii]

ꞁ En tanto oyo la reyna doña Belenguera que el rey de Leon entraua por ꞁ Castiella por ganar el regno τ con conseio del conde don Aluaro quel aiu-ꞁdarie el, que lego a Castiella. La reyna enuiol dezir τ rogar con los obispos ꞁ [fol.72v] ꞁ que non enbargase el regno asu fijo don Ferrando, que en cabo maguer que quisiese **no podrie**; pero ꞁ el non lo delexo por eso, paso Pisuerga τ quando

---

[i] See p. 15 above.
[ii] _DRH_: VIIII.v
[iii] Again, the organizational principles of _EG_ differ significantly. See above p. 15.

lego a Burgos fallo y do*n* L*op* Diaz τ | todo el poder de Castiella; τ uido q*ue*
andaua en uano τ tornose p*ara* Leon. El[i] rey | do*n* Ferrand*o* alçado rey, los
estremadanos enuiaro*n* p*ro*meter s*us* ser*ui*t*io*s granados a | la reyna, Auila τ
Segouia τ todos los ot*ro*s. Esto*nz* la reyna enbiol alos obis-|pos de Castiella a
do*n* Aluaro q*ue* les diese el cuerpo del rey do*n* Enric por enter-|rar; fuero*n* τ
reçibiero*n* el cuerpo τ uiniero*n* co*n* el a Pale*n*çia. Qu*an*do saliero*n* luego |
cerçaro*n* un castiello q*ue* dize*n* Muño τ fico y el rey do*n* Ferrand*o* co*n* las
huestes, y su | madre doña B*elenguera* fue enterrar su he*r*mano a Burgos τ pues
q*ue* torno ya ala | çerca falo ya el castiello p*ri*so. Despues p*ri*siero*n* Lerma τ
Lara, q*ue* tenie el *con*de | do*n* Aluaro. Desend tornaro*n* a Burgos τ reçibiero*n*
los *con* pro*ç*esion. Pues[ii] la rey-|na espisiera todos sus tesoros; puso mano a
oro τ a plata laurada τ por la-|urar q*ue* no*n* cu*m*plie*n* las re*n*tas por dar a
cauall*er*os. Esto*nz* p*ri*siero*n* Uilforado τ | Naguera τ tornaro*n* a Burgos. Los
castillos[550] Q*ue* tenie el *con*de do*n* Garcia **como eran fuertes nonlos**
quisieron cercar, dona Berenguela τ so fijo don Fferando seyendo en
Burgos. El conde don Aluaro τ el conde don Garcia co*n* s*us* a-|yudadores
pasaro*n* por Otor de Aios τ por Q*ui*tana τ destruyero*n* a Uilfora-|do, asi q*ue*
peso el rey τ ala reyna τ asi tornaro*n* as*us* lugares. Enta*n*to el | rey τ la reyna
pusiero*n* por yr a Pale*n*cia co*n* s*us* ricos om*ne*s de Castiella; aca | el *con*de do*n*
Ferrand*o* puso s*us* azes enla carrera, el *con*de do*n* Aluaro pusose en | Ferrera
por enbargar[551] alos q*ue* pasasen.

Dela prision del conde don Aluaro[iii]

| El miercoles adela*n*t, q*ue* era qu*a*tro te*n*poro de setie*n*bre, el rey τ su mad*r*e |
la reyna diero*n* q*ue* curiasen los paños q*ue* se tenie*n* del *con*de do*n* Aluaro, | τ
saliero*n* ala **don** Suer Telez τ el *con*de do*n* Aluaro salio de Ferrera por faz*er* |
ueyrayre τ co*n*tene*n*t τ gra*n*dia ala reyna de gra*n*d poder. τ pues Suer Te-|lez τ
Alfonso Tellez pusiero*n* se entre la uilla τ ellos, p*ri*siero*n* al *con*de do*n* | Aluaro
sin ferida τ sin golpe τ asi lo aduxiero*n* ala reyna τ al rey, p*re*so | ante si. Co*n*
est*o* entraro*n* a Pale*n*cia, pues[iv] tornaro*n* se a Burgos τ pusie-|ro*n* al *con*de en
p*ri*sion. Enta*n*to pusiero*n* pleyto q*ue* diese el *con*de los castiel-|los q*ue* tenie de
Castiella τ q*ue* fuese suelto: Co*n*te, Alarco*n*, Amoya, Echare-|[fol.73r] | do,
Çesare, Uilla Fra*n*ca, la torre de Uil Forado, Naguera, Pa*n*crudo τ q*ue* fuese
q*ui*to. | El *con*de do*n* Ferrand*o* tenie Castro Xeriz τ Orzeio*n*. τ el *con*de do*n*
Aluaro asu costa τ asu | misio*n* deue traher çie*n*t caual*er*os τ aguardar al rey
fata o combrase[552] el rey | estos castiellos sobre dichos. Al co*n*de do*n*

[i] *DRH*: VIIII.vi
[ii] *DRH*: VIIII.vii
[iii] See above p. 15.
[iv] *DRH*: VIIII.viii

Aluaro[553] diole por guarda a do*n* Garcia Royz | fasta q*ue* diese estos castiellos. Entre ta*n*to el rey do*n* Ferrand*o* çerço al *con*de do*n* Ferrand*o*, asi q*ue* | pleteo *con* el q*ue* **deuino**[554] su uasallo *con* la q*ue* tenie τ asi fue. Toda esta t*r*ibulatio*n* | ouo cabo **en** vj meses, q*ue* cuydaro*n* q*ue* nu*n*q*ua* lo abrie τ p*u*s fue Dios loado **asaz**[555] | bie*n*. Enta*n*to[i] los *con*des uiero*n* se abaxados del poder q*ue* solie*n*, come*n*çaro*n* de | correr toda Ca*n*pos; aca el rey do*n* Ferrand*o* co*n* su madre τ *con* los ricos om*n*es | **fueron** co*n*tra ellos τ salioles al ual q*ue* **dizen de Junquera;**[556] ellos uiero*n* q*ue* no*n* podrie*n* | aturar al rey, fuero*n* se p*ara* Leon τ *con*seiaro*n* al rey q*ue* guerrease asu fijo, | τ come*n*ço la guerra el rey. Enta*n*to algunos de Castiella q*ue* entraua*n* **contra** Sala-|ma*n*ca falaro*n* al rey co*n* gra*n*d poder τ pusiero*n* como dize*n* en Medina de Ca*n*-|po τ el rey cercolos ali. El *con*de do*n* Aluaro come*n*ço de calçar sus brasoñeras | τ p*r*isol gra*n*d mal. Alli fablaro*n* de paz τ de *con*cordia entre padre τ fijo τ | tornose el rey p*ara* Leon. τ el *con*de do*n* Aluaro leua*n*tolo enfermo a Colero,[557] τ reci-|bio y el abito de Ucles τ fino τ fue pues enterrado en Hucles. Su h*er*ma-|no el *con*de do*n* Ferrand*o*, fuese a Miramoni*n* τ fue y bie*n* reçibido τ adolescio en | Elbora, un burgo cabo Marruecos τ *con* todo eso fizo se leuar a Marue*cos*; | τ ali p*r*iso el abito por mano de frey *Gon*çalo del Espital, familiar del p*a*pa Innoce*n* | çio iij° τ fino y; pues fue aducho τ soterrado, **en Fitero**[558] **en** el obisp*a*do de Pa-|le*n*cia τ fue y su mug*er* doña Mayor τ s*u*s fijos τ muchos ot*r*os.

Como caso el rey don Ferrando con doña Beatriz[ii]

| Todas estas guerras *fechas*[559] finco el regno[560] | en paz al rey do*n* Ferrand*o*, et **asu madre, y ella demostrol man*er*as deso auuelo por tener la tierra en paz** τ asi lo touo fasta los xxv años q*ue* regnaua. P*u*s | adela*n*tose[561] casamie*n*to *con* doña Beat*r*iz, fija del rey Felip, ele*c*to q*ue* fue enp*er*ador | de Alimaña τ fijo de doña M*ar*ia, fija q*ue* fue de Corsar, enp*er*ador de Costa*n*tino-|pla, q*ue* fue muy fermosa; τ fuero*n* por ella do*n* Mamio,[562] obispo de Burgos τ do*n* | Ped*r*o, abbat de Arla*n*ca τ do*n* Rod*r*ig*o*, abbat de Rio Seco, Pedro Odario, p*r*ior del Espital. Estos | [fol.73v] uiniero*n* se a Frederico q*ue* era electo enp*er*ador τ dema*n*daro*n* gela q*ue* el la tenie en co-|mie*n*da τ alo*n*go la respuesta bie*n* **iiij**[563] meses; en cabo enuiola *con* muchas | dones.[564] τ uiniero*n* por Fra*n*çia τ recibioles bie*n* el rey Felip. La reyna doña Be-|le*n*guera co*n* los obispos *con* muchos ricos omes, saliero*n* la a reçebir *alende*[565] Uic-|toria τ uiniero*n* a Burgos. τ el rey seye y espera*n*do co*n* gra*n*d poder τ oyero*n* | su misa enlas Huelgas *tres dias*[566] ante de Sant Andres. Dixo la el obis-|po do*n* Mauriz. Dicha la misa, **cinjo**[567] su espada sobre el altar τ su ma-

---

[i] *DRH*: VIIII.viiii
[ii] *DRH*: VIIII.x

ₗdre _descinio_⁵⁶⁸ gela. A terçer dia p*us* de Sant Andres dixo la misa el obispo ₗ en Sa*n*ta M*ari*a de Burgos τ uelolos aly; fuero*n* todos los pr*e*lados τ los ricos ₗ om*n*es, de cada uilla los mayores. A[i] pocos dias de p*us*, enuio por Ruy ₗ Diaz, q*ue* fiziese de derecho delos malos fechos q*ue* fiziera τ fezie, ₗ τ dela ti*er*ra q*ue* tenie. Do*n* R*odrig*o era cruzado por yr a ultra mar τ uino a Ua-ₗladolit τ fue muy mal co*n*seiado; q*u*itose dende q*ue* se no*n* espidio del ₗ rey. El rey fues irado τ toliol la ti*er*ra. Do*n* R*odrig*o retouo lo q*ue* pudo las ₗ fortalezas, q*ue* gelas no*n* q*u*iso dar men*os* de xiiij. mill m*ar*auedi*s*. que de-ₗma*n*daua por retene*n*cias. A cabo del año do*n* Garcia P*er*ez de Molina, por ₗ co*n*seio del *con*de do*n* Sa*n*cho,[ii] come*n*ço guerrear a Castiella de _Molina_;⁵⁶⁹ el rey ₗ do*n* Ferrand*o* fue τ cer*c*o Cafra τ no*n* la pudo p*re*nder, p*er*o enta*n*to uino la reyna do*ñ*a ₗ Bele*n*guera τ puso bie*n* su*s* conue*n*e*n*cias τ torno el rey ala ti*er*ra. A pocos di-ₗas *u*ino el *con*de do*n* Sa*n*cho, q*ue* se era pasado a moros τ no*n* pudo ganar gra*ci*a ₗ ni*n* merçed del rey τ tornose otra uez a moros τ enfermo en Bayne, ₗ cerca Cordoba τ ali murio.

Que fijos ouo el rey en doña Beatriz[iii]

ₗ El rey do*n* Ferrand*o* ouo fijos en doña Beat*ri*z: el mayor do*n* Alfonso, p*us* el *con*de ₗ Ferico,⁵⁷⁰ p*us* el *con*de Ferrand*o*, p*us* el *con*de Enric, pus el *con*de Felip, a q*u*i el arcob*is*-ₗpo fizol coronar τ diol calo*n*gia τ prestamos en Toledo; τ ouo ot*r*o si a ₗ do*n* Sa*n*cho. Aq*ue*se mismo do*n* R*odrig*o el arçobispo fizol coronar en Malago*n* τ diol ₗ calo*n*gia τ diol p*re*stamos en Toledo; otrosi ouo fijo a do*n* Manuel τ ouo ₗ una fija dona Leonor, q*ue* poco uisco τ ot*r*a, doña Bele*n*guera, q*ue* fue[iv] ₗ [fol.74r] ₗ mo*n*ia en Burgos. Pues el rey do*n* Ferrand*o*, por *con*seio de su mad*r*e, no*n* q*u*iso treguas ₗ co*n* moros τ fue por Baeça τ por Ubeda τ p*ri*so Q*ue*sada co*n* el arçob*is*po do*n* R*odrig*o τ ₗ diola ala ygl*es*ia de Toledo τ uino Guadalq*ue*uir aiuso τ taio Iahet qua*n*to ₗ alca*n*çar pudo τ uino ala ti*er*ra por q*ue* fazie gra*n*d yue*r*nada. P*us* fizo otra hueste ₗ τ p*ri*so Baeça τ Anduiar τ Martos τ diolas alos frayres de Calatraua. ₗ τ tornose ala ti*er*ra otra uez **priso** Samach *τ* _Go_dar τ Garçes τ lexolas co*n* pod*er*es, ₗ τ torno a Toledo. Esto*n*z andaba por la ti*er*ra el legado _don_ **Johan**[v] obispo de Sabina. De ₗ otra yda p*ri*so al rey Eznatoraf τ Torre de Alboh, Cueuas de Sant Esteua*n* ₗ τ Chiotana. Otra[vi] uez

---

[i] _DRH_: VIIII.xi
[ii] _DRH_: 'comitis Gundisalui'
[iii] _DRH_: VIIII.xii
[iv] _EG_ alters the present tense of _DRH_, 'in regali monasterio degit uirgo Domino consecrata'. Berengaria died in 1279. See above p. 9 ff.
[v] Translator's error, 'erat in Hispaniis legatus Romane Ecclesie Iohannes de Abbatis uilla, que est in comitatu Pontiui, Sabinensis episcopus cardinalis...'.
[vi] _EG_ omits mention of Ximénez de Rada's fever.

cabo Sant Iuh*an* τ ce*r*ço Iah*en* τ no*n* la pudo p*r*ender, ⎸ mas p*r*iso Fega⁵⁷¹ τ
Halma τ destruyolas a suelo. Ot*rosi* p*r*iso^i Capiela, tornose a ⎸ la t*ie*rra a cabo
de xiiij selmañas. Esto*n*z el rey τ el a*r*çob*i*po echaro*n* la p*r*i-⎸mera piedra enla
ygl*e*sia de Toledo, q*ue* ante estaua como fuera en tie*n*po de moros.

De Abehut

⎸ En dias deste rey do*n* Ferrando se leua*n*to un ⎸ moro, Habe*n*hut, en t*ie*rra
de Murçia, asi q*ue* apocos dias fascas todos ⎸ los de aq*uent* mar le obedeçie*n*. τ
fizo descabeçar qua*n*tos **almohades**⁵⁷² ⎸ fallo τ p*r*iso Murçia τ ot*ra*s muchas
fortalezas τ fizo s*us* señales τ s*us* ⎸ armas negras en señal q*ue* todo yrie amal.
Este gano toda Andaluzia, si ⎸ no*n* fue Pale*n*çia q*ue* se _iunto_⁵⁷³ Iah*en*. Era de
linage delos reyes este Abe*n*hut, mu-⎸rio en **Almaria**,⁵⁷⁴ q*ue* lo mato un su
uasallo en q*u*i fiaua, Aberatona*n*, q*ue* lo en_uia_-⎸ra τ lo descabeço enel baño.^ii
Pues este Mahomat Abenalhaiar, **que** _era labr_-⎸ador, pusose aello τ fue rey de
Argona τ de Iah*en* τ de Granada^iii **τ de Baeça**. ⎸ τ p*us* q*ue* murio Abe*n*hut,
p*ar*tiose la t*ie*rra, asi co*n* muchos reyes τ muchos seño-⎸res τ por aq*u*i se
p*er*dio la t*ie*rra τ la ganaro*n* ch*ri*st*ia*nos, bendicho Dios, _q*ue* non_ ⎸ ouo en ellos
acuerdo. De ot*ra* yda ce*r*ço el rey do*n* Ferrand*o* Iah*en*, el q*ue* _enuiara por_ ⎸
engenios, oyo q*ue* **su padre el rey** de Leon era finado;^iv τ fue por alla _a_
_iurar_⁵⁷⁵ ⎸ el regno. Su madre doña B*e*lenguera era yda p*r*imer*o* ante q*ue* entrase
la t*ie*rra,⁵⁷⁶ **en bolli-**⎸**cio** τ enuiara ya por su fijo. Fuero*n* co*n* el el a*r*çob*i*po
do*n* R*o*drigo, do*n* L*o*p Diaz, **don Gonçalo** ⎸ Royz, do*n* Garcia Ferrandez, do*n*
Alfonso Tellez τ ot*r*os ricos om*n*es. Como yu_an_ ⎸ [fol.74v] ⎸ entra*n*do daua*n* le la
t*ie*rra τ reçibie*n* lo bie*n*; los de Toro uiniero*n* τ fiziero*n* le ⎸ omenaie. Anda*n*do
por la t*ie*rra⁵⁷⁷ dela reyna, ouiero*n* me*n*saie q*ue*las ifantas ⎸ doña S*an*ch*a* τ doña
Dolça, h*er*manas del rey de padre τ a q*u*i el padre dexara ⎸ el regno, q*ue* se
alçaua*n* co*n*las fortalezas τ q*ue* no*n* lo reçibie*n*; pero^v los obispos lue-⎸go lo
reçibiero*n* co*n* s*us* aiudadores.⁵⁷⁸ Fue adela*n*t, entro en Leon la çibdad τ fue lu-
⎸ego reçibido; τ alçaro*n* le luego y rey como lo solie*n* τ lo deuie*n* faze*r*; ali se ⎸
llamo rey de Castiella τ de Leon. Qua*n*do^vi lo oyo la reyna doña Teresa,
enuio fa-⎸blar de adobo τ de paz; esto peso alos caual*er*os q*ue* amaua*n* la
guerra τ ⎸ por q*ue* la t*ie*rra fincase en paz, por ruego de do*ñ*a B*e*lenguera finco el
rey en Leon τ ella ⎸ fue fablar co*n* doña Teresa de adobo. El adobo fue atal

---

^i *DRH*: VIIII.xiii
^ii This detail is not from *DRH*.
^iii *DRH*: 'hodie principatur', Muhammad I the first Nasrid king died in 1272, see above p. 8 ff.
^iv *DRH*: VIIII.xiiii
^v *DRH* emphasises the role of bishops in coronation, see Ward, 'Rodrigo', and above p. 18 ff.
^vi *DRH*: VIIII.xv

q*ue* las infant[a]s⁵⁷⁹ **rendi-**|esen la ti*er*ra al he*r*mano τ q*ue* ate*n*diesen **bien y** me*r*çed del. Esto fecho, otro dia uinie-|ro*n* a Benaue*n*t τ asi asigno les alas ifantes por mientre uisq*u*iere*ń* cada | una⁵⁸⁰ xxx mill m*ar*aued*i*s en oro en q*ue* uisq*u*iere*n*. Asi cobro todas las fortale-|zas, pues fue a Çamora τ a Salama*n*ca⁵⁸¹ τ a Ledesma τ a Çibdat R*odrig*o; τ | fue bie*n* reçibido τ fiziero*n* le omenaie. Esto*n*z dio el rey al arçob*i*spo | do*n* R*odrig*o Qu*es*ada por he*r*edat τ asu ygl*es*ia, q*ue* aun⁵⁸² gela auie p*ro*metida q*ue* aun | y auie moros. P*us* **a tres meses**⁵⁸³ fue ala el arçob*i*spo con su hueste τ echo | e*nde* los moros; τ*ii* ouola poco a poco con su te*r*mino: con Pelos τ Troya τ Locra, | **Dosin**, Fue*n*tilla*n*, Torres d'Alteu*n*fio, Mayuela, Eruela, Dos He*r*manos, Uilla | *Mon et N*i*e*bla, Carçorla, Co*n*cha, Chiellas. Pues el rey do*n* Ferrand*o* p*r*iso *U*beda τ | *torno a* *T*oledo era mill cclxxij. Murio la reyna doña Beatriz τ fue | enterrada en Burgos, enlas Huelgas co*n* los reyes.

Dela prision de Cordobaⁱⁱⁱ

| El año pasado q*ue* fino el rey de Leon, almogauares, por co*n*seio de un tor-|nadizo q*ue* era en Cordoua, leuaro*n* de noche escaleras τ p*r*isiero*n* una tor-|re en el exarq*u*ia de Cordoua. Desend enuiaro*n* por ayuda τ lego y luego Ordo*n* | Aluarez, luego a pocos dias do*n* Aluar P*er*ez de Castro. Desende enuiaro*n* | *por el* rey do*n* Ferrand*o* τ mouio sus huestes τ ce*r*çola τ asi la costriniero*n* q*ue* de | *fam*bre q*ue* de guerra, asi q*ue* se ouo de re*n*der. τ*iv* dio el rey ala ygl*es*ia Luce- |[fol.75r]|na, el arçob*i*spo do*n* R*odrig*o fiço ende obispo a do*n* Lop τ*v* consagrolo el, poblo se bie*n* de *ch*ist*i*anos. | El rey fal*o y las* *cam*pañas en la mezq*u*ita, las q*ue* aduxiera Alma*n*çor de Sa*n*tiague τ en-|uiolas ala τ*vi* reçibiero*n* las en Sa*n*tiague con p*ro*ces*ion*. *Cuando* Cordoba fue puesta en bue*n* | estado tornose el rey a Toledo τ fue y recibido con p*ro*cession. Pues*vii* el rey do*n* Ferrando | caso con doña Iuhaña, fija del co*n*de de Po*n*tiz, *nieta del* rey Loyz de Fra*n*çia, fija del co*n*de | Simo*n* de Po*n*tiz τ dela co*n*desa doña M*ar*ia. Entro en Burgos era mill cclxxv, et oyda | la misa, fue alçada reyna; τ ouo en ella dos fijos τ una fija: do*n* Ferrand*o* τ do*n* Loys | τ doña Leonor. Pues el rey do*n* Ferrand*o* torno a Cordoua τ p*r*iso Ecija, Almodouar | τ Luch τ Lucena τ

ⁱ 'toto tempore uite sue', *EG* has previously referred to the death of the infantas.
ⁱⁱ This represents a much abbreviated version of all the basic elements.
ⁱⁱⁱ *DRH* : VIIII.xvi
^{iv} *DRH*: VIIII.xvii, the details of seige have been cut down to a bare minimum but all the concessions to the see of Toledo and details of the new bishop are preserved intact.
^v *DRH* detail greatly reduced with a resulting (disproportionate) emphasis on matters ecclesiastical and religious.
^{vi} Observation of the details chosen for inclusion suggest that this is not intended to be seen as a royal chronicle. Amongst other significant excisions is a passage of praise for Queen Berenguela.
^{vii} *DRH*: VIIII.xviii

Sietefila τ otros castiellos q*ue* serie lue*n*gos de co*n*tar. Fata aq*u*i ǀ esc*ri*pso[i] el arçob*i*spo do*n* R*o*dr*i*go, año d*o*m*i*ni m cc xliij, era mill cclxxxj, alos xxvj ǀ años q*ue* regnaua el rey do*n* Ferrand*o* τ alos xxxiij. años q*ue* el fue arcobispo; τ ǀ uaco ento*n*z la siet de Roma un año τ viij meses τ x dias, muerto Grego-ǀrio; despues fiziero*n* a Sinobaldo q*ue* fue lamado Inoce*n*tio quarto.[ii]

---

[i] The translator alters the first person reference of Rodrigo.
[ii] The reference to Innocent is not from *DRH*. Innocent became Pope on the 25th June, 1243.

APPENDIX 1

Rubrics:

Del diluuio de Noe
De fijos de Noe
Los fijos de Noe que generation ouieron
De Espan e los que uinieron a Tubal
De Hercules τ delos griegos
De fechos de Hercules
Dicho como fijos de Dabal poblaron España pues como los echaron ende
los grie- gos, agora delos godos
Delos fechos delas almazonas
Delos reyes go ǀ dos de Chepre
El primer concilio de Toledo
Que concilio fizo Recaredo.
De fechos delos reyes.
El quarto concilio de Toledo
El quinto concilio de Toledo
El sesto concilio de Toledo
Delos reyes godos
El sesto concilio de Toledo
De Taio, obispo de Cartageña
Del rey Cidasyundo
El septimo concilio de Toledo
El viij. concilio de Toledo
El ixº concilio de Toledo
El x. concilio de Toledo
Del bien de Reçesuydo
De la uida de Sant Illefonso
DEL REY BAMBA
El xj. concilio de Toledo
El xij. concilio de Toledo
El xiij. concilio de Toledo
El xiiij. concilio de Toledo
En este concilio escusaron al de Narbona
El xv concilio de Toledo

El xvj°. concilio de Tole- do
El xvij conci- lio de Toledo
Delos reyes godos Egica
Todos los fechos delos godos, como fueron uençidos
Delos bienes de España
Que mal sufrio España
Que peccados fi- zieron los reyes godos
Dela conquista de Taric en España
Como leuaron de Toledo Asturias las reliquias
Qui leuo las reliquias a Asturias.
Delos que dizen de la primaçia fue en Yspalis
De la muerte del conde don Iulian
Del rey don Alfonso el casto
De la batalla de Roncas valles
Aqui torna al rey don Alfonso el casto
Del rey Ueremundo
Como legaron paganos
Del rey don Alfonso
De Roncasvalles
Froyla
Delos godos alcaldes de Castiella, onde se leuantaron los condes τ los reyes
De Muño Rasuera
Delos reyes de Asturias
De batallas de Almonzorre.
Delos reyes de Nauarra
Delos reyes de Castiella
Del primero rey + del Castiella
Delos reyes de Aragon
Delos reyes de Nauarra
Como el rey don Ferrand de Castiella ouo Leon
De como el rey don Ferrando de Castiella mato al rey don Garcia de
Nauarra
Del rey don Ferrando que partio los regnos
Delos bienes de Castiella. Como el rey don Sancho echo sus hermanos de
tierra τ como murio el
Quando torno don Alfonso en Castiella, muerto don Sancho
Como fue ganada Toledo
Como perdieron en España la costunbre gotica

De don Bernaldo, que fue arçobispo
Como don Bernaldo fue a Roma τ en Toledo fizieron otro obispo
De Ruy Diaz
De su linage
Del rey de Castiella
Del rey d'Aragon como ouo Castiella τ Leon
Como alçaron rey al que fue enperador.
Dela batalla de Fraga que se perdio el rey d'Aragon
Del enpera-dor de Castiella
Delos reyes de Portugal
Delos reyes de Castiella τ del enperador
Como uino el rey de Françia en España
Del rey don Ferrando de Leon
Delos freyres de Calatraua
Quando regno el rey don Alfonso.
De la discordia entre los de Lara τ de Castro
Del rey don Ferando de Leon
De la guerra entre Leon τ Portugal
Del rey de Leon, como guerreo τ adobo con Castiella
Del rey don Alfonso como gaño tierra del rey de Leon τ de Nauarra τ
d'Aragon
De Alarcos, como guerreaua a Castiella christianos
Dela batalla de Ubeda
Del conseio sobre la batalla
Como uino el rey d'Aragon ala batalla
Como se tornaron los ultramontanos
Como uençieron christianos
Los golpes
Quando fue fecha la batalla
Muerto el rey don Alfonso fino don Endric
De muerte del rey Enric
Como alçaron rey a don Ferrando.
Dela prision del conde don Aluaro
Como caso el rey don Ferrando con doña Beatriz
Que fijos ouo el rey en doña Beatriz
De Abehut
Dela prision de Cordoba

ENDNOTES

1 N: "compiezsa"
2 N: "travaiase"
3 302: "es asi [??] yo me trauie"
4 N: "Ydacio, Sulpicio"
5 N: "Trogo", marg: "Trogo Ponpeyo"
6 A later hand has deleted "habitar" and added "morar" between the lines. N: "habitar".
7 N: "Iauhet", marg: "por Japhet".
8 N: marg: "pro Thanays"
9 302: "septineaial"
10 N: "Terra"
11 N: "Magog, Cubal"
12 N: "satmatos…ficlos".
13 N: "Plafigonia", marg: "pro plafagones"
14 302: "dizen"
15 302, N: "rano"
16 N: marg: "pro hunnos"
17 N: marg: "pro Yauan"
18 N: marg: "pro uando"
19 302: "fazie"
20 N: "cabio", marg: "robo".
21 N: marg: "sclauones"
22 N: marg: "Bascones"
23 N: "Fataij"
24 302: "alauie", N: marg: "el auie"
25 N: "en Esperia un omne"
26 N: marg: "Vulcano"
27 302: "cerro"
28 N: "Yspano"
29 Missing in 302
30 N: "quando…ageño"
31 N: "fue para ala"
32 N: marg: "Pro Anteo"
33 302: "querien"
34 N: "fabla…enuenenada"
35 N: "rabio", marg: "robo".
36 N: marg: "Scancia"
37 N: "et los…et los"
38 N: "manera"
39 302: "g. mc"
40 N: marg: "Scilicia"
41 302: "Dia. Pues"
42 302: "pues", N: "Pitus"
43 N: "Fracia"
44 N: marg: "pro conquisieron"
45 N: "secula"
46 N: "almazonas"
47 N: "maltrato"
48 302: "foueste fuese"
49 N: "Ydaspi"
50 N: "Sithacus"
51 302: marg: "Baruista", N: marg: "Barcosta"
52 N: marg: "forte Scylla" "De cineus"
53 302: marg: "curso"
54 302, N: "elcus don"
55 302, N: "tamptouieron"
56 N: "pato"
57 Missing in 302, N
58 N: "ca pues"
59 N: "Goberendo"
60 N: "las ydolas"
61 302: "elos como eran" is repeated, and struck through by a later hand.
62 N: "Graçiano"
63 N: "mar"
64 N: "crebanto"
65 N: "sueuos"
66 N: marg: "pro silinigios"
67 302: "oocsio"
68 N: "predar"
69 N: "Alaricus" deleted.
70 N: "Radagayso" *passim.*
71 N: "Salicon"
72 N: "toparon Alioia".
73 N: marg: "alias Roma"
74 There is a space left at the end of this line, and the words "en era de" appear in the margin in the same hand.
75 N: "España"

[76] N: "burgundiones"

[77] 302: text illegible, in N the word "tostranarian" is deleted and "costranauan" appaears interlineally.

[78] N: "Gunthemando, Frasamundo τ Histirico"

[79] 302: "que"

[80] N: "las ydolas", 302: "lidia"

[81] N: marg: "Atila"

[82] N: marg: "saxones"

[83] N: "ydolas"

[84] N: "Tendeto (marg: "Teudedo")...rey...Arderico"

[85] N: marg: "Turismundo"

[86] N: marg: "Cathalaunicos"

[87] 302: marg: "murieron en esta batalla de cataluña cccv honbres"

[88] N: "Çepidas"

[89] N: marg: "ganivet pro cuchillo"

[90] N: "topar", marg: "pro robar"

[91] N: "Frantran"

[92] N: marg: "pro Arelato"

[93] 302: "matolo τ peyelo"

[94] N: marg: "Amalasuindo"

[95] N: marg: "chico"

[96] N: marg: "Amalasuentis"

[97] N: "pertie"

[98] 302: "cado"

[99] N: "sino"

[100] 302: "Uinçio"; N: "Tuncio"

[101] BN Res/278: "como"

[102] 302: "oyese"

[103] 302: esterrados

[104] Rubric missing in N, a blank space is left for it.

[105] BN Res/278: "condepnar...secta...creyola"

[106] N: "franceses"

[107] 302: "gillianso", N: "gillianso" corrected to "glorioso" in the margin.

[108] 302: Interlineal addition.

[109] 302: "el" deleted, "este" between lines. BN Res/278: "el"

[110] 302: The words "Enel ijº concilio de Toledo", which would have served as

rubric are deleted. 302: "este c. f. f. contados..."

[111] This rubric has been deleted in 302 by a later hand. At the mention of the first council, the later hand has added in the margin "Este fue el terçero Conçilio de Toledo. Del pimo y segudo no se haze mención en este libro, mas de lo que se apunta en la plana passada del segundo consilio". The same hand has altered the rubrics of the following councils, from tercero to quarto, quarto to quinto, quinto to sesto and sesto to septimo. N has the amended rubrics.

[112] 302: "Emendiro"

[113] BN Res/278: "τ despues entata"

[114] 302: "nõbre"

[115] BN Res/278: "razon"

[116] 302: "tres"

[117] N: "Gondemaro"

[118] N: "Yspalis"

[119] BN Res/278: "vascones"

[120] 302: "subrago"; N: "oceano...subiugo"

[121] 302: "iuntaron τ obedes-¡çian"

[122] 302: "iutaron τ obedesesçia""

[123] 302: "cien"

[124] BN Res/278: Recheniro"

[125] N: "maneras"

[126] N: "Andre"

[127] N: "temporal"

[128] N: "Cintila"

[129] N: "septimo"

[130] N: "an" marg: "pro ante"

[131] 302: "logras"; N: "lazras" marg: "lazerar, id est te afliges"

[132] N: "uenien"

[133] 302: "respuso trolos dos"

[134] 302: this word appears between lines.

[135] 302: "solo"

[136] N: "Cindasuindus"

[137] N: "donde fueron"

[138] 302: "son"

[139] 302: "fue al"

[140] 302, N: "miedo"
[141] N: marg: "pro real"
[142] N: marg: "pro diciembre"
[143] 302: "unas" corrected by a later hand.
[144] N: "os aurii", DRH: "os aurium"
[145] BN Res/278: "fechos"
[146] 302: "aribes"
[147] N: "maneras" *passim*.
[148] 302: "uinieron le"
[149] 302: "fiziesen"
[150] N: "Atigio"
[151] BN Res/278: "obedeçer"
[152] 302: "conuersen"
[153] 302: "puso"
[154] 302: "señas"
[155] 302: "aluoses"; N: marg: "aleuosos"
[156] 302: "desa-|prisieron unas letras"
[157] 302: "Catalinbo"; N: marg: "Concoliberi hoy Colibre"
[158] 302: "territañea"; N: marg: "cabe Ceritania o Ceretania hoy Cerdeña"
[159] N: "Uictimuro"
[160] N: marg: "Cerdeña"
[161] 302: "la diesen"
[162] N: marg: "Besiers"; BN Res/278: "τ Acde"
[163] N: marg: "Pezenas et Neumauso hoy Nimes"; BN Res/278: "en Mauso"
[164] 302: "non pudieron" repeated and deleted by second hand.
[165] BN Res/278: "Et assi acoreron se"
[166] N: "marauedis"
[167] 302: "yubas", N: marg: "pro yerbas"
[168] 302: "fama", N: marg: pro "fambre"
[169] 302: "dixo"
[170] N: "xv"
[171] N: "dominira"
[172] N: "suelto"
[173] 302, N: "Eues"
[174] 302: "echara"
[175] 302: "años"
[176] 302: "τ"
[177] N: marg: "pro Sinderedo"
[178] 302: "Cangi"; N: "Fangi"
[179] N: "Vitiza"

[180] N: "exulado...tolial"
[181] 302: "por Rodrigo"
[182] N: "etentar"
[183] N: "dicien"
[184] 302: "τ la"
[185] N: "a unos"
[186] N: "alos moros τ" missing
[187] N: marg: "concordia...Leouigildo"
[188] 302: "tanto en"
[189] N: marg: "bori, id est ebone"
[190] 302: "τ sus"
[191] 302: "fazienda a cutiano"
[192] N: "oriella"
[193] N: marg: "hunos, ahe qe humanos"
[194] 302: "subiugase", N: marg: "subiugada"
[195] N: marg: "Gothica, Runconia, Alava et Viscaya"
[196] From this point onwards calderones no longer appear in 302 as a textual marker. See above p. 4 ff.
[197] N: "mencal" marg: "pro metal"
[198] 302, N: "lieuan", on this occasion, as on other similar ones, the copyist of N indicates his puzzlement over the reading provided by his source.
[199] N: marg: "lee finco"
[200] BN Res/278: "Leonegildo"
[201] BN Res/278: "una neanu"
[202] BN Res/278: "tamaños"
[203] BN Res/278: "que fizo"
[204] N: "Exia"
[205] BN Res/278: "Mogey Arromj"
[206] 302/N: "τ"
[207] BN Res/278: "alçosse"
[208] 302: "pleruo" N; marg: "pro capitularon"
[209] 302, N: "yerua τ despetada"
[210] BN Res/278: "estos Gibel..."
[211] BN Res/278: "emparasse"
[212] BN Res/278: "Salua"
[213] BN Res/278: "uençido"
[214] 302, N: "estarie"
[215] N: marg, BN Res/278: "Merita"
[216] 302, N: "alçaron"
[217] 302, N: "yo, quando quiero"

[218] BN Res/278: "pensosele de achaquir"

[219] 302: "ayudar", N: "ayuda" BN Res/278 "en dar"

[220] 302: "amoscca antagonça"

[221] BN Res/278: "fuera"

[222] N: marg: "pro Ruchonia"

[223] BN Res/278: "Gegion"

[224] 302, N: "Mumia"

[225] 302, N: "mudauales"

[226] N: marg: "leese Pelayo", 302: "Paulo"

[227] N: "maiadura"

[228] 302, N: "murio".

[229] 302, N: "carta"

[230] N: "partas"

[231] 302: "algo escupartas con ti compaña τ si non nico ternas", BN Res/278: "pro dellos"

[232] 302: "respuso" deleted.

[233] BN Res/278: Adds: "los que los echauan"

[234] 302: "fiziera" deleted.

[235] 302, N: "murieron"

[236] N, 302: "Paulo"

[237] 302: "cesar"

[238] 302, N: "uestitutos"

[239] 302, N: "Iuhan"

[240] BN Res/278: "mano", rubric is repeated in BN Res/278.

[241] BN Res/278 "quinto"

[242] N: "Esebero"

[243] N: marg: "lee Pelayo" passim 302 and N: "Paulo" passim.

[244] 302: "muto yfafilar", N: "muto fafila y fafilar"

[245] 302, N: "en"

[246] N: "Çelsonia"

[247] 302, N: "τ"

[248] 302, N: "fija" DRH: "tercium filiul ex ancilla"

[249] 302: "de echutro"

[250] 302, N: "so"

[251] N: marg: "pro dcccx" passim

[252] 302, N: "h."

[253] 302: "scla"

[254] 302, N: "Iulian", DRH: "sancti Iohannis"

[255] BN Res/278: "honrra"

[256] N: "ouose"

[257] 302: "uestiçion"

[258] BN Res/278: "clamaron"

[259] BN Res/278: "a Leo"

[260] BN Res/278: "al su fijo fizolo…"

[261] BN Res/278: "caprouiesse"

[262] 302: "Eboles"

[263] BN Res/278: "Piteus"

[264] BN Res/278: "poridad"

[265] 302, N: "des…la tercia"

[266] BN Res/278: "podrias"

[267] N, BN Res/278: "por ello"

[268] BN Res/278: "partida"

[269] BN Res/278: "se osaua"

[270] N: marg: "Vbique"

[271] 302, N: "su alto"

[272] 302, N: "Mouenco"

[273] N: marg: "Nauarra. Ca…"

[274] BN Res/278: "Hules"

[275] BN Res/278: "Catachuey"

[276] 302, N, "Go"

[277] 302, N: echare"

[278] BN Res/278: "Abolabez τ Inelhy"

[279] 302: "toraznaua"

[280] BN Res/278: "plego su hueste luego en una…"

[281] BN Res/278: "lx" DRH: "LXX"

[282] BN Res/278: "migeros"

[283] BN Res/278: "dccclxxxviij"

[284] BN Res/278 "de"

[285] 302, N: "acorer"

[286] BN Res/278: "finco"

[287] N: marg: "ha se ser fico"

[288] 302, N: "las puertas"

[289] N: marg: "ha de decir pasaron Mauretania"

[290] 302: "uillania"

[291] 302: "calo"

[292] 302, N: "fizo"

[293] 302, N: "perlados"

[294] N: "gurerro"

[295] N: marg: "Ordoño"

[296] N: marg: "parece falta fue"

297 N: "mont"
298 BN Res/278: "dixo"
299 302: "es"
300 BN Res/278: "contassen"
301 BN Res/278: "encalçamiento"
302 BN Res/278: "compescado"
303 302: "Tunteso"
304 BN Res/278: "Carneja"
305 N; marg: "Cauria...Lomego"
306 N: "Theudemiro"
307 302, N: "fijo"
308 N: "Almotaphen"
309 N: marg: "Avempaz. De uno de este nombre hace mencion I Gines Sepulveda en su Epist^as como natural de Cordoua"; BN Res/278: "alcayt"
310 N: "Amontarap"
311 N: "ad"; BN Res/278: "Almotaroph"
312 302, N: "mando"
313 302, N: "el"
314 BN Res/278: "doto"
315 N: "Valviquenta"
316 N: "Rudena"
317 BN Res/278: "dieron refretas"
318 302, N: "destruyeron"
319 N: "Nedegado"; BN Res/278: "Andregodo"
320 302, N: "uino"
321 BN Res/278: "del Rey Froyla"
322 N, BN Res/278: "iogo"
323 BN Res/278: "esleyron"
324 N: marg: "Lee Lain τ Flain"
325 BN Res/278: "juyzios"
326 302: "don Nuño don Nuño"
327 N: "Veremundez", BN Res/278: "Uermudez"
328 BN Res/278: "Ximena"
329 302: "ça" added by later hand, BN Res/278: "Gomez"
330 BN Res/278: "finco"
331 302: "Nuuias"
332 302,N: "fincase fija de rey o de | linage τ casar non quisiese, sacando ende la uida dela monges, on-|drada en lo otro quisquisiesen", BN Res/278:

"que uisquiessen las dueñas que casar non quisiessen".
333 N: "conuigra", in the margin the later hand has attempted to reproduce the Gothic script of the original.
334 BN Res/278 "leujanozo de coraçon", 302: "primero"N: "premio"
335 BN Res/278: "uoto"
336 302: "meses de meses e fra"
337 BN Res/278: "Xemena"
338 BN Res/278 "torno el Rey don Remiro"
339 302: "con conseio", BN Res/278: "ouo su conseio"
340 302: "silio"
341 N: "comer"
342 Added to 302 by a later hand.
343 302, N: "demouio"
344 N: "a"
345 BN Res/278: "de allent"
346 BN Res/278: "a terçer dia"
347 302: "τ"
348 N: marg: "pro creyolo"
349 302: "misma"
350 302: "o qui mesielo"
351 302,N: "de ramen", BN Res/278: "Ramiro"
352 BN Res/278: "Agilo"
353 302, N: "acorren"
354 BN Res/278: "demando"
355 BN Res/278: "aluergada"
356 BN Res/278: "enla yglesia...soterraron lo" missing, possibly due to a homoioteleuton.
357 302, N: "τ"
358 BN Res/278: "fueron...Borietorexi", DRH: "Borgecorrexi"
359 302: "τ"
360 302: "perder" corrected by later hand to "prender"
361 302, N: "Cata", N: marg: "Pro guardate"
362 302: "fizo"
363 302, N: "fueros"
364 302: "fue ferido" deleted by same hand.

365 BN Res/278: "caprender los pobres"
366 302, N: "Garcia Ferrand*es*"
367 N: "fablando"
368 BN Res/278: "barrearon el"
369 N: marg: "tembloso"
370 302, N: "sos"
371 BN Res/278: "de guisa que"
372 302, N: "τ"
373 302, N: "lo dizie*n* esta doña Mayor q*ue* pues fue dicha, ¡ este caso co*n* doña Eluira. Muerto, regno su fijo do*n* S*anch*o el Mayor sea q*ua*lq*u*ı́-¡er,", DRH: "Post mortem eius filius eius Sancius, dicitur Maior, successit in regimine Nauarrarorum et duxit uxorem filiam comitis Sancii de Castella, que Maior uel Geloyra secundum alios dicebatur..."
374 302, N: "los ricos ¡ om*n*es q*ue* uiniero*n* touiero*n* se por el no*n* lo uiero*n* por tres uezes q*ue* fuero*n* ¡ ael; los ricos omes maltrechos,"
375 N; marg: "Nagera"
376 N: "que", BN Res/278: "destoruara"
377 302: "ella" deleted
378 302: "el finado" deleted
379 N: "que"
380 302, N: "dela"
381 BN Res/278: "desçercasse"
382 302: "τ heredo"
383 BN Res/278: "Pitheus...gracioso"
384 N: marg: "Cap de Estopa. Cita en Barcelones o Lemosin."
385 302: "no*n* pudiero*n* los des-¡çerca*r*la τ alço"
386 N: "Delza"
387 N: "Polonia", BN Res/278: "Palerma"
388 302: "fue"
389 BN Res/278: "uaron...fino el sin" missing.
390 Line missing in N due to homoioteleuton.
391 302, N: "agota"

392 BN Res/278: "pireus"
393 BN Res/278: "Luesia"
394 BN Res/278: "era"
395 302,N: "lados"
396 302, N: "con el"
397 BN Res/278: "del Rey...τ ouo en ella un fijo don Alfonso" missing in BN Res/278.
398 302, N: "fue deue...comencaron"
399 N: marg: "pro reyno"
400 BN Res/278: "violes"
401 BN Res/278: "Violant"
402 N: "comienza"
403 302: "Ferrand Garcia"
404 302: "rey" corrected to "rio" in margin.
405 302: "del uino para"
406 BN Res/278: "desfuyr"
407 N: "Seruando"
408 302: "ro" deleted.
409 N: marg: "caveria pro caualleria"
410 N: "desconataro*n*"
411 302: "tramosa"
412 BN Res/278: "Loruano"
413 BN Res/278: "solie dexir que"
414 BN Res/278: "cerca"
415 302, N: "catoles"
416 N: "contando"
417 N: marg: "Bierzo...Villa Franca", BN Res/278: "Xv"
418 N: marg: "Berlanga"
419 302, N: "Catalona"
420 N: marg: "Aluido"
421 302, N: "desende de"
422 302,N: "al onbre"
423 302: "como" deleted
424 302: "de" deleted
425 N: "gouernauase", 302 "gozauase" which may or may not be intentional, DRH: "Aldefonsus ei tanquam matri in omnibus defferebat et eius consilio se regebat".
426 N: marg: "Golpeiera", 302: "Golpenera"
427 BN Res/278: "leuado a Burgos preso"

428 302, N: "fizo y fincar"

429 N: "uint"

430 302, N: "uiera"

431 BN Res/278: "pesol al"

432 302, N: "dos"

433 BN Res/278: "fazienda"

434 302, N: "enterrose"

435 BN Res/278: "ouieres"

436 302,N: "iuuar"

437 BN Res/278: "guerrear"

438 N: "sotalaña", marg: "so Talauera"   .

439 302,N: "ella fizo"

440 302: "tugo"

441 N: "Vicente"

442 302, N: "uio so"

443 N: marg: "que ley non..."

444 302: "cubre"

445 N: marg: "ioven o moço", 302,N: "uiuo", DRH: VI.xxiiii.10: "Hic cum fuisset ab infancia litteratus".

446 N: marg: "Aurencio"

447 BN Res/278 has an extra rubric "Como perdieron la costumbre gotica en España" at this point.

448 BN Res/278: "conseiero", 302, N: "de como mandar"

449 302: "mayor" deleted by original hand and "daño" (N,BN Res/278: "mal") added by a second hand.

450 302: "alos" deleted

451 302: "fue el y"

452 BN Res/278: "guiaua"

453 BN Res/278: "τ a Layn Nuñez τ a Diago Laynez" missing

454 N: "Golpigan", BN Res/278: "Golpinga"

455 N: marg: "pro Velido Adolfos", BN Res/278: "Vellido Adolfos"

456 N: marg: attempt to mimic gothic hand of 302 suppression. BN Res/278: "τ Xristiana" missing.

457 N: "lidiando"

458 302: "los moros" is added by a later hand.

459 302,N: "pudo"

460 BN Res/278: "iogados"

461 BN Res/278: "*con* ┆ blueços [...] do*n* Pedro" missing, possible homoioteleuton.

462 302: "Gomez", however, the Count died in the previous sentence...

463 The opening words appear in BN Res/278 as the final words of the previous chapter.

464 302: "don vm."

465 302,N: "si"

466 BN Res/278: "Lamego"

467 302: 'dõ'

468 BN Res/278: "de Pontiz", "aquella...reyna" missing

469 N: "Trastamara"

470 302: "reyna", this rubric appears in BN Res/278 only.

471 302,N: "grand"

472 BN Res/278: "ael"

473 BN Res/278: repeats "quel prometio"

474 N: marg: "de Ienua pro Genua Genova"

475 BN Res/278: "genoueses"

476 BN Res/278: "quisieron leuar"

477 302: "ome" deleted

478 N: "agueros"

479 302,N: "descudos τ del"

480 302,N: "falleçer"

481 N: marg: "pro Minerua"

482 302,N: "Finta"

483 N: "Ucles"

484 N: "entrar", BN Res/278: "criar"

485 BN Res/278: "*con* do*n* Nuño [...] la t*ie*rra" missing, possible homoioteleuton.

486 N: "Lubeygal"

487 BN Res/278: "he*r*mano de Roy Gutierrez" missing

488 302, N: "tornasemos"

489 302, N: "pe*ro* delos sanos"

490 N: "Caso con"

491 BN Res/278: "con"

492 BN Res/278: "Cancet"

493 302: "frey" deleted

494 BN Res/278: "comienço"

495 BN Res/278: The rubric "Dela batalla de Alarcos" appears at this point, and the following rubric in 302 does not appear in BN Res/278. The order is obviously more logical therefore in BN Res/278.

496 N: "Ceguirhaghy", BN Res/278: "Cegurhaghi" BN Res/278: "por Portiello Miranda"

497 N: marg: "Carcasona Beziers"

498 N: marg: "Folchalguer"

499 N: "hospital"

500 302: torñqro"

501 BN Res/278 folio 90 is missing, folio 91r resumes here.

502 N: "Navas"

503 BN Res/278: "su hueste"

504 302: "quedara morien"

505 302, N: "que mengagero"

506 302: "lidiar" deleted

507 BN Res/278: "cuydaron"

508 N: marg: "alungada p. alvergada"

509 N: marg, BN Res/278: "Ucles"

510 302,N: "la fas"

511 302,N: "pudiesen"

512 302: "Alcatan"

513 N: marg: "Parthos"

514 BN Res/278: "costaneros"

515 BN Res/278: "τ los añafiles"

516 BN Res/278 "τ tomeste [...] que aqui" missing.

517 BN Res/278: "podremos"

518 N: "morit o uiuit con nos"

519 302: "letania"

520 N: "Oyent Abasceti", BN Res/278: "çeyt"

521 N: "desnodados"

522 BN Res/278: "cauallos"

523 BN Res/278: "los reyes"

524 BN Res/278: "fuyeron"

525 302: "aca paso aiuda", N: "a uida" marg: "a cada"

526 302, N: "tornaronse"

527 BN Res/278: "Eznauexore"

528 302, N: "moros"

529 BN Res/278: "fablo"

530 BN Res/278: "regno"

531 302: "de monta de ", N: "demanda"

532 302, N: "τ ala"

533 302, N: "tierras"

534 N: "aguardavan"

535 302: "Alfonso"

536 BN Res/278: "entendiendo"

537 BN Res/278: "fiziese"

538 302: "con"

539 302, N: "algo uos"

540 302, N: "Alfonso"

541 302: "amolo [...] Alfonso et que", N: "y solo"

542 This is an addition suggested by Lidforss. 302: "Alarcon priso este τ los que sopieron que amauan τ se otorgauan con la reyna"

543 N: "sino"

544 BN Res/278: "nin se podrien ni defender se non | tornase a España a honta" The emendation is from Lidfors's edition.

545 BN Res/278: "moros"

546 BN Res/278: "non quisieron dezir ninguna cosa [...] por otra razon aduxieron"

547 302, N: "cantauan"

548 BN Res/278: "catassen"

549 302: "naturazela"

550 302, N: "castellanos"

551 BN Res/278: "enpeçer"

552 N: "ocombrase" marg: "que combrasse pro cobrasse"

553 302: "Alfonso"

554 302, N: "enuio"

555 302: "aca"

556 302, N: "diablo nunqua"

557 N: "cabro"

558 302: "enfermo"

559 BN Res/278: "apaciguadas"

560 302: "fizo el rey" corrected by same hand.

561 BN Res/278: "andaronle"

562 N: marg: "mauriz"

563 302, N: "tres"

564 302: "dodones"

565 302: "dende"
566 302: "d"
567 302, N: "si uio"
568 302: "dauio"
569 302: "pie lieua"
570 BN Res/278: "fredigo"
571 BN Res/278: "Pego"
572 302, N: "almocadenes"
573 BN Res/278: "Valencia", 302: "panto"
574 302, N: "Alimaña"
575 BN Res/278: "entrar"
576 N: "por a Valladolid", 302, N: "obelito"
577 BN Res/278: "las arras"
578 BN Res/278: "ciubdades"
579 Second hand in 302 corrects "infantes" to "infantas".
580 BN Res/278 "uiujessen [...] año"
581 N: marg: "Talamanca sed videtur potuis Salamanca", 302 "Talamanca"
582 BN Res/278: "ya ante"
583 302, N: "otros meseses"

BIBLIOGRAPHY

Ainsworth, Peter, *Jean Froissart and the Fabric of History: Truth, Myth and Fiction in the 'Chroniques'* (Oxford: Clarendon Press, 1990).

Almagro Basch, Martin, *Historia de Albarracín y su sierra. T.III El señorío soberano de Albarracín bajo los Azagra* (Teruel: Instituto de Estudios Turolenses, 1959).

Álvarez Borge, Ignacio, *La plena edad media: siglos xii–xiii* (Madrid: Editorial Síntesis, 2003).

Amador delos Ríos, José, *Historia crítica de la literatura española*, Gredos reprint (Madrid: Gredos, 1969).

Busby, Keith, *Codex and Context. Reading Old French Verse Narrative in Manuscript*, 2 vols. (Amsterdam, New York: Rodopi, 2002).

Catalán, Diego, 'El Toledano romanzado y las estorias del fecho delos godos', in *Estudios dedicados a James Homer Herriott* (Madison: HSMS, 1966), pp. 9–102.

——, *El Çid en la historia y sus inventores* (Madrid, Fundación Menéndez Pidal, 2002) .

——, *La 'Estoria de España' de Alfonso X: creación y evolución*, Fuentes Cronísticas de la Historia de España, 5 (Madrid: Seminario Menéndez Pidal, Fundación Menéndez Pidal & Universidad Autónoma de Madrid, 1992).

——, *De la silva textual al taller historiográfico alfonsí: códices, crónicas, versiones y cuadernos de trabajo*, Fuentes Cronísticas de la Historia de España, 9 (Madrid: Seminario Menéndez Pidal, Fundación Menéndez Pidal & Universidad Autónoma de Madrid, 1997).

——, 'Monarquía aristocrática y manipulación de las fuentes: Rodrigo en la *Crónica de Castilla*. El fin de modelo historiográfico alfonsí', in Martin ed., *La historia*, 75–94.

——, *El español. Orígenes de su diversidad* (Madrid: Seminario Menéndez Pidal, 2002).

Cooper, Louis, (ed.), *El Liber Regum* (Zaragoza: Institución Fernando el Católico, 1960).

Doubleday, Simon *The Lara Family: Crown and Nobility in Medieval Spain* (Harvard: University Press, 2001).

Escalona Monge, Julio, 'Los nobles contra su rey. Argumentos y motivaciones de la insubordinación nobiliaria de 1272–1273', *Cahiers de linguistique et de civilisation hispaniques médiévales*, 25 (2002), 131–162.

Fernández-Ordóñez, Inés, 'La técnica historiográfica del Toledano. Procedimientos de organización del relato', *Cahiers de linguistique et de civilisation hispaniques médiévales*, 26 (2003), 187–222.

——, ed. *Alfonso el Sabio y las crónicas de España* (Valladolid: Centro para el Estudio de los Clásicos Españoles & Fundación Santander Central Hispano, 2000).

——, *Las Estorias de Alfonso el Sabio* (Madrid: Istmo, 1992).

Funes, Leonardo, 'Las variaciones del relato histórico en la Castilla del siglo XIV: el período post-alfonsí', in *Estudios sobre la variación textual: prosa castellana de los siglos XIII a XVI* (Buenos Aires: SECRIT, 2001), 111–34.

——, Dos versiones antagónicas de la ley: una visión de la historiografía castellana de Alfonso X al Canciller Ayala, in *Teoría y práctica de la historiografía hispánica medieval*, edited by Aengus Ward (Birmingham: Birmingham University Press, 2000), pp. 8–31.

García de Eugui, *Crónica d'Espayña de García de Eugui*, ed. Aengus Ward (Pamplona: Institución Príncipe de Viana, 1999).

Gómez Redondo, Fernando, *Historia de la prosa medieval castellana, I: La creación del discurso prosístico; el entramado cortesano* (Madrid: Cátedra, 1998).

——, 'La materia épica en la *Estoria delos Godos*', *Cahiers de linguistique et de civilisation hispaniques médiévales*, 26 (2003), 267–82.

Gonzalez González, Julio, *Alfonso IX*, t.I (Madrid: CSIC, 1944).

——, *El reino de Castilla en la época de Alfonso VIII*, 3 vols. (Madrid: CSIC, 1960).

Guenée, Bernard, 'Y a-t-il une historiographie médiévale?', *Révue historique*, 258 (1977), 261–75.

——, ed., *Le métier d'historien au moyen age: études sur l'historiographie médiévale* (Paris: Publications de la Sorbonne, 1977).

Faulhaber, Charles, *Medieval Manuscripts in the Library of The Hispanic Society of America. Religious, Legal, Scientific, Historical, and Literary Manuscripts*, 2 vols. (New York: The Hispanic Society of America, 1983).

Hernández, F.J. and P. Linehan, *The Mozarabic Cardinal: The Life and Times of Gonzalo Pérez Gudiel* (Firenze: Sismel, Edizioni del Galluzzo).

Jerez Cabrero, Enrique 'La Historia gothica del Toledano y la historiografía romance', *Cahiers de linguistique et de civilisation hispaniques médiévales*, 26 (2003), 223–40.

Lassiter, Linda Elizabeth, *An Etymological Vocabulary and Study of La Estoria de los Godos, 1243*, Spanish Studies 25 (Lewiston, Queenston, Lampeter: The Edwin Mellen Press, 2004).

Lacroix, Benoît, *L'historien au Moyen Age* (Paris, Montreal: Institut d'Études Médiévales, 1971).

Linehan, Peter, *History and the Historians of Medieval Spain* (Oxford: Clarendon, 1993).

——, 'D. Rodrigo and the Government of the Kingdom', *Cahiers de linguistique et de civilisation hispaniques médiévales*, 26 (2003), 87–99.

Maravall, José Antonio, *El concepto de España en la Edad Media* (Madrid: Instituto de Estudios Políticos, 1954).

Martin, Georges, ed. *La historia alfonsí: el modelo y sus destinos (siglos XIII–XV): Seminario organizado por la Casa de Velázquez* (30 de enero de 1995), Colección de la Casa de Velázquez, 68 (Madrid: Casa de Velázquez, 2000).

——, *Histoires de l'Espagne médiévale (Historiographie, geste romancero)*, Annexes des *Cahiers de linguistique hispanique médiévale*, 11 (Paris: Séminaire d'Etudes Médiévales Hispaniques de l'Université de Paris-XIII, 1997).

——, 'El modelo historiográfico alfonsí y sus antecedentes', in *La historia alfonsí*, pp.9–40.

——, 'Le pouvoir historiographique (l'historien, le roi, le royaume. Le tournant alphonsin)', in *Histoires*, pp. 123–136.

——, 'Paraphrase (transcription/traduction; approche lexico-sémantique)', in *Histoires*, pp. 69–105.

——, *Les Juges de Castille: mentalités et discours historique dans l'Espagne médiévale*, Annexes des *Cahiers de linguistique hispanique médiévale*, 6 (Paris: Séminaire d'Etudes Médiévales Hispaniques de l'Université de Paris-XIII, 1992).

Martínez Díez, Gonzalo, *Alfonso VIII, Rey de Castilla y Toledo*, Colección Corona de España, Serie Reyes de Castilla y León, 21 (Burgos: La Olmeda, 1995).

Menéndez Pidal, Ramón, ed., *Primera crónica general de España que mandó componer Alfonso el Sabio y se continuaba bajo Sancho IV en 1289*, 3rd ed., 2 vols (Madrid: Seminario Menéndez Pidal & Gredos, 1977).

O'Callaghan, Joseph, *The Learned King: the Reign of Alfonso X of Castile* (Philadelphia: University of Pennsylvania Press, 1993).

Orcastegui Gros, Carmen, ed. *Crónica de San Juan de la Peña: versión aragonesa* (Zaragoza: Institución Fernando el Católico, 1986).

Orduna, Germán, 'La élite intelectual de la escuela catedralicia de Toledo y la literatura en época de Sancho IV', in *La literatura en la época de Sancho IV: Actas del Congreso Internacional 'La literatura en la época de Sancho IV', Alcalá de Henares, 21–24 de febrero de 1994*, edited by Carlos Alvar and José Manuel Lucía Megías (Alcalá: Servicio de Publicaciones, Universidad de Alcalá,1996) pp. 53–62.

Pattison, David, 'The legend of the sons of Sancho el Mayor', *Medium Aevum*, 51 (1982), 35–52.

Sánchez Alonso, Benito, 'Las versiones en romance de las crónicas del Toledano', in *Homenaje ofrecido a Menéndez Pidal. Miscelánea de estudios lingüísticos, literarios e históricos*, 3 vols. (Madrid: Hernando, 1925), I, 341–354.

Soldevila, Ferrán *Els primers temps de Jaume I* (Barcelona: Institut d'estudis catalans, 1968).

Spiegel, Gabrielle, *Romancing the Past* (Berkeley, University of Califonia Press, 1993).

Van der Walt, Carol Ann, 'A critical edition of the *Toledano Romanzado*', Unpublished PhD. Diss, (University of Birmingham, 1999).

Vones, Ludwig, 'Historiographie et politique: l'historiographie castillane aux abords du XIVᵉ sicle', in *L'Historiographie Médiévale en Europe*, edited by Jean-Philippe Genet (Paris: CNRS, 1989), pp. 177–188.

Ward, Aengus, 'La *Estoria de los godos*: ¿la primera crónica castellana?', *Revista de poética medieval*, 8 (2002), 181–198.

——, 'Rodrigo Ximénez de Rada: Auteur et Acteur à Castile à la fin du treizième siècle', *Cahiers de linguistique et de civilisation hispaniques médiévales*, 26 (2003), 283–94.

——, ed., *Teoría y práctica de la historiografía hispánica medieval*, (Birmingham: University of Birmingham Press, 2000).

——, 'Iberian historiography and the Alfonsine legacy', *Hispanic Research Journal*, 4 (2003), 195–205.

——, ed., *'Crónica d'Espayña' de García de Eugui*, Historia, 9 (Pamplona: Departamento de Educación y Cultura, Gobierno de Navarra, 1999).

Ximénez de Rada, Rodrigo *Historia de rebus hispaniae sive historia gothica*, ed. de Juan Fernández Valverde, Corpus Christianorum, Continuatio mediaevalis 72 (Turnholti: Brepols, 1987).

——, *Estoria de los godos*, Colección de documentos inéditos para la historia de España LXXXVIII (Krause reprint, Vaduz: 1966).